Insignia
Scars of Lumierna
Kelsea Koops
I0712819

Pronunciations:

Stirling Bakere	Stur-ling Bake-eer
Amiria Rey	Aa-meer-ee-aa Ray
Ignis	Ig-nus
Taika	T-eye-kuh
Calix Gautier	Kay-lix Goe-tee-air
Ealdian Dietrich	Aal-Dee-un Dee-trik
Giles Bakere	Jeye-ls Bake-eer
Dicun	Deye-kun
Wyverna	Weye-ver-nuh
Lumierna	Loo-meer-nuh
Uviktiland	Oo-vik-ti-land

ISLES OF WYVERNA
Purdy Graveyard
Kresibo
Koobritz
Milline
Monikove
Villisa
Mishenibey
Sophicheua
Fuessdou
Milhoaks
Duscrona
Deveriou
Kiesheou
Jamespield
Indijeannie
Lumierua
Abram Canyon
N
E
S
W

LUMIERNA
WINGED CAVALRY BASE
THE CAVE

Prologue

The king of the western coast kingdom had to make a difficult decision. To its north, The Kingdom of Uviktiland was expanding its borders south. The rampaging army was marching down the coast and turning towns into ruins and gardens into graveyards.

There was no warning of the invasion, and the king took the best action with an army at its gates. He deserted his land leaving behind a large percentage of his people to save a small number. He rang the warning bells, and his people watched the sails drop while the invasion began. They stood on the docks with horror-stricken faces as their city glowed in the night, the hungry flames devouring what they had once called home.

Families gather in clumps stacked upon each other like bags of grain below the rocking deck. The masses swayed with the rolling waters; each person kept sitting up by their neighbor as the fleet of escaping ships cut through the water's currents. Fathers stay on guard protecting their families and mothers pull their children's tear-streaked faces into their chests as if hiding them from the events unfolding before them, would cast a spell to make reality forgotten. It turned into a dream that faded away from their memories when their eyes opened.

Chased from their lands, the fleet carrying a large portion of the city set sail to a channel of islands off their coast. The largest island was beyond the horizon, unable to be seen even on the clearest day.

This distance of travel is not alone in what would protect his people, but the geographical layout of the island is a fortress. The island was shaped as if it is a giant crater raised from the depths of the ocean, a bowl large enough for God himself. Rocky peak mountains with jagged cliffs drop off straight into the ocean encircling the entire island like towering impenetrable walls encasing the kingdom-sized valley like a nest.

If you did not possess the ability to scale the steep rock faces or fly above the peaks there is only one practical entrance into the valley. Facing the north was a natural harbor leading to a narrow passage slicing through the dense rock splitting the mountains with enough room to carry wagons of supplies.

The kingdom owned the island but before they arrived on its shores searching for refuge, no person inhabited the land. This was due to the fear of scaly beasts with spikes and talons able to tear into stone as they grip the mountainous cliffs.

Wyvern dragons ruled the island. They were believed to be vicious beasts that knew nothing more than aggression and killing. The king soon learned the myths were wrong. The dragons were aggressive creatures, but they were intelligent.

Wyverns had a sense of respect that would be given to someone who proves themselves worthy by their natural intuition. Bonds between a dragon and a person can be formed, and once the bond is strong enough, the dragon will allow the person to ride upon its back. This feat, given out sparingly by the dragons, resulted in many lives being threatened when the wyvern disapproved of the person standing before him or her. The seldom few, including the king, who was able to tame a dragon became the new defense system.

Hearing of a gemstone that glowed as if an everlasting fire sat in the heart of an obsidian stone, the Kingdom of Uviktiland decided to send their army to the island's harbor. They were met by a Cavalry of Winged Riders who showed no mercy when deflecting the second invasion. The few dragons that breathed fire set light to the Kingdom's ships as the other Riders used their dragons to smite the survivors in the water fleeing from the inflamed ships turning the harbor crimson. It didn't take long for the Kingdom to pull back and retreat. They created a treaty with the newborn island kingdom that declared themselves the Isles of Wyverna.

Uviktiland never again attempted an invasion or war; instead established trade routes with one another with the agreement the wyverns were forbidden over the kingdom's land. In doing so Uviktiland cut off all ties the Isles of Wyverna has with the rest of the continent, secluding them to the ocean.

The Isles of Wyverna set up its capital at the most southeastern point of the valley, furthest from the harbor passage being a week's ride on horseback. Laws were enacted to prohibit citizens from attempting to ride a dragon unless they inherited the right from their parents for their own safety.

The King believed this to be efficient in protecting his people and to help the nation grow efficiently, he extended the law to every career and trade in the entire nation. He grew obsessed with controlling his people and creating a nation where there was no unemployment, no poverty, and no homelessness. To keep order amongst the different social classes and succeed in his dream, a strict law was enforced, so that you are to never stray away from your assigned profession, by marking you with an insignia on your right forearm at the age of ten.

You are born into the line of work you will be in for the rest of your life. You will take over the occupation your parents held as they did for their own parents, continuing down the family line. Practicing another trade or profession can land you hanging from a noose.

While illegally riding a dragon, which was seen as the most heinous of crimes, resulted in the criminal being publicly drawn, and quartered. A punishment worse than death itself is saved for those who commit high treason. Your neighbors watch you beg for your last breath while your last moments are spent in agonizing pain.

This made it impossible to change who you are.

One

S everal hundred years later.

The chainmail over a blue gambeson rattles as the City of Lumierna's guard in his formal attire persistently pounds on the weak wooden door. He drops his arm, listening for any reply from inside the quaint bakery deep in the heart of the condensed merchant district. This district, through the guard's eyes, is nothing more than a cluster of dilapidated shops with the owners' homes built on top. The sagging buildings lean into one another morphing into an indistinguishable strand of walls snaking through the lower-class neighborhood. Market-goers keep a steady pace as they pass by, their eyes stopping on the guard's broadsword before swiftly diverting to another shop.

The bakery guild sign creaking above the door gives its only distinguishing feature from the rest of the drab buildings made of wattle and daub where the walls are made from woven wooden strips daubed with a material consisting of clay, soil, straw, and even animal dung.

Two more guards stand by waiting patiently beside the single horse-drawn wagon parked just outside the steps of the bakery's patio. The building is raised several steps off the market streets. Dirt roads are saturated with trash thrown from the shops and puddles from sources people choose to ignore.

Inside the bakery, the father's firm hand grips the young boy's wrist.

"I don't want to!" he cries.

"It's not your choice. You've come of age. The guards are waiting." His father, a man barely over thirty, lectures as he drags the unwilling boy towards the front door to hand him over to the guards who will escort them up to the chancery at the base of the king's castle. There he will have the insignia for the lower-class bakery occupation bestowed upon his right forearm.

The disgruntled father opens the front door to the awaiting guards who stand attentive at the sight of the father and son. The guard standing in front of the door turns on his heel to open a path for the two of them to pass by and step up to the wagon.

The young boy stares wide-eyed. His eyes focus on nothing in particular but everything simultaneously as they dart frantically around his surroundings. The father heaves the boy up into the wagon, the wooden frame barely making a sound under the boy's feathery weight. He stands in the middle of the wagon his tunic hanging loose around his thin frame despite his father making sure he wore a new belt around the top to dress appropriately for the occasion.

The wagon is nothing more than a quickly nailed-together wooden frame with a floor and wheels. The boy's arms cross, curling into his chest as the intimidation from the guards' appearance dwells on him. The father grabs the edge of the wagon with a single foot on the wooden wheel and hoists himself halfway up. The young boy sees his opportunity and darts, leaping past his father out of the wagon.

Not thinking of his escape route clearly through his head, the thought of wanting to go back inside the bakery to his mother's side clouds his vision. He jumps too close to one of the guards whose rapid response time catches the boy before his feet can even touch the ground. The father finishes hoisting himself into the wagon and angrily reaches down to the guard. He takes the scruff of the boy's tunic in his hand and yanks him back in.

He leans down, pulling the boy close to his face as he lectures, "Not only is this a very important event, it's the law. Do you hear me, Stirling? Not attending this ceremony is illegal!"

His voice is a growl, only loud enough for Stirling to hear as two of the guards join them inside the wagon while the one who had knocked on the door slips beside the wagoneer on the bench attached to the front. The guard pulls a scroll out from where he had it tucked in the front of his gambeson and reads off a name and location to the wagoneer. The wagoneer shouts to his horse and with a flick of the reins, they begin moving along the market streets.

Stirling can feel the eyes of all the people staring at him as they step out of the way of the wagon. He knows everyone knows where he is heading and what lies ahead of him since they too have experienced it and so have their parents, siblings, and children.

He doesn't understand why it was illegal and what truly will happen if he doesn't succumb and get the insignia. He once overheard his father talking to his mother about how they would be arrested alongside him since he was under the age of sixteen and was still their legal responsibility.

Stirling was born into the baker business, a commoner's job. Their shop is owned by his parents, Giles and Jannell Bakere. The aged shop has been passed down through the Bakeres, his father's side of the family. The building was built generations ago when Lumierna was first established on the island. His mother was born and raised in a smaller village in the center of the valley. Her elder brother was in line to take over the village bakery she grew up in. She had the choice of marrying one of the wheat farmers on the outskirts of town or remaining unwed while continuing to work at the family bakery. Instead, she decided to set out to the city to marry and start a baking business and family of her own.

He does not see the family history and pride in the bakery. He sees a mundane life that he doesn't want to wake up to for the rest of his life. A bread baker is not a career a ten-year-old boy aspires to be when he grows up, especially when he knows of so many other positions, he could only dream of being born into.

Stirling's eyes were shut tight in hopes this isn't real and when he is to open them again, he will be back home, or even better, somewhere out of the city. He begins to tap his thumb to each fingertip repeatedly in a nervous tick. They have stopped twice to pick up two other children and a parent to be their witness and guardian to sign the documents.

He has kept his eyes shut the entire time; he doesn't want to acknowledge the other children. He keeps tapping his thumb to his fingertips to give his mind a simple sensation to occupy itself with. He doesn't want to know their feelings about today, whether or not they are scared or excited. His father explained to him all the kids born within the month would get their insignias on the same day whether or not they had turned ten yet. This is to condense the workload to a single day because the Chancellor and the chancery don't want to be bothered with making the preparations and gathering in the ceremonial room for a single child.

He can hear the wagon's sounds and movements alter as it changes from rolling along the dirt and mud lining the city's districts to the wooden bridge taking them over the moat into the castle's grounds.

Stirling lets his eyelids open, revealing his eyes. The immense hazel irises of golden brown with moments of green like the bright sun shining through a tree's leaves track a guard walking far above them on the thick wall. They had passed the gatehouse of the outer bailey into the outer ward, consisting of the castle's personal livestock and the ancillary buildings to help manage the castle and hold its supplies. The golden eyes cannot resist taking the cut stone's handholds and crawling up the wall of the inner bailey and to the castle looming just beyond it. The towers' peaks block out the early sun, casting down a heavy shadow and leaving the air as chill as the night. A shiver runs through Stirling's body.

They travel across the property to a large stone building jutting out from the inner bailey wall. Two separate parents and their children sit on a bench outside. Both children with tear-stained cheeks, hold a cloth over their right arm.

They slow to a gentle stop. Without saying a word, the guards leap out from the wagon and line up shoulder to shoulder about a step apart from each other perpendicular to the wagon and a heavy wooden door. Giles picks up Stirling holding him with one arm as he lowers both of them out of the wagon to the ground as the two other groups wait their turn to slide out.

A creaking sound fills the quiet air as the heavy door slowly swings open, the hinges groaning from the weight of hopes and dreams it has been left with by the children crossing its threshold.

A man with wiry hair slicked back into a short ponytail stands in the doorway eyeing Stirling and the two other children. He steps aside letting a mother and daughter step through the door frame adding another disregarded wish at its threshold to stand with the other families.

He holds up a parchment quickly reading to himself, his eyes leave the list and inspect Stirling. "Are you Stirling Bakere?"

Stirling stiffly nods in response, his fingers tapping rapidly at his side. His eyes glued to his reflection in the strange man's eye.

The man smirks and says nasally, "Such a suitable name. Come on, hurry up now. You're not the only kid getting marked today."

He makes an ushering motion for them to enter the building. Stirling leans back in protest as his father pushes on his back leading him down the line of guards and through the open door. The man announces to the families still in the wagon they will wait for their turn on the bench and the ones on the bench will take their place in the wagon to return home.

Stirling's eyes slowly adjust to the yellow light given off by the candles hanging around the room and what light the slender windows in the stone wall allow to penetrate the room, creating elongated rectangles patterned across the floor. Three wooden tables line the center of the room, each with a small stand holding unknown objects beside it. Four people crowd the furthest table chatting, a young woman sits on top and swings her legs as she smiles at the current topic.

Past the empty tables is a raised wooden desk occupied by a row of four men with papers neatly piled in front of them. A fifth chair at the end is empty and pushed back from the desk as if someone has recently got up. The man who had greeted them outside the door shuffles past them and takes his seat in the end chair.

A pampered man in the middle stares down at paperwork. Without lifting his head, he studies Stirling and his father, then continues reading and writing down some notes. Coming to a conclusion, Stirling assumes the one in the middle must be the Chancellor with his embroidered robes and feathered beret on top of his bathed skin and combed hair. Stirling's face is smudged with dirt and his loose curls stick out unruly in all directions as he never tries to tame it.

The Chancellor lifts a new paper off the top of his stack. Without as much as a glance regarding Stirling he reads off, "Stirling of the Bakere family, today in the month of your tenth birthday, you shall be marked with the insignia of the baker occupation lower class. I, the Chancellor, and four clerks from the chancery who are chosen by myself and King Dietrich will stand witness to the branding ceremony."

The Chancellor finally brings himself up from his paper, his gaze landing on Giles. "I will now need the signature belonging to the legal guardian of the child named Stirling Bakere binding him to his insignia and will be kept here in our records vault."

Leaning against the wall, not talking with the other tattooists, is a tall greasy man with his hair tied up into a bun on the top of his head. His assistant, a young woman beside him, gives off the vibe she is overly pleased to be here to help bind these children to their insignias. The tattooist pushes himself from the wall and strides over to Giles and Stirling. His long spider-like legs stretch across the room with his head and shoulders hunched as if to avoid hitting his head on the candles hanging above, or maybe from years of hunching over a table marking forearm after forearm. His face is blank as his sight crushes down on Stirling, who stares back wide-eyed.

A skeleton hand reaches for Stirling. Stirling takes a half step back as the hand the size of his head seizes him by the shoulder. The boney fingers dig into Stirling's skin as he is pulled to the table in the center of the room. Stirling strains his neck seeking the help of his father, who steps up to the chancellor's desk to seal the future of his only son in the bakery business.

Don't let them do this! Stirling's eyes plead as he sees his father pick up the quill. Even if he could hear his thoughts, Stirling thinks to himself, his father won't help him. He is ecstatic for the day he can pass down the bakery to Stirling and this was one step on the way to *his* dreams. But not

Stirling's, he had no say in his future.

He struggles in the tattooist's grip in an attempt to free himself before his life is permanently chosen for him. Making no progress against his hold, Stirling is lifted from his feet effortlessly and splayed out on his back upon the first table, his limbs thrashing in resistance.

The other tattooists and their assistants end their conversation to watch the child they are glad isn't the one assigned to them.

The tattooist presses both his hands on Stirling's shoulders, pinning him down as his assistant saunters over. Her smile is warm and caring like a mother arriving to help a frightened child. She picks up a leather strap attached to the table. Wrapping the strap around Stirling's wrist and pulling it tight, the notch skips over holes to lock in until the strap cuts into his skin.

He wriggles his arm as she switches sides of the table to do the same to the other. Stirling tugs on the straps. The skin of his hand wrinkles and folds as it catches on the strap, making it impossible to pull free. The leather only digs deeper into his skin, leaving behind indented marks.

Stirling breathes heavily as she finishes locking down his other arm. With his heart racing, he tests the second restraint. No use, he twists his wrists in the restraints ignoring the sawing sensation.

"I've never seen such a persistent one. Should I lock his legs down too? He might try to kick you," the assistant states with genuine concern for the tattooist and little for the well-being of the child strapped to the wooden table.

"Go ahead." The tattooist mumbles as he steps over to the small stand, picking up his ink and tattooing equipment containing two separate wooden rods. One rod is constructed with a sharpened rake shape made of needle-sized dragon bones. It's designed to be dipped into the ink and then placed against the skin. The second rod is merely used to tap against the side of the first rod striking the sharp edge into the skin and inserting the ink into the desired design.

A single tear slips from Stirling's fear-filled eyes as his body becomes completely immobilized, leaving behind a salted trail led by decisions dictated to you far beyond your control.

Stirling twists his neck in an attempt to view his father standing near the table of clerks. Each wears the same distasteful expression on their face as they watch him displeased with the hassle Stirling is putting up, prolonging the allotted time given to him for the ceremony.

The man with the spectacles now satisfied that Stirling's marking has begun checks the name next on his list and excuses himself to escort the next child and parent in.

The Tattooist picks up a large stamp sitting on the stand and brushes a lighter shade of ink across the markings. He steadies it over Stirling's forearm as the assistant stretches the skin taught to ensure the stamp clearly shows the baker's insignia. Satisfied with the centering, he presses down on Stirling's skin, the cool ink leaving behind a perfect outline.

Letting out a sigh of relief, Stirling turns his head to examine the lightly stamped ink on his arm. "Is that it?" Stirling squeaks.

The Tattooist lets out a bellowing laugh but does not answer Stirling otherwise. Instead, he reveals the two rods. Dipping the pointed end of the rod into the ink, he sets it on the new outline. Stirling sucks in the air and holds his breath as he strains his head to turn away, bracing himself for the worst.

With the assistant still holding Stirling's forearm stretched, the Tattooist begins to tap the ink rod driving the small rake-like spikes into Stirling's skin. The air contained in his lungs races out as he gasps. The pain radiating up his arm slowly crawls across his entire body consuming him. *Tap, tap tap*, over and over again. The only sound echoing in the room as the Tattooist works away at the insignia for what feels like hours. *Tap tap tap.*

Relief washes over him as a damp cloth wipes his sore arm clean, soothing the irritated and slightly bloody skin. Stirling hears the clunking sounds of the leather cuffs coming loose and dropping back on the table beside his arms. He knows in reality the restraints are off, but he feels they are even tighter than before. Stirling checks over his shoulder to the other children who lay quietly accepting their fate. They had not put up a fight; their tears were from the pain alone.

"Where did all the spark go, boy? Huh?" The Tattooist smirks as he leans over, inspecting the sweating child who refuses to make eye contact. "Time to get off my table," he says in a crass tone.

Stirling's father walks over from the side of the room where he had been waiting. Slipping a hand under Stirling's back, he helps lift him into a sitting position. Stirling slumps as if he has a stone tied to each of his arms pulling him down with the weight of gravity.

Patting him on the back, his father asks, "See, that wasn't so bad now, was it?"

Stirling purses his lips and remains silent. Dropping his head, he watches as his damp cloth slides down his forearm revealing his insignia, a rectangle shape consisting of intricate lines twisting at the corners with a handle running down the length of his forearm designed like a paddle, like the one his father uses to bake bread on. Locking him in the baking business for the rest of his life. *Such a commoner's job*, he thinks to himself.

Stirling slides to the end of the high wooden table, his feet dangling in the air. Giles holds out his hand to assist him. Shrugging him off, Stirling leaps off the table, landing with a hard thud on the stone floor.

Giles places his hand on Stirling's shoulder and guides him back to the front door. Glancing backward, Stirling sees the Tattooist and assistant have already lost interest in them. They don't look up from their station as they clean and prepare for the next child who is waiting just outside. He looks ahead as he steps out the heavy wooden door as an official baker.

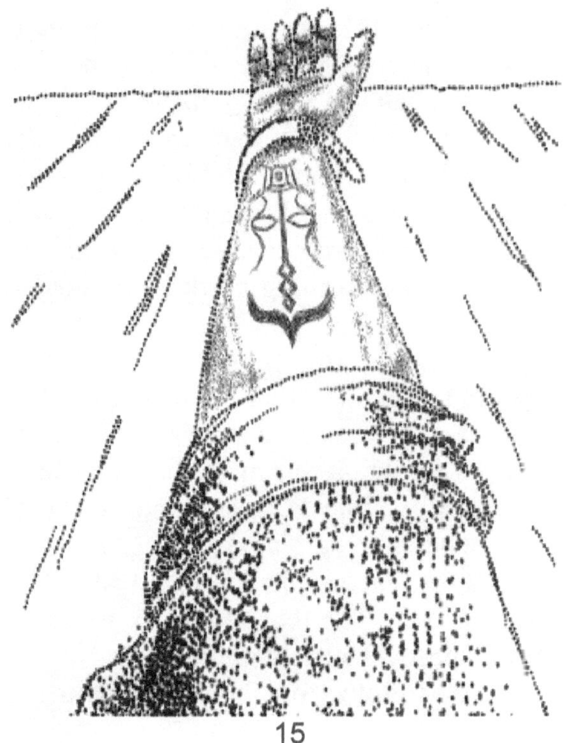

The wooden wyvern flies through the air with the help of a small hand. Lying on his back in the center of the only room on the second floor beside a small bedroom above the bakery, Stirling plays. The room is bare, except for minimal furniture; a mattress made of discolored linen sheets sewn together and stuffed with straw, a few shelves holding candles and kitchenware, a wooden table with benches, and a brick box that's top is opened and filled with smoldering coals warming a pot of mashed peas and carrots.

Stirling's mind is far from the small dusty room as he imagines the dragon being a real beast soaring through the clouds above. He only owned a couple of wooden toys in his life due to the cost and this was by far his favorite.

His mother, Jannell, kneels on the hard floor beside him. "Stirling, dear, what are you playing"

Stirling sits up, ecstatic. "I'm a Winged Rider!"

"A Winged Rider?" she repeats. "Why would you want to be one of the those? Seems dangerous"

"They fight and protect our kingdom!" Stirling throws

his hands enthusiastically and wildly as he talks, emphasizing his words. "The Bard who can read told me all about the history of the Winged Cavalry and sang songs about some of the Greats like Hildwulf who led a team of four to victory against a hundred Uviktiland ships! And Ravenor on his all-black dragon, completely invisible in the night. No one knew he was coming until his arrows were sticking out from their chest." Stirling grabs the imaginary arrow protruding from his rib cage and falls back to the floor dead.

Jannell smiles. "That's nice dear. But being a baker is fun too."

Stirling frowns. "Yeah, sure it is."

Becoming a Winged Rider for the Winged Cavalry is the most prestigious career in the Isles of Wyverna. Due to this fact it comes preassigned with the highest training difficulty. The young Riders experience grueling and vigorous lessons, starting the moment they receive their insignia.

Winged Rider parents strive for their children to be at the top of their class by teaching them the knowledge they will need to know starting as soon as they can walk. Anything they can do to get them a head start before they are sent to actual training.

The Winged Riders are a small selective portion of the nation as the highest ranking in the military. Even if your parent was a Rider, there is still a chance you will not be deemed fit to serve and will be demoted to a guard if you cannot prove yourself by graduation at the age of sixteen. For the few children born each year and the fewer who survive long into adulthood to have families of their own, they live among lords and never understand the value of money. For all they do to protect the population, they receive the highest respect from the kingdom's people.

Stirling dreams of being born as a Winged Rider. What young boy doesn't want to live the exciting life of fighting in the clouds? He stares at his wooden dragon as Jannell pats him on his head before returning to the table and picking up her wooden pestle and mortar. He watches his parents momentarily, his mother grinding the ginger, humming quietly while his father pokes at the hot cinders. Stirling pushes himself off the ground and shuffles his way over to the table.

Resting his chin upon the dented and chipped wood Stirling makes a exasperated sigh.

Giles jabs the iron poker into the coals and turns around to face Stirling. Staring down at him, he says with a stern voice, "For the hundredth time Stirling, you should be honored to be born a baker. Everyone has their place and you have the privilege of inheriting an important business.``

"A lot of people depend on bakeries," Jannell adds.

"It's not the same," Stirling complains, shuffling his way over to a stool sitting below the window.

Stirling ignores his father's grumbling voice behind him as he speaks to his mother, "Ungrateful. Nowhere in the holy words does it say life shall be full of dreams."

"Giles, he's just a boy," Jannell shushes.

"But he won't be forever."

With a little bit of force, Stirling pushes the weather-warped shutter caught on the sill open. Breathing in the pungent city air, he crosses his arms on the windowsill and lays his head down watching the townsfolk socialize below.

"It's not fair," he mumbles to himself as he inspects his insignia, "I don't want this."

Stirling's attention perks as four city guards appear from the market's crowd. People quickly scamper out of their way, but their rubber necks stretch with their eyes shackled to the guards. The curiosity to see whose home they were marching towards is too strong for them to ignore.

Stopping several shops down the dirt road, the guards step up to the tailor's shop. Stirling stands up quickly, kicking the stool out from below him he lets it crash to the floor. His parents startle at the sound as he leans out the window for a better view.

"What on earth are you doing?" Giles shouts as he stalks over to the window and peers out over Stirling to witness the guards bust through the shop's front door.

People begin circling as the guards disappear inside. A commotion coming from the depths of the tailor's home can be heard all the way to the bakery.

Suddenly a barrel is lobbed out the front door. It lands with a crash on the market road splintering open.

The liquid escapes through the cracks, saturating the dirt around it.

Two of the guards emerge with the Tailor, his hands tied behind his back as they escort him out of the shop.

The other two guards follow behind, holding another barrel together.

They begin swinging it between them and once the guards with the tailor step off to the side of the door, they lob the second barrel into the street. It crashes on top of the first, repeating the action as it bursts open, adding to the expanding puddle.

One of the guards who helped throw the barrel pulls out a parchment and announces to the crowd. "Durwin Macon of the lower-class tailor occupation has been found guilty of illegally brewing mead without being part of the innkeepers, alehouses, or brewery occupations. He will be brought to stand before King Dietrich who will decide his sentence.

Giles reaches out and pulls the shutters closed. Stirling jerks his head back in time to avoid being hit in the face. "Enough of that."

"What is happening?" Jannell asks.

"The Tailor is being arrested for brewing mead. Serves him right. You break the law, you deserve to be punished. Simple as that," he answers.

Stirling stares at the closed shutters, the people in the commonly noisy atmosphere of the market have grown eerily quiet. They must be watching as the guards take the man away, afraid to speak up so they aren't the next to be walked off in shackles.

"Stirling, honey, step away from the window. Come on and eat some lunch, then you can help me finish making this gingerbread. I know it's your favorite," Jannell says, her voice luring Stirling away from the window's trance.

He slides onto the wooden bench at the table, wondering what will become of the tailor.

Three

Two weeks later, Stirling wakes to the sun shining brightly into his home through the open window. His blankets are littered across the floor as the house grows too warm by mid-morning. By the time he awakes, his parents are already hard at work the aroma of baking bread, pretzels, and a few sweet treats in the bakery below.

Rolling off his straw mattress in his braies, rubbing his tired eyes, he stumbles across the room to the kitchen table where a loaf of rye bread is sitting out. He tears a chunk of the loaf and nibbles at the stale bread as he stares out the window past the rows of thatch and wood-shingled roofs towards the eastern mountains of the capital nestled at the bottom of the southernmost point of the island.

An unusual urge to venture out into the mountains suddenly develops and bubbles up inside of him. Stirling takes large dry bites of bread. Coughing up crumbs, he throws his short sleeve tan tunic over his dingy white undershirt. He pushes the long sleeves of his undershirt up to his elbows and ties the laced front of the tunic closed.

Hopping towards the staircase, he slips into his trousers with a tied top and synch around the ankles.

He ties the rope cord belt around his hips and whisks down the stairs to his mother's side. She wipes some flour off her face with her apron and peers down at her anxious son.

"Ma, Ma, Ma, Ma, can I go exploring?" he asks impatiently.

Pausing, she rests her hands on her hips as she thinks it over, "Hmm, we do have everything handled here, so that's fine as long as you don't go too far. Oh, and be home before the sun starts to set. You don't want to be out past curfew, or you'll make me worry."

Without any hesitation, Stirling slips on his leather turnshoes coming up to his ankles and takes off out the bakery door. Bumping into a woman standing in one of the many condensed groups of people flooding the streets, he utters a quick "sorry" and takes off sprinting through the market. He weaves his way through the bustling morning crowd throwing out routine apologies. Down on the trampled dusty ground, he can see nothing but worn and frayed tunics. He can't see the towering mountains past the rooftops, but he knows the direction.

Lumierna, a city at the bottom of a mountain, is on a noticeable incline with the castle perched at the top. He makes his way up from the flat grounds of the lower district market to the middle class and upper districts. The streets begin to widen, accompanying the homes and shops growing dramatically in size, each affording to have their own land between them. Even though there are only a few people on foot in this area, no one seems to take notice of the wandering child as he follows the dirt road.

Nearly out of the city, Stirling reaches the wealthy class neighborhood. The homes are grossly oversized with pristine yards. He passes the last house on the city line and comes to a stop at a stone wall standing twice the height of a man. It runs along most of where the city and the mountain meet like a gray seam to keep any tumbling rocks, animals, or other creatures hiding in the woods from reaching the houses at the bottom.

High up on the hill, he can see out across the city that encloses him all the way to the farmers' fields full of harvest and livestock. From here, his view is too good. He sees the gallows where the tailor's figure hangs. Shying his view away, he heads to a hole at the base of the wall, hidden behind bushes created by children long before him who, too, wanted to escape the claustrophobic feeling of the dense inner city and explore the thick forest creeping along the mountainside.

Crawling through to the other side on his hands and knees, he breathes in the pine-filled air, thin and fresh in his lungs. It's a relief from the thick air of indistinguishable scents of the market. With one long drawn-out breath, Stirling sets out into the forest, following a new path, slowly being worn into existence as he begins to further his escape into the mountains. He knows his way around the bottom of the forest reasonably well, but he awaits the time he finally knows every rock, branch, and bush in the place. He likes to think of it as his home away from home.

Feeling blissful with his current freedom, his smile doesn't falter as he trips and stumbles his steps along the rough terrain; hopping over raised oak roots and boulders, balancing on fallen silver fir tree trunks, and running his hand along the coarse bark of cedars as he passes trees who are older than Lumierna itself. The sun casts streaks of light down through the breaks and gaps between the overlapping treetops above like golden translucent ribbons.

Slowing his pace, Stirling notices the forest has grown quiet. Not the quiet he has become familiar with as he leaves the sound of the industrial world he is accustomed to, but instead an overwhelming, unnatural silence. The occasional rustling sound as small critters scurry through the brush and the whistling of birds has long faded to only the crunching of leaves, pine, and fir needles below his shoes.

A weary and uneasy feeling settles in his stomach as he pushes through a thick bush. Stepping out into a clearing surrounded by birch trees, he stops dead in his tracks. Stirling is speechless, his body as still as the white trees around him. A dragon fledgling lays basking in the sunlight, its autumn orange scales like fallen leaves glistening like a crackling forest fire. Lifting its head, it locks its golden eyes on Stirling. Stirling's heart begins to race with excitement and adrenaline. Building up enough courage, he uproots his foot and takes a small step forward.

The fledgling instinctively leaps to its feet in a fight or flight stance. Seeing it stand, Stirling instantly becomes aware this dragon is not built like the ones owned by the Winged Cavalry. Dragons were once caught from the wild but are now most commonly bred in captivity. They are of the Wyvern species, the only species he's ever known to exist, their bodies shaped similar to a bat with two hind legs and their arms and wings being one.

This dragon instead stands on four legs with its feathered wings puffed out from its body to give its body a larger appearance, along with the feathers on the tip of its tail fanning out like the fletching of an arrow.

Two small horns were beginning to sprout from the top of the fledgling's head, slanting to the point opposite of his snout.

His hands begin to shake as the adrenaline surges through his body, his knees feeling weak and ready to buckle as his leg muscles tremble. Slowly extending his right hand out, palm up, Stirling tries to show the dragon he means no harm like he would let a dog sniff his hand.

The fledgling drops its tail and feathered wings taking a few timid steps forward, extending its neck out as far as it can towards Stirling's extended hand. Without any known reason to Stirling, the fledgling becomes startled and swipes at Stirling's arm with his claws before swiftly leaping out of view into the thick forest.

"AHH!" Stirling yelps, immediately pulling his arm into himself. He holds it tight against his chest with the other hand without inspecting the damage. Stirling stares at the tree line where the dragon left with such grace and speed, he feels he had almost dreamt it.

With his adrenaline fading away from his recent encounter, he can now feel the searing pain coming from his arm and the warm liquid running down his elbow before watering the forest floor. He pulls his arm away from his body to check his wound. He sees three long gashes slashed widthwise across his insignia mutilating the image.

Stirling wobbles feeling woozy at the sight of his blood and the severity of his wound. He swallows his urge to vomit. Ignoring his revulsion, he quickly pulls off his outer tunic wrapping it around his arm as tight as possible. Already feeling lightheaded and beginning to sweat, Stirling staggers down the mountainside.

His feet drag heavy with each step he takes.
Left, right, left.
The buildings around him tilt and rock.
He's almost home, only three more blocks to go.
Or is it five?
He squints through his failing vision.
Where is he?
His toe catches on a rut in the road. He lies there in the dusty street, his tunic now soaked with blood beside his face. Sole after sole, he watches the faceless shoes pass him by.

Kelsea Koops

Four

Jannell sets the dress she was mending a torn seam down on the bakery table as she hears the front door open. A well-groomed man with broad shoulders steps into the shop as she hides her needle and thread under the dress itself. Standing up from her seat she shrieks at the site of the man's otherwise clean button-up yellow jopula smeared with blood as he holds Stirling limp in his arms.

Stirling, who has grown pale from the loss of blood, is barely able to keep his eyelids open, he rolls his fading sight to his mother.

"Stirling! Dear Lord, what on earth has happened to you?!" Jannell shouts with urgency as she rushes up to Stirling and the man.

Stirling opens his mouth to speak but is unable to form the words.

The middle-aged man replies for Stirling, "He seems to have been scratched by some kind of animal. I found him lying in the streets."

Anguished, Jannell cups Stirling's face wet with perspiration in her hands, and her voice catches in her throat.

Her hands fall to the man's arm to stabilize herself. She can barely stand.

"I should set him down." His voice is eerily calm.

Her toes almost tripping over the hem of her dress, Jannell clings to the man as he sets Stirling in the chair she was occupying moments before. She follows his movements and lowers herself beside Stirling with a significant thump as her knees hit the ground.

"My baby." She is on the brink of tears. With shaking hands, she pulls back his tunic revealing the three long gashes still oozing blood across his insignia. She lets the tears go, unable to hold them back any longer. She needs to save him, but not while the man is still here.

She doesn't remove her focus from Stirling's arm as the strange gentleman speaks, "I've got a daughter at home." He pauses. Sensing a flux in his voice she peers up at him. He has a pained expression. His face flattens out returning to normal. He continues but it's not his complete thought, "I do understand."

She is gracious for his help, but she knows he needs to leave so she can help Stirling without him seeing she knows how. She pulls a braided leather bracelet the color of fall from her wrist with the pattern of leaves stamped into the strips and holds it out to the man. "Here, for your daughter, as a thank you."

The man raises an eyebrow taking the bracelet from her. Checking his sleeves, he seems now to realize the fact they are painted in blood. Turning away, he pushes his sleeves up hiding the majority of the stains.

She knows she didn't see his insignia right. It is the adrenaline starting to surge through her veins playing a trick on her mind. Members of the Winged Cavalry do not take casual visits to this lower-class market district.

The sound of the bakery door closing is her marker to start her race. Jannell hurries over to the bakery's oven shaped as if it is a hut made of clay sitting on top of a rock-layered platform with a removable wooden door of its own. She picks up an iron poker and jams it inside the oven and practically leaps to where a stack of supply crates is lined against the wall and pulls out a bottle of spirits distilled from potatoes.

"Ma." She hears his fading voice. She has to hurry.

Rushing back to Stirling's side she cradles his chin in her hand lifting his face.

"Ma?" It's barely a whisper. His heavy eyelids drooped halfway down over his eyes.

"Honey, this isn't going to be pleasant, it's going to hurt a lot but you're going to be strong for me right?"

His head bobs in response, his skin a clammy gray. Jannell takes Stirling's wrist resting in his lap on top of his ruined tunic. Using her teeth, she uncorks the spirit bottle and pours the alcohol over the wound letting the liquid rinse the deep gashes free of foreign substances. Stirling's eyes widen. He jerks his arm at the invading sensation of the inside of his wound being scraped clean. Jannell keeps control of his wrist. The blood turns the clear spirit to red wine, staining his trousers and the wood floor below him.

She reaches behind her back, pulling the knot tying her apron around her waist free, and presses it to his arm. Lifting Stirling's arm, she lets the drenched tunic fall in a clump at their feet. She stands up and lays his arm on top of the table.

Returning to the oven, she picks up a small scrap of cloth turned into a rag and pulls the iron poker out of the burning embers. The tip of the dark iron rod resembles hell itself, glowing radiant and orange at the bottom of a long dark tunnel.

Jannell steps carefully back to Stirling and hands him the rag. His glazed eyes rise up at her confused and she signals for him to bite down on it. He does as she says and she kneels back down beside him. His eyes are stricken with horror.

"Nooo." He groans as she holds the iron poker near his

arm. Still a thumb's length away, he can already smell the hairs on his arms burning away. Running off instinct, Stirling wretches his arm away, the iron tapping the outside of his thumb.

The rag falls to his lap as he lets out the beginning of a pain-filled wail. Jannell's hand clamps over his mouth.

"SHH! Shhh!" She holds her hand firmly. "Shh."

Removing her hand from his face, she refuses to let their matching hazel eyes meet. Not while she will be putting him through pure agony with her own hands. For his survival, it needs to be done.

She puts the rag back into his mouth, "I'm sorry Stirling."

Placing her hand on Stirling's cheek, she gently pushes his face to turn away. Wrapping her hand around his entire arm she uses her weight to pin it to the table. Lining up the glowing poker with Stirling's wound, she presses down.

The excruciating pain is white hot as it shoots through his arm. He lurches, trying to pull away from the scolding heat singeing and cauterizing his wound, but Jannell keeps his arm locked down. His spasming body falls from the chair to hang halfway suspended as his arm stays trapped in place. He wants to scream, to cry out for it to stop. This is far worse than receiving the insignia. He spits the rag from his mouth, feeling the sour bile climbing its way up. What in reality, is no more than a few seconds feels like an eternity until Jannell lifts the iron from his skin. The removal of the rod doesn't stop the pain. The vomit finishes his ascent and with a convulsive heave, he throws up.

Jannell's jaw quivers as she keeps herself together with a few overstretched threads.

Sobbing tears flow down Stirling's cheeks. His small hand grabs the hem of her gown and tugs on it pleadingly. Her breath hitches. She bites down on her lip and places the iron down on the next gash. His mother's pleading instructions for him to remain quiet are obsolete compared to his involuntary shrieks of pain-ridden misery.

When the third is completed, Stirling lies exhausted on the ground cradling his arm, the scent of burnt flesh suffocating him. His eyes turn dull with his consciousness retreating to the depths of his mind to protect himself from the torture he is enduring.

Jannell steps back to the crates of supplies and picks up a jar of honey.

Squatting down beside him, Jannell takes Stirling again by the wrist and pulls his arm away from his body. His wounds are no longer bleeding to the same degree, and small amounts of blood trickle over the skinless chunks of revolting burns. His arm throbs as if it has a heartbeat of its own.

Unable to protest, Stirling doesn't move as Jannell takes a scoop of honey, smearing it over his freshly cauterized wounds. Picking up the apron that fell from the table as he did, she wraps it tightly around his tender forearm.

Jannell scoops up Stirling under his armpits, helping him stand up. Squatting down, she carefully picks the frail child up into her arms. His head, too heavy for his neck, rests on her shoulder. He drops his rag-doll arms, falling limply to his sides. Jannell closes her eyes and nuzzles her face into Stirling's messy loose curls. The curls he inherited from her that she keeps contained in a knot on the top of her head.

"What did this to you?" she whispers into his hair. "How far did you go? This didn't come from any animal here in the market." Jannell slowly begins to climb the stairs, Stirling's limbs swaying with the rocking motion of each step. "You're going to have to stay home for a while. This wound is bad and I don't want to risk it festering. I'll tell you when I think you are fit to go out again." She reaches the top of the stairs and wobbles across the room to Stirling's bed.

Cradling his head, she gently lays him down. She removes her hand from under his head, resting it on the flour sack pillow. Stirling's body is too weak to even open his eyes. She pulls the blankets sprawled on the floor back over Stirling, tucking him in.

Gently touching Stirling's cheek, she tells him, "Stirling, look at me." Stirling's eyelids flutter as he struggles to keep them open. Jannell continues, "Stirling, this is serious. If that man didn't help you, you could have…" Bringing her free hand to her mouth, she breaks off as the words catch in her throat.

Pushing a few curls that sprung free from the knot behind her ear, she regains her composure. "When your father gets home from his deliveries, he's going to throw quite a fit about this. So let's make a deal. I'll keep your father off your back if you in return don't tell him that I was the one that tended to your wounds. There wasn't enough time to find a mender, and I know a trick or two that I shouldn't. Do we have a deal?"

In barely a whisper, Stirling musters out, "Deal."

"I told you not to make me worry, I love you so much. Get some rest. I'll make up a hearty supper to help you regain your strength," she tells him with a kiss above his brow as he slowly drifts off into a dreamless sleep.

He spent the rest of the evening in bed only waking momentarily for his mother to feed him a vegetable and barley stew, but it wasn't until late into the night Stirling finally started to dream. The dream itself is peculiar. He had never dreamt of anything like this before. It felt so real as if all of his senses were awake while he lay there sleeping. He could smell and taste the damp air as he emerged from a cave hidden under the base of an enormous tree. He could feel the cool air on his face and the leaves beneath his toes. He takes off sprinting faster than he could have possibly imagined before. The trees are a blur in his vision; despite the speed not once did he falter as he weaved through the trees, bushes, and boulders.

The ground cracks and fissures beneath his claws, it quickly crumbles and disappears leaving only an empty sky under him. The forest trees, without their solid support, tip and shatter into millions of butterflies around him. Completely alone he pumps his feathered wings, soaring effortlessly.

Laying on his back Stirling's eyes slowly open to the dark emptiness of his home.

Five

Past the bakery, the shops of the market district, and the homes on the outskirts of Lumiera's limits, Jannell crosses the city border. She checked on Stirling after feeding him breakfast and told Giles she is visiting a friend and stopping by the apothecary for Stirling. It's a harmless white lie. She is visiting a friend, but she is not stopping by the apothecary.

She treads over a hastily put-together bridge of laid down thin trunks allowing her a safe passage over a running creak to a small cottage at the edge of the woods. Calling it a cottage is more than generous. The small one-room hut is structured of branches and small trees tied together with a thatched roof. A place for an herbalist to rest her head at night or hide from the pouring rain.

The herbalist's garden is her legacy. In her eyes, who needs a house with many unused rooms when she has the colors of the rainbow surrounding her? Green of mint, purple of flowering thistle, orange of marigold, and yellow of St. John's wort. There isn't an elaborate archway in the castle that compares to her web of twine strung across her yard with drying bundles of sage, lavender, and chamomile.

Jannell can hear the wind chimes of metal and hallowed wood sing in the gentle breeze as she steps through the morning glory arch leading into the mystical garden. White petals line the curling currents of the wind. She holds her hand out to catch one on her palm as one would catch a snowflake. She lifts it to her nose to smell the sweet aroma. Smiling, she blows on it lightly, returning it to the dance in the wind.

"Faerydae!" Jannell calls out.

A woman with straight brown hair that flows like silk down to her hips pokes her head up from a batch of elderflowers, "Nell!" She jumps up with excitement. The multiple colors of fabrics sewn into a layered skirt bounce individually with the movement.

Barefoot the tall and slender woman runs soundlessly over to Jannell, nearly knocking her over as she wraps her arms around her. Jannell returns the embrace, hugging her friend, who always smells as if she fell asleep in a daisy patch, and knowing Faerydae, she probably has.

Jannell pulls back, holding her loving friend by the elbows. "Why do you always act as if I haven't seen you in ages?"

Faerydae pouts her bottom lip. "Because last week *was* ages ago."

Dropping her hand, Jannell slips her hand into Faerydaes', giving it a supportive squeeze. Her friend, her sister in her heart if not blood, is one of her few lifelines. Giles is the wall keeping her safe. Stirling is the sun brightening her day. Faerydae is the root keeping her grounded when life blows through with razor winds.

Faerydae sees the ripples in the leaves of her dandelion-haired friend. "What is it?"

Sighing, Jannell tells her, "Stirling, he got severely hurt while playing." Faerydae gasps, covering her mouth with her hands. "I closed the wounds and put honey on it, but I still worry about infection. He feels warm to the touch and the area around the wound is red and angry."

"Oh, hon," she says, pulling Jannell into another hug for reassurance. "I've got just what you need. My favorite little man will be better in no time." She leaps away from Jannell, her long legs dancing gracefully through her garden.

She stands on tiptoe as she floats through the flowers, not a single delicate plant disturbed as she passes them. Stooping down, she picks the white flowers of coriander, the leaves of the purple flower periwinkle, and the entire stem of musk mallow.

Holding up her medicinal bouquet matching the floral design on her arm, she breathes it in. She loves her job and all it entails. She lives each day to tend to her babies in her garden. She blooms awake in the morning with her flowers to spend the entirety of her day under the blue sky soaking up the sunlight. When customers come by, she can't help but be excited as she talks about the healing remedies of each plant. The best way to steep the leaves, dried versus fresh. The differences in properties between the flower petals versus the leaves. How thyme can taste good but can also fight against infections.

She twirls back to Jannell who is leaning over a patch of nettles observing a butterfly float from flower to flower.

Jannell pokes her finger to the top of a flowered nettle, soft and free from the spines, and watches it bobble back and forth. "I wish I got to live out here in nature."

Leaning her head back, Faerydae lets the sun kiss her cheeks. "I wouldn't want to be anywhere else." Her attention is caught by a robin flitting around the branches above. "Why did you move to the city, to begin with?"

Jannell tilts her head back watching the robin. "I love to bake, and I wanted my own shop. I didn't want to be just help around my brother's shop. I came to the city in search of that dream and I fell in love with Giles, he gave me everything I wanted, a shop to call my own and a son to call my world."

They stand there momentarily lost in the beauty of the earth. Faerydae speaks first, returning her gaze to Jannell, "Still don't see what you see in him. I guess he's all right looking. But I am glad, adorable little Stirling takes after you, curly hair and all."

Jannell listens to the running creek as her mind wanders back. "He's not the grumpy man he appears to be. There's a sweet side reserved only for me. He is nothing but kind and caring, though." She drops her gaze. "I wish he showed that side to Stirling more. I'm afraid of what effect that will have on him as he grows up. His father never showed any love for him."

"Then you'll just have to give him extra cuddles to make up for it. When he is better, bring him around next time. It's been a while since I've seen that smile of his," Faerydae suggests.

"Trust me, he isn't a day without my snuggles." Jannell's smile lifts Faerydae.

Faerydae hopes to have what Jannell has one day. She can do without the frowning male spouse, but she wants to love someone the way Jannell loves Stirling. The unconditional love a mother can have for her child. The way the world doesn't turn unless she sees him smile.

She will find a companion who compliments her and her trade. Someone who helps her garden grow and doesn't make her leaves wilt.

Her shoulders sink.

She just hasn't found her yet.

Maybe a beautiful alchemist will visit her garden in search of ingredients.

She sighs, letting go of her fantasy, she shakes it off and returns to her sprightly ways.

Faerydae grins holding out her bouquet of herbs to Jannell.

Jannell graciously lifts her hands to accept.

Faerydae pulls it back teasingly, she wags her finger. "No no. First, you have to promise me you're going to come by and spend the whole day with me soon. I'm more than just herbs you know."

Jannell gives her a heartwarming smile. "You know I will always come by to spend a day with my best friend. If I weren't so worried about Stirling, I would stay today."

"You should steep the coriander in hot water, it will help with his fever. You can wet the periwinkle leaves and put them under his wrappings. Smash the musk mallow into a paste, that will help with healing his wound." Faerydae takes Jannell's hand, closing it around the bouquet. "Now go take care of your boy."

"Thank you," Jannell says to her friend. She begins to pull away from Faerydae's grasp but her grip tightens.

"Nell." Her eyes are the size of the moon. "Don't forget to take care of yourself, too. Remember, I'm always here for you. Even if you have a cough, come by to see me, and I'll make you better."

Jannell pulls her friend into a final embrace. "I'll come by every time I sneeze."

A giggle ensues in Faerydae and she nuzzles her cheek into Jannell's curls. "Well, if that's so, then I'm going to sneak ragweed into your house." She steps back, taking in a full view of Jannell. Reaching up, she pulls on one of her loose curls and watches it spring back into place. "Give Stirling a hug for me."

"Will do. I'll see you soon," Jannell says, backing up.

With her hair flowing in the breeze, Faerydae watches her favorite person leave the circle of her small garden world.

Time ticks by over the next two agonizing weeks as Stirling lays anxious and bored on bed rest. He feels as if he has regained all his energy, but his mother insists on keeping him inside, saying he is still too weak to leave the house. Tired of watching the same four walls and the reoccurring neighbors passing by, he starts yearning for his dreams of running through the forest.

Even lying awake staring at the ceiling, he could feel his mind slipping as if his thoughts were not his. He'd catch himself thinking about catching a grouse or finding a nice spot in the sun to bask. The dreams are always similar, but never the same. The majority of the nights, he flew alone in a world of endless blue sky, he would dip and twirl with the absence of gravity. Some nights he ran through an ever-changing forest, the trees would move as if they were alive. Their branches reach down like arms to grab him or they would sway and wiggle as if even the thickest cedar were only a sapling in a strong storm.

Seven

Sitting on the stool below the window overlooking the street, Stirling rests his head in his hand. After gaining enough energy to leave his bed, this was the only place other than his dreams where he could feel as if he wasn't stuck inside this house. Checking over his shoulder, he glances around the empty room. The only sounds coming from the house are the creaks of the wooden frame breathing as the sun rises into the sky, warming the land. Both of his parents had gone to sell their products at the joust, leaving him alone at the house.

He lightly touches the cloth bandage around his right arm, his healing burns still tender underneath. Thoughts begin to seep into his mind, calling him to the forest.

He spins around in his stool to face the room clutching his right arm in his hand. He stares listening intently even though he knows no one will be home until the evening.

Standing up from the windowsill, Stirling casually makes his way down the stairs out of the bakery's front door.

Weighed down with a strong sense of familiarity, Stirling is still nervous as he treks through the forest. He follows the path he had climbed a few weeks ago. Before he wandered free-spirited without care, now he jumps at each crack of a twig, fearing what other beasts are lurking in the unmapped terrain. He knows he should turn around. He should head back down the mountain before repeating his ignorant mistake again, but a lingering itch in the back of his mind tells him to continue forward.

He hesitates as he approaches the glade where he encountered the fledgling. Checking his surroundings, he sprints across the empty space and back into the false security of the trees.

Finally, he slows his pace. Stepping out into another small clearing, he comes upon a beech tree, its webbing roots raised from the ground as it sits on top of large boulders protruding out from a naturally made wall of rock, extending towards the pyramidal mountain peaks, a ridge made of jagged points like spikes on a monster's back unattainable to hike by foot. However, the distance straight up isn't far. Tilting his head, he sees the almost hidden cave between the rocks that can easily be mistaken as a deep shadow.

Stepping up to the boulders, he reaches out and strokes the tree's root, gripping the boulder as if it is glued. The tree is perpetually stuck in the position of sliding off the boulders and closing the entrance for good. He stands there with his hand still resting on the root as he stares into the cave that eats any light trying to enter it, making the depth and contents waiting inside unknown.

He taps his thumb to his fingers. He peers into the beckoning depths, then to the bright forest around him. A breeze comes from the abyss with a low whistle. The cave is calling for him to enter. He taps his fingers faster. Swallowing hard, he shifts uneasily on his feet.

With unsteady footing, Stirling descends into the cave. He glances back at the friendly forest behind him and slows to a stop. Halfway turned around, he feels another breeze with a scent he's never known. The whistle tells him to keep walking. He balls his tapping fingers into a fist and carries on deeper into the tunnel. Beginning to shiver as he runs his hand along the smooth cold wall for guidance as the light disappears and the shadows engulf him.

The distance of the tunnel is longer than Stirling expected as he continues to walk through the pitch-black world, his eyes straining to take in light that can help him find his footing along the path. Just as he starts to believe he will never reach the end, he begins to see the outline of his hand on the wall as the tunnel slowly grows to shades of gray as a dim light fights against the darkness pushing it away.

He steps out of the cramped dark tunnel into a vast cave three times the size of his home. The shape of the cave is a dome with the center of the ceiling being higher than the outer rims sloping down to the cave walls. The cave floor is scattered with various sizes of rocks, from pebbles to boulders up to Stirling's knees. Directly across the cave is a large opening giving away to the mountain's fortress cliffs that are a sheer drop to the rocky waters of the unforgiving ocean a mountain's height below.

His mouth gapes open in awe as he slowly steps across the center of the cave, rocks tumbling across the ground as he shuffles his feet, too distracted to watch his foot placement. The view of the neverending field of blue slowly comes into view as he nears the mouth of the cave. What he has been smelling is the ocean. He breathes in deep, memorizing the new salty scent.

Stopping around ten or so steps away from the ledge, he twists his neck taking in the entirety of the opening the whole bakery could easily fit through. He turns back to face the massive room wondering how it came to this shape. He figured it had to be natural, but how? Was it from the wind? Or the water, but the water was so far below. Did the mountain form with a pocket in it, like when you trap air while folding the bread dough?

Stirling considers the apple-sized rock by his feet.

If this formed like the dough's air pockets, are you a crumb or are you the excess flour that helped cause it? He thinks to himself, then lightly kicks the apple rock back into the shadows in the direction he had come from.

The sound gives off a subtle echo through the cave before settling down into its new spot.

His heart skips a beat.

The sound of another rock skipping across the cave floor fills his ears and fear leaps to the front of his mind. The rock tumbles from the shadows into view as it comes to a rolling stop a step away from him. He breathes in deep and sharply through his nostrils as he focuses on steadying his nerves. His thumb instinctively taps each fingertip over and over as he stares down at the rock he knows is not the one he had kicked. He begins to calm himself by convincing himself the rock had tumbled over to him because the one he had kicked must've knocked into it.

That has to be the explanation. His heart doesn't listen to his reasoning and picks up pace in his chest.

An uneasy dread looms over him, telling him this is likely not the answer and that maybe he isn't alone in this cave. He squints his eyes scanning back and forth across the cave shrouded in darkness. Even with the heavy shadows, there was enough light shining in he could make out any objects if they were to move. His eyes dance from shadow to shadow, waiting for whoever or whatever is there to reveal itself.

"I'm lunch. I served myself to a large animal for lunch." Stirling mutters under his breath, his voice quivering. Then his eyes lock on an object.

A large form stands directly in front of his only exit. The form is nothing more than a heavy shadow indistinguishable from any distinct animal features, but its eyes glow gold with the reflection of the subtle amount of light.

The creature takes slow cautious steps forward, and in response, Stirling steadies his quaking knees as he steps backward in an attempt to keep his distance. The creature's steps are abnormally silent except for the occasional rock shifting under its weight. Finally, the unknown animal steps into the light reaching halfway into the room, the dark earthy orange scales glistening.

Stirling, once again, stands staring at the fledgling.

He can feel his right arm throb as the not-so-distant memory of their last encounter pangs through the permanent mark left across his forearm. He coddles his right arm against his chest as the pain resurfaces and continues to back up until there isn't anywhere else to go—his heels at the edge of the cave mouth. One more step and he will plummet to his death.

The strong winds from the ocean push on his back as if warning him there is nothing to stop him once he makes that final step. But stepping forward doesn't feel safe to him either. He almost didn't make it home alive the last time he had encountered this peculiar dragon.

The dragon, whose body stands to Stirling's shoulders, not factoring in his elongated neck, cocks its head as he watches the frightened boy before him.

Unknowing how to escape his current predicament Stirling squats down and hugs his knees. Burying his face already streaked with tears of fear, all he can do is hope the dragon will leave him alone.

Silence, he can't hear anything except the sound of his heart drumming in his head and the whistle of the wind. Then he feels it. A warm breath hits his head sending goosebumps down the back of his neck.

"This is it. I'm dragon food," he whimpers as he continues to feel the constant breaths of the dragon.

Mustering up the courage to convince himself to sneak a peek, Stirling peels his face away from the safety and comfort of his knees. He wants to see the dragon one last time before he meets his end. What an awful irony his life is to be cut prematurely by the animal he is so desperately in love with.

The dragon's face is close—any closer and their noses would be touching. Both of their golden eyes lock for a brief moment. The fledgling's expression becomes excited as it jumps backward in a playful manner.

The sudden flash of movement spooks Stirling, his body jerking back reflexively. He teeters on the edge for a moment before finally losing his balance and toppling backward. His short life flashes before his eyes revealing nothing more than his life at the bakery, sunrise to sunset in the market district. Then there were the small amounts of times he escaped to the freedom of the mountains. The only times his happiness was pure.

Stirling opens his eyes, his body feels weightless, but the cave's ceiling remains in place. It isn't leaping towards the sky as he falls to the watery depths. He isn't falling. His heels are still dug into the hard surface of the cave's ledge, but the rest of his body hangs suspended above the daunting ocean beckoning for him. Holding on to him is the dragon, his tunic clamped firmly in its jaws.

With a body built with raw power and strength, it uses its muscular neck and hooking claws to dig into the condensed mountain ground and pull Stirling back up to the safety of the cave.

Once he is safe and sound on the solid surface, Stirling fleetingly crawls away from both the cliff's edge and the dragon who watches him with amused curiosity. Stirling pulls his dirt-coated knees back into his chest, recoiling from dragon terrified, "Why is it every time I meet you, I almost get killed!"

The fledgling bows its head and takes a single step towards Stirling, testing if he is allowed to continue forward.

Stirling defensively holds his hand palm out, "Don't!" He cowers away with eyelids squeezed shut. The dragon ignores the cowering demands of the boy and tenderly steps up to him. It sniffs Stirling's hand and then pushes the space between its two horns on top of its head against Stirling's palm.

Stirling's eyes shoot open. He yanks his hand back as if he had been bit. His eyes slowly turn to meet the fledgling's. He bounces between his unharmed hand to the peculiar dragon. Stirling doesn't understand. What are the dragon's intentions? What does it want from him? One day it attacks him. Then it saves him.

Pretending to be brave, Stirling spits his words, "If you're going to eat me, then just do it already."

"*I'm not going to eat you.*"

Stirling blinks. Did the dragon talk? He shakes his head vigorously, *no, no, nope, nope*. He's lost his mind. Keeping his eyes on the unknown creature, he crawls backward slowly. The fledgling takes a single step forward. Kicking pebbles in his wake, Stirling's turnshoes skid as he tears off for the tunnel in the back of the cave.

"*WAIT!*"

The voice of a young boy rings in his head. Stirling doesn't listen to the voice, doesn't turn around as he flees through the tunnel. Blinded, he runs with his hands stretched out in front. He can hear the claws of the dragon clacking against the hard ground behind him. It's gaining on him.

Stirling lets out a whelp as he trips. Falling through nothingness he slams into the invisible ground. Groaning he curls his already injured arm into himself as he rolls onto his side.

It's close, he can't see it but he can feel its presence practically on top of him. Panicked, he scampers back to his feet. His sense of direction gone with the absence of light, he collides with the wall. Spinning around, he presses his back against the wall and side steps in the direction he believes is the exit.

"*What—*"

The voice cuts itself off as Stirling makes a break for it.

He keeps his fingertips dragging along the wall for stability, his feet, with ankles bending with the small rocks rolling underfoot, work hard to propel him forward. Stumbling several more times, the light blooms to life before him. With the gift of sight, he picks up his pace in his race for survival.

He passes the boulders of the entrance into the open glade; his freedom is short lived as the neckline of his tunic chokes him. He's forced backward, his feet slipping out from under him he falls flat on his back.

The golden eyes appear above him, *"I said I'm not going to hurt you!"*

Stirling covers his ears, the disembodied voice shouting inside his skull. He's already weeping. The voice is stating innocence but his instincts are screaming danger. He's going mad. He's going to die here, and his body will never be found. His mother will never know what happened to him.

He fetals up with his hands still pressed to his ears. Can you even bury a madman on sacred ground?

"Yeah, you're correct. You are crazy." The fledgling sits down, *"Are you done with whatever it is you are doing?"*

Stirling uncovers his ears, the voice still loud and clear in his mind. He peeks at the dragon who cocks his head with a flick of his tail. It can't be possible. This wild dragon cannot be talking to him.

Wyverns in the Cavalry are bred in their captivity and when a Rider comes of age, they are walked down a line of suitable dragons for them to choose from. The Wyvern will then accept or deny the partnership. If accepted an incredible bond is granted by the dragon to the human allowing them to become as close as two beings can be *without* sharing a mind.

But to exchange thoughts with the dragon, to hear it speak to you, to communicate directly has only been achieved by a selective amount of elites over the entire Cavalry existence. Even then, it took most of, if not their entire career to master the ability. An ability they brought with them to the grave, never sharing the secret of their success.

"This isn't real," he says. Sitting up cautiously, he closes his eyes. He pinches the brim of his nose. "It's another one of those strange dreams I've been having. Where they feel real, but they aren't."

"*Those were mine,*" the fledgling replies even though the words weren't aimed at him.

Stirling pauses. He opens his eyes, focusing past his hand on the dragon. "What?"

"*I said, those were mine.*"

"I've truly lost my mind." Stirling shakes his head in disbelief.

"*I don't understand. How did you 'lose your mind'*" the fledgling asks naively.

"People with—" He holds his right arm up to show his insignia but drops it, changing his phrasing. "People like me, don't *talk* to dragons. We can't. It's not possible."

"*Then what are you doing right now?*" the fledgling says, cheeky.

"Leaving." Stirling gets up, brushing the dirt from his clothing. He stops mid-brush, his gaze landing back on the dragon. "So what did you mean, 'those were mine.'"

"*Your dreams, running through the mountains, wiggly trees, forever flying.*" The fledgling wags his tail. Stirling stares blankly, unsure of what to say. The fledgling continues, "*Those are my dreams. But this is all new to me, so I don't have full control over it. I guess they leaked into your mind.*"

Stirling stands idle as he comprehends what is being presented to him. A dragon is telling him his dreams are leaking into his subconscious?

"You're acting like this is normal."

"*Is this not normal?*"

Stirling can hear the honesty in its voice, or what he perceives to be its voice, "No. This—" He motions to the two of them, "Isn't normal."

The fledgling shrugs its shoulders, "*Seems normal to me.*"

"What, do you go around talking to people all the time?" Stirling counters crossing his arms.

"*Never spoken to anything before. You're the first thing I've ever met I could communicate with. I guess I got a little excited.*"

Stirling drops his hands. "Not even another dragon?"

The fledgling shakes his head. "*Nope. I've seen them out over the ocean. But I've never met any of them.*"

Stirling's curiosity begins to take over, replacing the fear he was being controlled by earlier. "What about your parents?"

"*Never met them.*" The fledgling appears unconcerned about the matter.

"If you never met them, then do you have a name?" Stirling takes a daring step forward.

"*Nope.*"

"Then what do you go by?"

"*Nothing. Did you not hear me earlier? I've never spoken to someone before.*" His words come off brash.

"Right." Stirling's eyes wander to the surrounding trees as he contemplates. This is real. How is this real? He returns to the dragon who hasn't moved, the round golden eyes watching, waiting for him to carry on the conversation. A conversation he shouldn't be able to have, but he is having it. Accepting the strange reality, Stirling speaks again, "I can give you a name."

"*You're going to give me a name?*"

"Well, yeah, if we're going to talk to each other, I can't call you nothing all the time. You need a name."

The fledgling leaps up to his feet, excited. "*We're going to be friends!*"

Friends, Stirling thinks, *with a dragon.* His first friend by description sounds like a figment of his imagination. He observes the bandage around his arm, but it is real indeed.

"Sure."

"*So, what are you going to name me?*" the fledgling pesters, bouncing on his claws.

"I'm thinking." Stirling racks his brain. He has never had to name anything before. "Cauis?"

"*Cai-a what?*"

"Never mind." Stirling runs his eyes over the orange dragon, with feathered wings. Orange, like the color of fire. Fire. He squeezes his eyes shut, traveling back to his visits to the monastery. They had told him words in Latin. Fire, Latin. It was? It was? "Ignis?"

"*Ignis?*" The fledgling mulls the words over in his mind. "*Yeah, I like it.*"

"There, your name is Ignis." Stirling checks the sun overhead. "It was nice to meet you Ignis, but I do have to get going."

"*Go? Go where?*" Ignis takes conservative steps toward Stirling.

Stirling responds with a step back. "Home. I don't live in the mountains, and I do have parents who will be mad if they find out I'm not home."

"*Can I come?*"

"NO!" Stirling touches his neck; he thinks of the tailor's body swinging from the noose outside the city. Ignis drops his head, yielding at the rise in Stirling's voice. "You-you can't come to the city! It's dangerous for both of us!"

"*Why?*"

Stirling drops his gaze to his shoes, lowering his voice to a mumble, "It just is." Sighing, he brings himself to meet Ignis' eye. "I do need to go though. Just-uh—" He puts his hand up as if talking to a dog, "Stay."

Turning his back to Ignis, Stirling heads towards the tree line to start his descent. He hears the scuffing of dirt behind him. Stopping, he checks over his shoulder.

Ignis freezes midstep as if he had been caught red handed.

"I wasn't going to follow. I swear."

For the first time in over a week, Stirling smiles, this is not how he pictured a dragon, "I'll be back. I promise."

Staggering up the bakery steps, Stirling slips in through the front door. He pauses in the entranceway, listening.

Good, he thinks with a sigh of relief.

The house is exactly as he left it, empty. His mother will never know he had broken their deal, even though—he feels the presence now in the back of his mind. The call to the mountains, the lingering itch, it was a muffled voice. A voice now loud and clear in his mind as he opened the once locked door to it.

His knee gives as his muscles are unable to support him as he steps up onto the first step of the staircase. That was something his mother was still right about; he isn't fully recovered, and rest is still needed.

Climbing the stairs on all four like an exhausted dog, Stirling crawls the distance of the room. His eyelids droop, cutting half of his vision. He blindly crawls onto his mattress and rolls up in the blanket. With the blanket tucked up past his chin, he drifts off to sleep, returning him to his dreams of the mountains.

Eight

His hand is in his mother's but his eyes are on the mountains, where he spoke to the dragon. No, he had named the dragon. Where he spoke to *Ignis* yesterday. He closes his eyes checking his mind, he can still feel Ignis' thoughts. He doesn't hear them but knows they are there. They aren't for him to hear, like watching someone mouth words under their breath to themselves.

He opens his eyes. There's a sparse number of houses outside the city limits, those who need the room for their trade. Stirling's attention is caught by the tanner pulling a goat hide taught on a wooden frame. He's tugged forward. His mother is practically skipping as she guides him down the familiar path away from the city.

"How much longer to the flower lady's house?" Stirling asks.

"It's Faerydae remember."

"I know."

They cross the wobbling bridge and step under the morning glory arch into one of the mystical lands reserved for the tales told by the puppeteer in the town's center. His eyes dazzle as he watches the flowers dance in the wind and the bundles of plants float above his head as if suspended by magic.

"You brought him!" Stirling hears shouted from the sky. He investigates the garden around confused, he knows the voice but he can't determine where it came from.

"Yeah, his arm is healing quite nicely thanks to you!" his mother calls up at the bright green elm tree.

He follows her gaze up to the branches overhead. The flower lady's hair shimmers in the sunlight as she hangs over the edge of a hammock hung between branches halfway up the tree. Stirling doesn't understand why an adult woman is resting in a tree, but he never understands anything the flower lady does. That is the reason he agreed to accompany his mother in visiting. He's always been intrigued by her quirkiness. You won't meet anyone in the market district that relates more to the wildlife around them than their closest human neighbor.

Faerydae swings from her hammock and with the agility of a squirrel, she hops down the overlapping branches until her bare feet stick firmly to the soil beside Stirling.

"My favorite little human!" she squeals, wrapping her arms around Stirling. Stirling "oofs" as he is swallowed up by the tall woman. Faerydae pulls back from the overly welcoming hug and uses both hands to play with Stirling's hair. "Look at these wild curls!" She pinches both of his cheeks. "You're so cute!"

Jannell smiles, she knows there's no containing her wild friend. This is her response every time Stirling has come by to visit with her since he was a toddler. He's never stopped her, even now, he stands politely accepting the affection. She puts her hands on her hips. "You know one day he's going to get too old for that."

"Oh daffodils, he'll always be my adorable little Stirling." She pats him on the head and then raises her hand high above her as if he was growing. "Even when he grows up to be a strong young man."

Stirling stares up at the flower lady with fascination and her playful mannerisms, to her, life is beautiful and each breath is a gift. She can be overbearing at times, like in this moment, but his mother explained the flower lady's reasoning. She doesn't have a child of her own and lives vicariously through Jannell and Stirling.

His eyes remain on her as she kneels in front of him. Her long and slender hands touch the bandage on his arm, her voice now taking on the role of his mother's. "How are you feeling? Does it hurt? Itch? Tell me and I can fix it." She ends with certainty, emphasized in a nod.

Stirling bites his bottom lip becoming shy. With a hunch in his shoulders, he dips his chin and tells the sprouting blades of grass. "It doesn't hurt much anymore, it kind of itches, I guess."

"Then I've got just the thing." She takes Stirling's left hand and stands back up, she meets Jannell's eyes. "And I can stir something up for you, you seem tired." She turns, pointing her finger at her single-room home. "To the hut!"

Jannell takes Stirling's right hand, careful not to hurt him, and they walk together like a family across Faerydae's garden.

Pulling back the curtain door of her home Faerydae releases Stirling's hand. Hopping over to her ingredients, she runs her hand along the sides of small wooden boxes neatly stacked and organized on a shelf. "Ah hah," she exclaims, pulling one of the boxes free. "Nell, can you fill that pot with water from the rain trough?"

"Sure." Jannell grabs the small pot hanging from a hook on the wall and takes it outside.

Stirling watches in silence as the flower lady, who is beginning to hum and bounce to her own beat, squats beside her small stove. Moving the coals, she stuffs new tinder into the stove to feed the sparks and small flames. She grabs another pot and sets it on the coals to begin warming.

"Here," Jannell says, holding out the pot of water.

Faerydae practically sings the words, "Thank you!" Taking the pot, she splits the water between the two pots and sets the second on the fire.

As if she is performing a dance, her body moves like it's made of water in fluid, rolling movements.

She takes a handful of mint from the previously grabbed box and drops it into one of the pots.

With a spin, she skips back to her shelf of ingredients and grabs licorice root.

She points it at Jannell. "This one is for you, it'll help give you energy, plus it tastes good."

Intrigued, Stirling is practically underneath the flower lady as she works. Each time he has traveled here with his mother, he watches the flower lady intently. What herbs does she grab? What is each of them for? How does she prepare them? Faerydae twirls a knife in her hand and quickly slices the root into even pieces. Without the concern of tripping on Stirling underfoot, she bends and twirls as she steps around him and returns to the empty pot of water to drop the roots in.

"Does mine taste good?" Stirling asks, now peeking into the pots.

"Most likely, mint always tastes good, but you aren't going to drink it. This is going to go on your skin." She taps her right arm, "I'm going to make enough for you to take home in case the itching returns. Same with you, Nell." She talks over her shoulder. "I'll give you all of my licorice root, so you can boil it whenever you're tired."

Jannell leans against the one small table in the room observing her best friend doing what she does best. "You spoil us Faerydae."

She turns to Jannell. "Well, I have to. If I want us all to live a long life together, I need to make sure your health is in tip-top shape." She squats beside Stirling finding his eyes.

Her voice is a serious tone he has never heard from her before. "I know you are watching closely, Stirling. Don't stop, okay? Stay curious. Do you understand?"

Stirling thinks he understands her meaning and nods.

She pokes his forehead. "You're a bright kid, don't ever stop learning new things". The shifting of dirt below Jannell's feet means Faerydae has said too much. She smiles up at her friend, apologetic. She turns back to Stirling. "Why don't you go try and catch me a grasshopper before this mint is done boiling."

"Okay!" Stirling agrees.

"Get ready, set, go!"

Stirling takes off running out of the hut. She stands up and takes a seat on the table next to Jannell swinging her legs.

"That's what I'm worried about," Jannell says without context.

"About what?" Faerydae inquires, but she knows the answer. She knows Jannell and she knows Stirling's knack for picking up skills.

"I'm worried that he won't stop trying to learn and expand his knowledge, and you want to know what scares me the most." Jannell turns her head to meet her friend's eye. "I don't want him to stop."

Faerydae squeezes her friend's shoulder. "Then we'll encourage his dreams, but we will keep him safe at the same time." Jannell cups her hand over Faerydae's as Stirling rushes inside with his hands cupped together above his head.

"Got one!" he shouts.

Faerydae leaps off the table throwing her hands in the air. "You win!"

Nine

It was not long after his trip to the flower lady's home, that his mother gave him permission to start venturing from the house again.

Going around town with his mother was nice but he was still in desperate need to escape the repetitive days of the bakery into the unwritten forest. Stirling would pass the long days talking to Ignis. He was slower to adjust to the newfound friendship, but with Ignis' chatty personality, they were laughing like old friends soon enough.

Taking advantage of his mother's trust, he tries to make his way up to visit Ignis as much and as often as he can. Walking up the steep incline every time he visited became easier with each passing day. It didn't take him long to become accustomed to it. After weeks of this schedule, his breathing barely differed by the time he reached the cave entrance.

Each day Ignis waits eagerly below the overhanging tree so they can walk side by side to their new favorite spot together.

There is a small canyon hidden in the mountains with pillars made of earth rising up inside the carved-out land like rock-formed trees refusing to be torn down while the rest of the land eroded away. This canyon is used as the training grounds for the Winged Cavalry. The training base is at the start of the canyon, where the bottom of the mountain's slope is level with the canyon's floor. For stamina training and the eventual combat courses, the classes are frequently held at the top of the rising canyon walls until it plateaus for the length of an hour's walk, cutting through the mountains until it drops off to the ocean.

Sitting on a nearby bluff overlooking the stretch of land cleared of trees between the forest and canyon's ledge Stirling and Ignis hide, concealed by cypress trees, ferns, and small field maple. They are able to watch the young Winged Riders' class silently without being detected.

Stirling runs his fingers over the grotesque scars on his forearm that have healed in place of the wounds given to him by Ignis a few months back. His fingertips can feel the bumpy, soft skin below but he has no sensation besides pressure on the scars. The thick scars give off the appearance of what they are, melted skin, stretched, and swirled. It has distorted his Insignia to the extent of being unrecognizable.

A class of five students stands along the canyon's ledge. They aren't the only class, but they are the only entry-level class made up of children in their tenth year. Compared to the previous class sizes consisting of two or three children, their class number is relatively high. This class will remain together for the rest of their training, moving up in skill and technique as a unit until they graduate at the age of sixteen. Afterward, they will be separated into their appropriate sections where they will get specialized training for each unit.

The class Instructor Aldred, a retired Captain of Unit Lapicidina who still gives off the presence he can fight off a full-grown grizzly bear, walks down the line of children with a stern expression.

"Before you learn to do anything with your dragon, you

must gain each other's trust. Not until then will your dragon respond to even the simplest of commands, such as to come and stand by your side," he says to the children who remain in an attentive stance listening intently to his every word.

"I will assume you have all been building a bond with your dragon, am I correct?" He pauses to see the children nod lightly before continuing. "I have sent your dragons down into the canyon. You will need to space yourselves along the ledge and use your personal whistle to call your own dragon over to your side.

Stirling watches eagerly, a coverless journal sits on the grass in front of him. The pressed parchment was bound together waiting to be filled with a multitude of sketches as a substitute for written notes.

Whistles begin to fill the air as the students begin to blow on the small metal tube strung on a leather cord around their neck at their own timing. Instructor Aldred stands back and observes as the students attempt to call their dragon to them. He walks to the beginning of the line, still giving them distance, and peers over the edge into the canyon. Three of the dragons have turned their heads and are listening in the direction of the whistles, while one doesn't even bother to acknowledge them. Shaking his head with disappointment, he keeps his mouth firmly shut giving no further direction to help the students.

What catches Stirling's attention during this exercise is the girl at the end of the line. She has a thin frame with her long dark hair pulled back away from her face into a ponytail. Her dragon is a simple beige color, its scute-style scales similar to that of a crocodile all dragons possess, appearing smooth from a distance. This only made the sharp cone shape spikes protruding from its face and down the back of its neck much more apparent. Unlike Ignis' eyes which seem to smile as he takes in the world, this dragon's eyes are fierce. The instinct to kill glinting off like the reflection of light.

Except this is not the only fact that caught Stirling's attention, it is the fact her dragon, as fierce and as stubborn as it appears, responded to her on her first call and sits obediently at her side. While the other students continue to struggle with their dragons. The scaly creatures slowly respond to their commands and crawl their way out of the canyon to meet their riders.

"Amiria, wonderful! Excellent job!" Instructor Aldred says proudly. "Now that's what I call a bond."

"Pft, she's got nothing on us, right, Ignis?" Stirling gloats, bumping his shoulder on Ignis who has been watching beside him,

"*I don't know. She seems like a natural to me.*"

"You're supposed to agree with me," Stirling points out.

"*Oh, I mean, yeah, she'll have to train a lot more to beat us,*" Ignis says, correcting himself.

"A little late now," Stirling says snidely.

After all the other dragons have finally made their way to their rider's side, taking longer than Instructor Aldred had hoped for, he begins to speak.

"I can see some of you exceeded my expectations," he says, narrowing down at Amiria. "Then some of you couldn't even meet them," he mentions, stopping in front of the kid whose dragon took the longest to even acknowledge the sound of the whistle.

The dragon behind him, an olive green color with ram-like horns, twitches its head, its attention darting around at everything in the vicinity while making a small chirp now and then.

Instructor Aldred scans the rest of the class as he speaks, "If you cannot even get your dragon to acknowledge you, how will you ever expect it to let you not only ride it but also command its movements? Dragons need to trust their riders with every scale on their body. If they don't, they will not dive into battle for you. They are intelligent creatures just like you. They understand they are risking their lives to do so."

The boy with the olive-green dragon raises his hand.

"Go ahead, Clyde," Instructor Aldred allows.

"So, are we not going to learn how to ride our dragons back today?" Clyde questions with a hint of disappointment in his voice.

"Oh, you young lads make me laugh. The answer is a definite no. Your dragons are not big enough to carry you yet. And you—" Instructor Aldred glares down at Clyde "— have a lot of training to do before then." He sizes up the rest of the class, "I've got something better planned. We are going to send your dragons to fly back to base alone and we are going to jog the entire way back. Now how does that sound?"

"That has to be half the island!" one of the other students, whose name is Nellie, complains.

"If we jog quickly, we can make it in less than an hour, maybe faster since it's downhill," Amiria chimes in with an encouraging smile. "We already jogged the distance uphill, so down will be easier."

Nellie rolls her eyes with the cross of her arms. "Says only you."

"Why do we need to do so much running? Aren't we going to be traveling by dragon?" Garret standing beside Amiria asks. The last student, Warrick nods in agreement.

"Have your parents taught you anything?! A Rider must always be in top shape. They must be able to survive and maneuver in and on any terrain they are deployed to. However, many of you may never leave your guard post on this island. Tell me this, what would you do if you no longer had access to a bow and had to take your fight to the ground? What would you do if your dragon was taken down and you were deserted a day's walk away from the nearest town? You have to be prepared for any situation that could possibly come your way. Question time is over, period. Send off your dragons!" Instructor Aldred directs.

The young dragons awkwardly lift themselves off the ground into the air at the command of their rider, their bodies tilting and swaying with the flaps of their gangly wings. With a flick of her wrist, Amiria directs her dragon to return to base. It spreads its chiropteran or bat-like wings with the membrane skin stretching between nimble elongated fingers lifting it off the ground with a single flap taking off in the direction of their base.

A disgruntled frown takes form on Stirling's face as he watches Amiria. "Well, isn't she going to be a showoff?"

Ignis proposes, "*Maybe she is better than us, I won't do something because you flick your wrist.*"

"She is not better than us. I don't need to go flicking my wrist because I can just talk to you. I bet her parents have been training her for years. That's not fair I…"

"*Look at you making up excuses.*" Ignis chuckles.

"Yeah, yeah, yeah. Shut up, Ignis."

Remaining in their hiding spot, they watch the class jog away trailing behind Instructor Aldred. One by one like little ducklings following their mother.

A week later, Stirling stands in a location further along the canyon the class never reaches and is out of sight in case they do show up to their regular location. The treeless stretch of land makes it a perfect spot for Ignis to practice flying without any obstacles in his way. He can see why they use this terrain for practice and eventually use the canyon itself for more advanced techniques like leaping from the canyon walls and parrying from attacks using the canyon's pillars for cover.

He holds his journal close to his face as he tries to

decipher the sketches he had jotted down previously while watching the class.

"Okay, so we got the bond part down. We need to get you off the ground or we'll fall way behind the class and it'll be hard for us to catch up." He states, closing his journal and tucking it into his waistband.

"If you want to stay caught up with the class maybe you should start running." Ignis teases.

"We're not here for me, plus that walk up this mountain from my home is not an easy hike. You don't even walk half the distance I do in a day. Now you got me off-topic. Flying. It can't be that hard. Show me what you got." Stirling rants.

Ignis makes a sound that mimics a sigh before spreading out his sleek feathered wings. He tries to repeat what he saw the other dragons do by giving his wings a large pump. Dust fills the air but Ignis' feet remain firmly on the ground.

"Okay, well, that was a good try. Let's try and figure out what they are doing differently than you. That sounds like a good place to start." Stirling explains. Ignis responds by mentally rolling his eyes and mutters something in the back of his thoughts Stirling couldn't comprehend.

Stirling begins to pace along the side of the canyon with Ignis trailing at his heels. He thinks of the men back at the monastery. How they would flip through books and scrolls, researching facts to answer their questions. He pictures the imaginary pages of his brain as he rummages through trying to think of a way to get Ignis flying.

Staring down at his feet, he loses himself in his thoughts, the rocks and dirt moving as he shuffles his steps. He pauses. He continues to stare down at his feet and lifts them one at a time as he realizes something that now seems so obvious he feels like an idiot he hadn't noticed before.

He spins around abruptly facing Ignis, who pulls back his head startled.

"What, what is it?" he asks, confused by Stirling's sudden actions as he shifts his weight back and forth on his four

limbs waiting for Stirling to finally speak.

"That's it! Your feet!" Stirling exclaims.

Ignis glances down then back up at Stirling. *"My feet? Excuse me?"* Still not comprehending, he says, *"There's nothing wrong with my feet."*

"No, not that there's something wrong with them. It's that you have four of them!" Stirling begins to explain, "All the other dragons only have two, then their arms are their wings," Stirling flaps his arms, "with that skin stuff spreading out across the length of their body. Even though your feathers seem to extend from your shoulder blades to your hips you're more shaped like a tall dog than a bat."

Ignis scoffs, offended at Stirling's remark.

"No, listen. You need more than just wing flapping to get yourself off the ground. You need to use your leg strength to give yourself a jumping start."

Ignis examines his body. He had never thought of his appearance as different from the other dragons until now. *"So you figured that out. Now, what's your plan?"*

Walking about thirty steps away from Ignis, Stirling announces, "I've got an idea. I'm going to cup my hands like a step and you're going to run at me and use my hands to vault yourself into the air. I will try and give you a lift at the same time, okay? But don't tackle me."

"I think that's a crazy idea, you want me to run at you?" Ignis questions.

"Yeah! It'll work. You have to trust me!" Stirling says, trying to convince him.

Ignis thinks it over for a brief second before replying, *"Fine, but if you get hurt, this was your idea."* Ignis backs up a few steps getting into a ready position by lowering his head and forelegs while sticking his rear up into the air, his feathered tail fanning out above him.

Stirling bends his knees into a shallow squat holding his cupped hands at knee height. "All right, on the count of three!" he shouts. "One, two…THREE!"

Ignis takes off sprinting. Approaching Stirling in only a few bounds, he leaps into the air as he spreads out his wings with the tips reaching for the sky. His claws barely touch Stirling's hands as he pumps his wings down with all the force he can muster. The force of the wind created by his wings pushes Stirling's thin frame to the ground.

He lies flat on his back as he witnesses Ignis soar into the sky. He hollers with excitement before coughing on the dust circulating around him.

Still lying on his back, he relaxes putting his arms behind his head as a pillow to take in the view of their success. Ignis wobbles in the air as he slowly circles around above. He can do this. Even with no one to show, without the threat of his family being hanged, he will soon be able to fly.

Ignis tips in the air, "*Ope! Uh oh, oh no.*" He counterbalances and tips in the opposite direction and crashes to the ground. "*I'm okay!*"

Stirling sits up, he stands corrected, one day he will be able to fly.

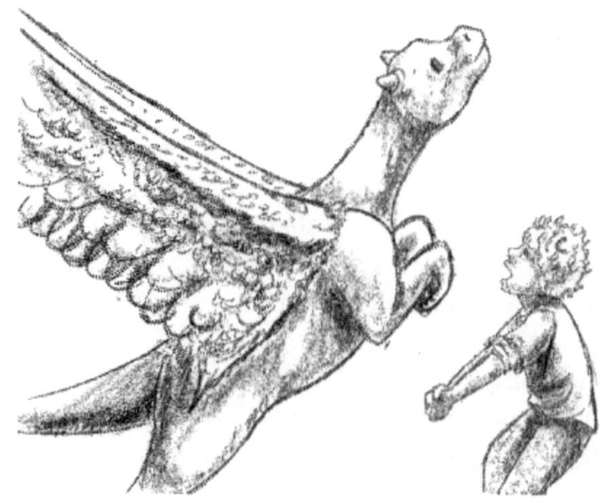

With his cheek pressing against the back of his hand, Stirling daydreams out of the second-floor window while his parents finish preparing supper.

"Stirling," his mother says, trying to get his attention away from the window for the first time since he had come home that day.

He turns around to acknowledge her.

"As your mother, I should have asked this a long time ago, but where is it you go all day? I'm worried that I'm not being a good mother if I'm too busy to even know where my own son goes off to almost every day."

"I just made some friends with some farmer kids. They've got a plot of land to play on and some good climbing trees," Stirling lies.

"I'm glad that you have made friends, but that seems a bit far," Jannell retorts.

"It doesn't take me long if I walk fast. It's not much further than the flower lady's. Sometimes I hitch a ride on the back of a cart to shorten my time. I don't really get along with any of the kids in our market area. They all seem more interested in their family trade and that's it," he adds in defense.

His father, Giles, peers up from the cheese and bread he is slicing on the kitchen table and declares, "As it should be. You too should start learning the bakery business. It's a respectable trade. You might be all play right now, but one day you're going to have to step up to the podium and take over this place like I did when my parents grew old. And if you don't want to go out of business, you are going to have to know what you are doing. Know what will make you stand out from the rest of the bakeries other than location and convenience."

Stirling rolls his eyes as he gets up from the window. He swings his leg over the table's bench and sits down begrudgingly. He bites his tongue as usual. He's learned to never say anything back to his father because no matter what he says, it will lead his father into lecturing him longer about the importance of your place in society and the bakery business.

Giles picks up a chunk of barley bread and a slab of cheese and sets it on the table in front of Stirling. "Now eat your supper with no more talk of these so-called friends of yours, and Jannell, this is your doing. Showing him it's okay to travel that far for playtime by bringing him to that herbalist's hut all the time."

Jannell disregards her husband's accusatory banter by reaching over and tousling Stirling's curls. She lowers herself on the bench next to him and when Giles turns to check the coals on the open-top stove keeping the house warm.

She whispers in Stirling's ear, "Having friends is good. I'll make sure you can go play while you're still young."

She sits up straight and smiles down at him. He returns the smile graciously but quickly hides it when his father turns back around and joins them at the table.

Eleven

The night's chilling tendrils creep through the cracks of Faerydae's cottage. She doesn't seem to notice anymore with her skirt of color, scraps of fabric spread out like petals of a flowering meadow. Her skin flushing, she leans over the hot coals of her alchemy set. She finishes grinding the last of the beetle wings in her mortar. Setting down her pestle, she adds the dry ingredient to a bowl already containing dried rosemary and honey.

Taking a freshly sharpened knife, she folds the end of her hair over the edge, and with a fluid movement, she cuts a small lock off. She whispers words as she sprinkles them into the bowl. She sets the bowl over the glowing coals and pumps the bellow, breathing a fresh breath of air across them. They ripple and flicker with life, melting the honey into a softened liquid.

Reaching over to a box of clay bottles, she runs her hands across the corks until she sees one with a pink painted dot. She plucks it from the rest and pours the rosewater into her mixture while simultaneously stirring. Removing her concoction before the rosewater heats up to a boil, she pours it over a fresh pigeon heart.

Her eyes shoot up from her alchemy set at the sound of boots treading heavily on the gravel path of her garden. With the skip of her heart beating in her eardrums, she grabs the third bowl with her almost completed love potion and throws it to a corner of her room behind her storage crates. The contents saturate the dirt giving up the properties they once held.

Still sitting on the ground, she spins around to face two guards pushing through her curtain door. "Faerydae Rhoslyn, you are under arrest for the practice of witchcraft."

She can't run. She can't scream. Her body is rooted to the ground in fear as the two guards trample through her home over to her. Eyes wide with terror, she stares up at their hands reaching down, ripping her from the earth.

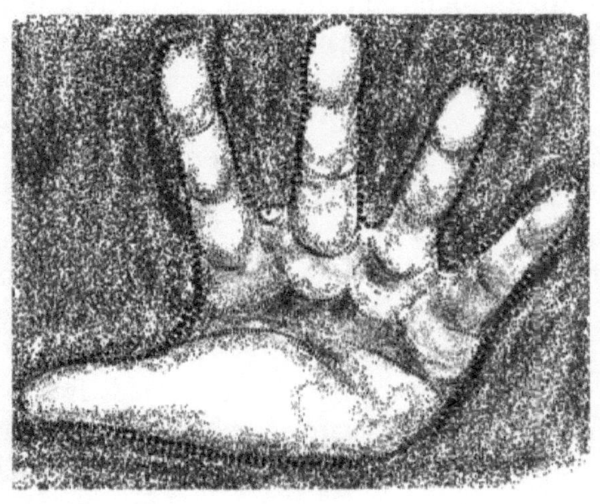

Twelve

Stirling stirs awake, reading the lack of sunlight in the upstairs room he can tell it's sometime in the early morning. He can hear his father's voice downstairs. His low tone barely penetrates through the floorboards. He strains his ears to listen, but he can't hear more than a murmuring sound. Intrigued, he listens harder and can make out another muffled sound. It sounds like the distinct features of crying.

His parents move closer to the stairs allowing him to hear the last sentence, his father telling his mother, "Take some time off, go rest your head."

He doesn't know what he expected from what is overheard. He knew he heard someone crying, but he is still caught off guard at the sight of her flushed and tear-stricken face. Her cheeks are as red as her stinging eyes. His mother, the woman who has given him life, stands broken at the top of the stairs.

"Stirling," she chokes out. She's across the room in a blink of an eye wrapping her arms around him.

He doesn't know what to say. She is the person who comforts him when *he* is crying. How does a child comfort a parent? His small arms curl around her, the fabric of her gown twisting in his fingers as he holds onto her. She nuzzles her face into his hair dampening his curls.

"I love you so much, Stirling." She tips over. Stirling, encased in her walls, collapses with her. Straw escapes the opened stitches with a puff of air.

He doesn't ask what had happened. That isn't what his mother needs from him. His father is there for her when she wants to talk. What she needs is for him to be beside her. To let her hold him and feel the warmth of his small frame. He stays there for her. He can hear the soft breathing as his mother succumbs to her emotional exhaustion. He doesn't need the safety of a blanket to sleep with her arms around him. His eyes grow heavy in the comfort of her, and he slips back into a slumbering ignorance.

Thirteen

Humming to himself, Stirling kicks a pebble along the road. He had slipped out while his mother was still asleep and his father was too preoccupied to notice. He never did ask her why she was so distraught.

He kicks the pebble again; it skips across the pressed dirt towards the hanging hill. The freshly sprouted daisies turning the green hill white lay flat and trampled in a recent floral massacre. Stirling stops at the bottom of the hill. His eyes trail the carnage up to the top.

Petrified, he can't even tap his thumb to his fingers. His heart ceases to beat, the blood no longer flowing through his body. He can do nothing but stare numbly.

A body hangs from the gallows stationed at the top. Each one of the strips of her multicolored skirt blows in the wind like all the different flags at the joust. Her silken hair caught up in the rope around her neck.

Tears fall from his eyes, the only moving item on the immobile boy. His lungs spasm as he struggles to breathe. He doesn't go to the mountains. He falls like the daisies and silently waters them as he weeps at the bottom of the hanging hill.

Jannell never patched the missing piece of her heart after losing Faerydae. She finds herself preparing to make the small journey to her friend's house, only to have the ugly reminder reopen her old wound. It's like seeing a stunning rose. Infatuated with its beauty, you forget it has thorns until you reach for it.

So here she remains in the bakery day after day, distracting herself from her heartache by busying herself with work. Growing lonely, she leans to her son for companionship, someone whose eyes shine as bright as her friends, but he is rarely to be seen.

Jannell watches her only son leap from view day after day over the next few years. She feels as if she is watching him grow up through a gallery of paintings. As if she is walking down a hall of pictures of him side by side, representing the days, weeks, and months as he grows up. Taking only a few minutes to examine each one before moving on to the next.

They barely speak to each other anymore. When he was a small child, he would confide all his thoughts, dreams, and hopes to her. She remembers teaching him of her beliefs in the stars one night, cradling him in her arms even at the age of six when he was getting too big to hold. He was always so full of curiosity and questions. Questions she often did not know the answers to; how was the furniture or supplies in the house made, what's beyond the mountains, what's beyond the ocean, why do I have to be a baker?

Some of the days Giles forces Stirling to stay home and work on chores, but even when they are in each other's presence, standing in the same room, sitting at the same table, his mind is distant, distracted by something unknown.

She misses her son, but she can sense he is miserable when he is kept indoors. She would take over his duties, relinquishing his daily shackles to the bakery and allowing him to run off to wherever it is he goes each day.

S tirling," Jannell says.

Stirling stops midway through slipping his shoes on. He gapes up at her as if he didn't notice she was even there until she spoke.

"Stirling, I was able to get the ingredients and make some gingerbread. Do you want to eat some with me before you go?"

He stares at his mother while making his decision, her hands with interlocked fingers held up to her chest.

He thinks of Ignis patiently waiting for him at the cave. "Can I take it to go? My friend is waiting and I want to leave before pa assigns me tasks."

Jannell's hands drop to her sides. "It won't take long."

"I really need to go. Maybe next time?" Stirling edges towards the door impatiently. Even being only thirteen years of age, he has grown almost as tall as Jannell.

Jannell sags, disheartened. "Let me wrap the gingerbread up for you."

"I hate when they practice down there. I can barely tell who's who," Stirling says, referring to the class of Riders they have been religiously watching the past few years.

They are in the midst of practicing the basics of flying at the Winged Cavalry base planted at the entryway to the canyon.

Stirling and Ignis sit lifted above the trees on a tor, a rocky outcrop rising separately from the rest of the canyon's incline. Stirling cups the gingerbread in his hand as he picks off a pebble size piece and pops it into his mouth, savoring the strong spices with an underlying sweetness.

Including Ignis, the class's dragons have grown a substantial amount. They were not to their full potential size but they had reached the size and stature to support a young Rider on their back.

Stirling sets his gingerbread off to the side and pulls out his journal and stick of sketching charcoal. He opens it up to an unfinished sketch of him flying on the back of Ignis.

"They still haven't gone full airborne yet. The only person who can make it around the track without any issues is Amiria," Stirling says, adding a condescending emphasis to his voice when he says her name.

"First thing tomorrow we can give it a shot," he adds.

"*Give what a shot?*" Ignis wonders.

"Flying together," Stirling clarifies.

"*Why don't we try it right now,*" Ignis suggests.

Stirling peers down over the steep incline of the massive stacks of rocks they were perched on. Climbing up and down is easy enough. There are plenty of hand and foot holds for a safe passage. When Ignis flies up or off their perch, he makes a steep dive, gliding down into the coverage of the trees and out of sight. Stirling's stomach lurches as he imagines diving head-first into the solid ground.

"Nope! No, we—uh—don't want to get spotted. Let's go to the spot where you practiced flying. There's not enough time today to hike all the way up there and still have an amplitude of practice time," he answers by making up a reasonable excuse to save his face from kissing the rocks as gravity pulls him into her arms.

Shaking his nerves off, he turns his attention back to the class who have taken a break from flying to begin practicing hand-to-hand combat.

Nellie hides, trapped below her wooden shield as Amiria hounds on the roof, wielding two practice swords made of durable wood to prevent them from splintering under the stress of multiple strikes.

Amiria has chosen to wield two swords over a sword and shield, allotting her the favor in speed over Nellie, who had now lost her sword when Amiria was able to trap it between hers, casting it to the side. Amiria's movements are a blur, her swords following one another as if they are connected.

Thump, thump. Thump, thump.

Nellie can't find any relief as the swords pound down one after another against her shield. She grits her teeth, adjusting her wide stance, her shoes grinding across the gravel to balance herself under the pressure.

The beating stops. She blinks as the sound and vibration of the continued blows cease, her stance softening now the heavy blows are no longer weighing her down. Faltering, she can't resist peeking around the shield.

With a smile on her face, Amiria takes advantage of the fact that Nellie has loosened her tensed muscles and she kicks upward at the wooden shield. Her leather boot hooks behind the lip and wrenches it free from Nellie's right hand, still hanging on with her left hand as it flings up and to the side with the momentum.

Before Nellie can pull the shield back in front of her, Amiria is on her, holding the rounded wooden edge of her sword to her neck.

Nellie throws her shield to the ground, upset. "I don't want to be paired with you anymore. They pair me because no one willingly chooses to practice with you. It's not fun always losing."

Amiria steps back, her face flat. "It's not my fault you always lose."

Nellie raises her lip mocking Amiria, "'It's not my fault you always lose.' Yeah, it is, when *you* have no life but practicing."

In her head, she intends to be sincere but her words come out patronizing, "Then maybe you should practice more."

"You might be perfect at everything else but you suck at people skills," Nellie bites out. "I'm going to practice with the guys because they are my *friends*. Do what you do best and practice alone." Turning with a huff, she storms off to join the group of Clyde, Garret, and Warrick, who were practicing together.

Amiria purses her lips and mumbles to herself, "You don't have to get upset, I just said you should practice more."

Standing alone, Amiria watches as the four classmates clump together. The three boys lean in as Nellie tells them something. The group bursts into laughter, but it subsides into low snickers as they all turn. Amiria quickly drops her gaze to the dusty ground. Their dagger-like eyes bore into her, slipping through the cracks. Their cuts leave no traces on the skin, but they dig deeper, dealing pain to her already damaged mind. She draws a swirl in the dirt with the tip of her sword. Sighing, she makes her way over to the straw dummy where she begins practicing alone.

Stirling squints, trying to make out the class better. "Why do you think Amiria went off on her own?"

"*Isn't there an odd number?*" Ignis points out, disconnected as if he doesn't care whether Amiria practiced alone or with classmates.

"Yeah, but they still usually practice in a group in some way," Stirling says, still fixated on the fact.

"*Maybe, she thinks she's too good for them,*" Ignis suggests.

Stirling sits back satisfied with the answer. "Yeah, maybe. I can see that."

He picks up his gingerbread and begins mindlessly nibbling on the corner as his mind begins to drift to a daydream.

The sunlight reflects beams of white as it strikes his new polished armor etched with the Winged Cavalry's insignia. Amiria squints as she peers up at the orange dragon swooping down to her. Stirling pulls his sword from its sheath and leaps from Ignis' back before his enormous claws cause the earth to shudder under their impact. She pulls her blade out in time to block. Stirling's sword strikes perpendicular to hers.

He towers over her, pressing the weapon down into hers with his weight. Her smug expression vanishes as her non-dominant hand catches the blade's flat side to help hold against his strength. Using his advantage, Stirling pushes against Amiria, thrusting his arms out, and knocks her backward. As she stumbles over her footing, he strikes repeatedly with his sword. With each blow, Amiria's reaction time becomes more and more delayed as he overpowers her. She finally succumbs to his advancements tripping over her heel. Stirling stands glowering down at her, her face contorting into a hideous scowl.

He points the tip of his sword at her throat. "You're not so perfect now, are you?"

Back on the tor, Stirling smiles to himself as he imagines himself beating Amiria in hand-to-hand combat.

"What are you so giddy about?" Ignis asks knowingly. If Stirling is deep enough into thought, he can mistakenly project the visions in his mind over to Ignis. Flashes of his daydreams or dreams at night as he has seen Ignis'.

Stirling, still smiling to himself, replies, "Just picturing us if we were allowed to be down there."

"I saw what you saw, and even if we could be down there.

You'd be that straw dummy."

"Shut up, Ignis." Stirling plays it off, resting his head on the rocks behind him, and stares up at the cumulus clouds floating through the sky like sheep in their pasture.

Sixteen

Stirling sits straddling the back of Ignis who has grown to the size of a horse. Stirling's legs fall in front of Ignis' folded wings swaying as they dangle around his neck as they traverse through the familiar forest on their way to practice flying together. Ignis' head held high like a swan assisting in keeping Stirling seated at the base of his neck.

Holding Ignis' neck for balance, Stirling advises, "Let's check and make sure there isn't a class going on. They aren't usually training on Saint's days. They are too busy having a feast over on the castle's grounds."

"Whatever you say."

Ignis steps up to their viewpoint on their bluff that remains out of sight from anyone who is standing below beside the canyon. Stirling leans to one side, peering around Ignis' thick neck.

The beige dragon with the amplitude of spikes strikes at Amiria like a snake striking at a rabbit, then recoiling back in preparation to strike again. She dodges each strike with ease, using the dragon's size and momentum against it by doing no more than side-stepping out of the dragon's path and turning her shoulder to lessen her exposed surface area in the direction of the threat. The cloth of her tunic ripples from the wind force as the dragon's head whips past her again and again.

"Her dragon is attacking her!" Stirling exclaims loud enough for only Ignis to hear.

Using Ignis' neck for stabilization, he scampers to stand up on Ignis' back, his head now even with Ignis. Gripping one of Ignis' two horns the length of Stirling's forearm, he leans for a better-heightened view. Ignis' head tilts as he supports Stirling's leaning weight.

"*No,*" Ignis says, trying to straighten his head. "*No, I think they are sparring. Also, is pulling on my head necessary?*"

"Sparring?" Stirling repeats, ignoring the question about Ignis' head as he continues to hold onto the horn for support.

Ignis sighs, his head twisting to the side. "*My guess is she's practicing her reflexes with something faster than, you know, a human.*"

"Oh, so she thinks she's too good to practice with slow regular people." Stirling scoffs.

Amiria dodges the dragon's strike once again. As the head passes her, she raises her fist tapping the underside of the dragon's jaw where the skin is soft and weak, free from the thick armored scales covering the majority of the body. With her spare hand, she grabs the largest spike protruding from the top of the dragon's head in the same location where Ignis' horns are placed. The dragon rears its head back at the touch dragging Amiria along with it until her fisted hand that had tapped the under jaw is now punching against the base of the dragon's neck where the collar bones are hidden below the dense muscle.

"Got you," she says, letting go from the spike, the soles of her boots silent as she lands back on the ground.

Stirling stares in bewilderment, completely enrapt by her

movements. Her swiftness is impeccable. The fluid way she is able to step and roll her shoulders away from the crushing jaws. She is like a leaf on the water's surface moving out of the way of your scooping hand as it flows with the water.

Stirling ponders, even if he trained alongside her in combat would he be able to keep up, or are they truly different breeds? Winged Riders in the Cavalry bred in their own category, like prized stallions and compatible mares to breed the perfect warhorse.

"Come on, let's go. We have our own training to do," Ignis suggests, already turning them away from the viewpoint to head back down the sloping backside of the bluff.

"Yeah, okay," Stirling agrees, his knees bending as he attempts to keep himself balanced while standing on a now-moving object. Before slowly lowering himself, he stretches his neck over his shoulder to catch one last glance at Amiria.

Amiria has turned away from her dragon and is sitting on the very edge of the canyon's ledge. She pulls her knees tight into her chest hugging them for comfort as she loses her thoughts to the view of the canyon and mountains beyond.

They step out into the clearing between the forest and canyon where Ignis had learned to fly. There is enough distance between Amiria and themselves that she won't be able to hear them if Stirling spoke at a regular volume.

"You ready?" Ignis asks, referring to flying.

"Yes, no. Give me a second." Stirling replies, lowering his chest to sit flush against Ignis' shoulder blades. He presses his face against the back of Ignis' neck, his thumb and fingers tapping rapidly.

"You've said that five times now."

"You've already gotten used to flying. I've never been off

the ground before. Be patient with me." Stirling barely lifts his face from Ignis' neck.

"I was patient, but at this pace, I'm going to die of starvation before we take off, and I only eat once a week."

"Okay, okay, okay." Steading his breathing, Stirling reaches around Ignis' neck and wraps his arms around the thick muscle mass. His fingers are barely able to touch the opposite side.

"Here we go," Ignis states, taking off in a canter parallel with the forest's wall of trees.

"Wait!" Stirling shouts in their minds

"Too late!" Ignis cheers with glee.

Ignis only takes two long galloping strides before attempting to take off; but unlike the usual steady stream of his normal walking or even the canters they have done through the forest to shorten their travel times, Stirling responds as if he is hit sideways in the rapids. Without anything to hold onto for support as Ignis bounces his body preparing him for flight, Stirling is immediately stripped off the side of Ignis landing on his shoulder in the gravel.

"Ahh!" He cries out. Wincing, he checks his shoulder for any damage. He brushes the dirt off the minor scrapes, "I told you I wasn't ready. Lucky we weren't in the air yet."

Stirling unties his belt letting it fall free of his waist to hang vertically in the air by one hand.

"Why did you take that off?" Ignis asks.

"So, I don't break all my bones." He rolls his sore shoulder.

Ignis shrugs and bows his forelegs, lowering himself enough to allow Stirling to climb back on.

Once seated firmly on Ignis' back, Stirling drapes the belt down one side of Ignis' neck. He leans around the opposing side, stretching his arm as far as possible without falling off. The tips of his fingers fumble with the leather until he finally obtains the belt, barely pinching between his middle and index finger. Very carefully, he straightens himself back upright keeping both ends of the belt from slipping out of his fingers.

He scoots back on Ignis, tucking his legs up like a frog on a rock with his chest pressing against Ignis' shoulder blades, his head now at the base of Ignis' neck. He stretches the leather belt older than himself as much as it allows, gripping it firmly in his hands, the tension of the belt pulls him firmly into Ignis' rough scales.

With a deep breath, the air slowly fills the expanding space of Stirling's lungs. He holds it there, feeling the pressure of the air longing to push its way back out.

Releasing the air, he tells Ignis, "Okay. I'm ready. But go easy. Can you try and leave the ground gently?" Stirling pauses then an afterthought arises, "Oh, and not too high."

"*You scared?*" Ignis teases.

"No," he lies, "I just don't want to die. That won't do either of us any good. Also, if we go above the trees, we might get seen by you know who."

"*Fine,*" Ignis reluctantly agrees, raising his wings from their resting place on his ribcage.

He moves one foot after another, gradually advancing into a trot with increasing speed to a canter and then to a gallop.

Stirling's knuckles begin to lose their color as he squeezes the belt firm in his grip keeping himself from being thrown off again. His eyes force shut, creating wrinkles in the corner. He can feel Ignis' muscles beneath him shift as he spreads his wings. Then with a few pumps, his clawed appendages leave the solid surface, free from the earth's gravity.

"*Are we doing it? Are we flying?*" Stirling says, his face pressed into Ignis.

"*Yeah.*"

Stirling opens a single eye and tilts his head, allowing his eye to perform its function of taking in light waves and interpreting them into sight for him.

He watches the green needle-clustered branches pass them by. They are around halfway up the height of the forest trees, which isn't high enough to be fatal to Stirling, but it is high enough to cause severe damage resulting in the inability to walk home himself.

"Whoa," He spouts, his second eye shooting open in astonishment.

He had done it. He is flying. He is actually flying. It might be slow and it might be low to the ground, but he is flying on the back of Ignis. Feeling brave, Stirling pushes himself off Ignis as far as the belt will allow. He shifts his weight to one side as he leans over Ignis' side to peak at the ground below them.

With a combination of the offset of his weight and the curvature of Ignis' back, Stirling begins sliding. Then, before he can comprehend what is happening, gravity has him in her clutches. The belt rings around to the top of Ignis' neck and his feet kick the empty air below him.

A scream escapes his throat for a brief moment as he clamps his jaw shut, cutting it short, remembering Amiria is within shouting distance. He clings to the leather, no more than two fingers width of worn leather from casting him down to the unforgiving earth.

"Let me down!" he screams in his mind at Ignis, his feet desperately kicking and reaching for anything for support.

"What are you doing?" Ignis ponders as if Stirling is doing nothing more than playing a joke.

"Trying not to die! DOWN! NOW!" he screams in terror.

"Okay, okay. Just hold on," Ignis says as he begins his descent.

"What do you think I'm currently doing?" Stirling growls.

Ignis' wings flutter, hovering themselves before they land. His hind legs stretch out, catching them while his forelegs remain curled into his chest. With his wings folding back into place, his full weight returns to him. He drops to his forelegs, his knees bending to absorb the impact as he catches his body falling the rest of the way down.

Stirling's legs feel as if the bones have been removed as he lands on the ground, his knees bending, refusing to hold him up. The only thing keeping him from falling onto his back is his hands locked around the belt. They are stiff, locked gripping to the thinning material. Focusing on one finger at a time, he commands his fingers to release their grip until both hands slip free of the fabric and he collapses to the ground.

Lying on his back, a shudder goes through Stirling's bones as he runs his hands over the gravel, feeling each small pebble roll from one side of his palm to the other. Solid ground. Good, safe, solid ground.

Ignis' face appears in Stirling's view as he stares up at the sky. "*You all right there?*"

"Yeah. Just... just give me a moment," Stirling replies, trying to speak over his racing heart, his soul slowly seeping back into his body.

There's so much to learn, he thinks to himself.

There is more to flying than purely sitting on a dragon's back. Balancing and gaining the muscles to maintain your position and posture while flying will come with continuous practice. But their movements and your movements, it all must flow together. Bonding is what allows a Rider to ride upon the back of a dragon, but training is what keeps them on their back. They have to move as one while in a world with three hundred and sixty degrees of turning possibilities.

"*Do you want to try again?*" Ignis asks, still standing over Stirling.

Stirling sits up, his back covered in dust. "Yeah, but let's lower the difficulty some more. Let's start with the jumping."

Ignis steps back as Stirling pushes himself up off the ground, the bones finally returning to his legs to support him as he stands up.

"*Explain?*" Ignis asks.

"I need to work on keeping myself seated. So, jump and maybe glide really really close to the ground. I don't want another scare like that one again anytime soon."

Stirling reaches out and places his palm on the bridge of Ignis' snout. The skin is smoother than the rest of the scales of his body, closer to resembling hard weathered leather. His bone features are smooth and rounded with two single straight horns of glistening white. He isn't threatening like the wyverns they've seen. His eyes smile with golden sunshine. This is his best friend. He couldn't care less about his insignia, the bakery, Lumierna, or the Isles of Wyverna, all that matters to him is being with Ignis.

Seventeen

Stirling nearly leaps down the stairs into the bakery. He is nearing his fourteenth birthday and has finally mastered flying below the tree line with Ignis. No matter which way Ignis decided to turn, Stirling was leaning along as if he was merely an extension of Ignis' body.

After several close calls to test how fast a person falls through the air, Stirling had brought a rope to help tie himself to Ignis. It saved him from breaking his limbs but he is still vulnerable to injuries if he falls. Stirling knows firsthand the type of burn and bruising a rope leaves behind on the soft skin around his stomach and lower back. Too nerve-wracking to take their height any higher, he remains below the treetops and away from the canyon's drop.

The weather the past week has been poor. A never-ending flood of water fell from the sky, keeping him captive in the bakery. He had put in a little effort to help with the chores as he chatted with Ignis through his thoughts. The rain kept most customers away, being in his personal favor rather than in the bakery's, keeping the tasks to a minimum.

His face beaming like the sun outside, he reaches for the handle of the front door with his turnshoes only half slipped on. His fingers glide around the cool metal and right as he's about to pull the door open, he hears his mother speak up from behind him.

"Stirling." Her voice is barely audible as if she is hardly able to exhale enough air to form the letters.

Then there is a thud.

One by one Stirling's fingers individually slides from the door handle. His hand falls limp to his side as if he suddenly lost control of the muscles. He stares at the door, his body refusing his mind's commands to turn around.

Breathe. She just dropped something. With jerking movements, Stirling convinces his stiff neck muscles to obey as he finally checks over his shoulder.

A vortex sucks the air into his lungs as he gasps, horror striking his every nerve. Stirling is choking on the air, unable to breathe in anymore and his body too frozen to push it out. The same breath sticks in his throat as he sees his mother lying there in the middle of the shop. Her body is so still as if she had decided to lie down in her flour and yeast-covered apron to take a nap on the hard wooden floor.

Stirling finds his body reacting before his mind this time, his knees skidding across the ground next to his mother in a panicked frenzy. He lifts her head into his lap, her sandy-colored curls falling loose from her bun.

He shakes her, to no avail. "Ma! MUUUUM!" Stirling glances around the room, his vision blurring with tears.

"Pa!" he screams. "FATHER! HELP!" he shouts again, his voice cracking under the strain as he chokes on the tears beginning to stream down his face.

What do I do?! What do I do?! he thinks to himself, his mind racing but coming up empty-handed.

The bakery's front door slams open, his father confused and unnerved at why Stirling would be shouting for him in such a frantic tone.

"Jannell!" Giles cries out.

He rushes across the room in two pounding strides, kneeling down beside his wife. His large hands strengthened from decades of labor brush a curl that had fallen into her face behind her ear, then cups her delicate cheek. Stirling lifts his gaze from his mother to gape at his father. His father is a man who is strict and stern. The man who has never shown any compassion or love in front of Stirling exhibits now as if his whole world is burning right in front of him, and he doesn't have a single drop of water to save it.

Giles scoops Jannell into his arms with ease as if she is the weight of a child. Stirling stands up alongside his father, his movements jerky and uncertain as he tries to comprehend what is unfolding. He watches his mother hang limp in his father's arms. He hadn't noticed how thin she had become. He searches his mind trying to remember the last time he had paid attention to her long enough to notice these important details.

Her curly hair that bounces with her steps has turned brittle like straw. Her once rosy cheeks are hollow, sinking into a face with sagging skin that has developed a bluish tint. The bags under her eyes are from more than just a single restless night, staining her face with dark purple.

"Stirling! STIRLING!" Giles screams, forcing Stirling back to the present. "Stirling, snap out of it. I need you to run to the apothecary down the road," he demands.

Stirling doesn't move, his feet nailed to the ground as his eyes dart from his father's worried face to his mother's fading appearance.

"NOW!" his father shouts urgently before turning away, carrying his mother up the staircase to lay her on their bed, a wooden box frame lifted off the ground filled with straw.

Stirling bursts out the front door and takes off running through the heavily crowded road. His shoes splash through puddles, spraying the murky contents onto the dresses and pant legs of the townspeople as he pushes through clumps of people moseying along the market district stopping at storefronts and merchant tables.

Many of the shoppers give him harsh stares after he knocks into them or their companions, and a few shout words of venom in his direction. Stirling doesn't notice, his mind recoiling, locking up tight. His vision tunnels, turning black around the edges as the people disappear from his vision.

They don't matter. None of this market matters to him. This kingdom doesn't matter to him. His feet act on their own as they guided him to the apothecary's shop. At this moment, all that matters to him is getting help for his mother.

Ignis, unsure of what Stirling is experiencing, can feel it. The invisible path connecting their minds slowly shuts. He feels as if his mind is being pushed out of an exit too small to fit through, his body battered and bruised until he stands on the outside. The exit slams shut behind him, leaving Stirling's feeling of dread dwelling inside him.

Stirling reaches the building where the apothecary's shop resides. As he bounds up the stone steps, his mud-caked shoes catch on the edge of the stair sending his body slamming against the front door.

A loud crashing sound startles the apothecary as he signs a parchment, his quill skidding across the carefully written lines as his hand jerks involuntarily, leaving a streak of ink.

"What in the world could that have been?" he says, his chair scooting back from his desk as he stands up.

He steps around his desk covered in papers and scrolls as an urgent knocking shakes his front door. Quickening his pace, he opens the front door cautiously, not knowing who it could be and why.

Stirling wheezes heavily as he tries to catch his breath.

Each word is exaggerated and deliberate as he forces them out. "My mother…She's unconscious. Needs…Help."

The apothecary examines the young boy standing at his doorstep in an attempt to make sense of the situation. "Is she ill?" he asks.

Stirling regains himself enough to answer. "I don't know, she's thin, bluish tint and cold, but she's breathing. She just fell over, and we couldn't wake her up."

"All right, boy, I will come and take a look at her," he says calmly. "Let me grab my bag." He straightens his houppelande, an outer garment with flaring sleeves, and shuffles back to his desk.

Stirling watches in a daze as the apothecary, a stocky man with a potbelly, gathers up items from various parts of the room seeming random and unnecessary. It is taking up precious time. The man hobbles around as if someone isn't in dire need of his help. The sound of snapping metal fills Stirling's ears as the apothecary finally clasps the bulky leather bag.

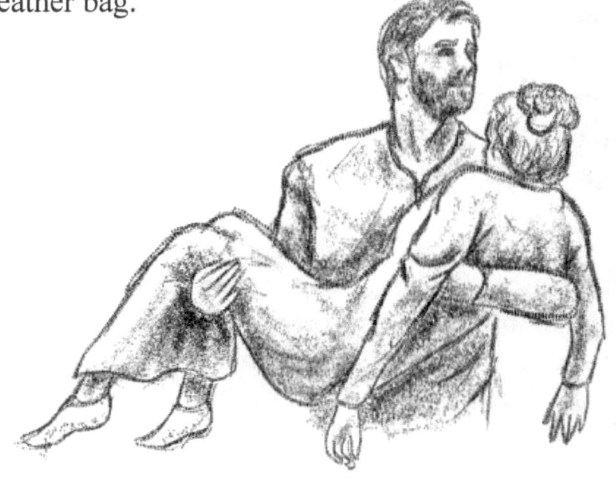

Eighteen

Stirling doesn't remember how he got back home or how long he has been back. His blurred vision slowly comes to focus as his mind returns to his body. He finds himself sitting on the floor of his parents' room, the scene before coming together.

He watches numbly as the apothecary hovers over his mother. His father is observing protectively from the corner of the room, his face set. If any of the emotions Stirling had witnessed earlier still lingered, he had locked them away. Forced away from the surface to the confines of his mind leaving behind a stoic expression firmly in place.

When Stirling felt ill, his mother would tend to him. She would place her hand on his forehead, tell him to rest up, and give him herbal concoctions she learned from the flower lady—Faerydae. He squeezes his eyes shut at the painful memory.

It's been almost four years but he can still see her body hanging from the noose. She was his mother's best friend who used to live outside of the city with a magnificent garden she let him play in. All until this kingdom took her away from his mother. Took away the second genuinely kind human being he has ever met. The one person who could have prevented this from happening with a skip through her garden. Instead, he was oblivious, caught up in his own life. Now he is dreading he is about to lose the one person he loves in Wyverna.

Stirling opens his eyes, releasing a new wave of tears. He can barely see the apothecary performing different acts; pulling open her eyes lids to check her eyes, taking an inspection of inside her ears and down her throat. He pokes and prods at her skin, seeming to have lost its elasticity. Her hands and feet are evaluated for any type of sign only he seems to know how to read. He interrogates Giles with questions about if she had been recently vomiting or having diarrhea.

How any of this would help his mother, Stirling will never understand. Why can't the apothecary pull one of his many miracles out of his bag and cure her?

"Do you know what's wrong with her?" Giles impatiently asks, hiding the undertone of his concern.

The apothecary stands up straight and turns to him. "Illnesses are tricky, are you familiar with the four humours or humourism?"

Giles shakes his head.

The apothecary continues, "It's the working of the human body, liquids produced by the person. When these are out of balance, either excess or a deficiency in one, the person becomes sick. Your wife is a bit tricky; she seems to have produced too much yellow bile, one of the humours, but she shows the qualities of the phlegm humour since her skin is cold and clammy. The state she's in, she must have been dealing with the actual symptoms for several days now. She's extremely dehydrated. I'm surprised she was still up and walking until today. It does a person no good to hide illness. Will only make things worse in the long run."

"Will she get better? Do you have any remedies for this?" Giles' his voice straining to remain calm.

The apothecary takes a moment before answering. "I have a few in mind, but they aren't miracle cures. They are designed to be ingested when symptoms first begin. I'm sorry, but with how long it was left untreated, the chances of recovery are low. I can give you some stuff that will help her rehydrate. I can't make any promises though. Rebalancing the humours can be tricky enough on their own and it appears that there is something sucking the life right out of her on top of it."

Giles glances down at Stirling out of the corner of his eye and says in a hushed tone, "Maybe, maybe we should talk about this in the other room."

Giles and the apothecary exit the bedroom into the main part of the home, leaving Stirling alone with his thoughts and his mother who lays in an unconscious slumber, her breaths shallow under the covers. The room begins to rock as his body sways, emotions pulsing through his veins. He leans his head back against the wall behind him to steady his body and hopefully his mind.

The pathway between him and Ignis creaks open enough to peak an eye through. Ignis accepts the invitation and opens the door, letting the pressure building up in Stirling's head barge in and consume him. The burden weighs down on him, but if the two of them carry it together, maybe just maybe, they will be able to lift it.

"I won't be able to hang out for a while, Ignis," Stirling says to him in their shared thoughts.

"Be where you feel is right, be with your mother. I can wait," Ignis replies, trying his best to comfort him from his cave in the depths of the mountains.

I can wait.

Ignis' words bring back a memory from almost a year ago. Where he had brushed off his mother's invite to sit and eat gingerbread with her. He had been so focused on getting to Ignis that he didn't even think of how she felt. He was growing up in the forest, growing up away from her.

His mother, the only one he will ever have, is the very person who had taken the time to hold his hand and teach him to walk. She stood alone, watching as he took off running without bothering to look back.

At the time, the moment was simple and insignificant, but the shadow of it is greater. It has grown larger as the light shifts from his new angle. Why couldn't he have given it to her? Why couldn't he sit down with her and share a smile? All she had wanted was some time with her son. Ignis would have understood, but he only thought of himself. Stirling brings his knees in tight.

She had always been there when he needed her, but he couldn't give her that small moment.

With his throat constricting, he buries his face to hide the tears lining his reddened cheeks.

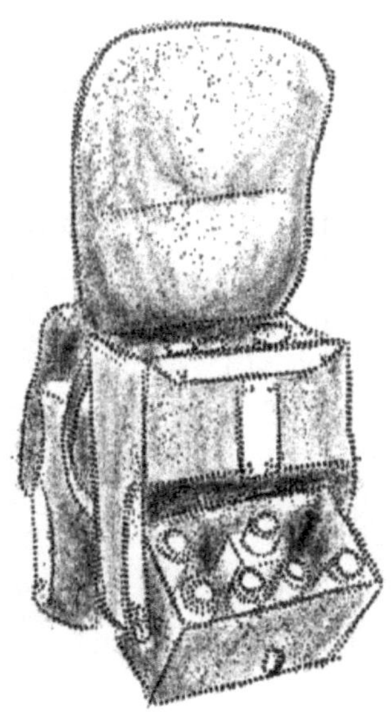

Nineteen

Over the next week, Stirling spent as much time as he could with his mother. The only time he left her side was to assist with the bakery when his father asked for quick favors trying not to keep him away from watching over her.

Stirling had pulled his stool away from the window over to his mother's bedside, but not before he had taken notice of the accidental embedded dips in the wooden floor, carved from the years the chair had sat in the same location. The spot Stirling escaped through the window and dreamt of a life away from the bakery. The memory of Stirling spending so many nights paying attention to the stars and the mountain's dark shadow cutting jagged lines into the twinkling sky. While his mother stood behind him as no more than an afterthought, tugs at his heart.

Maybe, if I had just paid attention to her, I would have noticed she was sick. Or, if I helped around the bakery when I was asked, she wouldn't have felt the need to work herself to... Stirling couldn't get himself to think the final word. He doesn't want to admit what he knows is inevitable.

He sits on his familiar stool in an unfamiliar spot as he watches his mother sleep.

He reaches his thoughts out to Ignis. *"Ignis, you said you don't remember your mother, right?"*

"Correct."

"I wonder what's worse; to have loved and lost, or to have never loved at all." His eyes fall to his mother. Her hair pulled free from the knot on the back of her head, letting the curls fall around her sunken features as he listens to Ignis.

"To have loved and lost. I'm thinking that even though losing someone dear hurts, it hurts because you got to spend time in this world loving them. The time you got to spend with them makes it worth it though."

Salted liquid clouds Stirling's vision as he lowers his head to rest on the mattress.

His father steps through the open door to the room to ask Stirling if he would like any supper. He stops himself before he speaks as he sees Stirling sound asleep with his head cradled in his arms on the mattress beside his mother. He decides not to disturb him, slowly backing out of the room. He retrieves the wool blanket off Stirling's bed in the corner of the room and carries it back into the bedroom.

Draping the blanket over Stirling, his voice no more than a whisper, he says, "I know it's going to hurt. But you're a strong-hearted boy, you'll get past this. We'll get past this."

He lays his hand on the top of Stirling's head. He pulls it back awkwardly and shuffles out of the room, silently closing the door behind him.

The next morning, Stirling scratches at a parchment sprawled out on the bed beside his mother, her upper body propped up by layering full flour sacks beneath her straw-filled pillow. The charcoal leaves behind black lines forming the shape of a dragon.

The remedies the apothecary had given her helped her

regain consciousness, but it is not curing her. She can't retain any liquids that Stirling has to help her drink.

She is too weak to lift her arms. Her body is failing her; dimming like a fire left unattended, consuming its support, slowly growing weaker until it finally fades out. All she has now is her son's tales about a friendly dragon.

"That's a silly sounding dragon. Four legs?"Her voice is a small breeze of the once strong wind it used to be.

Stirling pauses his story of a an orange dragon and touches his scar, "You know how I never told you how I got this?"

His mother, leaning back on the pillow, tilts her head raising an eyebrow quizzically.

Stirling, staring at his arm, takes a deep breath. His fingertips begin to tap his thumb. Index, middle, ring, pinky, ring, middle, index.

He slowly raises his gaze till their eyes lock, "I've lied to you all these years. I don't have any farmer friends. In fact, I don't have any friends except—except for Ignis. Although no one will ever believe me. But, Mother, Ignis is the dragon who gave this to me." He holds out his arm as if she had never seen his scars before.

Stirling feels as if he has cut himself open, revealing all the mechanics that make him tick.

He is vulnerable. His body shakes, but she needs to know the truth. He runs his fingers down the length of his arm remembering how she melted his skin closed.

The memory of the day he decided to walk off the trail his life was supposed to be on, is something he will never forget.

She eyes him skeptically. "Is this another story?"

"Yes, Mum, he's real and I'm teaching myself how to ride him. I go up to the mountains to train with him almost every day." Stirling's eyes are full of sincerity as he pleads, "He's real, I swear. Please believe me."

Jannell's lips quiver as she smiles softly. "I believe you."

Stirling feels the tension in his body drop with relief. Jannell's fragile hand trembles as she musters the strength to raise her hand up to touch his cheek. He cups his hand over hers, holding it tight against him, her fingers cold against his skin.

She speaks up again, her voice faint, "I know you will be a great man one day. You're going to make me so proud. Stirling, promise me, don't you ever give up."

"I promise," he manages to choke back the onslaught of tears.

He can feel his mother's hand become limp under as it almost slides from his grasp before he tightens his grip. He watches her through clouded vision as she falls back asleep with a faint smile still remaining on her face. Except she isn't asleep and he knows this.

His heart feels as if it had plummeted into his stomach, pulling his throat down with it. He can't speak, not a word. He can barely breathe, his chest constricting, suffocating him as he chokes on his tears.

He sits there holding his mother's hand, refusing to let it go. He lowers their hands to rest on his lap. Feeling as if letting go of her hand, she will disappear right in front of him, even though she is already gone. So, he remains there, on his stool, tears rolling down his face following his jawline to his chin where they drip one at a time onto his and his mother's intertwined fingers.

"Father?" Stirling runs his thumb across the leaves of the rosemary sprigs clamped in his hand. He steps into the threshold of the bedroom door.

His mother lays still on the bed, her body wrapped in a shroud with her face exposed. The smell of rosemary is strong in Stirling's nose. For the past day, each of his neighbors have set sprigs upon her sleeping body as they said their words of prayer.

"Pa?" Stirling's throat is thick from the tears he hasn't stopped shedding. The husk of what was once his strong father sits hunched beside the bed. "Father, they're here."

Giles' lifeless eyes don't leave his slumbering wife's face. With creaking bones, he reaches up, running the back of his index down her cool cheek. A gasping sob escapes his chapped lips, his red-stained face sunken with grief. He shifts, standing up from the stool. He leans over the woman he vowed to hold in sickness and in health. The woman he wanted to spend forever with, to grow old in this bakery with, to laugh with while their hair turns the shade of flour.

"I love you," he whispers to her, pressing his lips to her forehead. "I'm so sorry." Breathing a heavy sigh, he pulls the shroud down over her face and lays his hand on top of her head.

A man lays his hand on Stirling's shoulder. Stirling's red-rimmed eyes drag away from his mourning father and rise up to the older man. Dipping his chin, Stirling lets the man and his compatriot step into the bedroom. Unable to provide Jannell with the funeral she deserves, Giles hired men from the monastery to transport her back to her home village. Her family will be able to view her one last time and say their goodbyes before burying her on the church's grounds.

Stirling's back slides down the wall until he's sitting with his knees to his face. He throws his head back, letting it thump against the hard daub. Squeezing his eyes shut, he tries to hold back, composing himself in the presence of the monastery men. The rosemary crumbles in his crushing grip. His wet eyes open as the men step out of the room with his mother's wrapped body cradled in one of their arms. Choking on his tears, he slaps his hands over his mouth. The rosemary leaves rain down on his tunic as his body convulses with emotion. Whimpers escape through his fingers as the only person he has loved is carried out of his life.

Wiping the snot running from his nose with his sleeve, Stirling peeks around the door frame into the bedroom. His father lays on the bed with his back to the door curled up, the shaking of his shoulders being the only evidence he is weeping.

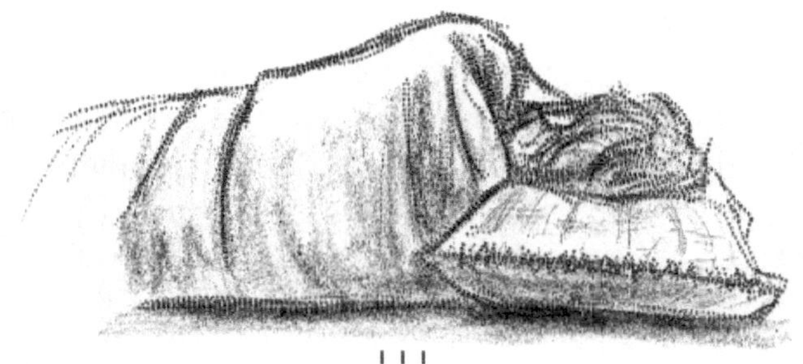

Twenty-One

The sun pierces through the treetops raining down on Stirling and Ignis in scattered storms. Stirling's light-colored eyelashes rest on his cheekbones while he lies with his back against Ignis', letting the dragon's stride dull his mind. It had been a few weeks since his mother's passing. She had missed his fourteenth birthday by only a few days.

That last day surges in his mind flooding his thoughts like water invading the boat that is meant to keep the sailors afloat through a crack in its walls. It is a constant reminder every time he closes his eyes. The image of her smile while she slips into her never-ending sleep. The last words she had said to him, the promise he had made.

He remembers sitting there until his father finally walked into the room to offer him lunch. He remembers seeing the tears his father shed; he had never seen his father cry over anything. His father always came off as the type of man who could shrug off any emotion.

He had seen what true love was that day. The way his father broke before his mother was as if half of his soul was tearing from his body. The way he stroked her hair before losing his composure. Stirling agonizingly let his mother's hand go as his father took his place on the stool. He didn't know how to comfort his father, so he had left. He left his father alone in his most vulnerable time to wallow in his sorrows. With tired and tear-burned eyes, he fell asleep curled up in a ball on his mattress in the corner of the room.

Ignis strolls through the forest to their usual hiding spot on the bluff overlooking the class by the canyon. There, already lining up along the edge of the canyon was the group of students they have been watching for years. Their dragons waiting patiently behind each of them.

He cautiously lies on the ground trying to not stir Stirling who had fallen asleep on his back. With a sudden jolt to the right, Ignis throws Stirling to the ground. He hits the patchy grass hard, waking him up in a panic.

"What! What's going on?!" He spins around in urgency trying to get a sense of his whereabouts.

"*SHHH! You're too loud. Now, take a look at that,*" Ignis says, motioning over at the class lined up. Stirling crawls his way across the ground pulling aside the leaves to peek through the field maple.

What he sees on each dragon is a saddle. Wyvern saddles are different from horse saddles. There are straps looped around the neck and tail attached to the seat resting between the wings starting at the base of the neck. The saddles' cantle is also more extreme; it cups the lower back, helping keep the rider from sliding or falling backward. The horn of the saddle is less defined though, a small bump for support but low enough it is out of the way when the rider needs to lean close to his or her dragon while diving or for other quick maneuvers.

It does not need to be pronounced since it is not used for attaching ropes or any other equipment. Items tend to be hooked out of the fighting zone on the back of the cantle. There are also no stirrups. A rider's legs do not dangle over the sides of a dragon. This could cause an increase in the probability of injury to either partner or cause drag while the dragon is trying to gain speed.

Instead, they have their legs bent and tucked up close to them in specialized holders they slide into but aren't tied down for quicker departure. Then each rider wears a designated harness with a latching hook that will attach to the dragon's saddle to keep him or her from falling off.

"Are they going to finally fly out into the canyon?" Stirling asks excitedly.

Ignis shrugs and responds sarcastically, *"I don't know, maybe they are just wearing the gear to try it on. Come on, of course they are going to fly into the canyon."*

Ignis' comment swerves right over Stirling's head as he replies, "This is going to be much more exciting than watching them fly around in circles at the base's track.

The past year and a half, the class had painstakingly trained at what Stirling deemed a snail's pace. They had started with getting used to sitting on a dragon's back. At the same time allowing the dragons to become accustomed to having someone riding and controlling their movements. They would crawl across the base grounds as the students awkwardly attempted to keep balance and control the direction the dragon needed to move in.

Eventually, they graduated into learning to take off from the ground and hover, strengthening their dragon's wings and their leg muscles as their knees dug into the saddle, keeping themselves seated properly. After long anticipation, the students were finally allowed to ride their dragons around the base's set tracks. Slow and low to the ground, they circled the base day after day.

Finally practicing with; obstacles that consist of non-lethal items being shot into the sky, full-grown dragons appearing from behind buildings, and weaving through and around tree trunks deliberately placed to act as diversions that can happen while flying. They had to maneuver and control all while maintaining a constant speed. If they faltered, they would have to run the course again until they beat the allotted time.

He watches the class with jealousy. They are ready to learn how to dive into the canyon and experience flying. While he stays here, stagnate, falling more behind in his practice. If only he had the same riding equipment.

The young students seem to stand on the tips of their toes as Instructor Aldred speaks, "This is it. This is the moment you can prove to not just me, but to yourselves that you are Riders. The only way you will succeed is if you can fully trust your dragon and its ability of flight. It will be able to sense if you waver. Would you trust your life with someone who doesn't trust you?"

Instructor Aldred pauses as the students shake their heads.

He continues, "If you crash, you cannot blame your dragon. It is not their fault. It would be your fault due to poor leadership. Do you understand me?" The students nod in acknowledgment. "Now, which one of you would like to go first?" he asks the class, his eyes stopping on each child.

Garret. Clyde. Nellie. Warrick. Amiria.

Everyone's arms remain glued to their sides. Not even a finger twitches as they nervously eye one another in hopes someone will step forth and sacrifice themselves to go first. Amiria glances down the line of her peers and lets out a sigh. Lowering her gaze, she lifts her hand level with her head. Garret side glances at Warrick, communicating with only their eyes.

"Ah, Amiria, my star pupil. May you show the rest of this class how one takes off flying from the canyon's edge? Since many of your guard posts will be on cliff sides much like this one and being able to dive off at a moment's notice is a fundamental requirement of your job," Instructor Aldred drills at Amiria and the rest of the class.

"Yes, sir," Amiria accepts.

Stirling watches through the field maple, anxious with a hint of annoyance. "Surprise, surprise. Look who's going first. Miss Perfect."

Ignis pushes Stirling aside with his head to peek through the same hole Stirling was watching through even though he could have easily picked another opening. Knocked off balance, Stirling throws his arm out to catch himself from falling over.

He flings his arms sitting back up and returns the shove. Ignis holds his position firm. Stirling growls and uses his shoulder to force Ignis' head to the side and get his viewing spot back.

Stirling nods, satisfied with the placement, "She's good, I know she is. That's why I've decided to declare her to be my rival. It's my goal to be better than her one day."

Ignis cocks his head goading. *"Oh, yeah? Your rival?"*

"Yeah, really. It's good to have ambition. Some competition, someone to compare myself to," he defends.

"Maybe you should start with that Clyde one. Start simple," Ignis jabs.

"Wait, hold on," Stirling says, putting his hand up to Ignis' face, purposefully ignoring his comment. "She's about to go."

Pulling on a pair of goggles, her skin pricks with the sharp gazes of her classmates. Her shoulders curl forward as she steps over to her beige-colored dragon; its spikes around its face and body have grown along with its overall size similar to Ignis'. The spikes protrude out of the dragon's jawline and up toward the back of its head where it meets with its long straight horns. They run down the dragon's elongated neck fading in size, disappearing before it reaches its shoulders only to resurface at the hips and continue to run along the tail increasing in size to gather at the end like a spiked club.

Amiria's face comes up short of the saddle before the dragon lowers its upper body for her. She grabs hold of the saddle lifting up onto the back of the dragon, settling her legs into place. She buckles her harness down and takes hold of the handles connected to the reins looped through a grommet in the saddle attaching to a separate band around the dragon's neck. If trained well enough by a Rider the dragon shares a bond with, it will be able to interpret the smallest of commands.

With a click of her tongue, the dragon leaps from the canyon's ledge, diving down along the rock face before expanding its wings. The thin membrane of its bat-like wings catches like a cotton sheet in the wind. With a strong thrust of its wings, they soar through the air halfway down the canyon. Amiria sits up, feeling the rush of the wind as they glide in the space once reserved for birds. Her long hair whips behind her in the wind. A smile bursts on her face like the morning beams of light blooming over the mountain peaks. There is nowhere else she would rather be.

Stirling's jaw drops as he watches Amiria fly out of view, "Did you see that? She's flying! Not like they did on the track or like what we attempted. But really actually flying! She's so amazing!" Cheeks flushing, he turns to Ignis. "Don't tell anyone I said that last part."

If Ignis had an eyebrow, he would have raised it as he mocks, *"Rival huh?"*

Stirling glares at Ignis with his furrowing brow and his mouth pulled into a thin line, an expression saying he is done with that topic. "Moving on, do you know what this means?"

"Not really, but I might have some idea what you are thinking of."

"It means we have a lot of work to do. I need to figure out a way for us to fly. I can't sit here playing with the bugs in the grass while the rest of the class flies."

"We don't have a safer way to keep you from falling off," Ignis informs in a way that doesn't discourage him but rather

just the opposite.

Stirling returns his attention to watching the next student line up at the ledge, waiting for their moment to take the leap.

He talks with his eyes glued to the Rider, "I'll go around town tomorrow and see what I can come up with."

Clyde is next in line. He is the stark opposite of Amiria as he sits straddling his dragon's back. They are as different as night and day. His olive-green dragon's single appendage at the crook of its wing digs into the crumbling ledge. His hands tremble as he peers around the dragon's head, its horns rounded like a mountain goat's.

He could see the opposing canyon wall running down and out of view.

"The sun won't be in the sky forever Clyde. You are wasting daylight and everyone else's time while we wait for you to sightsee," Instructor Aldred scorns.

"All right, all right," Clyde says hastily, his words breathy as he tries to calm his breathing. His dragon begins to lean.

Slowly the wall appears to grow as if it is a scroll unraveling to the true depths of the canyon.

He begins talking to himself to calm his nerves. Thoughts of crashing run through his mind psyching himself out. "You got this. You got this. Amiria did it no problem. Aw, that doesn't help at all. She's a freak. I wish I wasn't going second. I want to see how the others go."

Clyde closes his eyes, beads of sweat forming on his face from both the scorching sun above and his nerves. With his knuckles turning white, he grips the dragon's reins.

"Here goes nothing." He gulps. The olive-green dragon leaps from the edge.

Stirling can hear Clyde's curdling scream as they plunge into the canyon. He could barely see deep enough into the canyon to witness the dragon unfurl its wings, catching them into a steady glide in the direction of the base.

After watching Instructor Aldred take off on his dragon, ensuring the final student successfully leaped from the ledge into the canyon. Stirling removes himself from the viewpoint in the shrubs.

"Damn, they're gone already," he mopes. "I hate to say this, but I should probably be heading back home. I know my dad is going to have me clean up the entire bakery since I wasn't there to help during the day as usual and I need to think of a way to put together a makeshift saddle," he adds.

"*A makeshift saddle?*" Ignis repeats.

"Yeah, as in not a real one, just whatever stuff I can find to make something similar, or close enough," he explains. Ignis nods in recognition, still lying down as Stirling climbs up onto his back.

Stirling stares down at the ground as Ignis stands up, the patchy grass flattened where his heavy bulk had rested. Stirling could see the tiny bugs crawling around the leaves, scurrying into new hiding spots from the sudden disruption. He imagines them as the townspeople hustling to and from different shops and buildings as they carry on with their day.

Tomorrow, he thinks to himself, *I'm going to truly fly.*

Kelsea Koops

Twenty-Two

In the late afternoon, the front door to the bakery closes behind Stirling with a soft click as he steps inside the shop.

"Stirling," his father calls out to him from behind the hut-shaped oven.

He pulls away from the oven with two loaves balanced on a wooden paddle. Stirling stays mute as he aimlessly wanders over to the wooden work table. Giles turns around it as he tilts the paddle letting the loaves slide off onto the surface. Stirling watches as the flour on the table wafts into the air as each of the loaves disturbs its resting place like a dragon disrupting the dirt as it lands.

"Stirling, I need you to be home. I can't do all the work on my own all the time. You can't keep running off to go play anymore. You've been too old for that for quite some time now. You have responsibilities here as a baker," Giles lectures.

Stirling bites his tongue as he refuses to meet his father's eye, remaining focused on the loaf closest to him. He doesn't want to take over this shop, to live this uneventful life. "What do you need me to start with?" he finally manages through his gritted teeth.

"Since you've been slacking off. We've run low on supplies. We need to make a run before the sun sets. I need you to pull the cart," Giles states.

Stirling lets out an exaggerated sigh. "Joy, cart pulling." He mutters sarcastically under his breath.

The wheels of the small creaking cart bounce over every pebble in the dirt road sending the cart into a constant vibration as Stirling pulls it along, following behind his father through the market. Each hole in the road sends a jarring sensation shooting through his arms as it clashes with the uneven surface.

Stirling chuckles to himself as he pictures the two wheels popping off the cart as it hits its final straw, the wheels rolling off free through the market crowd. People comically leap out of the way of the out-of-control wheels gaining speed with no stopping in sight until they've left this town for good.

"Almost done," Giles informs Stirling as they stop in front of a shop he recognizes as the man who normally sells them the yeast and flour.

He stares at the pig feet pickled in the jar at eye level to him on top of a display set up with small clay compartments with types of grain, rye, and oats he has to offer. He remembers coming here with his mother and she would let him dig through the barrel of potatoes and pick out the ones she would prepare for dinner. He used to think the grocer's store was fascinating with all the variety of items set out front and hanging from the walls and above his head. Now it just seemed unorganized and random.

Growing bored, he leans against the slanted wooden

frame of the cart. It sits tilted forward with the two handles jutting out of the front and sticking into the ground on either side of him. As his father haggles over prices, boredom fills his young mind, compelling it to wander. Stirling scans over each shop barely regarding what each one was selling; not like he had any coins to bargain with anyway.

Then he stalls. It isn't the shop he delays on that caught his eye. He couldn't care less about the cooper making barrels. His eyes jump back to the shop right before it, a leather works shop. Strips of leather hanging out front blow lightly in the soft breeze over a table of finished products for sale. Those strips are exactly what he needs. That, some rope, a metal ring, and a fastener, then he will have himself a harness.

He can feel the cart shudder as the hefty bags of yeast and flour are hoisted and dropped into it, but his mind is on the leather strips. How is he going to be able to afford them? Even if he was paid for his work around the shop, it would still take him months to save up enough to even buy even one of those strips. He also knows there is no way his father is ever going to pay him.

He would say something along the lines of, If I start paying you, then you can start paying me for all the food you consume and the roof over your head. If you want to make money, start learning how to take over this shop.

Stirling rocks his body to assist in standing up from the cart causing it to roll backward on him slightly throwing his momentum off. Slipping, he lands back against the cart again, his weight pressing the cart's handles into the ground acting as breaks.

"Stirling, stop wasting time. Let's go," his father barks as he walks away.

Groaning, Stirling regains his footing and lifts the two handles to upright the cart. Hunching his shoulders, he mechanically follows his father pulling the cart behind him.

I have to steal them. The idea runs through his mind. It's

my only option if I want to get airborne anytime soon.

With his feet slipping in the trampled earth, Stirling struggles with his last steps as they reach the bakery. He feels as if the vindictive cart has a mind of its own and is personally throwing on its brakes to spite him. Each complete turn of the wheels feels like a feat on its own. His knees wobble, giving him a heads up before they buckle beneath him, sending him tripping to the ground at his father's feet. The items in the cart slide forward as the handles crash to the ground at his sides.

"You're weak," Giles growls. "That's not even close to the amount my father had me pull when I was your age, and that would be after I spent the morning working my ass off maintaining the shop."

Stirling keeps his head down as he curls his fingers in, the dirt bunching in his fists.

His father continues to belittle him. "What's that dream you used to have as a kid? Oh yeah, to join the Cavalry. Even if you were allowed to join, you would still have to give that dream up. You would never be able to pass their fitness requirements. I've heard some of those Riders have pulled their injured dragons to safety."

Stirling glances up, his father silhouetted by the sun resting on the rooftops. "You've listened to tales of the Cavalry?"

"No, definitely not. But us men, we do like to talk at the tavern," Giles bellows.

Frowning in annoyance, Stirling sits back on his knees, his trousers caked in damp dirt. He holds back any ill thoughts as he uses the cart to lift himself to his feet. Soon he will be soaring through the sky and moments like this will be insignificant.

He'll be soaring over the bakery with everyone gawking up at him. He'll run his hand through the once unreachable clouds and see distant lands. Even if his father shouted to the heavens, he'll be too far above Wyverna to hear his father's lectures.

It is late into the night as Stirling lies awake on his straw mattress. He stares at the ceiling painted black above him, as little moonlight is able to weasel through the closed shutters. Shapes he knows aren't really there float around his vision as he listens to his father's heavy breathing become a rhythmic pattern of sleep.

Now's his chance. It's late enough that all of the townsfolk will be fast asleep. Even the common drunks should be finished staggering home this long after curfew. He isn't worried about running into them anyway. They can barely remember how they made it home, let alone recall anyone they saw randomly walking along the road.

Stirling still fully dressed, slips from his covers and stalks soundlessly over the floorboards, each placement of his feet strategically planned out. He knows which boards creaked and where to place his weight to avoid any possible sounds. Carefully but swiftly, he makes his way down the staircase and out the front door. The clicking of the closing door is barely even audible to himself.

The crescent moon gives off only a subtle amount of light as heavy shadows line the sides of the narrow roads creating the perfect covering for Stirling to walk amongst.

This is the only time Stirling enjoys the city. The emptiness of the streets with everyone's windows shut to keep out the chill of the night air. The colorless buildings remind him of walking through a mountain passage with only the stars watching. It gives off an almost lonely feeling as he listens to the crickets chirping.

Hugging the sides of the buildings, he strolls down the road cloaking himself in the shadows as he navigates back to where the leather shop is.

Stirling jumps at the sound of a clay object shattering on the ground. "Hey, you Miss." A drunken man slurs, the only thing keeping him standing is the wall behind him across the road from Stirling.

Stay calm. He thinks you're a girl. You're still in the clear, he reassures himself.

Doing his best impression of a female voice, he calls back to the drunken man, "I'm sorry, sir, but I must be on my way."

The drunken man leans forward. "Aw, don'cha be like that, it's late. Come here bootiful, inshide wid me. I keep ya warm," he suggests with an exaggerated welcoming motion of his arm. Without the wall to stabilize himself with he staggers off balance bending at the waist. "Ohh ope ope ope," he mumbles, waving his arms to counter the way he is tipping over.

Stirling slips into the alley between the buildings he is in front of, squeezing himself sideways between the two daub walls. His feet are lost in the mud that never sees the daylight, he walks his hands along the rough wall as he sidesteps his way to the next market road.

He can hear the drunken man calling for him. "Where'd you go, miss?"

Stirling lets out a sigh barely audible over the sucking sounds his shoes make as he pulls them free. The rotten stench of stagnant water water wafts up with each step from the cement-like mud that threatens to pull his shoes off as he hears the man grumble something incomprehensible along with the opening and shutting of a door.

After scooting the entire length of the building Stirling pops out on the road the leatherwork shop is on. He scrapes the mud encasing his shoes off on a wheel of a wagon left outside a building. With his shoes now less likely to leave behind muddy evidence, he proceeds on his way to the leatherwork shop only a few buildings down, the display empty with all the merchandise pulled safely inside.

The owners, Stirling assumes, live above the shop, as do most of the merchants in the city. Inspecting the second floor, he waits to see if there is any flicker of a candle or clue they might still be awake. Nothing, he checks his surroundings, glancing up and down the road before casually walking up to the entrance door.

He grips the handle, unlocked, just as he guessed. He pushes open the door ajar enough to allow his thin frame to squeeze through.

Other than rooms in the castle, the gatehouses, and entrances into the castle ground, people around the city don't have locks. The citizens didn't have the need or urge to steal large amounts of items. Petty theft is around, but it is uncommon. Low-income families or rebellious children taking an apple off a fruit stand or a ring off a jewelry display does happen from time to time. But, most people refrain from the idea because they have the means to support themselves but also because of the severe punishment for any minor crime. No one wanted to have their head in the stocks while they slowly dehydrated in front of their peers as an example of what happens when you break the law.

Stirling stands inside the darkness of the shop, his fingers tapping rapidly at his side, his heart thumping in his chest.

Trespassing and burglary are outright unheard of. The only people who cheated and stole an extensive amount are the citizens from Uviktiland across the water. They pirate the trade route Wyverna's single harbor, Kitlsbo, in the north for expensive goods rather than paying the overly excessive import taxes.

An icy chill prickles down his spine as he imagines what the punishment for burglary is if petty theft is spending days humiliated in the town square hoping you will live out the sentenced duration.

No. Keep your thoughts on track, he thinks to himself, shaking off the feeling of dread stabbing into his chest.

He scans the shop's interior covered in various types of hides, from cattle down to rabbits. The strong scent of leather and oil lingering in the air coats his skin.

Stirling shakes his head, his thoughts getting off track again. He balls his hands giving them a pump of encouragement as he steps lightly and carefully over to a table draped in leather strips. He didn't have these floorboards memorized as he did with the ones he had grown up with the past fourteen years.

Lifting his tunic, he begins tying strip after strip around his stomach as a precaution in case he does run into someone on his way out. He prefers to avoid the whole ordeal of them questioning his arms full of leather and connecting it to the infiltration of the leatherworks shop.

The ceiling above creaks. He freezes mid-tie, leather strips already covering from his hips to his chest. He watches as the small dust clouds form from the rafters as if he can see the imprint of each footstep on the old groaning wood. A heavy foot lands on the first step at the top of the staircase leading from the loft down into the shop. The sound echoes through the house and Stirling's body, rattling his bones. He's surprised the whole neighborhood can't hear it.

An older gentleman with a burly beard and stocky stature

comes stomping down the stairs, making them creak and sigh as they support his weight. Not carrying a candle or lantern, the man feels his way around, dragging his hand along the railing. He steps off the last step into the shop, his eyes only groggy slits as he barely even scans across the lightless room. The man scratches his belly and strolls across the shop to the back door to relieve himself.

Stirling stands petrified, the man didn't see him. He hadn't registered anything was amiss. He had walked right past him without even noticing his presence. With his heart pounding on the doors of his chest, he imagines fissures splintering across his brittle ribs. Careful not to trip on his heels he cautiously backs his way out of the shop. But not before helping himself to a few metal rings and a large metal T-shaped hook.

His back bumps into the front door. Keeping his eyes locked on the back door the man exited, Stirling fumbles blindly for the door handle. His hands pat the wooden frame in a frantic manner, convinced the handle had been removed to trap him so he may be persecuted for the crimes he has committed. The cool metal appears beneath his palm and he vanishes from the leatherwork shop leaving behind only his haunting presence.

Hunching his shoulders, Stirling briskly walks at a speed barely slow enough to not be considered a jog. He wraps his arms around his body, his head hanging low as he stares at his feet. Step by step, pressing into the earth to propel him forward and away from what he had done.

Thief! His consciousness repeats over and over in his head.

Thief, thief, thief, thief!

"I know, I know," he whimpers to himself. Hunching his shoulders he moves through the streets with as much stealth as he could manage while keeping up with a quick and steady pace.

His near encounter, his sheer luck. The only reason he is currently walking free through this city street is similar to surviving combat because of a fluke. The sword didn't pierce his body due to the single fact that his attacker misjudged his body mass and struck through the long dark cloak he was wearing.

The impending feeling, if it wasn't for luck you should be dead because of your own poor choices, weighs him down. He keeps trucking forward through the invisible hands pulling at his shoes and pant legs. He isn't going to be able to settle down with the ominous windows belonging to innocent people lining the streets. With each cracked window, he swears he can see the whites of the watcher's eyes. He won't slip into a comfortable and relaxed state until he is far away from the shop, of all shops entirely.

Standing at the city wall separating the overbearing cage-like city from the open freedom of the mountain's forest, Stirling squats down, pushing aside the bushes concealing the rabbit hole in the layered stone wall.

With a last glance over his shoulder, he crawls on his hands and knees through the hole.

No longer ten years old, his shoulders brush the rough interior of the wall. Then without bothering to wipe the dirt from his palms and trousers, he sets off on his ascent through the forest.

Ignis perks his head up as Stirling enters the cave. "*You seem stressed,*" he points out.

"Well, no duh, I just robbed someone's shop. I stole supplies they need to make a living. It's like if someone stole the yeast out of the bakery," Stirling crudely responds.

"*Is that not something people do?*" Ignis naively questions with a tilt of his head.

"No, it's not something people do," he snaps.

Stirling sits on the floor in the empty pocket between

Ignis' body and his tail curled in a half circle around him. Lifting his tunic and undershirt, he begins untying the leather strips, dropping them into a pile beside him.

"People don't normally steal from each other. Well, not here, at least. I don't know how things are elsewhere. It's unethical. It's a sin. The laws are stringent and systematic. The slightest change must be documented, and the slightest challenge against the king will bring your life to an end."

He pauses and forces the repeating vision of him swinging by his neck on a hill full of daisies to the back of his mind as he gathers his thoughts. "I'm not a criminal. I– well I just couldn't think of any other way to get these supplies. I feel guilty. I hope it doesn't effect the leatherworker too badly," Stirling admits. "I wish." Stirling pauses, "I wish making choices in my life didn't involve committing crimes. Every day I talk to you I'm committing treason. I'm lucky to see each new day."

Ignis's neck curves like a bow as he eyes Stirling, "*I'm sorry.*"

"You haven't done anything except be my best friend. Even if my life is cut short, it was at least worth living because of you."

Ignis dips of his head, "*I hope it isn't.*" He still never understands these laws Stirling always refers to. Humans have such bizarre ways of living. All he understands is that laws exist. If you break them, you die in some horrible way and that is final.

"Me too." Stirling closes his eyes momentarily then claps his hands on his knees after dropping the final strip of leather in the pile, "All right, enough talk about the crimes I have committed, and let's continue committing more by getting this harness made."

Scooping up one of the straps, he leaps to his feet and motions Ignis to stand with him.

He holds out the strip against the front of Ignis' chest at

his collarbone. "Okay, I think I have an idea of how we can do this."

Circling Ignis, he proceeds with explaining, using hand gestures and pointing to help Ignis understand what he is describing. "We can have a strap looping all the way around your neck, at the top I will attach some extra leather to create handles, and at the bottom near the joints of your legs, there will be a bridge attaching to two leg loops to prevent the one around your neck from spinning around. Your wings come right out from the bottom of your shoulders, so I'll have enough room to have one more strip come up and over your back attaching the two leg loops without it rubbing against your wings while flying. At the center of this strap, I'll have a metal ring that I'll be able to attach my own belt to."

"*What?*" Ignis blinks.

Stirling picks up the metal T-shaped hook with curved ends from the pile of leather strips. "With this, it can slip through the ring but only at a specific angle. Otherwise, it's permanently fixed there. Especially if there's tension, that locks it in more. You got it?" Ignis blankly stares at Stirling. "Or just stand there. I got this," he says, cracking his knuckles.

He tosses the first strip over Ignis' back and begins tying the leather together with a slip knot and pulling them as tight as he can by having Ignis clamp down on one end with his teeth while he pulls the end, ensuring the knot won't come loose.

"*Once this is on, how does it come off?*" Ignis brings up.

Stirling stalls, not thinking that far ahead. "Uh, you might have to wear this for a few days until I can find some buckles and we can give the design an upgrade."

Ignis sighs with defeat. Piece by piece, Stirling constructs the support to help bring him one step closer to the clouds.

Twenty-Four

The twilight sky begins to turn the color of sapphire with amber edges as the sun prepares itself to grace the world with its first rays over the horizon.

Stirling, snoring softly, is sound asleep, leaning against the soft feathers of Ignis' wings, who is wearing the now completed harness. As the sun finally makes its debut over the edge of the earth, Stirling stirs awake, orange sunlight striking him across the eyes.

He bolts up straight as it dawns upon him morning has arrived. "Damn! How am I going to explain to my father why I'm not home? He's probably realizing it right now!"

Letting out a loud sigh, he falls back against Ignis hopeless, the feathers acting as a pillow catching his head.

Ignis opens his eyes, his pupils constricting into small dots in the glaring sunlight. *"Well, since you're already caught. How about you stay here and we test out this harness."*

With a wild grin, Stirling says, "You've got a point there. I'll be in trouble whether I return now or later."

Ignis stands up abruptly letting Stirling fall backward. He sprawls out into a lying position on his back unable to catch himself in time.

"*Then let's fly!*" he says enthusiastically.

Stirling leans up on his elbows, suggesting, "You want to head over to the canyon then?"

"*No need,*" Ignis responds. "*We can fly from here like I always do.*"

Ignis trots the short distance over to the mouth of the cave overlooking the ocean and rising sun.

Gradually rolling over onto his stomach Stirling pushes himself into a kneeling position considering what Ignis is suggesting. He unsteadily crawls himself to the edge of the opening. He peaks down at the sheer drop to the waves crashing against the rock wall below. His sight immediately grabs hold of the rocks jutting out of the water like spikes on the back of a sea monster.

"*You scared?*" Ignis teases. "*I thought this is what you wanted to do?*"

"Yeah, it is, but I just, it's just." He sways, feeling woozy staring down at the intimidating height. He backs away safely, not playing down his fear, "You want me to jump from a cliff. So yeah, I'm a—little bit nervous,"

"*I jump from here every day. I can't fit through the other exit anymore. So you're going to have to put some faith in me,*" Ignis says to reassure him.

"It's not you that I'm nervous about trusting. It's my maybe-not-so-handy work that I don't trust," he admits referring to the harness.

"*Well, there's only one way to find out if it works. I'll try and catch you if you fall off,*" Ignis says while kneeling on his forelegs so Stirling can climb up onto his back.

"Try? Don't you mean will?" Stirling says, unsettled.

"*Yeah, same thing,*" Ignis says, brushing it off.

Stirling slips on the belt he altered with the new hook

making sure it fits snug and isn't going to come undone. While steadying his breathing, he grabs the handles of the harness, the leather strips taut on Ignis' back, and hoists himself, swinging his leg over. Ignis stands himself back up. Stirling rocks with Ignis' movements as he settles himself in, his legs bent underneath him, resting at the base of Ignis' wings where the feathers flow down to his spine.

Ignis' claws dangle off the edge of the cliff, and clumps of loose dirt and pebbles crumble off under his weight tumbling to the rough current below. Stirling peeks over the edge. Immediately regretting his decision as his face contorts along with the twisting of his stomach. The distance between him and the water appears to be stretching.

Breathe in. Breathe out. Breathe in. Breathe out. Stirling focuses on his breaths trying to calm his nerves. He begins to tap his fingers on Ignis' back and has his thumb hooked around the handle. Index, middle, ring, pinky.

He forces his eyes shut as he reasons with his instincts to stay safe in the confines of the cave. He fights the losing argument trying to convince himself he is not going to plummet to his death. He breathes in deep, his chest expanding as he reaches the maximum capacity in his lungs. He holds it. Slowly releasing the air, he opens his eyes reflecting the golden color of the morning sun.

"Please don't kill me."

Without hesitating, Ignis leaps from the safety of the cave and dives toward the salty waters. Stirling can barely keep his stinging eyes open against the rushing wind. His stomach and the rest of his internal organs are left back in the cave as they free-fall at a velocity he never thought possible. The desperate urge to scream fights its way through his throat only to be met by the wind, forcing it back down as his jaw hangs open. The ability to cry and breathe is ripped away from him at the speed of a hurricane.

His fingernails dig into his palm, drawing blood as he grips the handles of the harness, his life depending on it as the ocean races to meet them head-on.

Ignis' vibrant wings explode open at the last minute, catching them before they collide with the water. Gales of salty wind thrown from the thrusts of his wings spray ocean water into a mist around them. Stirling's body slams hard against Ignis from all the force and sudden change in momentum. The muscles in Ignis' back rippled beneath Stirling's shins as they are propelled forward parallel to the water, the tips of his claws clipping the rising and falling waves.

They slow to glide over the water's surface sending rippling trails below them. Feeling a throb in his head from the whiplash, Stirling cautiously sits up.

He is weightless as if the world below him ceases to exist along with all the troubles that come with it. Nothing seems to matter anymore—the thoughts and opinions of the townspeople, the laws of the kingdom, the bakery, and his father. At this moment, here and now he has discovered the true feeling of freedom.

Letting go of the handle with a single hand he tests out his balance. Feeling brave with a dab of hesitance, he shakily lets go with his other hand. For a brief moment, the fear of falling off and being submerged in the deep cold water surges through him. He rapidly grabs hold of the handles once again to save himself, even though he wasn't going to fall off with his belt firmly hooked to Ignis' harness.

"Come on, don't be a chicken. The Cavalry isn't afraid of anything, especially not flying," he whispers to himself. Loosening his grip once again, he lets go with both hands, simultaneously raising them out to his sides.

Stretching them out, he lets his fingers separate as the feeling of the air cuts around his arms. He can feel the air pushing up on his hands as if it is solid and ready to support and lift him to the sky with wings.

"Is this how flying works?" he ponders, taking it all in.

He can't convey in words how he feels. How the possibilities from now on are endless. How this is a happiness, a love, he has never experienced before. He is miserable at the bakery, in the city, but here defying gravity, he has forgotten that life has ever even existed.

He wonders what he would appear like to someone else right now, a young boy with arms out wide on the back of an earthy orange dragon with a pastel sunrise painting the sky with pinks, oranges, and yellow in a serene backdrop. The water reflects the sun's rays onto Ignis' underside causing him to glisten as if he is built of crystal.

"I wonder if my mother can see me," Stirling considers out loud, speaking to no one in particular.

"*Probably,*" Ignis gives Stirling this small satisfaction. "*Hold on tight, we're going back to the cave,*" Ignis advises.

Stirling retakes hold of the handles for stability. Arching his body, Ignis banks hard, turning in the direction of the cliffs and slowly climbing their ascent.

As they reach the opening, Ignis back flaps his wings, his body hanging vertically in the air as he slows into a steady hover. His claws gouge deep grooves as he takes hold of the cave's ledge. His body hangs halfway out as he finishes pulling them inside.

Stirling unhooks his belt and slides off Ignis stumbling on the solid ground, "THAT WAS AMAZING!" he hollers, tripping over his feet as he bounces, still overcome with adrenaline. "We can start practicing every night. That way we can use the canyon too without anyone noticing!"

"*Will your father notice?*" Ignis inquires.

"Oh, he'll definitely notice. But, you know what? I don't care," Stirling responds. "I'll be in trouble today, tomorrow, next month, next year. But no matter what my father says or how many times I'm told I am forbidden to leave. He won't ever be able to get me to stay in that bakery."

Ignis' golden eyes flash him a cautious warning. "*Be careful what you say or wish for. You don't always know what your father will resort to if you keep testing his patience."*

"Yeah, yeah. My Pa and his lecturing," Stirling says, waving off Ignis' forewarning as he loses himself to the sun shining brightly into the cave and reflecting off his hazel eyes. The green and gold glow with radiance.

With his head still in the clouds, Stirling peels himself from the sunrise back to Ignis with sudden urgency, as if he had just remembered something. "I'm going to head back, okay? I'll be back tonight."

"You're leaving?"

Stirling rubs the back of his neck awkwardly. "Yeah, I uh, you are right about my dad and I should head back to help during the day."

He takes a few steps back, putting his hands up apologetically as he slips towards the cave's exit.

Ignis stands dumbfounded at Stirling's sudden alteration in character. *"Oh, uh, okay. See you tonight then."*

Stirling walks the rest of the way casually in the cave while still in Ignis' line of sight; but once he is hidden in the dark cloak of the tunnel, he takes off in a sprint.

Kneeling in the field maple on top of the bluff overlooking the class' training ground, Stirling pushes enough leaves out of the way to peek through.

Amiria stands at the clearing between the forest and the canyon's ledge with her dragon. She is in her full practice gear; simple leather gauntlets, riding boots, a leather chest plate, goggles, and her harness similar to what Ignis wears looping around her waist, connecting to another loop around each thigh on the front and back of her.

Like he guessed, she would never miss a morning practice before class.

He has a feeling in his gut that it's odd for him to be watching her alone like this. He isn't with Ignis watching her class for learning purposes. Though he can't take his eyes off her. Her sleek dark hair is pulled back as always with subtle waves at the bottom. She isn't composing herself in the unique behavior he has observed to be common amongst Winged Riders as if they are ready to turn and fight but combined with elegance like a noble at a royal ball. She stands with the hunch of someone who has been given too much weight to hold.

Amiria steps closer to her dragon, closing the gap between them. She gazes into its eyes as she places the palm of her hand on the snout of the massive creature's face, the size of her torso. It lets out a sigh of comfort, the breath rippling Amiria's shortened tunic as it closes its large brown eyes, pressing into her touch. A small smile of pure love emerges on her face as she leans, touching her forehead against the dragon's.

Stirling is awestruck as he watches her. He knew they had been trained to bond with their dragon to gain its trust to be able to ride with full potential, but he had only seen her fly and train with her dragon as if it were merely a tool. To see her here and now with her compassion worn on her sleeve is a new side he never thought he'd see of her, or any Winged Rider if he is being honest.

He's locked, frozen in a state where the forest vanishes around him, the trees, the grass, all of it fading away until the only thing he can see is her. The way her neck curves as she holds her head pressed to her wyvern's. Their eyes closed, softly breathing in each other's presence.

Stirling can't control himself as he leans forward through the field maple he is concealing himself in in an attempt to get a better view. It is as if some kind of force had taken over his body, and it wants to be close to her. Longing to stand beside her and be part of this moment with her, to share who he was with her. He could feel his heart thumping in his chest. The rhythm isn't fast, but it feels off as if it has skipped a beat.

He freezes at the sound of a twig snapping under the weight of his hand. His chest restricts, holding his lungs at a standstill, so not even the sound of his breath escapes his lips.

Amiria's eyes shoot open like a predator hearing the footfalls of its prey. Her attention immediately locks on the boulders and brush blocking Stirling's trembling frame from her view.

She leers, unmoving, her hand still resting on the dragon's snout. Waiting and listening for another sound to confirm she had heard something other than a small animal.

Letting her hand drop to her side, she puts her weak foot forward and her strong foot back in a bladed stance and faces her whole body in Stirling's direction.

Stirling wants to run away, to leave this spot he is planted in before she decides to come and investigate, but he can't conjure himself to move, afraid he will cause more commotion if he high tails it out of there. He can't even get himself to scoot backward slowly, his limbs refusing to budge as if he is cast in stone. He is well concealed behind the field maple, but he can feel her eyes burning like a raging fire through the green leaves and straight into him leaving him incapacitated.

Amiria tentatively steps closer to her wyvern's side placing her hand on the saddle, her eyes not leaving the thicket on top of the bluff. With a swift movement, she leaps onto her dragon's back and with one last glance at the leaves rustling lightly in the breeze, she gives out a whistle, and her dragon rockets into the sky.

Stirling's arms buckle, casting him to the grassy floor gasping. He doesn't get up right away as the control of his muscles returns, but instead, he lies there for a moment. Amiria had terrified him, but he can't stop himself from smiling.

Twenty-Five

The moon, full like a silver coin in the sky, hovers at the highest point, making the pale-colored buildings glow with a soft light in a colorless world. It is a perfect night for flying.

After years of training in the sky, Stirling and Ignis' minds have completely synced. While in the air, they are now capable of making decisions as one entity rather than a rider commanding the dragon to move as they deem to be the most effective flight. With their mind in unity, the results are quick precise movements, changing at a moment's notice. They feel as if there isn't anything they can't do.

Stirling holds his hand behind him, keeping the door from slamming shut as he sneaks back into the dark bakery.

"Stirling," a voice speaks out from the shadows of the shop.

Stirling jumps, startled at the unexpected sound. Searching, he squints into the familiar room as his eyes adjust to the absence of light.

Giles stands in the middle of the shop.

"Stirling," he says once again, "you're sixteen. You are a legal adult now. You can't go sneaking out into the night anymore. You need to be awake during the day. You have responsibilities here."

Stirling opens his mouth to protest, but his father cuts him off, "Don't try and weasel your way out of this one. At first, I thought it was some phase you were going through after your mother's passing. I thought maybe you'd grow out of it. But after all the lectures, the grounding, the extras chores, here you are. Still acting like a child, sneaking out to who knows where after curfew. What is it? Some secret? Have you joined some group of vandals and gotten into mischief?"

Stirling balls his hands into useless fists hanging at his sides.

Giles continues to berate him, ignoring the veins popping on the back of the clenched hands, "Or maybe it's a girl? No, I doubt that. What kind of girl would be interested in a boy who can't even perform the basic tasks of his job? How would you be able to support her? Support a family? You wouldn't be able to, because you can't do anything right. You're useless."

"Just shut up!" Stirling shouts, finally reaching his boiling point, unable to contain his composure after years of belittlement from his father. "Why does it always have to come back to being about this damn bakery!"

"This bakery is our life!" Giles yells, frustrated.

Stirling holds his voice in a normal pitch, unlike his initial outburst, but he speaks hard and stern with words full of the despicable truth of how he feels, "No, Father. This bakery is your life. This is not the life I want. I've never wanted it. Why do you think I always leave at every opportunity I'm offered? I hate this place."

With his jaw set and his eyebrows furrowed, Stirling turns away from his father in the direction of the staircase. His body is rigid as he moves his tense muscles.

With one foot firmly on the bottom step, Giles speaks up again. His voice is a low growl, halting Stirling, whose neck disappears into his collar as he raises his shoulders, his hands clenched at his sides.

"I'm going to give you only one more chance, Stirling. The day after tomorrow, well, technically tomorrow since the new day has already begun, we have a huge commitment to fulfill. I've collaborated with the fromager and the butcher from down the street to set up a stand together at the Joust. It's an important event even people from the small neighboring villages will be attending. I will need you to be here today and tomorrow."

Giles waits for Stirling to speak, his eyes locked on the back of his head and Stirling's pinned to the white-washed wall. The words he wants to say are written across his hidden face.

"And what if I don't?" he finally replies through his teeth.

"If you leave, then I will be sending you to your mother's parent's bakery in Milleoaks. Maybe being far away from the city will do some good for you. Keep you away from wherever it is you sneak off to."

Stirling drops his shoulders. He glares over his left side at his father, entirely lost of words. He rummages through responses he can pull out, but all end with the result of him being banished to his grandparents' bakery before the sun rises. His grandparents live in a small village in the center of the crater-like valley making up the entirety of the nation. Even traveling fast on horseback it is a several days ride away.

Stirling bites the inside of his cheek, refusing to say anything that would satisfy his father. He doesn't know how to win an argument against his father. If he agrees, he has forfeited. If he speaks any form of opposing words to him, he will only prolong his loss.

What is even worse, Stirling thinks to himself, is his

father doesn't even understand the extent of his threat. His father is threatening his very existence. Threatening to cast him away, stripping him of what holds him together. Ripping him away from the mountains where he spent the happiest moments of his life with Ignis. Anchoring him to the ground where he can no longer feel the wind lift him into a world given to birds but stolen by him alongside his best friend.

The taste of iron saturates Stirling's tongue. He releases his cheek from the entrapment of his teeth and turns away from his father once again. Silently he sulks up the stairs in defeat.

When morning finally arrives, Stirling wakes up exhausted. He managed to rest his eyes for no more than three hours before his father woke him with an aggressive demand to get up and ready for the day.

Laying on his straw mattress in the corner of the room, Stirling can only wish he was allowed to roll over and fall back into blissful sleep. His blanket pulled up to his chin creating a pocket of warmth protecting him from the chill air that had snuck into the house overnight through the gaps in the door frame and around the window's shutters.

"Time to get up Stirling." Giles grunts.

Stirling yanks his cover over his face in obstinacy. His father's footsteps disappear down the stairs, preparing to start his daily work. Frustrated he rips the blanket back off, his clenched fists landing at his sides. With a scowl of averseness, he rolls up into a sitting position. Grabbing his slim-fitting dark brown trousers from the side of his bed, he slips each foot through and pulls the twine at the bottom, tightening the fabric around his ankles. In one movement, he stands and pulls his pants up around his waist.

Sighing, he shrugs on his short lengthed blue tunic ending past his hips. The fabric closer represents a grayish tone than blue after it had been dyed poorly, allowing his father to haggle down the price from the tailor. He pushes up his dingy white long undershirt sleeves up to his elbows.

Stirling finishes looping his belt around his waist at the landing of the stairs. Stirling recalls the confrontation he had with his father just hours before. He glances across the room at his father, who is already working hard at getting the straw and wood lit to heat the furnace of the stone oven. Stirling knows as soon as they burn to ashes in a minimum of two hours, his father will clean them out to the floor for Stirling to sweep out onto the streets. Ingredients are organized in order on the old table, waiting to be combined into a melody that will sit and rise until it's time has arrived to move into the hell-like cocoon, where it will undergo metamorphosis.

"Don't stand there. Get to work," Giles commands.

Stirling clenches his jaw, his teeth grinding as he traps any protest that comes to mind. Grudgingly he shuffles across the room. His feet drag as he refuses to exert the energy into picking them up properly. He slides the mixing bowl to the furthest corner of the table to begin making the first batch of dough.

Without measuring, Stirling scoops a handful of yeast into the bowl. He reaches over grabbing the water pitcher and pours a rough estimate over the yeast and begins sifting it through his fingers as his mind wanders out to Ignis.

"I just started and I'm already bored."

"What is it that you are doing?" Ignis asks, yawning as if Stirling had woken him up.

"I don't really know, stirring yeast until my father realizes how long I've been doing the same thing for," he says with a chuckle.

"Don't ruin this. Remember he's going to send you to your grandparents' bakery if you keep acting up," Ignis

reminds him.

Stirling stares at the soaked yeast, then up at his father who is stretching out his back after hunching over the fire for an extended period.

"*Yeah, I don't want that to happen,*" Stirling says in a tone Ignis finds peculiar, as he can't tell if he is being serious or sarcastic.

"What are you doing?" Giles asks, observing Stirling. He lectures, "You need to add the other ingredients before you start beating it like that. Useless, completely useless. No, you're worse than useless. You're a burden at times because you do nothing but waste time. You take, but you don't give. You couldn't be your mother's son. You've put her talents and humbleness to shame."

Stirling's hands stop. The tacky substance glued to his skin. He keeps his head down as his eyes dart up to his father at the mention of his mother.

The thoughts of all the responses he would love to tell his father came rushing in, almost knocking him forward as he can feel them slam against the front of his skull. Don't bring her into this. We are more alike than you think. She had more skills than you know but she kept it all a secret. I wish she was here and not you.

Stirling doesn't say a single word as he stares fixated on his father. He holds his tongue, fighting down his pride, and returns to work in silence. Is this what his life is going to be like? Constantly having to hold back everything he is thinking, never expressing his thoughts and opinions? Is living a life where you're always told what you can and cannot do really living?

Picking up his pace, Stirling begins putting in actual effort into his tasks. He isn't trying to impress his father by proving to him he can be a hard worker and do the job correctly. He wanted to show his father he was capable of it.

By the end of the day, he is drained of all his energy. He sits slumped on the bench at the dinner table. A loaf of barley bread baked fresh that day sits cut between him and his father as the rest of the barley and rye loaves, pretzels, oatcakes, and sweet fig bread was either sold or are being set aside to use for the stand at the joust.

Pieces crumble off the dry chunk of bread as Stirling fumbles with it in his calloused hands solemnly. Pretending he was someone he wasn't mentally exhausted him, but his father is satisfied with his work for once.

Giles tears into his food with the satisfaction of a hard day's work well done. Brooding in his chair, Stirling momentarily watches his father. Just like his mother before she had passed, he had never taken a moment to consider his father. He was always too preoccupied with his life. He notices wrinkles have set into the corners of his eyes and across his forehead. The evidence of exhaustion is worn into his skin. It isn't from being sick or from working a job he loathed, but from aging with time and taking care of a misbehaving child on his own.

"I'm going to bed," Stirling mumbles as he drops the bread on the table half eaten.

He swings his leg over the bench and shuffles his feet over to his bed.

Giles leans across the table snatching the leftover bread, replying, "Goodnight," not thinking much else of it.

Twenty-Six

Stirling's eyes open on cue as if his internal clock with years of programming knew the time to ring the alarm in his head. Like a rooster crowing to start the day on a farm, it announces to him this is the moment for him to slip from the shackles of his home to the perfect dreamland he brought to life.

He lays awake. His eyes scan the shadowed room, his father's faint snores coming from behind the bedroom door. That is his sign. He slips out of bed and runs across the room. His foot placement is precise, memorized from years of practice. He slides his feet into his turnshoes without the backs pulled over his heels as he slithers out the front door into the night.

Hopping down the main street on one foot at a time, he tugs his shoes on properly and takes off sprinting without a single concern about who might see him.

In a slow jog, Stirling emerges from the forest to the bare patch of land leading to the canyon's ledge holding a pair of eye goggles he had made himself. Wispy strands of hair caught in the breeze, tickle his face like the loose strings of a spiderweb. Scanning the clouds to his right he smiles as his sight secures his ride.

Ignis descends from an overpassing cloud, his color dulled from the faint moonlight but still distinct as he vanishes into the canyon below. With the sound of gravel grinding below his shoes, Stirling takes off in a full sprint at the canyon pulling a pair of goggles over his eyes. The edge draws closer as if the ground is being pulled out from below him, and, without hesitating, he leaps from the ledge.

He free-falls through the air, his limbs flailing as if they are searching for something solid to grasp. Something to stop the imminent threat of falling to his death. Ignis' eyes widen as Stirling plummets past him, just two short wing bursts away from catching him.

Folding his wings in tight to his body like a falcon, he arcs diving after him. With Stirling's body spread out flat, the air pushes against him slowing his descent in comparison to Ignis' aerodynamic posture helping his lifeline catch up with ease. His forelegs extend out forward, his claws reaching for Stirling who goes static, stiffening his muscles to hold his arms still against the wind's force. As Ignis's claws loop around Stirling's biceps. He immediately releases his wings, spreading them out and stopping their rapid descent. Stirling's chin hits his chest as his head whips down, sending a jarring pain down his spine.

Sailing low through the canyon, Ignis helps Stirling crawl up around his body onto his back. Ignis attempts to assist by pushing up on Stirling's feet, giving him a lift instead of letting them dangle free. Stirling grips the harness, refusing to let the wind yank his feeble body off as they push through it.

Flopping his torso over Ignis' back, Stirling lays across him perpendicularly. With a hook of his belt, he safely swings his leg over, sitting up properly.

"WOOOO! I bet little miss prodigy wouldn't try that!" he shouts, adrenaline surging through his veins.

"*I think she would. But I think she would actually be able to land on her dragon's back.*" Ignis teases.

"*Hey, one of these days, I'll time it right. It's not just on me, you know. You play a part in it, too,*" Stirling retorts.

"*Yeah, my part is keeping you from going splat on the canyon floor,*" Ignis mocks.

"*Okay, fine. Let's move on. Let's practice a wall turn around to a fly, sprint, fly,*" he says, changing the subject.

Stirling and Ignis have been working on maneuvers only they will be capable of achieving using Ignis' four legs as the main factor.

They bank hard to the side, turning their direction to head straight at the canyon wall. As they close in and are nearing a head-on collision with the rough rocky surface, Ignis lowers his head, tucking it under his body until he is able to see his tail. His body in reaction contorts to follow the guiding movement by turning to correct itself. His feet as result, make a crashing contact with the wall.

Rocks break off from the impact, tumbling to the ground below as smoke-like dust rises around his claws. This all happens in a matter of seconds as Ignis shoots back off the wall using the combination of his legs and wings to launch himself off, creating a quicker alternative to turning around in tight quarters instead of conducting a large sweeping turn.

In a gradual slope, they lower to the base of the canyon. Ignis' front legs straighten out, bracing for the impact of the solid ground rising steadily closer to them. As soon as his claws touch the ground, he pulls his hind legs forward in a running motion. His body's weight shifts over his front legs until the momentum steals them from their contact with the ground, his body suspended for the blink of an eye. The claws of his hind legs strike the ground, his nails digging into the dirt as he launches into a gallop.

Galloping along the bottom of the canyon with his elongated neck stretched out in alignment with his spine, his claws grazing the dusty land with such elegance that it appears he is still flying. Merely gliding low across the earth's surface like when he would dip his toes in the cold ocean's water as they sailed over.

Over the last two years, Stirling had to steal more supplies to adjust Ignis' harness, whose shoulder height is in line with the top of Stirling's head, who has had multiple growth spurts resulting in a long lanky body. It was a little more than a year after his first robbery when he stole again from the shop. They had noticed and reported that items were missing, but they had no evidence to pinpoint a suspect and their guard soon dropped. They became complacent after a year of no misfortunes. Stirling had felt an overbearing amount of guilt for what he had done to his neighbors. Still having to convince himself whenever he sees the shop that what he has done is wrong but necessary. Even heroes aren't perfect and have to make some harmful decisions to succeed in the long run.

Another addition he had made to the harness was leather pads the size of his feet attached to the harness strap directly in front of the joint of Ignis' wing and back. The pad drapes over the corner of the wing, giving Ignis' feathers protection and Stirling's knees grip as he presses into Ignis' folded wings while he gallops, assisting Stirling in flowing with Ignis' movements.

Spreading out his enormous wings twice his length, he leaps into the air in sync with the propulsion of his wings. The force thrusts him from a gallop to a skyward climb in one continuous motion.

The chill of the night air nips at Stirling's face, coloring his cheeks and the tip of his nose with a soft pink.

Staying low in the canyon, they glide like a silent ship drifting through the currents of the midnight ocean. Stirling leans himself back, lying where the feathers meet on Ignis' back. He lies on the soft cushion as he gazes up at the stars above him. The thick bright clusters illuminate the black canvas past the end of the grayscale stone walls. They appear so close as if they are painted on the canyon's ceiling. As if he can reach up and simply touch them. As if he can pick off one of the glowing dots and hold it close to him in the palm of his hand, letting it light the path one step at a time.

When he was a little kid, his grandparents on his father's side passed away. His mother told him people turn into stars when they leave their bodies on earth. Eventually, he stopped believing as he grew older, but at times it is still a comforting thought. His eyes drift shut as he imagines his mother watching from the stars, her smile twinkling along with the lights.

Stirling's eyes flutter open. Leaves rustle above him in the gentle breeze. Ignis twists his neck, nudging Stirling, who was still strapped to his back.

"You fell asleep," Ignis states.

"Oh, sorry. I was just so relaxed." He yawns.

"It's fine, you haven't been able to get much sleep," Ignis reassures.

Sitting up, Stirling stretches his muscles, raising his arms high above his head with a yawn. Glancing around, he recognizes where he is. Ignis had flown them out of the canyon once he had noticed Stirling had fallen asleep and walked them over to their viewpoint on the bluff.

The sun beams unveiling from the mountain tops dye the clouds in the sky a mixture of pinks and oranges with such vibrancy that if you described it to someone who's never seen the sunrise, they wouldn't believe you. The forest remains in the heavy shadow cast by the mountain peaks.

Stirling's mind drifts to his father, who always wakes as soon as the sun peaks its shining eye over the mountaintops.

Something moves in the corner of Stirling's eye tearing his focus away from the sunrise and away from his father.

"Get down!" he says, in a haste. His voice is hushed but commanding.

Ignis, who is still standing, drops his bouldering weight down to the ground with a quake. Stirling barely catches himself by grabbing hold of the harness' handles. If it wasn't for him still being buckled down at the waist, he would have been thrown off.

"*What is it?*" Ignis requests with more curiosity than concern.

"Look there," Stirling says, pointing at a beige wyvern arriving over the treetops.

Its back flaps over the clearing, lowering its hind legs to the compacted dirt. Folding in its wings, the dragon tilts forward, unable to balance on two legs alone. Extending its folding wings to the front, it catches itself landing on the middle joint of the wing where a single claw appendage protrudes.

"I didn't think they would have training today because of the joust. Guess she's too good for any social gatherings." Stirling sighs as they see Amiria perched upon the dragon's back in full training gear.

Over her long-sleeved cream-colored tunic, she wears black treated leather gauntlets with gold-plated grommets, their stark contrast even noticeable from their distance. To protect her chest, she has a matching leather breastplate with a binding down each of her sides starting at the armpit. Resting snug on her face is her eye protection designed by and for the Winged Cavalry only. The glass shaped perfectly into two medallions fits snug into their bronze metal rims carved with delicate designs keeping the glass lifted from the wearer's face. Leather padding outlines the inside for comfort as the goggles are fastened behind the head by a durable leather strap.

Stirling pulls his misshapen goggles off his head. He brings them down to his lap and analyzes them with a grumble. He had put so much time and effort into finding broken clear glass bottles that were also the right size. He had secretly heated the glass in the bakery's oven, softening them as he ground the jagged and sharp edges, smoothing and thinning them till they were wearable. He formed the leather holding the glass by wetting it, stretching and molding, drying and repeating until he finally got it right after weeks of trial and error.

Stirling's attention snaps back at the sound of a high-pitched whistle. Amiria's dragon leaps into action, curving its body into a dive, disappearing into the canyon and out of sight.

Stirling and Ignis lay low in the thickets waiting for a sign on if they should run or remain hidden.

Amiria and her dragon come rocketing out of the canyon. They spin, climbing higher and higher towards the pink clouds brushed in the sky like the blush on a woman's cheek. The beige dragon leans back, arching its neck backward and tucking its wings in tight. They begin to fall as gravity pulls them into a nosedive and the forest is their water. The dragon turns itself upright as its wings shoot open, catching them as they graze the treetops. The dragon's talons clip the tips of the trees as the branches toss around in the windstorm below its beating wings.

Leaves rain down on Stirling and Ignis. The branches above them sway as the massive creature swoops by.

"Nice move. We should try that later," Stirling compliments.

He knows she is a showoff but he can't help himself being impressed by her. He'll never admit it to Ignis but he admires her.

Stirling lowers his gaze back down to the goggles still in

his lap. Just because he didn't have specialized equipment, a military-bred dragon or the mark on his arm doesn't mean he can't learn to outfly them all.

"Let's get out of here before she sees us. Or— "He scans the sky through the treetops, "What if we raced her?"

"*Excuse me? Crazy said what?*" Ignis asks, whipping his head around to Stirling.

"Come on. What if we raced her?" he brings his eyes back down to meet Ignis'

"*Are you ill? After all these years of you explaining how you need to hide this and having to sneak out to fly. You suddenly want to reveal yourself to one of the most military pets there is?*"

"Oh, imagine what it would be like to race someone," Stirling teases.

"*No, no, no. No way. That is a horrible idea. Plus, what about your father? You're already late.*" Ignis reasons as he refuses to stand up.

"Since when did care about that?"

"*If she sees us, then what? You're arrested? You're put to death? That's even worse than you moving far away. You won't exist anymore. I can't talk to you ever again.*" Ignis begins to panic as he runs through the possibilities.

Stirling touches his neck and swallows his mind flashing to the woman swaying above the trampled daisies, "You're right. I'm just playing. I would never actually confront her. Let's go."

"*YES PLEASE!*" Ignis jumps up.

Stirling covers his head as a storm wreaks havoc through the trees around him. Debris cuts around him, flung by the powerful gales of wind. "What's going on!" He cries out over the snapping branches.

Twenty-Seven

The sound of a horn bellows above them. Without uncovering his head, his neck creaks, turning for him to stare directly above. His eyes water from the gusts of wind slamming down on them from the beige wyvern's wings. The tips of the trees open and close with the pulsing air revealing them.

"Ignis." Stirling's voice is flat. His soul has already escaped. Thumping below him, Stirling can feel Ignis' heart pounding through his thick rib cage. Completely inert, Ignis stares up at Amiria above them. "Ignis, please for the love of god, run."

Ignis tears from the trees, bounding across the clearing for the canyon. The sound of Amiria shouting at them to give themselves up is overtaken by the wind and blood rushing in their ears. Stirling slips his goggles back onto his head.

Ignis vaults into the canyon, mimicking the way Amiria had earlier, but instead of only twisting his body one hundred and eighty degrees he keeps his wings in close with the subtlest offset the air slipping through, spiraling him the entire way down.

Amiria grips her reins commanding her wyvern to follow in pursuit. Her face contorted in a fury of confusion, her long hair tied up above the strap of her goggles whips behind her in the powerful wind.

Ignis slows his spinning to a halt as they near the canyon's floor. He lifts his head and with a robust beat of his wings, he makes a sharp L-shaped turn sending them flying parallel to the ground. They catapult forward through the canyon.

Amiria's dragon takes a slower, more gradual swoop to straighten themselves out in tail with Stirling and Ignis. She scowls as she reads the distance has grown between them. They are far enough away from her that she can cover the sight of them up with her hand.

She flicks her reins, pushing her dragon to pick up speed. She follows behind Stirling as he and Ignis make swift maneuvers around the natural pillars left over from when the now dried-up river had once carved through, breaking off into smaller streams snaking and winding, eroding a path through mountains over thousands of years.

She sees her chance. They come up to an opening between the groupings of pillars. A large enough span between them that Stirling and Ignis can no longer wind strategically through them and have to resort to flying straight.

"Now I've got them." She smiles, impressed with herself as she begins closing the distance.

Squinting through her goggles, she tries to comprehend what she is seeing. They were moving too sporadically before for her to get a good view of who they are. Now being able to see them clearly has only raised more questions. The image in front of her isn't possible.

The dragon is oddly shaped. From what she knows of dragon anatomy, its body shape is all wrong. His wings are so smooth as if they were painted into the air with a fine-tipped brush, unlike the dragons she was so accustomed to where even from a great distance, you can see the elongated bones through the thinly stretched membrane substance.

She crawls closer to the strange dragon and what she believes to be a boy riding it. He hadn't answered her before when she instructed him to present himself and bare his mark for her to see. He took off without answering any of her questions, eluding her arrest. This only makes him more guilty. Then this dragon he is riding. Does this dragon have four legs? This isn't her first time seeing an orange dragon, although it is uncommon since most are bred to be earth-tone colors for natural camouflage. Never has she heard of a four-legged dragon. Not even in the myths.

Now she is only the length of her dragon away, and she can see everything clearly. The dragon's wings are smooth like polished honey maple wood, but they are feathered, along with the tip of the tail where feathers fanned out like an arrow's fletching for balance and control.

This boy can't be from Wyverna. His clothing is of a commoner, a simple short tunic, and trousers with no riding gear other than goggles. Is he a spy? Is he sent here from Uviktiland to infiltrate our military training, but why? Except the Uviktiland doesn't have dragons. Their only known habitat is the island adjacent to Wyverna. That is the main advantage and has kept the nation safe from another invasion. Her mind runs wild with possibilities of who this strange unknown boy and dragon might be.

Ignis' tail is now only about a head away from Amiria's wyvern's jaw, open wide and ready to snap down and throw their enemy to the canyon floor. She needs to find out who they are. It doesn't matter to her whether they are dead or alive when she figures it out. She knows by their appearance they aren't part of the Winged Cavalry and that is enough proof for her. She needs to apprehend them at any cost. This is the sole reason for her existence.

Stirling turns around, seeing how quickly she has gained on them.

Amiria flinches at the sight of the boy's frightened face. This is the face of someone who understands death is inevitably near. Her dragon clamps down. Feathers caught in its jaws as Ignis appears to defy gravity by running sideways along the canyon wall. They slowly lower down the rock face at an angle until he is far below Amiria. Using his wings and hind legs, he pushes off the wall returning to the air in Amiria's dragon's shadow.

Amiria snarls in frustration alongside her dragon as they race after their prey. Ignis banks around a pillar as they reach another cluster, hindering Amiria from gaining her full potential speed.

A realization dawns over Stirling. Amira is an excellent flier but she has never flown for the sake of flying. It is always training moves she had learned from class or from her parents. Movements carefully stitched together by masters before her. Movements a team can follow. There is nothing unique or creative. Therefore, she might be fast and she might be strong, but all she knows is her Winged Rider manual. She's never tampered with making up her own moves or flying free.

Ignis flies uncomfortably close to the pillars and canyon wall as he snakes around them. He nearly misses colliding with them by either grabbing them with his front claws to pull himself around to the other side or by kicking off to abruptly change directions. Making his movements sharp and unpredictable. Amira struggles to keep up.

She has no issue with avoiding the pillars altogether, but her swooping style of turns and the excessive amount that Stirling is causing her to have to perform are significantly impeding her speed.

Stirling barely has time to register the scorching inferno as they dodge the incoming flames.

"WHAT THE—!" Stirling's yell turns into a cough as the immense heat radiating from the fire feels as if it is cooking his lungs.

His skin becomes flush and hot to the touch even though he isn't burned.

He and Ignis whip their heads around to see Amiria. Her face is set and serious, she is a wolf and they are a fleeing deer. Her dragon opens its spiked jaw far enough for you to see the back of its throat, a small flame sparking to life by where the uvula would hang. The dragon's chest expands as it sucks in an extra amount of air, filling its lungs to the max.

"IT CAN BREATHE FIRE!" Stirling shouts as the dragon releases its captive oxygen, sending out another wave of flames.

Almost being incinerated, Stirling and Ignis take cover behind a pillar. The flames ricochet off the pillar and blossom out to the sides around the round structure, leaving the rock with scorched black marks.

"What kind of high-class family would she be from if she was given a fire-breather," Stirling panics aloud, his voice a frantic squeal.

They dodge another burst of flames. He can feel the hair on his arms singe, curling, and falling away from his skin. Beads of sweat form on his face from the heat and his exertion of energy in his attempt to survive.

He knew she was talented, yet he had still underestimated her. He didn't expect her to possess that kind of ability since she had never displayed it during her training. He thought he knew her after all these years of analyzing her and her class. Only those born with the expectations of a leadership role are given the species of wyverns who are able to breathe fire.

"*Ignis,*" Stirling says in a hurry. "*We need to lose her before she kills us.*"

"*The end of the canyon, it's a small slit between the rock walls. It's too small to fly through,*" Ignis suggests as Stirling finishes his thought.

"*But wide enough to run through.*"

Picking up their speed, they push their known limits as

they head straight for the end of the canyon not far from their current position. Amiria, now familiarized with their tactics, is steadily closing in on them.

They reach the last stretch of the canyon, a straight shot to the end as the walls begin to close in on them, giving Amiria the higher advantage.

She sneers as her dragon takes in another large breath believing she has her deer lined in sight of her arrow. The canyon walls are now a hand's length away from the tips of both dragon's wings. A single alteration in their flight can cause them to clip their wings, potentially sending them crashing to the ground.

Her dragon releases its breath, sending one more wave of fire at Stirling and Ignis. Pulling back on her reins, she watches the fire consume the small amount of space between the walls filling her view with a deadly cloak. Her dragon back flaps into a hover, beating its wings in place, knowing this is as far as she can fly into the narrow pass. Keeping her eyes on the flames as they dissipate, she knows it would have been near impossible for anyone to dodge it.

Seeing no one flying down the pass, she drops her gaze to the canyon floor to inspect her prize. Tendons in her neck bulge as she seethes. She had failed. Galloping down the narrow path both Stirling and Ignis continue to escape unharmed from her flames.

Amiria screams out in frustration. Her eyes are furious as she and her dragon shoot up into the air, climbing their way out of the top of the canyon.

Ignoring the fact that Amiria is no longer in pursuit of them, Stirling and Ignis continue forward with their goal of escaping out the end of the canyon that once used to be a waterfall flowing out of the mountain range encasing the island and falling into the ocean below.

They can see the opening. They can see the rising sun shining through, a celebration of their success Amiria was unable to catch them even with all her training and birthright.

Stirling is excited he has survived but he also feels a little letdown. That is the prodigy? This is all the "best in" her class has to offer? Though he'd rather never repeat this encounter. Being burnt to a crisp is not something he had planned on doing today. He just needs to make it out of this canyon and he can return to his cave to form a plan on how to avoid Amiria finding them again.

The early morning sun shines bright through the canyon's opening, illuminating the gold in Stirling's hair and eyes. A shadow emerges blocking out the rays pouring into the canyon pass like closing the door on the finish line.

Twenty-Eight

Locking his legs, Ignis' claws grip the ground the best he can manage, forcing them to come to a skidding halt. They slide all the way to the edge of the cliff, rocks kicked up and broken loose are sent tumbling over the ledge to their new home at the bottom of the ocean's shore.

Oh no. Stirling hunches on Ignis' back, unable to hide. He holds his hand up to block the light from his eyes as he stares out at Amiria, her dragon hovering a stone's throw away in front of them. He can feel the gust of wind hit Ignis and himself each time her dragon beats its wings holding itself steady in midair.

He bites down on his lip. He had thought about racing her, but he didn't want to be caught. He doesn't want to die. There's nowhere for him to go. He can turn and run again but she'll easily catch back up. She knows he exists now, and she won't let him out of her sight. Not when she stumbled upon someone committing high treason of riding a dragon.

He's going to have to attempt to talk his way out of this situation. He taps his thumb to his fingers as he thinks. Why didn't he run as soon as he saw her? She wasn't just born into the Cavalry, she has consistently proven herself suitable to be at the top ranking and he knew that. He wants to kick himself. He had gotten too complacent in the woods as if the trees could hide a massive orange figure without ever giving them up.

Stirling gives in, putting his hands up in defense, his insignia now in plain view. Amiria's eyes dart from Stirling's face to his arm. Dropping his arm down, he sees her narrowing in on his insignia in an attempt to read what it is.

She peels her focus from his arm back to his face and declares, "You have been witnessed and caught illegally riding a dragon which is, by law, punishable by being drawn, and quartered."

She watches as the boy's aghast expressions droop, his face turning pale and dismal. As if this is a fact, he knew but the reality and acceptance are finally setting in. He is visibly shaking. Swallowing hard, he runs his trembling fingers through his sandy-colored hair.

Breaking out into a cold sweat, he manages to stumble through a sentence. "O-okay, I will tell you everything but p-please don't kill me."

She shakes her head confused. Do criminals usually make demands? "You're going to tell me? Do you understand anything? I don't care about why you are on a dragon. I have visual evidence that you are. That is all I need. I will seize your dragon for evidence and bring your lifeless body back to the Cavalry. Then they will be able to tell me who you are."

Stirling blinks, casting his eyes down as he searches his mind for a reply. What should he do? What can he do? He's not good with words. He wants to puke, not talk about his death sentence.

"Stirling. Hey, Stirling."

"What?"

"Your mark. Use it as leverage."

"How?"

"She needs it to identify you."

"She says she doesn't care."

"But she does. I can tell she's curious. She was trying to read it earlier," Ignis advises. *"Use that to your advantage."*

Stirling returns his gaze to Amiria, her dark eyes like swords slicing through him. He closes his eyes, retreating mentally. Sure, I'll just convince death glare here that my identity is more important than her responsibility. That will totally work. Stirling jumps at the sound of Amiria yelling.

"COME WITH ME WILLINGLY OR DIE HERE!" she commands, her wyvern's jaw unhinging with the preparation of setting them ablaze.

"STOP!" Stirling holds out his left hand. "If you kill me with that fire you won't be able to identify me!"

"You do not need to be recognizable," Amiria responds, not calling off her dragon. She has grown annoyed by the boy refusing her directives. She didn't think apprehension would be this difficult. She has never witnessed a commoner question authority, not even a town guard. She is here in the name of the Winged Cavalry. Alone the name should be enough. As a Winged Rider, commoners won't even make eye contact with her let alone speak to her. Why did it have to be her that discovered him? She's not ready for this conflict.

Amiria bites her lip, fretting. Doubts of her capabilities begin to seep through the cracks in her confidence, the ideas that she had given her life to training and it was all a waste in the end. This is what she's dedicated her entire being to and she's failing.

She's saying her demands correctly, isn't she? He isn't doing as she says. Instead, he's attempting to manipulate her on what she should do.

"But you're curious," Stirling confronts, throwing out

Ignis' guess.

"What?" Amiria asks, scrunching her nose.

Stirling's voice quivers as he fights through the submissive instinct. "You're curious. I saw you trying to check my insignia. You want to know who I am." he says, casting out his bait.

"A crime as severe as this does not require a trial with the substantial amount of evidence I have. So I do not need to hear your excuses," she spits.

Covering his insignia with his left hand, Stirling raises his right arm into the air waving it back and forth with a false facade of assurance. "Come on. Do you really want to spend the rest of your life not knowing who I really was? There's only one way to find out. What do you say?"

The bait is there, and she is nibbling it.

Amira clenches her fists as she holds herself back from killing the boy on the spot and getting this over with. Any other Winged Rider would. Why is she hesitant? Why is she holding back? She puts forth the commands that have been drilled into her but she doesn't believe the words she is spouting.

He is right, she is curious. She wants to know who this boy is. She wants to know what kind of dragon that is. She releases the tension in her hands with a sigh. She has already botched her career before she even graduated. How dare some malefactor tell her as the authority figure what to do.

With a rolling of her shoulders and a crack of her neck she regains her composure and plays her part. "I understand your terms. I will accept. Meet me at the top of this cliff where it plateaus. But if you try escaping my so-called curiosity will vanish. I will kill you with no hesitation. Deal?"

"She's just as scary as I imagined," Stirling whimpers to Ignis, believing her threats. "Deal!" He yells back to Amiria.

Stirling and Ignis leap from the ledge and take off upward to the plateau with Amiria following close behind but keeping enough distance that she has time to react if Stirling decides to turn around and attack.

They land on the flat surface one after another. Ignis trots out his landing gracefully and stands tall like a massive Clydesdale. While Amiria's dragon lands harshly with a slide, hunching over with the knuckle of its wing dug into the dirt for stabilization before arching its head up like a cobra ready to strike.

Stirling hooks his goggles to his belt before unlatching himself from Ignis' harness. He swings one leg over, sliding off Ignis' back, his hands remaining stuck to the harness as he presses his face into Ignis' side.

"Breathe," he tells himself. Taking a few shallow breaths, he turns only his head to peak at Amiria before returning his forehead to press into Ignis' scales. He squeezes his eyes shut. "Be calm, Stirling. Be calm." He takes one more deep breath and, turning on his heel, he faces Amiria.

I'm so dead. He turns back to Ignis, grabbing hold of the harness for stability. *I'm going to die. Oh god, I'm going to die.* He twists his neck to see the menacing girl scrutinizing him. His body hunches forward hanging from his grip on the leather harness. Cursing under his breath, he reluctantly pushes back from Ignis and takes several unsteady paces forward until he stands in the middle of the two dragons.

Eyeing him suspiciously, Amiria commands, "Don't take another step closer. Raise your hands and state who you are."

Stirling complies, raising both of his hands up to eye level, stating, "I am Stirling Bakere." He winces after saying his last name. He can see it on her face, even with her goggles still on. She knows from how his introduction started how it will end, "Bakery occupation of the lower middle class.

"A baker boy! On a dragon!" she remarks, raising an eyebrow. "And strangely shaped one."

She lifts her goggles with one hand pulling them free

from her head. With a shake, her hair pulls along the leather strap before tenderly falling back to place with a sway. She keeps her head high as she scours down at Stirling from her dragon, a similar size to Ignis despite their difference in stature. For the first time since Stirling had started watching her class six years ago, their eyes meet.

He had only a vague idea of what she looked like from the safe distance of his perch. He has never seen her this close before. They are only around ten steps away from each other but even from here, he could see the details of her face he had never noticed. Her olive skin is tan and dark from the frequent exposure to the sun, glowing with adrenaline and excitement from the recent chase. Her hair is smooth and clean, another sign of her status. It is pulled back away from her face as always but now he can see the strands blown loose from the wind lining her face.

She hooks her goggles to her belt before unbuckling herself and leaping off her dragon's back. Bending her knees into a low crouch as she lands. In one motion she stands up turning on the ball of her foot, squaring her shoulders to Stirling.

A glint of light in her hand catches Stirling's attention.

Holding a dagger, she announces, "Bear your insignia for me to see it clearly."

He clenches his jaw. His insignia has always embarrassed him when he is in town. The design of a bread paddle mutilated by three burn scars.

Gripping her dagger with such poise as if she is going to carve a work of art, Amiria marches over to Stirling with a clear amount of confidence, stopping just an arm's length away.

His already thumping heart races faster in his chest. He swears to himself, it is impossible that she can't hear it. Half of him begs to glance back at Ignis for reassurance. He can feel the familiar orange dragon's golden eyes protectively watching him, but he is too scared to take his eyes off

Amiria. They dart to her dragon, its brown eyes glaring at them from behind her.

Are its nostrils smoking? He wonders as the dragon becomes out of focus behind Amiria's head, but he doesn't want to risk another glance.

Sizing him up, Amiria gives Stirling a full inspection. She can see the beads of sweat running across his brow and down the side of his face and she observes he is containing a his tremor.

So, he is scared? she thinks to herself.

Stirling is a good head taller than Amiria, she reaches barely above his shoulder but he knows nothing when it comes to actual combat. She will be able to take him down if she wants to with a few swift movements. But it is something else he can't quite put his finger on, making him so uneasy.

"Come on," Amiria says.

"What?" Stirling squeaks.

"Show me your insignia. Now," she demands.

Stirling touches his right arm subconsciously, pulling it close to his side. Timidly, he lifts it, holding it out for her to see. He watches her face intently as she analyzes it but he can't read anything. Her emotions are flat.

Finally, Amiria speaks up again. Stirling drops his sore and stiff arm after he has been holding his arm out for what feels like ages. "You can barely tell what it is, baker boy. But I know one would not lie about being a baker. Though it is impossible for one who does not have the mark of the Cavalry to bond and control a dragon."

"You just saw me fly, didn't you? I was pretty in control," he rebuts, speaking up for himself.

She does not speak. She leans back as she tries to assess the situation. Her dragon makes chattering sounds behind her as if it is getting antsy.

Keeping the dread from filling the silence, Stirling

nervously runs his mouth, "We can even communicate with our minds."

Amiria's stoic expression morphs to ire as she stops Stirling from saying anything further by yelling, "Lies! You cannot speak to a dragon! Do you take me as some kind of fool?!" She has been used by too many people because of who her father is. She can't let herself get played by a commoner.

Stirling flinches, taking a step back with the anticipation that she might actually use the dagger held firmly in her hand. But she doesn't. She holds her stance, her eyes burrowing into his.

He's not playing with fire. He's already been set aflame. He's going to burn no matter what. He decides to gamble the dagger is meant for her own protection. He gains the courage to counter again. "You don't see any reins on him, do you? And we performed some pretty tricky maneuvers, don't you agree?

Shifting her weight to one foot, Amiria leans to the side to peer around Stirling at Ignis. He towers behind, watching intensely. She runs her gaze along the harness for any evidence of something that can be used as reins.

Crossing her arms stubbornly, she returns to Stirling. "There must be another way you were controlling it."

"Ha, you admit it! That I was able to control him!" Stirling bursts, smiling and pointing his finger at her. His face sinking, he immediately retracts his hand. This isn't Ignis he is talking to; this isn't even his neighbor. This is a Winged Rider. He gulps.

Amiria puffs her cheeks flustered. She messed up her wording and she knew it as the words tumbled out of her mouth, but it was too late to stop them. She's caught off guard, surprised some baker boy was able to catch it so quickly. She thinks of the four others in her class. That got you, or I win, tones to their comments. How they would laugh off their friendly banter. She was never invited to participate in their games.

She analyzes the hazel eye boy. How did a baker boy fly so remarkably? He had almost succeeded in outrunning her. Almost being the keyword, but that shouldn't be possible. She feels drawn to this boy. He is correct. She does want to know about him. Who is he? Where did he come from? What is this outlandish dragon he possesses? If she kills him, she will never truly know and the mystery will eat at her. Her eyes drop to his twitching fingers at his side. His weight shifts unnerved.

Maybe she should hear him out. She only said those threats because she was doing what she was trained to do. She wants to find out what his story is before she arrests him and takes him in custody to the Cavalry.

Maybe I'll finally get words of approval. Show the others I'm more than just my name. I've dedicated myself, yet still only receive scrutiny, she thinks.

"Fine, your story then," she says in an almost uncouth tone, returning to her authoritative stance.

"Huh?" Stirling says, tilting his head.

"Your story. How did you come to accompany your peculiar dragon?" she clarifies.

"Oh!?" he sputters, his muscles going limp. "Uh."

Her eyebrows lift. "Or I can arrest you, I don't have all day, baker boy." She shrugs indifferently.

Knotting and untwisting his fingers, Stirling keeps his gaze down as he tells her, "Okay, I'll tell you everything."

Twenty-Nine

The sun steadily rises in the sky as Stirling talks. Amiria doesn't say a word as she listens to his story. Their legs dangle over the edge overlooking the sprawling ocean, with their dragons lounging within earshot. Ignis sprawls out, uncaring, basking in the sun while Amiria's wyvern keeps its unblinking eyes glued to her.

Stirling started from the beginning when he received the scar and his peculiar dreams. How he befriended the fledgling and named him Ignis. How they had watched her class train. How he handmade the harness and the goggles. How he had to sneak out almost every night to fly in secret. He told her everything except the details of his home life at the bakery. Some things he wanted to keep to himself.

Taking in all the information, Amiria watches the ocean shining, reflecting the sun's light like a new set of armor. She finally responds, "You've been watching me since we were ten?"

Blushing, Stirling stammers, "Well, um, no, not you exactly. It was your class to be technical."

A subtle smile creeps across Amiria's face. "Whatever you say, stalker. Here, let me see your goggles," she asks, reaching out as a signal for him to hand them to her.

Stirling's heart stops, his eyes landing on her wrist. At the end of her leather bracer where her wrist is exposed is a leather braided bracelet the color of fall with the pattern of leaves stamped into it.

His mouth goes dry as he tries to speak. "Your bracelet. My mother had one just like it."

"Oh, this?" Amiria says, pulling her hand back to touch the bracelet, "My father gave this to me when I was a kid." She spins it around her wrist slowly. It is the only gift he has ever given her. "You said she had, as in past tense. Did she lose it?"

Stirling intertwines his fingers to hide the trembling. "She didn't lose it. She gave it to some gentleman for…as a thank you."

He had left out the part about the man who brought him home when he told her the story. He had left out all the parts with his mother.

Amiria's eyes grow wide as she stares at Stirling. He doesn't lift his gaze from his hands as she finishes what he had meant to say, "For saving you after receiving that wound on your arm."

It is as if the world stopped turning. Time is standing still. The wind no longer carries the clouds. The waves stopped perpetually at their peak waiting to crash. A seagull midflight that will never land. Stirling, the only object in motion, whips his head around to her. He is close enough to see the light flecks in her dark round eyes before they both divert away self-consciously.

Amiria runs her hand through her hair. "Does she-does she want it back?"

Stirling winces as if he is jabbed in the heart. "She's gone now."

An awkward tension sets like a thick fog in the air. Neither of them raises their eyes from their laps. Stirling bites his lip as he tries to come up with a way to fix the conversation. He reaches, unhooking his goggles, relieved he can change the topic.

He holds them out to Amiria, who is still playing with the bracelet on her wrist. Her hazy vision slowly focuses on the goggles as she resurfaces from being deep in thought. She takes them from Stirling. Holding them gently in her hands as she inspects them silently. They are uneven, misshapen, and ugly. Yet, she observes, they are creative. He had put thought and care into making them for himself. She turns the goggles over in her hands a few times, debating hard on what she should do.

She knows the law. She knows what she is supposed to do. As she listened to Stirling talk, something was telling her otherwise. He has such a passion when he talks about flying. About his dragon. She hasn't heard any of the other students in her class ever speak in such a heartfelt way. They speak as if it is nothing more than their mandatory duty.

She doesn't get along with them that well anyway. In fact, she didn't get along with anyone. Even when she was only a small child, the other children avoided her, making her the pariah she would never grow out of. She doesn't see the difference in her behavior then everyone else. In the end, she comes off as cold and brash, but she doesn't mean to be. She only means well when she critiques them. The only time her father spoke to her was to criticize her, but it was to make her a better Rider.

Is that not how one shows affection?

With no one wanting her around, she's adapted to distancing herself. Why be on display at the castle's events as the lonely wallflower when she can fully dedicate her time to training?

"Leaders don't need friends," her father used to tell her. You have to command a team, not worry about your friends on the battlefield. It is a weakness the enemy can exploit.

She's close enough to this boy she had attempted to kill to feel the heat coming from his shoulder. She threatened to burn him to a crisp but instead of continuing to run, fight, or deny his crime, he made only one request. He wanted to be heard, to tell her the life that had led them both to this plateau, knowing after this session, he will be sentenced to death in the most torturous way set into law.

She glances over at Stirling out of the corner of her eye. He wears a hint of sadness over his whole body. It is obvious in his eyes but there is also a touch of it in the way his shoulders slump, the way he is nervously rubbing one of his hands in the other. Is it because he knows he will be dead tomorrow? Is it the bracelet or something else entirely?

Twisting around, she faces Ignis who is lying on his side with his head watching in her direction, wearing the same expression as if they really are connected.

He flies for the love of flying, not because he is told to. I wonder what it's like making your own decisions, she wonders to herself.

Untwisting, she sees Stirling had turned to follow her gaze to see what had caught her attention. As he returns to face front his eyes catch hers for a brief moment. Quickly, he adverts his focus elsewhere, trying to look anywhere but at her as she continues to watch him. Her eyes shift from his wild loose curls to his dirt-streaked face down to his right arm with the almost unrecognizable insignia tying him to a lifestyle he has no interest in being part of.

Pulling the strings on her bracers, she loosens it enough to pull up the sleeve of her training tunic, revealing her insignia—thin black lines woven together to create the shadow of a wyvern dragon smooth on her skin.

Her gaze makes its way back to the goggles still in her hand. It's never been apparent to her that someone might not want their insignia.

She reaches down to her harness and unhooks her goggles from her belt with her free hand and holds them out next to Stirling's. The differences are striking, it is obvious which pair is more appreciated.

Goggles are thrust in front of him. "Those aren't mine," Stirling points out.

Amiria turns her head away as she replies with a soft voice, "I know."

Stirling blinks at the goggles for a moment as Amiria continues to hold them out in front of him, her stubbornness-holding firm as she refuses to face in his direction.

"Thank you," he mutters, accepting them from her, still a little wary of her reasoning.

Amiria doesn't say you're welcome before standing up and brushing the dirt off her tights, "It's getting late in the morning. I've got training that I still need to complete."

Turning on her heel, Amiria's boot digs into the gravel. She raises her chin and walks off, returning to her dragon. Stirling's jaw hangs slack as he remains locked in place, watching her leave. He is unable to form words. Is he not being arrested?

Neither of them bid farewell.

Amiria pauses as she steps up to her dragon who is waiting eagerly to take off. Holding up Stirling's goggles, she slips them onto her head, pulling her hair through so it hangs over the strap.

Her dragon's chest nearly touches the sandpaper surface as it crouches low to the ground. Gripping the saddle, Amiria pulls herself up.

Stirling can hear the click of her buckle as she hooks herself to the saddle. She glares down at him through his goggles. "I don't know how you flew with these things on. You can't see a single thing."

Stirling snaps his jaw closed, and a smile as gentle as the

sunrise behind him leaks onto his lips.

She smiles, nothing more. Her dragon rears back on its hind legs, spreading out the webbing of its wings from its arm down to its thigh. Then with a blow of a whistle, they take off into the sky as if god pulled them up by a string. Taking a wide turn, they dive back down into the canyon.

Stirling watches as she vanishes from his sight. He scoots back from the ledge and carefully rises to his feet, slowly letting his mind catch up to what had unfolded. He pats his body in disbelief. *Yep, still alive.* In a trance-like state, he shuffles back to Ignis.

Ignis, who was still laying on his side, rolls onto his stomach with his legs bent underneath.

Stirling stumbles, dropping to his knees at Ignis' side. "Give me a moment." He lowers himself to the ground and rests his face on the gravel. He pets the earth, feeling the small rocks roll under his hand. "Nice dirt. Safe, secure dirt."

"*Umm. You all right?*" Ignis lowers his head to Stirling.

"Yep." Stirling doesn't care about the dirt sticking to his lips as he talks, "Perfectly fine." He pats the ground testing the solidity of reality.

"*Oookay. Now that you magically avoided one death sentence, are you ready to go face your father?*"

Stirling sits up, "Definitely not. I already know how the conversation is going to go," He shakes his head. "I can't go to Milleoaks, it would take me a couple of days by horse just to get back here and that's even if I'm able to get away at all. My mother used to tell me how strict her parents were."

Ignis brings his face close enough to Stirling, that his warm breath ripples the sandy curls. He turns to meet his friend's eyes. He studies Ignis, whose face is as long as Stirling's torso. He is a massive scaly beast used for a life of bloodshed, fighting, and guarding the Isles of Wyverna. He is meant to be fierce. He is supposed to be threatening. Ignis' golden eyes stare back at Stirling, gleaming with nothing but love and affection. He is Stirling's best friend. The one being who will lay his life down to protect him. Other than his mother and Faerydae he has never known of a human to show the compassion for another that Ignis displays.

"Ignis," His voice is hollow, "Ignis, she was wearing my mother's bracelet."

"*What does that mean?*"

"It means that it was her father who saved me all those years ago. A nobleman, a Rider in the Cavalry. What was he doing in a dirty marketplace like mine? There's grumpy people, mud, and waste," Stirling defines.

"*Do you believe everything happens for a reason?*" Ignis questions.

Stirling takes Amiria's goggles, slipping them over his eyes. Adjusting the straps, he answers, "No, not really. I guess I believe life happens, and it's up to you to determine how to live it." Stirling takes in a long breath at the rising sun. Hanging his head, he stands up, "Let's go."

Grabbing the harness strapped to Ignis, Stirling heaves himself onto his back. He holds his balance as Ignis stands up, his body rocking as his weight shifts along with his legs. Then without a single verbal command, Ignis sprints to the edge and leaps off over the water.

Thirty

Stirling stands in front of the bakery analyzing the walls built from wattle, daub, and a timber frame. The buildings to the left and right are so close together they melt into one another like wax candles set side by side. There aren't any guards or Winged Riders here to arrest him, so Amiria really did let him go. He stands there, still unable to comprehend how or why she left him. She hadn't said anything about changing her mind about his arrest, or did he miss some sort of cue in her words and expressions? He replays her smile as she wears his goggles.

He grins to himself.

Replacing his bashfulness with gloom, Stirling places one foot on the first step. Taking a deep breath, he opens the door and enters the bakery.

A young woman standing in front of his father sets a loaf of rye bread into her martebo sack with a hole cut through so she can have it slung around her neck, and a young boy standing beside her hangs onto the hem of her dress.

Both the mother and her son have a layer of soot on their hands and up their arms. Stirling notices the mother has a streak of black smudge across her forehead, reminding him of his mother and how she would always have flour on her cheek or in her hair.

The woman drops a coin into Giles' hand, the sleeve of her dress rolled up, showing off her blacksmith insignia.

Explains all the black smudges, Stirling puts together.

Seeing Stirling waiting patiently by the entrance, Giles negates his son and any attempt to show acknowledgment. In return, Stirling refuses to try and make eye contact with his father. He steps back, opening the shop entrance for the mother and child, overhearing their conversation as they leave to continue their errands.

The child tugs on his mother's dress whining, "When are we going to be done? I want to go home and finish forging some hooks so I can get Pa to show me how to make a knife."

Stirling courteously closes the door behind them before he is able to hear the mother's reply, probably something about one or two more stops, then they can work on it together as soon as they return home.

Straining his muscles, Stirling forces himself to look across the room at his father who continues to repudiate making eye contact by stubbornly beginning more of his tasks around the shop.

When Giles finally speaks his voice is calm but stern as if it was any other day and he is merely giving directions about chores or errands that need to be done, "I sent a letter to your grandparents earlier this morning informing them you are on your way and should be arriving no later than a week. I have a trade merchant friend who is already planning on heading out to the Kitlsbo and is willing to escort you in his cart."

"Sir," Stirling says, raising his chin. He will not be sheepish this time. He will be heard.

"No, Stirling. There's no more of your excuses that can

get me to change my mind. I'm tired of dealing with you and whatever it is you run off to do," Giles states in a disappointed tone.

"But, sir," Stirling repeats, keeping his head tall, his height being the same as his father's.

"STIRLING! I'M DONE!" Giles barks, slamming the wooden bread paddle down that he was moving from the stove.

Stirling flinches, momentarily losing his composure. He balls his hands at his side withdrawing into himself. Don't give in already, he chastises himself. "But I'm not done." He fusses.

"Excuse me?" Giles raises his eyebrows, baffled.

Finding his voice, Stirling tells him, "I've held my tongue for years so that I could avoid hearing you lecture me about this stupid bakery. I've told you before that I don't want to be a baker. I don't want this life. The only thing I can hope to accomplish here is mastering the rise of yeast." Anger grows inside of him as he runs his mouth, "No, screw that, I'm not going to waste my life here and I'm definitely NOT going to waste it in a poor farm village in the middle of nowhere. I'd rather live in a cave." Stirling rants, breathing heavily as if he had forgotten to take a breath between his words.

"Stirling Bakere!" Giles jabs his finger, his voice thick with outrage, "You listen to me now! You cannot be without a job! We have laws to keep people from being unemployed and homeless. It's been completely successful. There hasn't been documentation of a beggar since they created this law a few hundred years ago." His father retorts.

"Documentation! Everything is so heavily documented and we just accept it. I'm surprised there isn't a scroll out there documenting every time I said I didn't want to be a baker or how many times I've left the house so they can gather up all the evidence to arrest me for not following the ways of the land." Stirling bursts, fed up with all the rules and limitations. No one ever questions anything documented by the kingdom.

How do people even know the scrolls are an honest history? Those who are in power control history. How many things have been fibbed so people believe laws make the world go round?

Giles stares at his son in bewilderment. Stirling is an embarrassment to him.

His fellow mates would boast about the progress their child was making. How they showed enthusiasm for their trade with a promising future as they worked to master it. When they spoke of their children, Giles always hung back, refraining from mentioning Stirling and his shortcomings. He told them little about Stirling; lying saying he is always sick in bed, using the excuse he must have got something in his blood after he got the gruesome wound on his arm from falling on a pitchfork at the farm he played at as a child. He doesn't want to admit to people he was failing at raising his son.

When he was only a year older he had met Jannell. They married and Stirling was born by the time he was twenty. He was an adult and he gave up any childhood dreams to do what was required to take care of his family. But Stirling–Stirling behaves as if he will never grow up.

If only his mother had stopped him from dreaming so much. Giles' own mother had made him give up his dream of learning how to play the citole when the baker insignia was bestowed upon his arm. She had explained to him what it signified and it was who he is. Dreaming is a waste of time. Dreams are not reality. That is why they are called dreams.

"STIRLING! Where are you going!" Giles calls out. Stirling is already disappearing up the stairs.

"I'm going to pack my stuff" Stirling shouts from the top of the stairs as he marches across the room to his mattress laying in the corner. "ALSO! You better write two more letters!" He continues to holler as he pulls the few short tunics and his only spare trousers out of a small storage crate. "One to the chamber to state my change i recidency and one to my grandparents telling them I'M NOT COMING!" He pauses lingering as he holds the wooden dragon that can now lay easily in the palm of his adult hand.

Rubbing his thumb across the carved wood, he sets all his items, including his flour sack pillow, on the blanket and ties the knot tight around his only belongings. He stares at the grooves below the window frame as he hears his father screaming from the bottom of the stairs.

"STIRLING! If you leave this house and it's not with your escort, I will notify the gaurds. Then you will have all the time you want to dream FROM THE PILLORY!"

Rolling his eyes, Stirling swings his makeshift sack over his shoulder and heads back downstairs. His father stands at the bottom of the staircase. He drops his gaze, unable to meet his father's eyes.

"Go ahead, notify them." Stirling grumbles as he reaches the bottom step. Their shoulders bump as Stirling pushes past him.

Strolling across the room, he heads straight to the wooden shelves holding the finished bread loaves. "They'll need to know so they can document their first unemployed and homeless citizen," he says, picking up two loaves. He faces his father. "See this. I accomplished something. Are you finally proud of me?"

Giles watches his only son walk towards the front door. He can't help but wonder why his son can't be normal.

Why can't he conform to society like the other children? All he ever wanted was to have a family and work side by side in this bakery passed down through the generations. His already small family lost one member now he is losing another.

"You'll be back, you'll get cold, and you'll get hungry, and you'll be back," are the last words Giles says to his son. He watches useless as Stirling yanks open the front door.

Stalling halfway out the door facing the road where the fresh scent of bread meets the pungent city air, Stirling turns his head to the side and mutters to his shoulder, "I do love you. Maybe one day I can come back."

Stirling finally steps completely out of the doorframe, closing the door softly behind him. Leaving his father alone in his bakery.

He stomps down the wilted steps sagging beneath him as if they are tired of existence. The dirt crunches below his shoes as they strike the road. He adjusts the blanket sack hanging over his shoulder with the loaves tucked in his arm. A few groups of shoppers who have been standing within earshot of the bakery stare at him.

They must have heard us yelling. Nosy people, can't mind their own damn business.

Hiding his face, he scowls to himself and shoves past them. He stalks down the always-bustling road of the market and disappears into the sea of faces.

Thirty-One

The sun crashes through the open space free of trees in front of the cave entrance hiding deep in the forest below the mountain's jagged peaks, the beech tree perched on top hanging perpetually suspended.

Ignis doesn't move as he lies basking in the radiant light, his body relaxed and spread out, absorbing the heat as he speaks, "Well, look who's back so soon. I can see from your pack that it went well?"

"Yeah, I don't know," Stirling says, dropping his sack on the ground next to Ignis before plopping down. He leans back against his friend's body, his wings like a feather bed.

Ignis lifts his head to ask, "*What do you mean?*"

"I've never really tried to see my father's perspective of this whole ordeal until I saw how our neighbors were gawking at me when I left the bakery. I know that they overheard us yelling. So while I was walking up here, I thought to myself how I don't care what they think of me. Their opinions mean nothing to me. It doesn't stop me from wanting to live my own life because it's my life, not theirs.

But they aren't just watching me. They're also looking at my father and judging him. My father does care what they think. He's the one that has to live and deal with them on a day-to-day basis, not me. I realized that in the end, he wasn't trying to do anything except play by the rules. I then snatched the rules, crumpled them up, and threw them back in his face," Stirling admits.

"*Do you regret it?*" Ignis questions with a hint of sorrow in his voice.

Closing his eyes, Stirling rests his head, letting it sink into the orange feathers, feeling Ignis' chest move as it expands and deflates with his steady breathing. The fresh pine breeze ruffles his curls.

"No," he answers after a moment of thought, "I do have a sense of guilt but…I feel what I have done was worth it for my own sake. Selfish as it sounds, it needed to happen. You can't live your life in misery to make others happy. One day, when the timing is right. I'll go back. I'll apologize to him for the way I acted and what I put him through. Maybe one day I will be someone he is proud of."

"*Or you can be an utter disgrace and be sentenced to a horrific slow and prolonged public death,*" Ignis chimes in.

The blood drains from Stirling's face as he remembers that it's not hanging as the punishment but drawn and quartered. "Or, there's that." He shakes off the disturbing images flashing to the front of his thoughts. "Either way, I'm going to need to lay low for a bit until I know for sure no one has sent out a search party for me. So there's going to be no flying."

"*Why would they be searching for you?*" Ignis asks as he rests his head back down

"You're so full of questions, aren't you? Because someone doesn't move, marry, have children or die without it being reported. The king likes everything controlled. So some kid running away? They won't know what to do. They'll freak out that they don't have the proper paperwork to fill out for this scenario. I have a feeling if they don't find me within a few days, they will give up and label me deceased. That paperwork they do have. That way no one will know someone can successfully leave. They're too proud of their flawless laws to admit to something like that. It might start giving people the king's worst nightmare." Stirling pauses for dramatic effect. "Ideas."

"So you're dead if they find you and you're dead if they don't. Humans are fascinating," Ignis points out.

"Yeah, we are pretty weird." Stirling drowsily mumbles, his eyelids growing heavy over his stinging tired eyes.

It's been a long day. He hasn't managed to get more than a nap's length of sleep since yesterday. Stirling watches in a slumbering daze as his eyelids close, hiding away the sunny forest.

Thirty-Two

F ield Marshal Rey."

A newly promoted Lieutenant Colonel for the selected Winged Cavalry division that watches guard over Lumierna announces. He stands at attention outside the open office door to the Field Marshal, the most senior officer in the Winged Cavalry. His office is a standalone building at the home base outside Lumierna.

The log-structured building sits on a hill looming over the entirety of the base. A large desk sits on the far side of the rectangular room in front of an expansive window imposing on the training fields. Lining the walls are shelves with rolled-up maps, scrolls, and books. Articles of memorabilia are scattered amongst the stacks of papers, one in particular, being a drawing of a spinster. Her hands delicately hold the wool as her long dark hair slips over her shoulder.

Amiria's father, the man who had brought Stirling home after his first encounter with Ignis, is staring out the window with his hands clasped behind his back. His body remains fixed, unmoved by the man who has called for his attention.

Unsure of himself and if the Field Marshal had heard him, the Lt Colonel says in a sharp tone, "Sir."

Field Marshal Rey, uninspired by the Lt Colonel's introduction, turns around at a deliberately slow pace to acknowledge the man. His uniform is a golden gambeson with clasps decorated with wyvernite crystals reflecting the light like flames flickering down his chest.

"What may it be Lieutenant?" Rey asks.

The Lieutenant Colonel grits his teeth. "Sir, we have just received news; a young boy has fled from his home in the lower-class market district in Lumierna," he informs him.

For a split moment, something appears on Field Marshal Rey's face as the Lt Colonel mentions the lower-class market district, but it is gone as fast as it has surfaced. The Field Marshal's face is a book without a cover. The Lt Colonel remains standing still with his arms locked to his sides outside the entrance to the office. Rey stares at the man, too intimidated by him to step down.

Field Marshal Rey pulls back the chair at his desk, treated walnut wood with an elegant pattern carved into the back and arms. His fingers drum along the back as he continues to stare down the Lt Colonel. The intensity of his glare crushes like the pressure of being over a hundred feet below the water's surface. He motions for the Lt Colonel to come inside as he steps around his chair, taking a seat. The Lt Colonel takes only a few steps before stopping.

"No, no. Come on, come take a seat," Rey insists, pointing to the chair sitting across from his desk made from the same kind of wood but with a simpler frame.

Field Marshal Rey waits for the Lt Colonel to take his seat before he begins speaking again.

"Let me get this straight, lieutenant," he says, leaning back in his chair with his elbows resting on the armrest and his fingers interlaced across his stomach. "You come in here, interrupting me from my own work, to tell me what? That some kid ran off? He just ran, ran away, off into the unknown? As if something like that would matter to me?"

The Lt Colonel shifts uncomfortably in his seat. "Yes, sir. Witnesses reported that he and his father were arguing in their family bakery before the boy took off."

Field Marshal Rey lets out a bellowing laugh.

He unlaces his fingers, grabbing the ends of the armrests as he leans forward still laughing. "Maybe he went for a jog around town."

The Lt Colonel sits back rigid in the chair, uneasy.

Rey's face suddenly turns serious. "Hold on, did you say the bakery? Never mind, I don't have time for this. I've got more important business to attend to than some Peasant family feud. Do not come back to my office, Lieutenant Colonel, unless I summon you. Matters like this can be handled at a much lower level."

Swallowing hard, the inexperienced Lt Colonel remains still in his chair. "Sir, there has been a search warrant made for him. I've been commanded by my Colonel to deliver this to you."

The Lt Colonel slips his hand into his coat pulling out a scroll with King Dietrich's seal on it. He holds it out across the desk to Field Marshal Rey.

"EXCUSE ME!" Rey says, ripping the scroll from the Lt Colonel's hand, nearly pulling his glove off along with it. "You should have started with that! King Dietrich sent errand boys with orders for My Cavalry without consulting with me first!"

The Lt Colonel's face begins to sweat, "Sir, it was a rushed notice, sir. King Dietrich's scribe wrote out the warrant as soon as the news made it to the castle. It was to be delivered to you immediately. Sir."

"What does King Dietrich want with some child anyway?"

"He's more of a young adult; he's reached the age of

sixteen, sir. Apparently, he was saying things about not wanting to work at the bakery and that he would rather be out of a job and live in the streets."

Field Marshal Rey unrolls the scroll scanning the warrant. "And his father?"

"He is already under investigation," the Lt Colonel answers.

"Investigating his father won't do too much. He has no legal responsibility for the boy's actions anymore. The boy on the other hand shall be apprehended on sight," Rey recites short of a yawn, his eyes falling to the warrant. He grumbles under his breath as his eyes scan the information, "Didn't think the Cavalry was designed to play fetch." He glances back up at the Lt Colonel. "What are you still doing here? You delivered the warrant. Isn't there a search and arrest you and your division should be conducting?"

"Yes sir, thank you, sir," the Lt Colonel says, standing up stiffly, careful not to scrape the chair across the ground. Without taking the time to breathe, he shows himself out of the office.

Thirty-Three

The forest bursts into existence as Stirling's eyes shoot open. The sound of Ignis's voice booms inside his head, yelling his name.

Startled, Stirling bolts upright with the throw of his arms. The forest in front of them had changed since he had closed his eyes. The vibrant forest was full of life and the music of birds had grown quiet. An unsettling cloak of shadows has invaded the trees leaving behind a stark contrast, the light of the sun giving its last farewells behind the western mountains.

He had let himself fall asleep out in the open like that right after he had said people might come out searching for him. How ignorant can he be?

"*STIRLING!*" Ignis hollers. Stirling's attention snaps to him. "*I heard something! I think it's people on dragonback!*" Ignis informs.

Stirling immediately leaps to his feet. "Crap! Ignis, can you find a way into the cave without being noticed? I know wild dragons aren't some taboo thing but it's easier if they don't see you because you yourself are out of the ordinary,"

Stirling says in a panic.

They both freeze as they hear shouts coming from above the treetops. "Damn. Go, now!" Stirling hisses.

Stirling leaps up from the ground bolting across the exposed forest floor visible from the bird's eye as Ignis slinks his large body into the trees in search of a safe route.

Halting below the overhanging tree, waiting to conceal him in her depths, he hears the sound of dogs barking in the distance. He turns around. His blanket with his belongings is still laying on the ground where he had dropped it. Wasting time, Stirling stands still, his eyes darting back and forth between the safety of the cave and the danger of where his pack lays. Time is being counted down with each thunderous tick of his heart. Vicious barks and snarls echo from the forest as if the surrounding trees were the teeth of a gruesome smile.

Stirling grits his teeth and sprints back out into the open, deciding it is better to risk being caught now versus them finding his stuff later. Sliding to a stop, he grabs his pack and bread in one motion as he launches himself back in the direction of the cave, dust kicking up in his wake. Stumbling over his feet, he leans forward, his fingertips grazing the patchy grass keeping his balance.

Ignoring the fact he left behind skid marks; Stirling frantically throws himself into the cave as if a monster is nipping at his heels. His body disappears into the darkness of his new home.

Stirling staggers into the cave. The only light illuminating the open-air pocket in the dense rock is the rising moon from the east. The sun now vanished behind the western mountains. The small details in the cave are impossible to see, a black cocoon surrounding him. The royal blue sky steadily grows darker as if it is on the other side of a window. A massive glass wall separates him from the entire world as he floats out in a dark empty space.

Stirling can still hear the snarling of the dogs echoing into the cave. It reverberates off the stone walls, making it as if they are all around him. Their fanged mouths growl right into his ears. Their barks ring through his head as if they have torn straight through his eardrums. Dropping his stuff to the ground, Stirling's hands shoot to his ears in an attempt to block out the sounds.

They have to be right outside the cave. They must be able to smell him. How could they not? He came here almost every day; his scent is all over this forest leading to and from this exact location.

He falls to his knees, still cupping his ears. He can hear the men shouting now. This is it. They found him. He should not have made such a scene. Someone ratted him out. He proved nothing to no one.

He is a failure.

The sounds of men and dogs begin to subside into silence. Stirling releases his hands from his ears, the only sound around him now being the crashing of the ocean waves far below him.

He is alone, more secluded now than he has ever been before. Emptiness falls thick and heavy over him. He can feel the weight of it pressing down on his shoulders like being laid out flat on the hard floor and stone by stone is added onto him until he is slowly crushed to death.

With his arms wrapping around his knees, Stirling wonders if it is all even worth it. He has given up the little time he had with his mother and he has now thrown away what time he has left with his father. Any possibility of him changing his mind to go home and live his normal life as a baker growing old with a family is now gone. It isn't out of his reach. It is entirely out of sight. He is nothing more than a malefactor hiding from the military in a cave while they unleash a manhunt in search of him.

He did all of this for what? The already non-existent chance he will be accepted as any form of Rider, in the

Cavalry or not. Even the dream of being able to fly free without the noose looming overhead has been erased. They know who he is. If they don't find him soon, they will document him as deceased. People who are dead can't be resurrected.

What was he thinking? Convincing everyone he could disregard the occupation he is assigned? It isn't as simple as stocks and pillories. It isn't as easy as death by hanging as it is for practicing other trades. No, his life will be seen as treason, and treason is taken seriously. Torture as you slowly die is a punishment set to the extreme for the high severity of the crime.

He risked this possible outcome because why? Because he believed in himself? Because he's been breaking the law for the past six years? Not only has he been training himself how to ride a dragon, but he has also been stealing, ignoring his occupation, and teaching himself other traits a baker has no need of knowing; like how to craft tools, stitch clothing, and mend shoes.

They aren't going to be like Amiria, who took the time to understand his side. The Cavalry isn't going to sit on a cliffside and watch the sunrise while he explains his past. He was lucky with her. His whole life, he has been nothing more than fortunate.

"Where's Ignis?" Stirling moans.

Feeling something trickling down his cheek, he brushes against his face with the back of his hand. Pulling his hand up to his eye level, he attempts to make out what it is but to no avail with the lack of light in the cave. He puts his hand back to his cheek as another warm drop runs down his face. He's crying.

"What have I done?" He murmurs, pulling the blanket over his head and resting his forehead against his knees as he feels the weight of the stones finally crush him.

Stirling doesn't know how long he has been lying there when he opens his eyes. The blanket is the only barrier separating his face from the cold hard ground. His body lies slightly uncurled, having tipped over when he fell asleep sitting up.

The cave is absent of light except for the stars shimmering through the foggy night sky. The air temperature had dropped drastically. Any warmth left by the sun is long gone and replaced by the damp marine layer creeping in from the ocean.

Wrapping the blanket around him tightly, Stirling shivers as the stone floor sucks the heat straight from his body.

"Ignis?" Stirling calls out in his mind.

"Stirling, you're awake," Ignis replies.

A rush of relief floods through Stirling's core as he hears Ignis' voice echoing in his head, *"Ignis! You're ok! Where are you?"*

"I'm on a spot overlooking the ocean. I'm waiting for them to leave the area before I fly out into the open." Ignis explains, his large mass attempting to crouch behind the trees lined up along the part of the forest's edge that drops off the side of the mountain's face.

"They're still out there?" Stirling wonders.

"Yeah, the dogs have moved on to another part of the mountain but they still have Riders circling all over. I guess they're trying to find any hint of your whereabouts." Ignis expands.

Stirling pulls himself into a tight fetal position as he feels his stomach wrenching. He doesn't understand how search dogs work and how they are able to track him, but at least the dogs aren't able to find him right away. Maybe the fact that he has been all over this part of the forest is throwing them off, or perhaps it's because this cave smells too much of Ignis.

With droopy eyes, Stirling begins to nod off again. The lingering dread of who will arrive first to the cave, Ignis or the Cavalry, lays thicker over him than his blanket.

Thirty-Four

The rising sun strikes across Stirling's face. He opens his eyes, blinking them rapidly, trying to help them adjust to the penetrating light.

He made it through the night, but Ignis is still gone.

Was he not able to find an opportunity to make it here? Stirling ponders, pushing up onto his elbow for support as he reaches to grab his pillow and loaves of bread.

"*Ignis?*" Stirling calls out as he breaks off a piece of bread, his stomach rumbling loud enough to echo off the cave walls.

"*Ignis?*" he calls out once again with a sense of worry. "*IGNIS!*" he yells with urgency.

"*Huh? What?*" Ignis' groggy voice comes to life in Stirling's head.

"*You weren't answering, so I thought something might have happened to you,*" Stirling says, his body and mind relaxing.

He doesn't know what he would have done if he had lost Ignis. He would have no one left to turn to. Ignis is all he has.

"I was sleeping." Ignis replies with a yawn, *"They were circling for so long I fell asleep. But you fell asleep before me so you can't say anything."*

"So they are finally gone? Are you able to get to the cave?" Stirling asks.

Stirling stares at the chunk of bread in his hand with anticipation as Ignis takes his time before answering. *"They seemed to have disappeared for now. I'll be there in a moment. Hold on."*

Releasing the pressure on his elbow Stirling lies back down. This time his head is resting on the straw-filled flour sack. His legs tuck up close to his chest on the uncomfortable ground as he takes a bite of bread.

He lets his eyes slide shut as the sun's rays cast over his body, returning the warmth that had been stolen from below him. He reminds himself of a reptile. His muscles refuse to move after stiffening up from staying curled up all night in the frigid air.

A shadow consumes Stirling. He doesn't need to open his eyes to see who it is because he can feel it. Ignis is an extension of himself, whether it is accepted or not.

Lowering his head, Ignis climbs into the cave. The vastness of the cave is well enough to encompass more than one full-grown dragon. Ignis takes precautions to avoid scraping his horns on any lower hanging spots on the ceiling.

Ignis drops his hulking weight down beside Stirling, who instinctively as if he is no more than a small frail child, shimmies up to Ignis, pressing the front of himself into the scaly underbelly. Even without their bond and without Stirling telling him, Ignis knows Stirling is upset. He can see it in his face and in his actions. He isn't the joyous boy he has grown up with. At this moment, he reminds him of the first time they had met in this cave. He was a young child new to the outside world. Now he is a young adult new to the reality and consequences of his actions and he is terrified.

Ignis relaxes his wing, letting it hang down his side, and drapes it over Stirling. He wraps his neck and tail around himself, enclosing Stirling in his protective ward as they both drift back to sleep again.

Giles' shaking hands loosely grip the bread paddle. He sticks the wood into the oven and slips it under the loaf of barley bread. Impatient, he pulls the bread out too fast and it drops from the paddle, tumbling to the ground. Already overwhelmed with frustration, Giles belts out in anger and whips the paddle across the room. It smacks into the far wall and clatters to the ground.

His son has been missing for two days now and he hasn't heard any updates from this supposed superior Cavalry. People talk as if they are a mightier species than the folk clustered in the market streets. These higher beings were sent to find Stirling. So why haven't they returned with him yet?

Why haven't they found his son yet?

Sighing, Giles picks up the loaf and sets it on the table before shuffling across the room to retrieve the paddle. He's stopped halfway by a knock on the door. Giles turns confused. This is a bakery, people don't usually knock before they enter his establishment. Cautiously, he makes his way to the front door as the knocking proceeds.

"Hello?" Giles asks as he pulls open the door.

A young guard with auburn hair swooping across his brow stands at Giles' doorstep. The boy cannot be much older than Stirling. A second guard, similar in age, with his dark short hair pushed back, stands at the bottom of the steps. They wear matching blue soft armor gambesons with Lumierna's City Guards crest pinned to their chest.

"Yes, hi, is this the household of Giles Bakere?" the guard asks.

Giles raises an eyebrow. The guard sounds as young as he appears, "This is, how may I help you today?"

The child in a guard's uniform coughs into his hand, clearing his throat, "I have been sent to inform you, that your son, Stirling Bakere, has died."

Giles' world tilts, his forearm shoots out, catching himself, he leans into the door frame, the boy's face fading from view. His words are barely audible over the rushing sound in Giles' ears.

"The Winged Cavalry found his body at the bottom of a cliff in the mountains. It appears he had fallen by accident. The report states he had perished before the Winged Cavalry was able to render aid. The Winged Cavalry and the city of Lumierna send their condolences."

The young guard waits for the ghostly man to speak, so he may answer any questions the grieving family may have. Giles goes limp, his arm slips from the doorframe and he falls to his knees. The boy backs down a step distancing himself from the man. Giles doubles over, shattering before the guards. He buries his face into his hands. The scream starts as a low rumble, growing into an alarming wail that tears at his throat.

"Come on, William. We passed the message. It's time to go." The second guard reaches up, snagging the boy by the wrist, and tugs him along. William lets his partner pull him down the market street. He checks back over his shoulder to the father, his mournful howls still ringing in his ears.

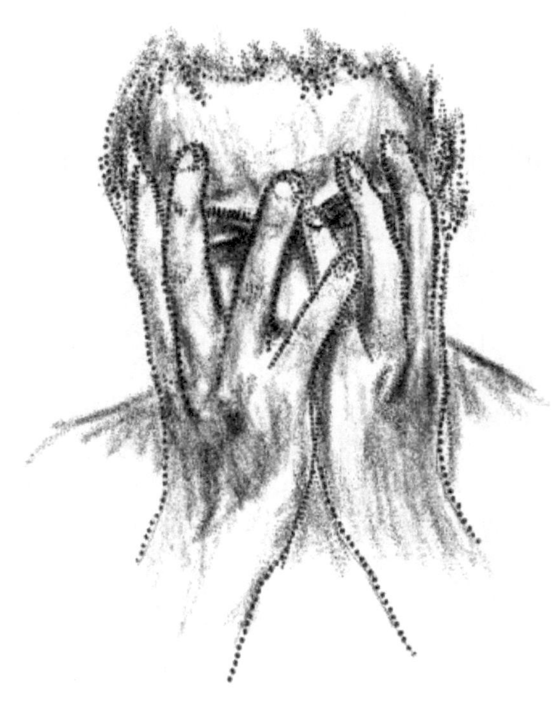

Thirty-Six

Stirling can't keep track of the times the sun and moon played tag across the sky. The shadows and light are in a constant dance across the cave. He assumes it must have been longer than a few days, maybe almost a week but has it been long enough for them to give up and pronounce him dead?

His body feels accurate to the label they will give him. He feels heavy as if his body has formed with the rocks around him, keeping him from even being able to roll over. His arms are filled with lead, lying useless beside him. He twitches his fingers to check if they are still his. They move on command but the numbness in his hands makes the movement feel foreign as if he is merely watching someone else's hand move.

He is so thirsty. His tongue is enlarged and scratchy in his mouth. He hasn't had any water to drink except one of the days, a downpour left behind small puddles at the rim of the cave mouth. They've dried up now.

Maybe he should get up in search of some more water or something to eat like a berry bush. He is so tired though. His

head throbs so hard he can see each and every pulse.
    Throb.
    He closes his eyes, hoping his headache will subside.
    Throb.
    He is just so tired.
    Throb.
    He'll just rest a little longer.
    Throb.

Thirty-Seven

Shivering, Stirling's entire body shakes beneath the blanket pulling him out of his dreams where he was home with his mother. A world where he had chosen the warmth and comfort of being by her side in the bakery. She was sitting beside his bed, tucking him in after a full supper telling him everything will be ok and she loved him.

He lies on his side as his eyes crack open. The cave comes into view as Ignis' wing is no longer covering him. Keeping his head planted on his pillow, he tries to check around the cave for Ignis.

The cave is massive but holds no sizable fixtures for a dragon to hide behind. Slowly he tilts his head north of himself.

His eyes strain to see above, his head only able to tilt so far without moving his body. He does not see the orange dragon he knows so well, instead, he sees an unfamiliar pair of human legs. They sit cross-legged, wearing a form fitting pair of black riding tights with a pair of dark leather boots.

Sitting in the stranger's lap are two items: a costrel with

two loops on either side of the corked top with a matching cord threaded through the loops and a large cross-shoulder bag crafted with durable suede leather with a flap hanging over the top and a string tied down to a button on the belly of the bag hiding the contents.

Stirling's eyes lock on the symbol burned into the side of the castrol, the Winged Cavalry emblem. He bolts up as fast as his feeble body will allow him. Even in his weakened state, he refuses to go down without a fight.

A wave of dizziness washes over Stirling as black dots form in his vision. His body, unable to keep up with the abrupt movement after lying stagnant for a prolonged time, tips over. He catches himself with his elbows before his head hits the ground.

His eyes fall to a slender calloused hand holding onto his shoulder. Following the hand up, he skims over a leather bracer, up the clean mauve cotehardie, a woolen button-up top, all the way to a tanned face with round dark eyes.

"It's fine. I'm not here to take you in." Amiria is calm and tender as she speaks. Her voice is soothing, like that of a person comforting a lost child.

Pulling her hand away from his shoulder, Stirling hangs his head, the tension releasing from his muscles.

Picking up the costrel from her lap Amiria extends it out to Stirling holding it down below his face. His eyes lock on her. His appearance and health are in a terrible state, showing he hasn't tried to take care of himself in the past week. His lips are severely chapped and flaking, the bags under his eyes hang low and vibrant while the rest of his face is flushed of all color.

Leaning onto one arm, Stirling's free hand trembles as he takes the costrel being held near his face. Amiria can hear the water sloshing inside as it shakes in his grasp. He brings it to his lips and leans his head back, letting the water replenish the moisture that has all but vanished like a rainstorm flooding the dry barren land of a desert.

It tastes like heaven to him, as if the water holds all of the answers to life. He can't control himself as he begins chugging. He can't consume it as fast as his body desires it.

"Whoa, slow down there, baker boy." Amiria advises as she reaches out to take the costrel back, "You'll make yourself sick."

Stirling lets Amiria take the costrel, gravity pulling his heavy hand down to the ground to hold himself steady as he attempts to speak. His voice is hoarse and scratchy in his throat as he forces out, "Where's Ignis?"

"I sent him out to stretch his wings and get something to eat. It was hard convincing him I was only here to help. He is really protective of you. If we hadn't met before, I'm pretty sure he would have tried to kill me," Amiria answers.

Nodding slowly, Stirling tries to picture Amiria attempting to persuade Ignis that she means no harm. She must have some impressive communication skills if she was able to convince him to not only let her remain in the cave but to also leave her alone while he was asleep and vulnerable.

Stirling's voice is grated as he tries to speak again. The words tear into an uninterpretable garble of sounds in his sore throat. Amiria hands the costrel back to Stirling, who takes another swig. He swishes it around his mouth before swallowing.

"How did you find me?" he finally says, his voice weak and raspy.

"I'm not sure what's worse, how the Cavalry wasn't able to find you or how easy it was for me to do so alone. I knew since you do not fly above the tree line, you must be within walking distance from both the canyon and the city. So that gave me which part of the wall I should start searching for clues on. Then I found this convenient little hole in the wall. With all those years you've walked the same path here, it's created an obvious trail that led me straight to you. I think they were relying too much on their aerial views and hounds, but you can't see people hiding inside a cave from the sky and dogs are going to avoid the scent of dragons. It usually means one of us or a wild one. They aren't going to go messing with wild dragons," Amiria explains to Stirling as he nods, only pretending he is following along with what she is saying as more questions pop into his mind.

"Are they done searching for me?"

"Yes and no. They marked your papers as deceased and that is what is being told to your family and the townspeople, but you are still on their wanted list. If they find you, there will be no trial, no jail time. You will be executed onsite in secrecy. King Dietrich will not want to make changes to his paperwork, nor does he want the townspeople to know he has lied to them," Amiria clarifies.

"What a nice man," Stirling mutters under his breath.

"At least dying by sword or arrow isn't as bad as if you were caught riding your dragon." Amiria's eyes drift to the far wall, her mind telling her his fate. Drawn and quartered.

"Reassuring," Stirling mutters as his stomach twists.

Then in the midst of his aching head, dehydration, and newly acquired nausea, he remembers something he felt terrible wasn't his first question. "My father, did they do anything to him?"

"No." Amiria shakes her head, "I heard from my father that he was interrogated about the situation and your potential whereabouts, but since you are sixteen, there was nothing more they could do."

Stirling is relieved his actions hadn't caused his father to be arrested or to lose his bakery. This can work out in the end. Yes, he is a fugitive, but he is also free, even if it's only that he is an outcast, to live alone in the mountains. A type of life he has already been living for years.

Now he can cut out the part about sneaking in and out of

the bakery every day with his father demanding answers and setting up restrictions and limitations. Now he is able to do as he wants, and go wherever and whenever he pleases. For once, he can take care of himself.

The sound of Stirling's stomach rumbles like thunder. He tries to cover it up by placing his hand over his stomach as it tries to digest a chasm in his guts. Amiria smiles and unties the bag's flap. She turns it upside down, spilling the contents between her and Stirling. His mouth regains the ability to salivate as he stares down at the cheese, apples, pears, some bread, and even dried meat laid out on display before him.

"I thought you might be hungry after being out here for so long. I took a guess at your reckless actions that you didn't prepare yourself ahead of time, and it appears I was correct," Amiria says with sympathy in her eyes.

Any small amount of saliva that had formed in Stirling's mouth evaporates as his mouth goes dry. I'm still being taken care of by someone, my mother, my father, Ignis, now even Amiria, he thinks to himself. One day I want to be the person taking care of another. Help someone else who needs it.

"Don't be disrespectful now. I brought this for you. Go on, eat," Amiria insists.

Stirling picks up one of the apples taking a large bite. The taste is sweet and delectable on his shriveled tongue as the juice brings life to the inhabitable wasteland.

Ignis appears gripping the side of the cave opening. The back flap of his wings, casts strong gusts across Stirling and Amiria, her hair whipping around and flowing with the gales of salted ocean air. Ignis' front legs cling to the cave floor as his hind legs hang over the edge, his claws gouging the side of the mountain.

Folding in his wings, Ignis finishes pulling himself inside the cave as he shouts excitedly with a wag of his tail. *"STIRLING! YOU'RE AWAKE!"*

Stirling's face beams with a sudden rush of energy as he

sees his best friend. *"Ignis! Looks like we made it!"*

Assessing the scene in front of him, Ignis bounces back and forth between Amiria and Stirling who is lounging on his side propped up on his elbow, and Amiria, who is sitting directly by his head. The only thing separating them is the food sprawled out.

"Oh? What is going on here? A little date with a girl, I see. I can leave again if you need some alone time," Ignis teases.

"It's not a date. We just met. She was showing me the food that she had brought," Stirling growls.

"Food she had brought? Definitely a date."

"Not a date."

Amiria studies Stirling's mannerisms for a moment, the way his head and body moved as if he was talking, but no words came from his mouth. She glances over her shoulder at Ignis and then back to Stirling. "Are you two talking to each other right now?"

"Huh?" Stirling turns his attention back to Amiria.

She puzzles over the thought. "So it is true. How very interesting."

"You didn't believe me?" Stirling says.

"Honestly, no. It's my job to assume guilty until proven innocent," she admits with a shrug.

Scooting his legs up, Stirling shifts himself into a sitting position face-to-face with Amiria. Stirling slouches, hunching his shoulders forward. She straightens, stiffening her spine as the small gap between them shrinks.

"I've got to be departing now," she says hastily. Avoiding direct eye contact, she finds another spot in the cave to focus on, "I have some obligations to attend to today. Our final evaluations are coming up."

Stirling cocks his head. "Then you will be assigned to your unit?"

Amiria remains turned away but her eyes dart back to

Stirling. "Yes, but it is all based on my evaluation scores. All the brass will be watching and...so will my father." Folding in on herself, she says quietly, "I need to be going. I've been here too long already." Standing up Amiria brushes the dust off her tights. "You can keep the bag and costrel. You will be needing them more than me."

Stirling picks up the soft leather bag. The hide must have come from a large animal since there is no stitching connecting multiple hide strips or tears. Stirling remembers the pouches his parents would carry made of old burlap sacks or the corner of a torn flour sack. How the seams tend to come loose, threatening to drop the items contained inside.

"Take care, the both of you," Amiria says as she nods to Stirling and Ignis.

She takes a single step towards the back of the cave when Stirling catches her hand. "Amiria, wait."

His touch sends a small shock across her skin. His ice-cold fingers make her feel warm as he stares up at her from a half-kneel. Their eyes lock for the first time today. Stirling seems to have lost his ability to speak properly. He stammers, trying to form his thoughts into words.

"Can we...you know...fly...us two together one day?" he finally manages to force out.

Amiria searches Stirling's eyes focused on hers, wide and nervous but filled with hope. She has never been invited to spend time with someone else before that wasn't preassigned by a higher-up. Even then, they didn't interact with her. They were assigned duties and a partner, not a friendship. Does he really want to spend time with her as an acquaintance, or does he have ulterior motives, some other intentions to use her? Use her like her classmates do when they can't accomplish a task on their own. Use her like the trivial low-ranking Riders who only speak to her in an attempt to speak with her father. Use her like how Wyverna will use her life as if she is disposable, sacrificing one to save thousands.

She watches as the ocean breeze brushes the few loose

curls hanging low across his forehead. Can people be genuine? Is it earnest that he wants to spend time with her, not the Winged Rider next in line Field Marshal Amiria Rey, but the girl Amiria? Her heart begins to drum in her chest.

She holds her voice steady as she speaks. "Sure, okay, why not." She smiles shyly, "I did enjoy outflying you. My next day off is a week from now. I can be here in the morning."

Stirling bites his lip suppressing the smile that is about to leap across his face as he lets his hand slip from hers, "Okay. I'll see you next week then."

Amiria turns her head before the grin breaks through the surface. She composes her face, conducting herself with practiced formality as she walks to the back of the cave and disappears into the darkness of the tunnel. The only remnants of her are the taping of her boots on the stone ground.

Taking another bite of his apple Stirling lets himself fall back to a lying position, his head landing on the straw pillow. Resting his hand with the apple on his chest, he stares up at the cave ceiling. It took him 16 years, but he finally did it. He made a friend besides Ignis. But not any friend, a girl, in the Winged Cavalry.

Shifting his shoulders on the rocky surface, Stirling frowns and struggles to sit up. His head feeling heavier than the rocks around him. He bites into his apple and swallows.

"I've got a lot of work to do if I'm going to be living here from now on."

"*As in what? This place seems fine to me,*" Ignis says, plopping down near the entrance where the sun is still able to reach.

"Warmth for one. I need supplies to make a fire. Maybe a wall to keep the wind from blowing on me and the fire. Then even some kind of structure for me to sleep on, something to keep me off the cold ground," Stirling yawns.

"*Humans are so needy. I think the cave is fine,*" Ignis

says, glancing over at Stirling, whose heavy bagged eyes are drifting off.

Stirling tries to rise to his feet, becoming lightheaded he slumps back to the ground.

"Maybe you should drink, eat, then start tomorrow."

With head falling to his pillow Stirling mumbles half awake, "Yeah, tomorrow."

"So, what do you need me to do?" Ignis asks, watching his wobbly legged friend.

Placing his hands on his lower back, Stirling leans curving his spine backward, making cracking sounds as his vertebrae pop, "You can help with moving some of the larger branches in here that I can tie together with leftover pieces of rope from your harness."

"And that will keep the wind off?" Ignis asks, confused.

Stirling takes a few large bites of a pear. His cheeks puff out as he talks, "Just trust me, I know what I'm doing. Well, I'm winging it, but I'm an expert at that."

He swallows the rest of the pear in his mouth and squats down, picking up the bag and costrel. His muscles are still weak, and he slumps, falling onto the side of his hip. Shaking off his fatigue, he slings both items over his neck and one shoulder allowing the straps to go across his chest. He struggles back to his feet with a few wobbling steps before stabilizing himself. Finishing his apple with several large bites, he lobs the core out over the side of the cliff.

"I'll call you when I need your help," he tells Ignis. With a sluggish gait, he shuffles out of the cave.

Outside, Stirling leans over picking up twigs along the tree line, adding them to a stack collected under his left arm. He only needs to collect enough to last him the night. This is his top priority. When he is better rested, tomorrow he'll begin compiling a substantial amount inside the cave, so he'll only have to replenish what he uses from his stockpile. Finding a way to make an axe and hatchet is another thing he realizes he needs to add to his list. He can't rely on fallen branches forever; he'll need to begin cutting down larger pieces and falling trunks.

He heads back over to the cave, arms full of varying sizes of branches from the thickness of his finger to the size of his forearm. He dumps the stack, adding them to a pile gathering below the tree perched over the entryway.

Turning back to face the forest, he stands there momentarily lost in thought as he runs over ideas about how he is going to make some sort of bed. He needs to create a barrier between himself and the stone floor or he'll freeze no matter how warm he makes the fire. The earth will still steal the heat from his body like the thief it is.

He has heard people who are charcoal burners or woodcutters living on the outskirts of the city in houses that are dug halfway into the ground. Nothing more than a thatched roof sticking out above the earth's surface. They are known for sleeping on the soft earth. Stirling dug deep into his memories, trying to recall what it is they slept on.

If he can find enough saplings, he can tie them together into a rectangular frame with a few going across like steps of a ladder. He'll need some fresh pine pulled down from the trees and layer it with rush, long string-like grass that will help create some padding.

Stirling sets off into the forest in search of his supplies. Noticing a bounce in his step, he slows to examine the sponge-like moss beneath his feet.

This will make good tinder, he thinks to himself.

His mind is still deep in thought of how he is going to execute his ideas. Kneeling down, he begins absentmindedly digging his fingers under to lift it up, he realizes it stays intact like lifting the corner of a floorboard.

"It can also help block the wind if I put it on the wall,

maybe even sleep on it. I wonder if I can roll it up." Proving his assumption correct, he slowly rolls the moss up like a rug for easier transport.

"For the wall, I can take some branches and tie them together. Then I could fill in any gaps with caked mud and this moss so the wind won't leak through. After learning some hunting skills, maybe I can eventually use some hides for the wall. No, that's stupid. I'm going to want to use the hides and pelts for my bed. This moss will be fine."

"Are you talking to yourself?" Ignis' voice chimes into Stirling's head over his thoughts, snapping him out of his concentration.

"No. Well, yeah, I was planning."

"Well, can you plan a little quieter? You were so deep into thought I started to hear it. You've only been away from the city for a week and you're already talking to yourself. You're not even that isolated. You've got me and that girl of yours to talk to."

"Oh, shut up, Ignis. Why don't you go find some long branches and bring them to the cave? Oh, and stay away from my thoughts that aren't directed at you," Stirling demands as he tucks the rug of moss under his arm.

"Then don't put your thoughts on display. Keep your boring thoughts about building to yourself. Oh and especially if you're thinking about Amiria, you can keep those personal too." Ignis mocks.

"I just met her!" Stirling yells, becoming frustrated.

"You've been watching her for six years. I call your bluff on the 'I just met her.'" Ignis laughs.

Shaking his head, Stirling swats at the air around him as if Ignis is a fly buzzing in the air. *"Get out of here, Ignis. Go find some branches and make sure they're fairly straight."*

Stirling can feel Ignis disconnect from his thoughts after a short chuckle. Standing back up, Stirling scans the pine trees nearby, inspecting them for one with low enough branches for him to reach.

Stepping up to one of the pines, Stirling stands below the lowest branch. He reaches above his head, his fingertips grazing the thin branch full of emerald green needles. Sighing, he glances around in hopes of an even lower branch.

Cursing under his breath, Stirling stares back up at the branch hanging over him. He stands up on his tippy toes extending a single arm maximizing the full extent of his reach. The tips of his fingers are now barely able to curl over the top of the branch. He snorts with frustration.

Clapping his hands, he rubs them together as he bends his knees. Leaping up, Stirling grabs hold of the branch firm in his hand. The fallen needles, piled loosely on the forest floor, slide as his feet make contact with the ground. Falling backward, Stirling grips the branch as it bows from the pull of his weight. The branch, no longer able to handle the stress, snaps, releasing Stirling from his suspension to meet the earth.

Lying on his back, he stares up at the canopy above him, the pine branch lying across his body. "This is going to be a long day."

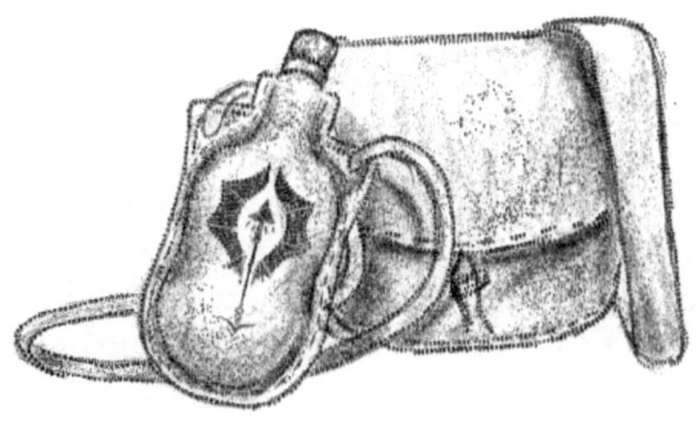

Thirty-Eight

The cave grows steadily colder as the light from the sun dissipates with the night moving in. Stirling stumbles across the middle of the cave dragging the last of the saplings. Despite the ocean wind, Stirling decides to set his camp closer to the cave mouth, allowing space for Ignis to sleep beside him. Reaching the front left corner of the cave against the wall, he drops the saplings and collapses to his knees, sitting back on his heels. He holds his arms out in front of himself and examines the fresh cuts and scrapes on his arms from carrying the firewood.

With a large branch still in his mouth, Ignis lands at the entrance of the cave. He steps over to where Stirling is still inspecting his arms and releases his branch, adding it to his accumulated pile.

Stirling drops his arms, placing his hands on his knees to keep himself steady. He has gone past exhaustion, arriving to the point of fainting as his heart goes into overdrive to keep his body functioning. He has spent more energy than he had to start with collecting all of the materials. His body can barely move.

"Damn, I still need to make the fire." Stirling groans as a shiver ripples through him. The dampness is beginning to seep through his skin to his bones. He can't even manage standing back up, his legs refusing to listen to the command signals fired from his brain.

Slowly leaning forward till the palms of his hands are placed on the ground, he crawls closer to the fire pit he has made with a few sticks enclosed by rocks the size of his fist to keep the embers contained as best as possible. His body and his mind screams at him to lie down, to sleep, to close his eyes, and let himself slip into the unconscious world.

Not yet. He shakes his head, suppressing the urge to close his eyes. He needs to make a fire at least, to help him through the night.

Stirling sits back as Ignis asks, *"Have you ever made a fire before?"*

"Yeah, but it was on the stove back home. So, it's different," Stirling answers as he stuffs some inner bark and leaves under the firewood.

He picks up two thin pieces of rock he is hoping will be flint. He had taken a guess while he was searching but he was in a race against the sun and didn't take the time to test them out.

Holding one of the rocks close to the tinder he strikes it with the other. Nothing. Stirling shrugs it off and strikes again. Still nothing, not even a single spark, as the cave only grows colder. He just wants to rest. He is malnourished and exhausted. There isn't time to play with rocks. He strikes the rocks together for the third time. Nothing. Unable to hold in his frustration, he begins repeatedly striking the rocks over and over.

An itch begins to form in the back of Ignis' throat. It resembles the need to cough with a hidden undertone. He watches Stirling with fascination. He isn't sure how rocks are able to produce fire. He was starting to doubt they even could after this display.

"Why won't these work!?" Stirling screams as he throws one of the rocks in a fit of rage.

The rock disappears into the shadows of the cave. Stirling hunches over in defeat as he realizes what he has done. His impatience has lost him the chance of making a fire. The last of the rock's tumbling echo finally faded. He doesn't have time to play around. He can barely function, the exhaustion taking a toll on his focus and balance, making him feel nauseous.

The itch in the back of Ignis' throat is now becoming unbearable.

Slumping his shoulders forward, Stirling stares down at his hands resting in his lap. He releases the grip letting the second rock slip from his fingers and it clatters to the ground. He can barely make out the outline of his body in the dim light.

Then a flash and everything is lit up. For a moment it is as if someone opened a window directly to the sun itself. The brightness and the heat overwhelm him like a slap in the face. Throwing himself backward Stirling attempts to stand up in reaction to the sudden burst of energy but he only manages to stumble, tripping on his heels and falling flat onto his back.

Propping up onto his elbow, he assesses the situation of what had happened. He peers down the length of his body. The cold fire pit he had been sitting at is now glowing warmly from the smoldering wood.

Stirling's eyes jump to Ignis, then back at the fire pit, then back to Ignis, who cocks his head, apparently as shocked as he is. "You can breathe fire! That would have been extremely useful information not just five minutes ago but maybe back when we almost got turned into ash by Amiria."

"I didn't know I could. I thought I needed to cough. Then boom, fire. You thought you were surprised? Imagine being

the one to suddenly have fire shoot out of your mouth," Ignis defends.

Stirling pushes up into a sitting position.

He scoots up to the fire and holds his hands out, letting the warmth bring life back to his fingertips. "This fire does feel good though. It's worth almost being roasted alive for."

A whip of cold air blows into the cave knocking the flames over so they lick the side of the fire pit. Stirling grimaces at the stack of long branches Ignis has brought in. The adrenaline allowing him to react to Ignis' fire was short-lived. The energy is fading, vanishing, and nausea from over-exhaustion is settling back in.

All he wants to do is curl up into a ball and cry. He isn't finished after making the fire. He still needs to build the wall before he goes to bed. Otherwise, the wind will threaten to put out his fire during the night. He doesn't know how he made it through so many frigid nights, but he doesn't want to test how many more his body can sustain.

Rocking his body, Stirling uses the momentum to help get himself up to his feet. He wobbles momentarily and staggers his way over to the pile. The branches aren't heavy, but they are around the same height he is, making it more of a hassle as he drags them along the cave, aligning them up side by side.

Taking leftover braided rope, he begins peeling it apart until only the thinnest possible stands were left. Branch by branch, he ties them together leaving the least number of gaps he can manage.

"I'll add the moss tomorrow. This will have to do for now," he says, his hands trembling as he pulls the last knot tight.

Squatting down, he slips his shaking hands under his new wall which is as long as it is tall. Straightening his legs, he attempts to lift the wall.

His fingers give out. The muscles and tendons are unable

to stay contracted. The wall slips from his open hands, slamming back to the ground. All he needs to do is stand this up at an angle supported by two sticks and he can finally go to sleep.

He needs to do this one last thing. One last hurdle separates him and sleep, but his body is fighting against him, making it nearly impossible to even move. It had given up long ago, but he kept pushing it with the promise of eventual rest.

His vision is starting to blur; he leans to Ignis for help. "Can you somehow help me lift this? I can't do it on my own right now."

"*How?*" Ignis questions.

Stirling picks up the piece of the rope he hadn't pulled apart and ties it to the top of the central branch. "Bite onto this and pull up. I'll put the supports in place. You just need to hold it."

Getting up from his cozy spot by the fire, Ignis takes the rope in his mouth as Stirling readies himself with a branch half the length of the wall. Ignis raises the designated top of the wall till Stirling tells him to stop. The tied branches form a steep ramp rising away from the mouth of the cave, with one side running along the cave wall.

Stirling takes a branch and sets it vertically below the wall.

"Okay, now gently lower it until it rests on the stick. But don't let go." He tells Ignis, who does as he is instructed.

Stirling lets go of the branch jammed beneath the wall and picks up the second branch. He shifts over to the other end and shimmies it into place.

"*Can I let go?*"

"Hold on a moment," Stirling says as he pushes a few rocks into place pinning the bottom of the branches.

"*Now?*"

"One last thing," Stirling says, crawling around to the back side of the wall.

"You keep saying that." Ignis groans. Still sitting on the ground, Stirling uses his feet to push a few more rocks against the bottom of the wall to keep them from sliding.

"Okay, now you can let go," he says.

Ignis releases the rope from his jaws.

Stirling holds his breath as the wall shifts settling into place. Stirling feels his whole body sigh with relief. It worked. Now he can finally sleep.

Struggling to stand, Stirling feels as if his breathing is slowing but his heart is racing. His legs waver beneath him as he tries to stand up straight. He takes one step forward. The world spins around him. His body slumps as his vision begins to leave him. Reaching out with nothing to grab onto, Stirling starts to fall forward.

Quickly extending his neck, Ignis catches Stirling with his snout. Stirling's face presses against the spot between Ignis' eyes.

"You all right?" he asks.

"Yeah, I just need…" Stirling mumbles without finishing, his eyes already closed.

"You need to sleep," Ignis finishes for him. *"Hold onto me."*

Stirling mindlessly loops his arms around, hugging onto Ignis' snout.

Ignis slowly backs up, guiding Stirling around the wall whose feet are useless as they drag across the ground. Ignis lowers his face gently laying Stirling down beside the fire under his new shelter.

Picking the blanket up, Ignis is careful to not catch it on fire as he covers Stirling who was already fast asleep with his head resting on his arm.

Ignis lies on the opposite side of the fire, his body acting as an opposing wall enclosing Stirling in a small room.

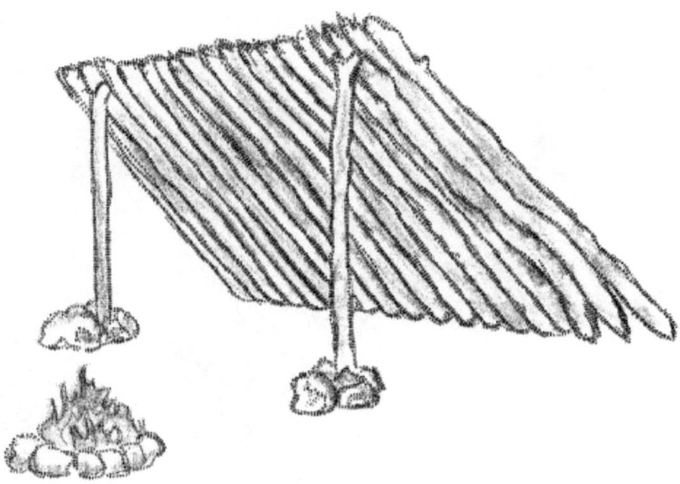

Thirty-Nine

Gray clouds roll in, covering the sky. Winged Riders act as if they are on holiday, spreading out around the grass hills emerging up around the training track of the bass to watch the next graduating class run through their final evaluations. The Field Marshal, General, Lt General, and Major General sit up on a covered deck, each with a quill in hand to mark their scoring. They are the top four positions in the Winged Cavalry. Their opinion is law in the Cavalry world. They will determine where each new Rider will be placed across the kingdom.

Sitting in a lavish tent is a surprise to everyone, King Dietrich.

Their king relaxes on a seat of plush pillows hidden from the view behind his canvas walls. Obscured in the shadows, he watches the testing class.

Riders whisper to each other with their theories of why their king has granted them this opportunity to relish in his presence. He has never made an appearance at an evaluation in the past. An event, special to those in the Winged Cavalry, is beneath any of those who work in the royal court. They wonder about the sudden change in character and what had enticed him to travel out here from the comfort of the castle.

A young Rider with sharp and handsome features holds out his palm up to the sky. "No rain yet," he says to a girl tucked under his arm as they lounge in the grass.

"I hope not," another says, clinging to his opposing shoulder.

A girl laying in front rolls over to her stomach resting her head on his thigh, "Calix, do you think any of these new Riders will join your unit?"

Calix laughs. "Doubt it. They don't just let anyone in."

"Then why is King Dietrich here?"

A fourth girl injects herself into the conversation, "Maybe he's bored. Calix is the best Rider they've seen in generations. The new guy will have to be compared to him to even be considered and good luck with that."

"Isn't the Field Marshal's daughter in this class?" The girl under Calix's arm mentions.

"I don't know," Calix says, disinterested.

The girl resting on his leg clicks her tongue, "Why does that matter?"

"Just wondering." She giggles. "Be interesting to see what his spawn is like. No one even knows what she looks like. She doesn't attend any parties."

"My friend knows someone who's met her and they could only talk about how awful she is. Truly spoiled and rotten to the core."

"Pfft, she thinks she's too good to grace us with her presence. I hope she fails. Won't that be amusing?" The girl on his shoulder laughs.

"They're starting," the girl at his leg informs.

Calix lays back in the grass, "Guess they are."

Closing his eyes, the girls snuggle up to him with their heads on his chest. He listens as the class begins. The whistles of their instructor commanding their drills echo through the base.

Calix doesn't plan on watching any of the class. Why does he care about some students taking a test? He's only here to take the day off and cuddle with his admirers in the daffodils. Maybe it's good that it's a chilly and cold day; a better excuse to sit close.

His face scrunches as he opens his eyes, staring up at the layers of clouds. The spectators gasp in reaction to something on the track. The girls groan and complain as he sits up to see for himself what has riled the crowd.

He regrets looking. He's becoming entranced. His eyes magnetized, stuck following everywhere the girl on the beige wyvern flies. He has never seen anyone move the way she does. The complete control of her dragon. Never faltering, no hesitation, no mistakes. Her executions of the drills are perfect. No, they are better than perfect; they are extraordinary. *She is extraordinary.*

"Calix?"

"Calix?"

Their calls to him fall on deaf ears. He doesn't hear the girls trying to grab his attention. He forgets they are there entirely. He is focused on one thing and one person only.

"Who is that?" he says under his breath.

"You were great out there!"

"I'm sure you will get a good placement."

"Outstanding job!"

Amiria hears the loving appraisals of family and friends surrounding her classmates. The training field is crowded with Winged Cavalry of all ages. Riders have traveled across Wyverna to attend and support the class taking their evaluations test as they do every year. Standing alone near the edge of the training field, Amiria tones the buzzing chatter out. She scans the field for her father, he was one of the judges after all, but he is nowhere to be seen. Her shoulders sink. He must be busy calculating the scores with the other brass. She convinces herself that is the reason. He's busy, that's it.

She catches her eyes slipping over to King Dietrich. He had shown up for her evaluation. Well, her class' evaluation. It was unexpected to everyone, even the top brass. He sits in the shadows of his tent on a seat cushioned with furs and fabrics. An unnerving tingle runs down her spine, she can't see his eyes but she can feel them. She turns away self-consciously.

Fiddling with her leather bracer, Amiria distracts herself to keep herself busy. She doesn't want to watch Nellie's parents pat her on the back, Garrett's father giving him a celebratory handshake, and Warrick's laughing brothers tackling him. There is no one here to give her words of encouragement. Awkwardly tucking a strand of hair behind her ear she pretends she has somewhere else to be and turns to leave the celebratory field. She stops short. A young man a few years older than her stands in the way.

"Hi," he says.

"Hi?" she replies, wary of the stranger.

"You were truly amazing out there," he tells her, leaning forward.

She leans back, uncomfortable. "Uh, thanks." She goes to step around him, but he sidesteps to remain in front of her.

"Sorry, I should have introduced myself. I'm Calix Gautier." He holds his hand out to shake.

Gautier. He must be the General's son. If she had attended even a single event at the castle, she would have known that. What she remembers hearing from her father, the son isn't the next inline General but instead, the younger daughter is. His father is a—is a— she doesn't know what position his father is in. She's rarely spoken to General Gautier and for

Winged Cavalry business only. She takes his hand with a faux disposition of respect.

"Gautier." She nods her head affirmatively.

"Rey." He plays the part back and gives her hand a firm shake. A perfect smile spreads across his face as he flirts, "I meant it though. You were clearly the best out there."

"I appreciate the compliment, but I have an engagement to attend." She keeps her voice formal and steps around Calix. He turns as she passes, keeping his shoulders squared to her.

Once past him, he trails behind her saying, "You're lying. I can tell."

Amiria dips her chin, her gaze landing on the patchy grass. What a master of deduction he is. Of course, she is lying. Today has been blocked out for any other Winged Cavalry business.

"Come on." He picks up his speed and steps in front of her again. "Come hang out. Let's celebrate your testing. We can—We can get something to eat." He throws out a suggestion.

Amiria doesn't slow. She pulls her shoulders up to her ears and walks around Calix, "No, no, thank you. I will wait to celebrate at the banquet after graduation."

She doesn't care who he is the son of. She has no interest in getting a bite to eat with a man she has just met. She thinks of traveling all the way into the unknown terrain of the mountains to find Stirling. She corrects herself. She has no interest in getting a bite to eat with *this* man she just met. Her mind wanders back to the perfect angles of his face but her eyes remain forward. No matter how handsome he is.

Calix tries to hide the aghast expression on his face. He blinks slowly. He has been rejected. He cocks his head as he comprehends the fact, that she rejected him. He had left behind the girls he had arrived with to speak to her, and she rejected him. What does one do when they are rejected? He wouldn't know. He could return to the girls, he knows they are still nearby, but he doesn't want to. He stands in place, no longer physically following Amiria, but his eyes remain riveted to her until she is gone from view.

Blindly feeling her way through the dark tunnel, Amiria's eyes strain to see what is ahead. Her hands run along the damp wall leaving its cold mark on her skin. Her feet step cautiously, relying on only the sense of touch after being deprived of the sense of sight she has grown too reliant on.

It had been a week since she first traveled through the tunnel, not knowing how long it would last nor what was at the end. This time she knows both answers, but her heart still speeds up with nerves and uncertainty.

She is never one to experience real fear. The fear that leaves you stopped in your tracks, the fear so deeply embedded you can't shake it off even after the threat is long past. There have only been a few things that have truly scared her throughout her life.

She remembers the first time she got separated from her mother in a crowd of strangers. She was at one of the few castle holidays she attended before refusing to show her face again. She had hidden underneath the banquet table until her mother's warm embrace found her and took her in. Another time she was scared. She had gotten herself stuck in a deep ditch, too small and weak to pull herself out. She struggled for half a day till her father came searching for her.

She had panicked and was frightened but when the events would come around again, she learned to remain calm, analyze her problem, and come to a solution.

What is different this time? Why is she not able to settle down? Why did every step she take make the feeling in the pit of her stomach worse?

Amiria squints as she steps out into the cave. Her eyes adjust slowly from the absence of light in the tunnel to the bright morning sun shining directly in from the cave mouth. Blinking the room into view, the changes Stirling had made are automatic. It is visibly apparent how he is quickly adapting and making this his new home.

She tilts her head. The curly-haired boy is curled up on a bed made of branches tied into a wooden frame containing pine and brush underneath a slanted wall. Ignis' lies to the side with his tail curled around as the only barrier between her and where Stirling sleeps. The remnants of his fire burned low in the pit.

Inventive, she thinks to herself, impressed by what he was able to come up with.

She wondered how he was able to do it. He is not born into a trade where he is taught to build anything, yet he is able to figure out how to assemble item after item to help him along. Help him live in a life not assigned to him, a life where he cannot rely on others to help him live comfortably. A life where you need to be well-rounded.

She feels a pang of jealousy. She doesn't have a creative bone in her body. Everything she ever needed was made by someone else. With all her training in combat and tactics, would she even be able to survive even in a house alone with no one to serve her? Yes, she would be able to hunt but can she figure out how to clean an animal or even how to cook it? She's never needed to figure out how to make anything from scratch. There was nothing that her coin couldn't buy for her, and the Winged Cavalry didn't provide for her.

To have the basic knowledge of multiple skills seems more essential for your everyday life than expert knowledge of one skill.

Amiria pauses as Stirling stirs to the sound of her footsteps. It has now become apparent to her that she isn't prepared, but she is always prepared. She stumbled her way in here with the intention to ask Stirling to come fly with her but all of sudden she is without words. This is the first time she is going to spend time with someone for fun.

It is as if her breath is caught in her throat, everything inside of her stops as Stirling sits up, his curls knotted on the back of his head. He turns to her, rubbing his eye with the back of his hand.

He pulls his hand slightly away from his face and squints. "Amiria?"

Her heart begins jumping widely in her chest. "Yes," she answers as calmly and collected as she can manage.

With his head remaining on the floor, Ignis opens his eyes to the sound of voices as Stirling asks, "May I help you?"

Amiria awkwardly fixes her cotehardie tucked under her harness as she regains her composure. "Um, we had an agreement. That I would be here on my next day off to fly together."

Stirling slaps his palm to his forehead, "Oh right, has it been a week already?"

Dropping his hand, his eyes dance around the cave as if he is deciding on what to do next. He pulls the blanket off his lap and scoots himself over to the fire pit. Amiria shifts on her feet, unsure about the direction this interaction is heading. She eyes Stirling as he sits himself in a kneeling position beside the fire and begins poking the embers with a twig.

Sighing, Stirling tosses the twig on top of the embers and returns his gaze to Amiria with a blasé expression.

Amiria's posture drops showing her insecurity. Her mind is running rampant with self-doubts. *He doesn't want you to be here. He just invited you to be nice. You're a fool for coming here. He's using you. He doesn't like you. No one likes you. Don't let him see you like this.* She pulls back her shoulders and puts up a front of confidence.

"Do you want to sit down and have breakfast? Sorry, there isn't much of a fire. I'm not the best at tending it overnight," Stirling says nonchalantly.

Amiria turns her head away, embarrassed at her thoughts. He was sighing at the fire, not at her.

"Sure," she mumbles, stepping across the middle of the cave to Stirling's camp.

Stirling scoots himself backward sitting cross-legged on the blanket cushioned by pine. Amiria carefully steps over Ignis' tail, who still hasn't moved a muscle. Only his eyes follow her movements.

Smiling up at Amiria, Stirling pats the spot beside him. She bites her lip hesitantly as he pulls the bag she had given him the week prior closer to him. He rummages through the contents removing a handful of berries. She is to become an official member of the Winged Cavalry in a matter of days; she should be able to handle having a one-on-one conversation with someone if she is to lead an entire team one day.

"You seem to be doing fine now," she points out, slowly lowering down beside Stirling.

Her legs tuck beneath her, and she leans heavily to the side, her body tilting away from him.

"Thanks, I'm getting the hang of the wilderness life. I do need to learn the whole catching animals part but I do know where some berry bushes are, and I stole some eggs from a bird's nest. When I was younger, my mother's best friend was an herbalist who taught me a lot, so I recognize plenty of edible roots and plants out here," Stirling says.

"Oh," Amiria says, remembering her thoughts about if she would even be able to feed herself if she lived on her own.

The Cavalry supplies the food in their packs when they are sent to their posts. She can't tell the difference between a poisonous plant and an edible one.

"What's that for?" she asks, referring to a thick log not much longer than it was wide.

"It's going to be for water. There's some streams not too far from here. I also found a nice spring, but it's a bit of a hike from here. So, I'm going to hollow it out to hold my water storage, so I won't have to make so many trips. Too bad there's not a spring in the cave." He tells her with a smile.

"Like an underground lake?" Amiria says, her voice barely over a whisper as she untucks her knees from beneath herself, pulling them up to her chest. She wraps her arms around her knees and sets her chin on top.

Shoving a handful of berries into his mouth, Stirling asks, "A what lake?"

Amiria becomes shy as she speaks. "I know we just met, but can I take you somewhere private and show you something personal of mine."

Stirling coughs, choking on his berries. Ignis lifts his head, giving Stirling a sideways glance as he slaps his chest with one hand and spits the berries out into the other. Amiria's lip curls halfway as she tries to hide the look of disgust as Stirling coughs out the word, "What?"

Other than being disturbed by Stirling spitting his food out into his hand Amiria disregards his reaction, explaining casually, "There's this secret spot of mine on one of the smaller adjacent islands. Most are too small to even bother but this one has some hidden wonders. I promised we would fly together and, well, we have to fly there. I've never told anyone about it, so you will be my first."

Smearing the berries in his hand on the ground, Stirling cocks his head at Amiria. "And what do I owe such an honor?"

Rolling her eyes, Amiria answers, "You shared a lot of personal stuff with me the first day we met, even though I tried to kill you. So I thought I'd share something with you. It's kind of like your cave here but you know…better."

"Oh? Where exactly is this so-called better place?" Stirling asks in a condescending tone.

Amiria almost leaps up from where she had been sitting uncomfortably. Stepping back over Ignis' tail, she walks up to the edge of the cave overlooking the ocean.

She blocks the sun's glare with her hand and points out to an island sitting on the horizon, a pyramid of rock on the edge of the water. "The dragon's nesting ground."

Stirling stretches his neck peaking around Ignis to get a view even though he has seen the island numerous times from the cave. "I thought it was uninhabitable," he brings up.

"It is but that doesn't mean you can't go there. It means it's not sustainable for human life," she explains as if Stirling is a child.

"I know what it means. I just assumed no one has ever gone over there." Stirling retorts, slipping on his shoes and lying beside his bag.

"Pretty much no one does, except for a monthly inspection by the Cavalry. But that is why I go. You being a renegade living in a cave, I thought you would be someone who understands why sometimes someone needs to escape." She crosses her arms, curling in on herself. "When you have to uphold a high standard criteria, you can't run away. People don't drop everything they've ever known on a whim. They're too afraid of the unknown. They're too afraid of King Dietrich. They will live by the rules whether they agree or not—to save their own neck," Amiria vents as if she has forgotten she isn't alone.

She feels vulnerable. She raises her shoulders to hide herself further. Maybe she had opened up just a tad too much.

With his head down, Stirling stops a few steps away from her as he fastens his belt around his waist. With his head tilted down, he glances up with his eyes through the mess of his sand-colored hair. His eyes are the color of a prairie changing seasons, a mixture of green and gold. Amiria feels her heart skip.

"Well then, let's go check this place out," Stirling says with a toothy grin.

Amiria can't help but return the smile.

"Taika!" she calls.

"Taika?" Stirling repeats.

"My dragon," Amiria confirms. A beige wyvern with a face riddled with spikes pokes its head up from below the mouth of the cave. "I wasn't sure about her coming in and startling you. So I had her wait outside."

"Say again?" Stirling says, raising an eyebrow.

"It's okay. Wyverns can hang on cliffsides by their talons for hours. They can even sleep like that." Amiria starts to explain before Stirling cuts her off.

"No, not that. I mean that–that dragon is a girl? She's just so…"

"Fierce? Scary? Intimidating? Are you saying those are not qualities a female can have? Or should they be prettier like your dragon over there—" Ignis perks up as Amiria continues with her defensive tangent. "All gleaming feathers and smooth scales."

Stirling puts his hands up in defense, knowing he struck a nerve and insights, "Oh no, they can definitely be terrifying."

"*Did she say I was pretty?*" Ignis butts in.

"Don't you start Ignis," Stirling says back.

"*You're just jealous because she didn't say you were pretty,*" Ignis brags.

Stirling blushes, "Get your pretty feathered butt up so I can get your harness on."

"You two talking is so fascinating," Amiria says with an admiring demeanor.

"Yeah, I guess, except now he's being all full of himself since you called him pretty," Stirling blurts.

"Well, he is pretty. In fact, he is actually beautiful. Like the last color in the sky before twilight," Amiria expands.

"Well, aren't you poetic?" Stirling says sarcastically.

"*Did you hear that Stirling? I'm a beautiful sunset,*" Ignis gloats.

Stirling groans. "And Ignis ruined it. You wouldn't be calling him pretty–"

"*Beautiful.*"

Stirling glares at him. "As I said, you wouldn't be calling him pretty if you had to listen to him all the time."

Amiria refrains herself from laughing. She can only hear one side of the conversation but the manner they appear to be talking to each other reminds her of how only best friends or siblings would speak to one another. Where you can be informal, rude, and downright insulting, but it's the fact that your love runs so deep that all the banter between you is still a form of endearment.

The pang of jealousy she had felt earlier returns to her like a sticker from a plant caught in her clothing jabbing at her side. She is going through vigorous training, yet he has accomplished something even in a lifetime of training she most likely won't be able to obtain. Though, she will admit that she has tried. Sitting alone away from the city with her dragon Taika, telling her about her day, her wishes, and her conflicts. She'll stare Taika in the eye, waiting for a reply that never comes.

She watches as Stirling loops the harness he made himself

around Ignis. Another realization ignites inside of her. Stirling is making his own choices in life. He is in charge of his outcome instead of following the path written on parchment for him. If he can do it, why can't she?

"All set," Stirling announces, tightening the last strap.

"Let's get going then." Amiria smiles.

Forty-One

The lapis-colored saltwater shimmers like gemstones in the sunlight. Amiria and Stirling are silent as they fly low above the water. They are over halfway to the island and neither one of them has said a word.

What does one talk about while flying together? Stirling tried to think of a topic to bring up but decided against it. He enjoys the silence while flying, just your thoughts and the sound of the wind as you break through the invisible mass.

Stirling subtly glances over at Amira. She is only a dragon's wingspan away. Ignis' and Taika's wing tips flying dangerously close to clipping.

So this is what it's like to fly alongside someone, he thinks to himself.

It resembles walking next to someone. When you are side by side, you feel equal. No one is leading the other. You are on this path together.

The island is larger than Stirring had pictured from the smudge on the horizon but is not much larger than the city of Lumierna. With the island now looming over him, he can see the hexagonal shapes of columnar joint rocks around the edges. There is no valley in the center like Wyverna. Instead, jagged andesite rocks surround the perimeter of the island, stacking up like a broken staircase to the highest peak far above sea level. The petrified ruins of a collapsed volcano.

Waving her hand, Amiria grabs Stirling's mesmerized attention, "We're going to land just past these cliffs. Then we'll go on foot from there."

They fly vertically, climbing the face of the island and over boulders the size of houses to a small gap of flat ground boxed in by walls of rock. The light gray colored terrain is harsh and barren. Stirling can't see much vegetation other than a few weeds popping through the cracks of dense stone.

Amiria pulls off the goggles she had replaced after giving Stirling hers. Clipping them to Taika's saddle, she unhooks herself and leaps off the back of her dragon. Pointing to a small channel between the boulders about shoulders width wide.

Amiria speaks over her shoulder to Stirling, "Come on baker boy. It's through this passage."

"Okay. But this better not be some sort of trap," he says, eyeing the narrow path, skeptical as he unclips himself and slowly slides off Ignis.

"Why would I want to trap you? Especially in such an elaborate way?" Amiria questions standing in the channel's entrance.

"You know, because I'm a wanted man and all," Stirling says, reaching her side.

"You're also documented as deceased already. I don't need to trap you to kill you. I could have just done that back in the cave where already no one will find you." Amiria smirks, skipping off down the narrow passage.

Unsettled, Stirling glances back at Ignis for reassurance, who only responds with a shrug. Taking a deep breath, he follows Amiria into the thin pathway. The open pocket and Ignis quickly disappear as the walls guide them away.

Following close behind Amiria, Stirling feels claustrophobic. The walls are barely wide enough for him to walk normally down the straight path. Every now and then, the rocks will change in shape and he has to squeeze past the uneven juts in the wall towering a story high. The sky, a blue ribbon above them.

"We're here," Amiria says after a long period of silence, halting in her tracks.

Stirling, who hasn't been paying attention, gazes up at the sky. He looks down in time to keep himself from running into her. He presses his palms against the rough wall as his body leans forward with the momentum left over from his sudden stop in movement. Being a head taller than she is, Stirling easily sees over her to glance at what she is referring to.

He doesn't understand. It's no different than what they've been walking through. They were still in this channel and it appears to be stretching on forever. The only difference now is a long crack in the ground with a section of the gap wide enough to fit yourself through.

"Um, wow. This is really something special. I particularly enjoy the cramped vibe it's got going on. Really adds to the ambiance," Stirling lies.

"No, you idiot. I'm talking about that," Amiria says, holding her hand out, referring to the hole in the ground. Kneeling down she motions Stirling to do the same. "Just listen."

Stirling squats down, the path being too narrow, and remains directly behind her. Hoping he doesn't bump into her, Stirling leans carefully over Amiria listening.

Water. He can hear the sound of rushing water. Even though he can't see it, there is water rushing below their feet.

"Is that a river?" he asks.

"An underground river," Amiria corrects. "Go ahead, climb in."

"Before this moment, I didn't even know about underground rivers. Now you want me to climb into one?" Stirling asks cautiously, trying to read Amiria's intentions on what she is getting him into.

"Where did you think springs come from?" she asks.

"Umm...underground rivers?" Stirling guesses.

She turns around halfway to face him. Her ebony eyes are soft, unlike the severe sharpness he had associated with her to always have when he watched her classes. He is close enough to see she has a few light freckles speckled across her nose and cheekbones forming constellations.

"You're going to have to trust me, okay?" she tells him.

Stirling locks his eyes with hers. They lag, lingering on her as his head turns to the gap, his heart beginning to race with fear in his chest, "Why don't you go first."

"Don't be a chicken. Maybe you should have stayed a baker if something simple as this scares you," Amiria says, egging him on.

Standing up, Amiria presses herself against the wall allowing Stirling enough room to squeeze past her.

Stirling frowns. She didn't need to make a comment like that but it worked. "Fine, I'll go."

Stirling sits back on his butt and inches himself closer to the gap letting his feet fall inside. He needs to prove to her whatever she can do, so can he. Carefully lowering himself into the hole, Stirling stands with his shoulders still above the ground. He can feel the water flowing around his ankles begging him to come along.

"Just sit and go." Amiria encourages, "Trust me, let go."

Stirling nods nervously, lowering himself slowly and gently into a sitting position in the water. His hands press firmly against the slick walls, keeping him stationary while the water pushes against him. He tilts his head back, the light bright in his eyes. Amiria peers down at him through the opening above smiling, the sunlight a halo around her.

Her smile is different from previous times. She reminds him of a child sharing their prized possession or playing a game with their friends full of pure merriment. Stirling doesn't take his eyes off her as he releases his hands from the wall, the image of Amiria vanishing as he's whisked away into the dark tunnel.

Water splashes over Stirling's face finding its way into his nose and mouth, depriving him of being able to take a proper breath. He feels helpless as the water carries him blindly speeding along the gulch. Dragging his hands along the wall, he tries to slow down, but with everything around him smooth from the countless years of erosion, there is no hope.

Then he is weightless.

Falling from a chute in the ceiling of an enormous cavern filled with a freshwater lake, Stirling doesn't have time to muster out a scream before he hits the water sinking deep below the surface.

He remains there, floating halfway between the surface and the bed of the lake. His hair flows with the water's movements like meadow grass waving in the wind. He stares up at the ceiling he had fallen from giving off a blue shimmering light in a trance. If he didn't know that he was underground, and it is not even midday, he would truly believe it is the night sky.

Another splash breaks the steadiness of the water, distorting the blue light above. Amiria sinks into the water as Stirling did, her hair fanning out around her. She hangs suspended in time. With his attention changing from one wonder to the next, Stirling turns his stupor in her direction. She gives a small smile and swims directly back to the surface without stopping to gaze up at the stars.

Bubbles escape from Stirling's mouth as his lungs beg for air. Giving into the need, Stirling follows Amiria. Breaking through the surface beside her, Stirling gasps, gulping in the oxygen.

Amiria raises an eyebrow, "Did you stay down there the entire time? I just realized I never asked you if you could swim. It's not usual for commoners, is it?"

"Thanks for thinking of my safety. This commoner is self-taught by the way." Stirling answers.

"Of course you are," is all Amiria replies knowing Stirling has been able to teach himself everything he knows.

"I was in some sort of trance. It was so…" Stirling begins but stops as Amiria starts to giggle.

"Before you finish, try looking up now," she insists as she tilts her head up to the ceiling.

Following her gaze. his jaw drops in astonishment. Stirling sees clearly now the ceiling of the cavern really *is* glowing. He can get lost in the serene surroundings; clusters of dots lighting the cave with a blue hue, the crystal clear water reflecting the pattern above almost perfectly as they tread peacefully beside one another.

Amiria studies Stirling as he beholds the cave in wonder. His hair, heavy with water is no longer sticking up in random directions, now hangs flat against his head, the ends beginning to curl, especially around his ears. Turning her head quickly, she pretends she is also taking in the sight around them as Stirling turns to her.

"What causes the glowing?"

"I don't know. I've wanted to ask my father or maybe someone like a scribe but I don't want them to know I've been sneaking off to this place instead of training. I like to think of it as magic," Amiria admits.

As Stirling listens to Amiria talk, he notices how the light reflects off the water droplets creating the illusion she is sparkling. She doesn't seem threatening anymore. Yes, she makes some insulting and crude comments now and then but so does Ignis. He isn't afraid she might pull a dagger on him anymore. Instead, she is—

"Beautiful." Slips out of Stirling's mouth before he can catch it.

"What was that?" She asks, treading closer to him so she can hear him better, leaning in with curiosity.

Stirling's stomach twists as he stumbles, clarifying, "The cavern, it's, it's beautiful. How did you find this place?"

Amiria's face drops. "By accident one day."

Slowing her tread, she sinks until the water is up to her nose and she soundlessly breaststrokes away. Hanging back momentarily, Stirling wonders if it was something he said.

Waist deep in the water, Amiria stops swimming. She finds footing in the fine sand and she walks up onto a sandbar at the edge of the cavern. Lying down on the soft ground, she stares unblinking, her eyes fixated on the glow of the ceiling. She can hear Stirling's clumsy steps splashing through the shallow water.

"Can dragons talk to one another, like how you and Ignis talk to each other?" She inquires without taking her eyes away from the glowing dots.

Stirling drops down beside her. He remains sitting with one leg extending and the other bent with his arm resting on top.

"Sort of. I asked Ignis the same question. It's the same but different, they are able to communicate with each other but it's not with our words. What I'm guessing is, when they speak to us, they are borrowing knowledge of the language from the person with whom they've bonded," Stirling explains.

Amiria nods. "Interesting."

The two of them sit in silence, the only sound coming from the water raining down from the chute they had fallen from.

Amiria unexpectedly sits up. "I found this place by accident."

"You've already said that," Stirling interrupts.

Amiria scowls at him before continuing, "I found this place by accident because it was after I had finally learned how to fly and my father was putting me through all this extra training before and after my classes. I would be dragged out of bed by my private tutor and trained until I was granted permission to crash from exhaustion at night. I wasn't even permitted a break until I performed to the standards my tutor set.

"Frustrated, I took off. I wanted a break. I needed to get as far away as I could, away from my duties, away from—everyone. Then I fell through that hole in the ground. For the first time, I didn't know the direction I was going in. I was scared. Even after I fell in here, I thought I was going to die. Trapped, not a single person knew where I had gone. I thought about my short life and was any of it worth it. Was I satisfied with it? No—"

She shakes her head. "I despised it. Don't get me wrong. I want to be part of the Winged Cavalry." She drops her gaze to the sand. "Sometimes I would like to slow down, enjoy life—before it most likely ends early—and I don't know, maybe have some more control over it? It is mine, isn't it?" Her eyes flit over to him. Stirling nods in agreement. Amiria sighs, "You're doing exactly what I've always wanted to do."

"What is that?"

"Living how you want to."

Stirling stays there, his shoulders hunched with his arm still resting on his knee. The other lay in his lap as he registers what Amiria is telling him. She is exposing a side he would never have guessed she had before he met her. He has always perceived her as a prude, too good to be around other people, and obsessed with being the best. He had misjudged her completely. He only saw her at surface level, saw the person she wanted to be seen. But now he sees the raw version of her. In reality, they are the same. Living a life that society had assigned them. How many others out there share this same view?

"It's funny," Stirling mutters.

Amiria scoffs. "What's so funny about me opening up to you?"

"No, it's not that. I actually admire you for the opposite reason. You were given everything I wanted, but I had to sneak around breaking the rules to acquire it," he says.

It dawns on Amiria, both of them aspire to be like the other. Their actions are that of Ouroboros, the symbol of the serpent eating itself. An infinite cycle of one's actions causes the other to react in kind completing the cycle.

"I never thought I would have so much in common with a peasant," she says, scrunching her nose at the last word.

Stirling shakes his head, insulted. "I'm not a peasant. I'm a commoner. Well, I was. But you don't have to feel ashamed. I don't have a lot in common with my assigned class anyway. So I'm not really sure where that puts us."

"Some branch off on its own?" Amiria adds.

"Yeah, a broken and gangly one," Stirling jokes. His smile fades and his eyes glaze over as he stares out across the water. Ripples spread across the glowing surface of the water, making the blue dots appear to dance to the sound of the waterfall. "I wonder what else is out there?" Stirling says in a distant tone as if his mind is far away.

"What do you mean?" Amiria questions.

"I've never been off our island before. Our island is massive. I've never even been to the northern side of the port. I've only been as far as the center when I was really young." Stirling continues to stare into the distance.

"You can't even see Uviktiland from here. I only know it's there from the maps I've seen and what I've been told. But the maps don't show much further than their coast. So, I wonder what is *really* out there," he finishes.

"I've been to Uviktiland, the main city, Vistjaldenne. It's not that great," Amiria admits.

"Why is that?" Stirling asks, intrigued.

"It's, the people there—especially around the port—were begging for all kinds of things. Money and food mostly. There were people with rags for clothing, people with open sores all over their bodies, and people who were no more than skin and bone sleeping on the ground. People doing unthinkable acts to make mere pocket change.

"Our nation is wealthy. The wyvernites are more valuable than you can imagine. Just a thumbnails amount of the crystal can buy a whole ship's worth of supplies. So we get the best of our own products and the best of theirs. Hence why the Cavalry was created, that empire took land, homes, and lives from our people once before. We weren't going to let it happen again. Maybe the rules they made really are for the better. We have an extremely healthy economy," Amiria explains.

"I never knew that. I heard our economy was well off, but I never knew the extent of Uviktiland. So I had nothing to compare," Stirling says, hanging his head. "Maybe I'm the fool. Maybe the way the kingdom is–is for the better."

Regret settles inside Stirling as he draws spirals in the sand beside him.

"Maybe it only appears better on the outside. Yes, Uviktiland is riddled with poverty but if you have a talent or gift, you're allowed to pursue yourself in it. You aren't forced into a job despite what you want. They and their families' lives aren't threatened if they deviate. They can choose to beg for money or they can choose to search for work," Amiria says, reassuring Stirling, who nods his head.

"Sure. But it doesn't stop me from wondering if maybe I am the one who is wrong."

"*Hey, Stirling,*" Ignis' voice pops into Stirling's head, who immediately perks up.

Amiria eyes him suspiciously.

"*Yeah?*" he replies, not knowing what it could be about.

"When are you heading back? Taika is creeping me out. She keeps staring at me, all spikey scary face, not much of a conversationalist," Ignis tells him.

"Seriously?" Stirling groans, dragging out the word. He is learning a lot about who Amiria is as a person. He doesn't want to go back yet. *"Fine, we'll head back."*

Stirling turns to Amiria, who is studying him with a confused expression. "That was Ignis. Your dragon is scaring him."

Her expression changes to a proud smirk. "That's my girl."

Glancing around the cave, Stirling asks, "How do we get out of here anyway?"

"Well, the water has to escape somehow, doesn't it? Otherwise, this place would be filled to the top," Amiria says.

Stirling stares, waiting for her to reveal the answer and skip the guessing game. "There's a tunnel over there," she answers.

Stirling examines the direction Amiria is pointing in. Less than half of the tunnel peaks above the water, a dark dome resting on the surface like a turtle's shell.

He turns back to Amiria, slightly peeved. "We could have swam here? Why the whole *slip and slide to my death* thing?"

Amiria shrugs, lifting the shoulder closest to Stirling to her cheek, accompanied by a mischievous smile. "I wanted you to experience it the way I did for the first time. Experience the fear, the confusion, and the wonder of it all." She pushes up and stands over Stirling. He stares at the hand offered out to him. "Come on, let's go then. Your dragon is crying for you."

Rolling his eyes at the comment, Stirling accepts her hand, letting her help him to his feet. The two of them swim across the lake into the tunnel. The low ceiling is only an arm's reach away, leaving the shimmering cavern behind.

"What's with tunnels always having to be pitch black? Can't one be lit for once? Maybe with more of those glowing dots," Stirling mutters under his breath as he slowly strokes through the water behind Amiria.

The ground gradually rises below their feet.

Ignis is perched on a rock jutting out of the ocean near the cliff face of the island. Taika's talons grip the opening of the tunnel, her body pinned to the wall above it. She peaks her head into the human size hole in the wall with a steady stream of water pouring out.

Ignis wags the tip of his tail at the sight of Stirling emerging from the shadows ankle-deep in water. His body hunched over with his hand tapping along the ceiling, careful to keep his head from hitting any rocks deciding to hang lower than the rest. Amiria strolls next to him, her height barely affected by the tunnel.

He puts his hand up to block the light of the sun, squinting while his eyes adjust, "Ignis, get over here so we can go."

"Noo, I don't think so. How about you come here." Ignis says not moving from his perch.

Stirling steps to the edge of the tunnel, the rocks slippery with algae. The water lapping up from the ocean gives off the impression the current below is strong and the dark royal blue warns you of the depth.

"How do you expect me to do that? You want me to swim to you?"

Ignis lifts his chin. *"Well, yeah. I'm not getting into the water. It's cold and my wings will get wet. I don't have talons to go climbing vertical walls like that. So, you're going to have to come to me. Plus you're already drenched."*

Stirling's eyes practically roll back into his head, his clothes clinging to his body as he listens to Ignis list his excuses. Ignis doesn't move any more than to adjust his feet remaining comfortably on his rock.

Stirling sees Amiria shake her head, ignoring his banter

with Ignis. She reaches up to Taika out of the corner of his eye while he starts to ring out the bottom of his tunic, his hair already beginning to dry. He does a double take as Amiria lifts herself off the ground, hanging from Taika's saddle.

"Wait, you can get on your dragon—" Stirling turns his head all the way sideways. "—upside down?"

Pulling her legs into her chest, Amiria grips the saddle, acrobatically raising them above herself, and places them into the braces. Her knees lock into place and her hips press into the saddle's horn. Taika pushes her head and chest away from the wall so she isn't completely vertical anymore, alleviating some of the strain on Amiria.

"A rider must learn how to mount their dragon under any circumstance," she brags, nodding her head over to Ignis. "If you can catch up, we can fly back together."

As she finishes her sentence Taika turns, scampering up the wall for a better height advantage, and launches off into the air leaving Stirling at the tunnel alone.

Stirling grins as he dances back and forth on his feet with the excitement of a race. "Ignis, come on, let's go! We need to catch up!"

"*If you care so much, you can come here,*" Ignis says stubbornly.

"AGH! IGNIS!" Stirling shouts, bouncing back and forth. He sees Amiria's shape shrinking as she leaves them behind, then back at Ignis, throwing his head and shoulders back in defeat, "UGH!"

Amiria slows her pace as she glances behind her, noticing Stirling approaching, his hair drying into messy curls and his re-soaked clothing beginning to dry in the airflow.

"I guess you won't have to fly alone after all," she shouts to him.

Stirling shakes the saltwater from this hair. "Yeah, no thanks to Ignis."

Stirling can feel himself smiling internally. He refuses to let the emotion surface for her to see. He knows she is faster than him. In reality, he could never have caught up to her. She would have left him in the dust with no hope of catching up, but she didn't.

Coming upon the cave, Stirling and Ignis land gripping the side and climbing directly inside, while Amira and Taika hang on the edge halfway. Stirling unhooks himself and slides off the back of Ignis and steps over to Amiria, who remains seated on Taika's back. He is close enough to feel the warmth coming off the female dragon, her muscles flexing and moving as she holds herself from a watery death.

Amiria's face is around the same height as his now.

His fingers tap near his leg. He needs to ask her something, but he can only get his voice to come out in a nervous hush, "Hey, I know we're still getting to know each other, but can I ask you for a favor?"

"Depends on what it is," she responds.

Through his light eyelashes, his eyes are wide and pleading. "Can you check on my father for me? I want to make sure he is doing okay."

She stares at him reading and searching for his undertone intentions. Does he have remorse, does he miss his home, or is it purely curiosity? His expression is strong and serious, but his eyes give away his heart. He is someone who grew up adapting his lifestyle of needing to conceal himself from the world, turning him into an excellent liar.

Right here in front of her, his mask is cracking. He is revealing himself to her. He is a child just like her. He is lost, hurting, and asking for help. She is trained to protect her kingdom but it makes her happy to be asked for something at such a personal level because that's something *friends* do for each other.

"Fine, but only under one condition," Amiria states, playing it down as if she isn't glad to do him a favor.

"Sure, what is it?" Stirling shrugs.

"Don't you ever go doing anything stupid to get yourself caught. You hear me, baker boy? Ever."

"What?"

"Swear to me and I'll go check on your father," she tells him, pointing her finger in his face.

He straightens his back holding his head high with a pleased smile. "I swear."

Amiria holds her hand out to him. He stares at it. She holds firm. "It's to finalize our agreement." Smiling, Stirling shakes on their deal.

"*Awe, she cares*," Ignis teases.

With his finger still twisted around Amiria's, Stirling begins to blush. He hastily lets go, feigning a cough to cover up his reddened cheeks before she notices. She smiles at his poor attempt before giving Taika a whistle and they leap from the edge sailing into the air. Their figures disappear around the mountaintop.

Stirling turns back to Ignis, "*Shut up, Ignis.*"

Forty-Two

The bakery appears incredibly ordinary to Amiria as she steps up to the front door wearing her practice gear of leather armor. The baker's guild sign hangs above the door as the only decipher between this and its neighbors. It is just another shop crammed amongst the multitude in the market. She would never have thought anything different of it, of the baker working hard inside if she hadn't met Stirling. She would have never come to this part of town at all if it hadn't been for Stirling, not when she can send the hired help to do the shopping and cooking. She's never stepped foot into either the pantry or the larder. She wouldn't even know where to start with replenishing the stock.

Even when it comes to her clothing, her family has a personal tailor who does house calls and measures her. She can see why her peers never step foot in the lower-class districts; the condensed buildings and narrow roads are claustrophobic, there is an unknown liquid running along the road even though it hasn't rained in over a week, trash is thrown out beside doorsteps, and animal waste lay smeared in lines as it gets repeatedly run over by carts. Then there is the foul pungent odor. She can't blame Stirling for running away. This place is suffocating.

She glances over her shoulder at the townspeople huddled together, eyeing her. She knows from the Cavalry's investigation, that the bakery she needed was somewhere around this block but to find out the exact building she had to ask a few of the locals for directions. They must be as nosy as the noble man's wives, sitting around the solar, speaking ill of those who aren't up to their standards. She wonders what kind of rumor these people will be spreading about her wanting to visit Giles Bakere after he had been confirmed innocent of his son's recent death.

Shaking off her thoughts and the people watching, she pushes open the door. The door opens too easily. Amiria is met face-to-face with a middle-aged woman on the threshold. They stop before colliding with each other.

"My apologies," Amiria says, stepping back from the door to let the woman pass.

The woman acts mystified as she stares eye-to-eye with Amiria. Their matching dark eyes meet for a brief moment before the woman shyly tucks a strand of her black hair behind her ear. Ducking her head, she slips past Amiria. Out of habit, Amiria's eyes dart to the woman's insignia, reading the spinner's occupation.

Remaining in the doorway, Amiria continues to watch, perplexed by the peculiar behavior of the woman. Hunching, she shuffles away down the market, glancing over her shoulder now and then to look back at Amiria.

"It's like that spinster woman has never seen someone from the Cavalry before," she says. Brushing the encounter off, she lets herself into the bakery.

Glancing around, she inspects the room. So, this is where he grew up. This room is no different in size than her bedroom.

She breathes in the delectable fresh bread aroma as she wonders what it was like to grow up here. Would she have run away the same as Stirling or would she have enjoyed the simplicity of this life? A family all working together to run their quaint shop, instead of her father, the Field Marshal who is never home, and her mother. Her mother had passed when pirates tried to infiltrate a trading vessel she was running security on. She saved the crew and the cargo, but she gave up her life in the process. That was the life for someone in the Winged Cavalry, always ready to die for your kingdom even if it leaves behind your five-year-old daughter.

A scruffy man with brown hair stands facing the shelves compiled with different loaves of rye and barley, biscuits, pretzels, and a few treats like date loaves and gingerbread. His unsteady hands fumble as he pulls the product closer to the front.

"How may I help you today?" Brown eyes, puffy and red from recently crying, turn to her.

His facial features are mundane, another citizen she wouldn't second glance at but there, in the structure of his face, she sees Stirling. The way his eyes turn down as if he is always worried, or how his nose is a little too big. She can see it there in the structure of his jawbone.

Giles sputters at the sight of her uniform. He spins back around and grips the shelves for support, "I–I don't want any more trouble."

"I'm sorry sir, I'm not here on any dealings." Amiria says calmly, "I'm here to purchase a pretzel."

Giles rigidly checks over his shoulder and grimaces. The sight of the Cavalry emblem tearing new holes in his heart, "I–please, just please leave. I–"

Amiria hears the splintering of wood. She gasps as the shelf Giles is hanging onto tears free from the wall spewing the baked goods onto the ground. Giles catches himself on the counter.

"Are you all right?" Taking a step forward, Amiria extends out her hand.

"I can't–" Giles' words catch thick in his throat. He picks up a loaf of gingerbread from the falling shelf and holds it to his chest. Tears begin to flow down his cheek and catch in his beard, "I can't do this."

A small hand appears on his shoulder. Sniffing back the mucus running from his nose, he meets the gaze of the young girl with dark round eyes.

"It's okay. Whatever it is, it's going to be okay." Her smile is small but it speaks a thousand words. A smile showing she means the words she is saying, a smile more genuine than the haphazard condolences from his neighbors.

He has heard them talking in huddled groups. A problem child they called Stirling. Bad parenting, they blamed Giles. Lost his wife and now his son, what a pity. The nails of his free hand dig into the wood counter. It's not his fault, he tried to protect Stirling, to keep him safe at home. It's their fault. He wanted to be like them. He glares down at the Cavalry emblem on the girl's leather armor. No, it's his fault for pushing him away. He had failed as a father.

Giles pulls away letting her hand hang in midair. He side steps away, the gingerbread still pressed to his chest. Amiria's smile drops alongside her hand. Wiping the tears from his eyes, he faces the broken shelf as he speaks, "Take what you need, free of charge. Please, just please leave."

Amiria's eyes begin to water at the sight of the broken father. He's shattered like broken pottery. You can glue the pieces back together but the fissures will always be there. She wants to tell him the truth. She knows she can help him, she can make it stop hurting, but she will only jeopardize him if the Cavalry ever comes back to interrogate him further. In his current state of mind, he won't be lying when he tells them he doesn't know where his son is and believes he is dead.

Understanding her uniform is what is causing Giles' distress, Amiria crosses her arms in an awkward attempt to hide the gear. "I'm sorry," She utters.

Giles takes several smaller steps away, the gingerbread in his hand beginning to crumble as he coddles it against his chest. Refusing to lay eyes on her, Giles points at the pretzels stacked on the still-intact shelf. Amiria's lips tuck into a thin line, her gaze dropping off to the side. She's doing more harm than good being here. She reaches into a velvet coin purse on her hip. She sets a stack of coins on the counter, enough to repair the shelving and pay for the spoiled food on the floor. Reaching up, she takes a soft pretzel.

"Thank you." She hunches her shoulders holding the pretzel close and backs up towards the door, "I'm sorry." She softly tells him and spins around.

Pausing at the door, she checks back at the grieving father as he slowly lowers himself to the ground, careful not to crush the gingerbread in his hand. Her lip quivering at the image, she removes herself from the bakery she plans on returning to. Someone has to help the baker who lost his support stand back up.

Forty-Three

The throne room is a vast hall with a stunning display of pewter gray granite flooring and towering pillars holding up the heavy vaulted ceiling several stories above them. The whitewashed walls with gold trim are painted with elegant depictions telling the history of their ancestors fleeing the old land to the island, which is only a fragment of what their nation used to be. There is an entire section of the wall dedicated to how their ancestors learned to tame the dragons and protect themselves so that never again will their land be stripped from them.

The smell of spring wafts through the room from freshly cut flowers in hand-painted vases of white and gold placed beside the red-painted oak benches lining the walls. Rainbows of light give life to the granite floor as the sun shines through the mosaic windows two stories tall.

At the end of the hall is the throne set higher than the rest on a vaulted granite dais. King Ealdian Dietrich, a broad man in his late thirties with well-groomed hair and a beard with the beginnings of graying sits leaning back on his throne made of wyvern dragon bones.

Ribs lined side by side rise above his head like an ocean wave ready to crash. Each of the throne's feet ends with the talons clawing into the ground. Vertebrae run down the right and left side of the throne's ribbed back to the ground where the tail bones swoop out away from the throne and curves back, so the tips of the tails point to each other in front of King Dietrich.

Sitting perched on top of the vertebrae sides, rest two skulls watching out in the opposite direction. Their jaws carefully wired opened in an everlasting roar. Glinting in each of the eye sockets are wyvernite crystals made from dragon bones heated to a precise degree only reached by the inferno breath of a wyvern.

With their arms crossed behind their backs, Amiria and her four classmates; Clyde, Nellie, Garret, and Warrick stand before King Dietrich in an attentive stance. She runs her eyes down the plush red carpet flowing down the steps of the dais from the throne like a waterfall of blood.

King Dietrich's scrutinizing glare falls heavy upon them from his seat of bones. His eyes gleam like the wyvernite stones set in the dragon skulls. Out of the corner of her eye, she can see the family members standing eagerly to see where their child will be placed. The captains are split evenly to each side of the dais facing the new recruits.

Field Marshal Rey, Amiria's father, and the General second in command stand closest to King Dietrich on either side. Their golden gambesons stand bright along the line of dark purple worn by captains. General Gautier, a woman with a pinched face, glares at Field Marshal Rey.

He takes one step forward, his heels snapping together with his back straight, "You have been brought here today to witness another class of brave warriors commit their lives to save the citizens of Wyverna. We the Winged Riders of Wyverna stand tall and fly high, honored to protect and serve this glorious kingdom. As their parents before them and their grandparents before them, these Riders have been training their entire life to be chosen to be part of the units that form the Winged Cavalry. Spread out across this land, they are separated by distance but in alignment with their integrity and their goals." His eyes scan the room and the members of Amiria's class. "We have taken in consideration not only your scores from your evaluations but your growth over the years to find the team most suitable for your contribution." His eyes fall upon her as he finishes his sentence.

She locks eyes with him, holding herself proud. Today is the day, Amiria thinks to herself. Today she will join Unit Castra in protecting the southeastern part of Wyverna, their jurisdiction is Lumierna, the base, and the surrounding lands. This includes the mountains touching the castle's back gates where Stirling has taken up occupancy. She will be stationed here at the home base and follow her father's direct orders preparing her to take his place as Field Marshal.

"And now you have the privilege to be addressed and provided your new placements by our majesty, King Dietrich." Field Marshal Rey turns about face and stiffly bows to the king. "Your Majesty."

King Dietrich nods at him in reply. Field Marshal Rey molds back into line, hardening into a statue.

King Dietrich's voice bellows across the room, amplified by the room's acoustics. "Nellie Gregory, step forth." He remains seated, reading from a parchment in one hand and waving her forward with the other in an almost bored manner. "Lady Gregory, you have been chosen for Unit Portus stationed in outpost Kitlsbo overseeing the trading docks. For what you lack in physical strength, you make up with your keen and watchful eye."

The captain of Nellie's new unit steps out of line and strides over. He shakes her hand firmly with congratulations and pins her division's crest onto the left side of her navy-colored cotehardie, the garment favored by women in the

Cavalry for its ability to be form-fitting and elegant without wearing a dress.

"You may step back in line," King Dietrich ushers. Nellie bows, taking her place in line as he reads off the next name. "Clyde Mannering, step forth."

Swallowing nervously, Clyde takes a single step forward. "Sir Mannering, your flying and combat skills are not up to par with the level required for the front line. You will remain here patrolling the castle grounds and monitoring the citizens' behavior in the city as Lieutenant in Lumierna's guards."

Utter shock flashes across his face. Fighting back the tears of his demotion Clyde holds up his chin as the Captain of his new guard unit pins their crest onto his jopula. Turning about face, he catches Amiria's eye. She can hear the hiss of breath through his teeth.

Amiria waits patiently as her two other classmates, Gareth and Warrick are called and assigned their new units.

Her heart skips a beat as she finally hears, "Amiria Rey, step forth."

This is it, she thinks to herself.

Where she is to be placed is obvious. She was going to be placed in Unit Castra, her father's old unit, as was her mother's, her grandparents, and the Reys before them. The unit that stands above the rest. The unit that produces Generals, Brigadiers, and Field Marshals. The position no other family has held the title of. It has always been her bloodline and it always will be. It is her birthright.

The King is leaning forward in his chair for the first time during the entire ceremony. His eyes scan the length of Amiria's body, "Miss Amiria Rey. You have received the highest marks of your generation, as we expected as an offspring from two of our top riders. You have been chosen by me for my personal guard."

What? Amiria is thrown off. *A guard? Only a guard?*

Why would I be demoted to stand with the guards like Clyde?

She tries to mask her confusion rising to the surface of her face like an undesirable blemish for fear of disrespecting King Dietrich. He personally wants her to watch over him. She should be honored.

A man that is not the captain of Unit Castra steps out of line to pin her with her new crest. The man's dark hair is combed back, exposing the ghostly gray color of his face, as if his olive skin hasn't been in the sun for years. His eyes are crystal blue, but they don't shine. They are flat and dull. The eyes of someone who has not only seen the light fade from enemies' eyes on the battlefield but also his comrades.

His pale eyes burrow into her as he pins the unfamiliar crest to her cotehardie. His lips, already a straight taught line, disappear as he pulls back the corners into a smile.

"We've been waiting for our next prodigy. Welcome to Unit Larua." His voice is barely audible.

Amiria remains fixated on the carpeted stairs in front of her as he speaks to her. From her peripheral, she can see the General. Her eyes latch on to her as she receives her pin, then she smiles as if she knows something Amiria doesn't. Amiria disregards the General, unable to see her father around the broad shoulders of the Major who pinned her.

Who is this man? The pin on his chest states he's a Major. Captains welcome the initiates, no one higher has time for this other than her father and the General. She has have never seen him or the crest before. *Unit Larua...Ghost? Ghost Unit?* Amiria wonders.

She bows appropriately and steps back in line. Her scores were top of the charts. The King had proved it by announcing it to everyone here. So, then how was she not selected for her father's old unit? Why was she chosen to stay in the castle over protecting the entire kingdom from those who try to harm it?

Her eyes drift to the spectators watching from the walls. She doesn't recognize any of these people. They aren't her family. They aren't her friends. The only family she has is her father and that is stretching the definition of family. The only friend she has. She thinks of Stirling. Does he consider them friends?

Her eyes stop on a young man with the same dark hair and light eyes as the mysterious Major. But his skin still has life and his eyes still shine. She recognizes him, it's the older boy from her evaluation, Calix Gautier. Who is he here to see? The graduation is by invitation only. Is he here because of the General? She catches him staring at her, but he doesn't break the gaze, his eyes unblinking. Amiria pulls away first, quickly diverting to the girl beside him. A shiver runs down Amiria's spine when she sees the uncanny smile on the girl's face.

She can hear the clinking sounds of the king's jeweled hands against the bone armrest as he lifts his towering body from the throne. Her eyes jump away from the girl, latching onto the shifting silk robes to keep herself from wandering back.

After generations of selective breeding, the kings have produced hulking men, each bigger than the last. King Dietrich's robes drape over his body, concealing his mass, pooling around his slippered feet. "And this concludes our initiation ceremony. May we give these young Riders a round of applause for their official entry into the Winged Cavalry. Welcome new warriors."

The King lightly taps his fingers on the palm of his opposing hand as the onlookers join in.

Amiria's class bows one final time in unison, holding the pose for exaggerated respect until King Dietrich announces, "You are now dismissed. A feast will be held in the grand hall for those who wish to join."

The light clapping subsides. Everyone remains standing in their current positions as the king stalks down the short dais stopping momentarily to eye Amiria before departing the room without another word, guards in tow.

Field Marshal Rey stands idle as the captains' formation breaks. General Gautier steps closer to the Major who had pinned Amiria and leans into his ear whispering. She glances at Calix, then at Amiria. Watching, Amiria can feel the tips of her ears warming as if she is being talked about.

Surrounded by praising parents and congratulations, Amiria stares across the room at her father in fear of the reprimand she will receive. Taking over his position is the whole reason she was born. He points to a secluded space in the corner of the throne room. Setting her jaw Amiria walks around the merry groups to meet with her father.

Stopping in front of him, she retakes an attentative stance with her arms crossed behind her back.

He reaches out and flicks the crest pinned to her. "I can't believe him."

Huh? Amiria is unable to determine the emphasis in her father's voice. Is he upset? Is he mad? At her? Whose him?

"Sir? I don't understand." Keeping her shoulders pulled taught, Amiria removes her hands from behind her back halfway relaxing her stance. She taps the crest, "Unit Larua? My scores were top of my generation. King Dietrich said that himself. How was I demoted?"

"King Dietrich's guards aren't what you think. I guess I owe you a *congratulations*."

"Congratulations?" Her composure slips. Her lips part as her jaw slacks. She stares up bewildered. She can't recall a time her father gave her words of approval. During the brief and rare moments they interacted, all she would hear from him is that he didn't have time and she can use some improvement.

"Congratulations Amiria." Her father's words are almost a sigh, "The King's Guards, Unit Larua, is a special operations group for classified and covert missions."

"Pardon?" Her head shakes slightly, her mind refusing to comprehend. "Special operations?"

"Yes." He's starting to sound annoyed, "Many of their dealings, I'll never know the details of." Amiria can see the detest in his eyes. He never liked it when King Dietrich gave the Cavalry orders, and this is a team he has sole command of. "You should take this as an honor. They haven't recruited a new member in five years."

She has managed to exceed even her own expectations, but she doesn't feel proud of herself. She wanted to learn under her father's wing. She wanted to work beside *him*, not King Dietrich. However, she should be honored as her father said. King Dietrich believes she is adequate enough to join the top riders in his personal guard, but she doesn't know how she feels about this.

"Come, Amiria, before the feast grows cold," her father directs, motioning for her to follow him.

She is going to be living a life full of all kinds of secrets. Will there be any part of her that is real to the world? Will anyone know all of her anymore? *Stirling.* Stirling, who is one of her secrets. He is the only person who will truly know her.

"Yes, sir." Amiria nods, following him along with the rest of the small crowd to the corridor leading to the grand hall.

One step past the threshold of the exit, she is caught by Clyde waiting in the corridor. He pushes himself off the wall he is leaning on beside the door.

"Explain to me," he starts. Amiria pauses, bringing her shoulders to her ears. Reluctant, she turns to him. Her father eyes them for a moment but carries on, following the savory smells wafting from the banquet hall. Clyde continues, "Explain to me why you get to have it all?"

Tucking away the introverted girl, Amiria brings out the Rider in her to confront him. She drops her shoulders and squares off to him, "I'm not following what you are getting at?"

Clyde's tone is bitter, rotted by years of disdain. "At first

I was elated to see you too, didn't make the mark, that you're not training to be Field Marshal beside your father, but then I was informed by Nellie on a secret only graduates of the Winged Cavalry know about, and of course…" He throws his hands in exaggeration. "You get picked for this special little team."

She keeps her face flat and emotions in check, "While you were having fun with your friends, I was training. So, you're wrong. I don't have it all." Amiria turns on her heel, leaving Clyde to boil in his loathing fumes.

"Your Majesty?" Field Marshal Rey addresses King Dietrich, the room behind him lively with the chatter and celebration of the new graduates.

"Yes, Field Marshal?" He sits upon an elegant golden chair accented with wyvern ivory. The royal family's table is raised on a small dais at the head of the banquet hall. He will remain there overseeing his guests as platters of food are brought to him upon his request.

The queen, Oriana Dietrich, sits beside him. She is unfazed by the Field Marshal. Her attention is absorbed in wiping the baby prince's face as he grabs a handful of mashed carrots. Two small princesses squirm in their chairs whining for their mother's attention. Rey stands at the bottom of the three steps keeping his focus on his king. He motions with his hands a request to step up closer.

King Dietrich waves, his hand beckoning. "Yes, Field Marshal, step up."

Field Marshal Rey waits until he is directly across from King Dietrich, only the table separating them. His eyes drift to the queen and their three young children, the eldest being around five. He promptly returns his gaze to King Dietrich. "I apologize ahead of time, and I am honored by the decision, but what made you change Amiria's assignment? She was approved to be part of Unit Castra to train by my side as the next Field Marshal."

King Dietrich's eyes quickly find Amiria as if he already knew where she is standing alone in the corner. He watches her pick at a plate of herb-rubbed chicken and several of the side dishes, "I want the best of the best on my team." His eyes flick back to Field Marshal Rey, "Do you have a problem with my decision, Field Marshal?"

"No, sire." He pauses. "It's just abnormal for someone in line for a leadership role to not start their training as soon as possible."

"Do you believe your daughter needs an exorbitant amount of time to train as Field Marshal? Do you believe she is not gifted in what she does?" The King's crafty words are underhanded. He despises the Field Marshal. He has always had a disdain for the Rey family, even as a young prince. The bloodline has upheld a certain characteristic. He recalls the previous Field Marshal, the pretentious arrogance of his own self-worth. They have always acted as if they were above the laws of Wyverna. The laws, his royal blood had set centuries ago. *They* run the Winged Cavalry. *He* runs the kingdom. They still fall under *his* order.

He eyes the slightly older gentleman. They have been in their reins of power for around the same amount of time, they've been in this quarrel for over a decade now.

"She is extraordinarily gifted." Rey crosses his arms behind his back, "Gifted enough to lead this private team of yours, then run the entire Winged Cavalry."

"As expected from a Rey." He returns his gaze to Amiria. "As expected." He tilts his head forward, shadowing his smirk.

"Amiria Rey."

She jumps, startled. The small roasted potatoes bounce and hop across her pewter plate. Calix watches the round potato roll to his boot. She was so engrossed with her solidarity as one of the plants decorating the room she hadn't noticed his silent steps approaching.

"Stealthy," she says. Composing herself, she returns her line of sight back out across the room filled with people who had already forgotten she was also one of the graduates, "I didn't even sense you."

"Stealth is the main part of my job," he says cunningly.

Her head turns slowly to meet the older boy's pale blue eyes, "You're?"

"Welcome to the team." He grants her his prize-winning smile.

Uninterested, Amiria returns to watching the room, "Thanks."

His smile dissipates at the dismissal. He steps in front of her crowding her view, "You mentioned waiting to celebrate at the banquet. Well, here we are."

She holds up her plate. "I've got my food already."

"Good, we can skip straight to the talking part. We should get to know each other, especially now that we're teammates." He takes a step closer.

Put off by his eagerness, Amiria maintains the gap between them, keeping a comfortable distance. She can hear Nellie squabbling with her younger sister, "Of course, she has the most handsome guy in the Cavalry after her. Ugh!" she exclaims. "Miss Perfect will get to live her perfect life in the castle while I'm sent to the harbor that reeks of dead fish."

Calix turns his ear to listen. "Huh, interesting. Did you hear that?" He takes another step, attempting to close the distance she had made.

"Unfortunately." She mentally curls into herself. She always hears them. They say their demoralizing comments with the purpose and intent of her hearing. They've been condoning this behavior since the first time she met another child. She's been outcasted to train alone, shunned to avoid all gatherings, and her peers have verbally expressed she is not wanted around. The true reason is unknown to her, is it because of her as a person or the person they believe her to be? This prodigy, who has been giving everything on a silver platter. She has been giving nothing but expectations she's exhausted herself to uphold.

"How about we talk somewhere private?" He takes another step forward. Amiria's back bumps into the wall.

She can feel the eyes of her classmates and the others close to their age group staring at her. Watching, judging, ridiculing. Why does she care what they think? She shouldn't care what they think. She was born to serve the citizens of Wyverna. She doesn't exist to cater to their opinion.

Her eyes narrow into slits as she glares up at Calix. "How about you leave me alone?"

He puts up a façade of being disheartened. "Aw. Don't be like that?" His voice is smooth, with a deep rich tone that you can't stop wanting to hear. He reaches out to touch her arm.

Amiria slaps his hand, she's done being talked down to by the others her age and she's done being used, "Don't touch me."

Calix's eyes switch from his hand back to Amiria. A muscle twitches in his tensed jaw. He exhales through his nostrils and drops his hand to his side, "You'll come around."

"I doubt it." She thrusts her plate into Calix's hands and pushes past him, "I'll see you at the first team meeting."

King Dietrich leans back in his chair, "This is going to be interesting."

Forty-Four

Wood is arranged neatly in the fire pit, stacked according to Stirling's trial and error, allowing an efficient amount of oxygen for the fire to breathe. Ignis blows lightly, igniting the wood with life and covering the cave with a warm crackling light. Stirling sits back, leaning against Ignis's body, his eyes slipping shut.

"Hey, I've been thinking," Ignis says.

Stirling's eyes remain shut, enjoying the warmth radiating from the fire, "About what?"

"Well, today was Amiria's initiation. She's officially part of the Cavalry and I know you've been all buddy buddy the past month but..." Ignis trails off, trying to figure out how he wants to word what was on his mind.

Stirling sits up and snaps, "You trying to ask how long before she is going to rat me out?"

Ignis shrugs. *"Well, I wasn't going to say it like that. I was going to say it more like give you away accidentally."*

"I don't think she ever will," Stirling defends. "I believe she is trustworthy."

"To whom? You or the Cavalry?" Ignis retorts.

Stirling returns to leaning against Ignis and stares blankly into the fire. "I like to hope, me. Even though the Cavalry has been her whole life and I'm someone she met recently. I enjoy hanging out with her. She understands me for the most part. Plus, it's nice to have, um, human interaction. No offense."

"Whatever, you just think she's pretty." Ignis sighs, laying his head down around Stirling.

"Shut up, Ignis," Stirling mumbles in denial, nodding off to sleep.

Forty-Five

Sitting outside the cave, Stirling leans against the boulder entrance. The afternoon sun is warm and feels like a blessing on his skin. He slowly uses his sharpened slate rock to cut a split branch that will become the handle of his axe

Ignis hangs to the side of the small clearing watching as the rhythmic tapping of the chisel filling in the silence of the forest.

"*Incoming,*" Ignis says as Amiria appears from the tunnel.

Stirling squints up at her, has it been another week already? The past three months Amiria had appeared in his cave once a week. That confirms they're friends, right?

Right? He has a– His mind drifts as he takes her in. She has a long bow looped over her shoulder with a quiver strung across her back alone with her usual mauve cotehardie, black tights, and leather boots.

"There you are." She reaches for her bow pulling it free from her shoulder, holding it firmly in her hand. "Drop what you're doing."

"*Good afternoon* is how most people greet each other," Stirling replies, raising an eyebrow at the bow.

Amiria unhooks the quiver, dropping both items beside him. "Good afternoon. Ready to do some training?"

"Training? I don't remember scheduling training."

"I decided it would be a good idea for you to learn how to hunt and defend yourself."

"True, cause Ignis doesn't help me."

"*You chose this.*"

Stirling ignores him and continues to listen to Amiria.

"I brought one of my old bows. It might be a little short for you, but it'll get the job done. For swordsmanship, we'll train with sticks for now. I don't want you getting hurt," she tells him.

Stirling squints at her comment. Scooping up the bow, he begins analyzing it. He knows nothing of the craftsmanship. He holds the bow out, pretending to weigh it. Plucking at the string, he can feel the bow hum in his hand.

This time it is Amiria's turn to raise an eyebrow at Stirling's inexperience. "Have you even seen a bow before, baker boy" she teases.

Stirling stands up handing it back, "Only on guards."

Amiria holds the bow up to her eye level. "Take in my years of wisdom." Stirling rolls his eyes. Amiria continues, "You should always check the condition of your bow, especially an old one like this that has been sitting in storage. Any nick or warp in the bow or string can cause your centering to be off and it won't shoot properly. So, you inspect the limb for any discrepancies like cracks or splinters. Then you check the string. Let me see your hand."

Amiria holds out hers. Stirling hesitantly puts his in hers with the palm facing up. Her small fingers are cold and dwarfed under his.

She raises his hand to the bow's string. "Curl your fingers around the string and run it through them. You're feeling for any frays or broken strands."

Stirling watches Amiria's hand as she guides his fingers along the string. She lets go of his hand when they reach the end. His hand drops to his side and he slowly releases the breath he had been holding, hoping she doesn't notice.

Stirling retrieves the bow back with new admiration. He holds it up to his eyes, inspecting the elegantly crafted wood. The striped wood grain runs longways like trails taking you nowhere except forward straight to your destination. Leather, he guesses is pig hide, wraps around the center so tightly it gives off the illusion of polished wood. Rubbing his thumb along the grip, he tries to feel for any distinguishable breaks between the strips. The lack of blemishes astonishes him as he can't find a single imperfection in the leather furthering the illusion. He can see for himself the quality of your items has a staggering difference when you have access and the coin for the true masters of the craft.

"Grab the quiver. We can test your shot on the tree over there," Amiria says, pointing at some thick firs on the opposite side of the clearing of Ignis.

"The what?" Stirling asks.

"The quiver, the quiver. The thing that holds the arrows," Amiria says with a groan.

"*This is going to be good.*" Ignis chuckles, crossing his front legs, getting comfortable.

"Shut up, Ignis," Stirling snaps, picking up the quiver.

He follows Amiria, who has him stand around twenty steps away from the tree.

"Is this not too close?" Stirling questions.

"I will decide that after you prove to me, you can hit the center of the trunk from here. Go on, let's see," she answers.

Stirling eyes her. "Are you not going to tell me how?"

"I want to see what I'm working with. Let's see if there is any raw talent in there. Then I'll show what you're doing wrong." Amira smiles.

"Thanks," he says sarcastically.

"You'll probably need to hold it for him too," Ignis mocks.

"She can't hear you," Stirling reminds him.

"Yeah, but you can." Ignis laughs.

Stirling frowns at his undermining comment.

Shrugging it off, Stirling slings the quiver over his back and pulls out an arrow. He studies the well-balanced stick in his hand. Reflecting the sunlight, the ink-colored fletching made from feathers glint blue and green.

Holding the arrow pinched between his thumb and index finger, he hooks the notch on the string and pulls. He can feel his muscles straining as if the bow and string longed to be side by side together again and are fighting tooth and nail against him.

He is surprised that such a delicate frame can be so heavy. He attempts to sight down the length of the arrow, lining it up with the fir tree. The tip of the arrow sways, rocking back and forth as if he stood on a boat. The muscles in his arms begin to burn from the strenuous hold. Giving into the will of the bow, he lets go. The arrow flies from his hand, embedding straight into the mossy forest floor.

Dropping his already exhausted arms in defeat, Stirling turns to Amiria, seeking help.

She purses her lips. "Well, that…that showed me everything I need. We'll start with how to even hold the bow."

"Told you," Ignis says.

Stirling strikes a glare at him as Amiria continues, "So hold the bow up how you would naturally without pulling back on the string.

Lifting his arms as instructed, he holds his body still, moving only his head as he watches Amiria circle around him. She stops off to the side in the direction his chest is turned to.

"First, let's fix your fingers." She reaches up, pulling the arrow out from being pinched under his thumb and replaces it between his index and middle.

"You can hold it like that but trust me, this will be easier. Then—well. Hold on," she says, placing her hands on his elbows and adjusting his arms.

Stirling's body becomes rigid under her touch. Stepping close enough that a deep breath would close the distance between their chests Amiria pushes up his arms, aligning his stance. It doesn't occur to her how close she is until she drops her hands, satisfied with her adjustments. She can now see the pulse in his neck beating rapidly. She breathes in. He smells of the forest and campfire, with no lingering stench of the market district, or the bread of the bakery. He's adapting to the world around him. Her eyes crawl up him, stopping at the curls falling across his forehead. His jaw pops as he refrains from looking down at her.

"Now what?" he nervously squeaks, his arms beginning to shake.

Amiria takes a step back, her voice returning to an instructive tone. "When you pull back you're going to find your anchor point. It's what you find most comfortable for you. A lot of people tend to go near the corner of the mouth. This is your go-to point when shooting for a consistent shot. Then after you reach it, focus on the smallest spot you can on the trunk. Then let go. Don't move. Just let go."

Stirling does as instructed, pulling the string back until his hand nears the corner of his mouth. His arms are already on fire from holding the stance. Picking out a piece of bark standing out from the rest, he takes a deep breath in. Holds it and releases. His fingers release the string from his grasp, letting it snap back to place.

Stirling yelps, dropping the bow as the arrow sails past the trunk entirely and is swallowed up by the thick brush. Amiria lets out a small gasp as Stirling hunches over, cradling his forearm.

"Did the string slap you?" she asks.

He lifts his arm, inspecting the bruise already forming below his elbow on the inside of his forearm–a thin red line dots across where the string had drawn blood.

"You didn't warn me about that," he manages through the pulses of pain.

"I never had that issue, so it slipped my mind. There must have been something wrong with your grip," Amiria admits.

Stirling examines the swelling of his arm, considering his options. Shooting a bow doesn't appear hard. He would never have guessed the difficulty and pain it would be to learn.

"Try again or quit. It doesn't matter what you choose. You're going to embarrass yourself," Ignis mocks.

Stirling can't tell Ignis to shut up this time because what he had said is exactly what he is thinking. He is going to embarrass himself in front of Amiria with his inexperience. It is his second shot and he's already harmed himself with it. Though what would be more embarrassing to him is if he quits.

Pushing past the pain, he picks up the bow, *"You gave me a worse wound than this, and I didn't give up on you."*

Amiria leans in to examine his arm, "You okay?"

"No." He pulls the arm into himself. "But I'll live."

He shakes his arm as if it will erase the pain. Huffing at the throbbing sensation, he picks up the bow and readies his position. Stepping up to him, Amiria ignores his presence and the warmth radiating from him as she checks over his elbow and his grip.

"Okay, now try," she says, stepping back.

Biting his lip, Stirling takes another deep breath. The arrow flies, whistling through the wind and sticking with a light thud into the trunk of the tree. It is off to the side and far below where he was aiming but he had done it. He hit the tree.

Turning to Amiria, he grins with pride slapped across his face.

"Good, but next time hit the center."

"Oh, come on. I was close enough," Stirling argues.

"Close enough? There's no close enough when it comes to life or death. Close enough can stand between a wounding shot and a fatal shot. In real life your target shoots back," she lectures.

"So, you're telling me you never miss? Never ever?" he says, skeptical.

"Give me," is all she says, holding out her hand for the bow and quiver.

Stirling hands them over with a devious grin. She throws the quiver on and before Stirling has time to blink, in one swift motion, Amiria pulls an arrow from the quiver and it is sailing across the space hitting the center of the trunk.

She turns, her torso remaining still as her feet pivot in the grass. She releases arrow after arrow hitting trunk after trunk unfaltering, all hitting the direct centers as she turns across the circumference of the small clearing. An arrow zips between Ignis' horns landing in a tree behind him with a *thunk*. Ignis blinks stunned. She reaches back to grab another arrow but finds the quiver has run dry. With adrenaline pumping, she grabs her dagger from its hilt on her belt. While still holding the bow in one hand, she turns around pitching the dagger at the original tree.

Stirling can't see the dagger fly past him. He can only hear a whooshing sound as it passes his head and a thud as it embeds itself beside her arrow. Amiria extends her arm handing the bow back to Stirling.

Looking him dead in the eye, she says, "Never, ever."

"*Show off,*" Stirling tells Ignis.

"*Did she just aim at my head?*" Ignis replies, still stunned.

"It's okay. You don't have to be intimidated. If you spent your entire childhood practicing, you would never miss either. The less I missed, the sooner I got supper."

Stirling stares down at the bow in his hands reflecting; of

course, she wasn't able to accomplish that overnight. She might be a prodigy, but while he was playing in the mountains and having fun with Ignis, she was dedicating her existence to training.

"I want you to try to work on this every day. You hear me, Stirling?" Amiria says, snapping her fingers in front of his face, grabbing his attention from the bow, "It's learning to hunt or starve. You can't survive off berries and the random food I bring you."

The food she will bring.

A spark lights inside of Stirling as he comes to the conclusion, "You mean you plan on continuing to come up here after you start going on your missions?"

Amiria's cheeks blush under her olive skin. "Well, yeah, someone has to make sure you're still alive and I'm the only one who knows you're here. I've already started coming up here on a weekly basis so it won't be so bad to continue the routine, so…"

"*She wants to be friends forever*," Ignis teases.

Stirling represses the urge to smile, "So, you *do* enjoy hanging out with us."

"Maybe." Amiria deflects and walks over to the tree, pulls her dagger out, and places it back in the sheath. "I can give you a quick demonstration on swordmanship but I'll have to be leaving soon after that."

"Why so soon?" Stirling asks.

"I can't lay around the woods all day. I left between my tasks saying I was going to give Taika her exercises."

Stirling defaltes a little, "So the sword?"

"Go grab two of those sticks." Amiria instructs.

Stirling picks up two long sticks he had brought to the cave along with the ones he used to make his bed frame. He tosses one to Amiria. She catches it one-handed, twirling it around her body. She gets into a ready stance, pulls the stick up to her head, and points it directly at Stirling. Her feet are in a well-bladed stance, aiming her chest away from him and her shoulder in his direction. Stirling faces directly at her gripping the bottom of the stick near his hips, the top pointing up at the trees.

"As a start signal, have Ignis make a sound or something," Amiria instructs, her eyes pinned on Stirling.

"*You're screwed*," Ignis taunts.

"He heard you," Stirling tells her.

Ignis takes in the moment as a bead of sweat forms on Stirling's brow. He snorts, blowing a burst of small flames from his nostrils. Amiria reacts, leaping forward instantly. Stirling barely has time to comprehend as he puts his stick up, deflecting her strike from above. He's surprised the stick doesn't snap in half as it sends vibrations reverberating through his bones. Distracted by the pain in his arms, he is oblivious to Amiria, who has retracted from the blow.

Pain in his side shoots through his ribcage replacing the discomfort in his arms. His vision clouding, Stirling drops the stick grasping at his side. His feet stumble below him. "Agh, what in the world?"

"I didn't even hit you that hard, come on, let's try again. This time I'll let you come at me first," Amiria says playfully.

Grabbing the stick he had dropped, Stirling lunges himself at Amiria, his swing a wide arch over his head. Amiria steps to the side, raising her stick to meet his at head height blocking his blow. Stepping in close, she places her foot behind his as she simultaneously pushes with her forearm and elbow against Stirling's shoulder and collarbone, sending him tumbling backward.

Stirling can hear Ignis bursting with laughter. Laying on his back, Stirling stares up at the clouds floating by.

The end of Amiria's stick hovers over his pulsing throat. "You're dead"

"You cheated! You tripped me!" Stirling says, batting away the stick from his neck.

"Never said a sword fight is fair. Did you think it was just hitting swords? If you think like that you will be dead as soon as you are challenged. In fights for your life, there are no rules. Remember that," she says, extending out her hand.

Accepting it, Stirling lets her help him sit up. She squats down analyzing him.

"What?" he asks.

"You have pine needles stuck in your hair." She laughs, plucking a dried needle from his tangled curls. "Now, I'm going to be late. I'll be back next week." Amira stands up. "Promise to work on your shot all right?

"Yeah, okay." His mood lifting after his painful defeat.

"Enjoy that bruise on your arm, and maybe the one on your side. Take care, the both of you," Amiria says with a nod in Ignis' direction, who returns with a bow of his head. She returns Stirling's smile. With a wave goodbye, she heads back through the cave to meet Taika waiting for her on the cliffside.

Stirling's eyes fall to his left arm, the purple swelling deepening and becoming prominent. He lifts his tunic to examine his ribcage. There are no marks yet, but the skin is tender where she hit him.

"*You got your ass kicked.*" Ignis chuckles.

"If you don't finally shut up, I'm going to use you for aiming practice," Stirling replies, peeved.

Rolling himself off the ground, he begins removing the arrows from the trees. *It won't take me a year to learn this bow. I'm going to show her.*

With all the arrows back in the quiver, Stirling slings it across his back and stands facing the tree. He removes an arrow holding it between his middle and index as she showed him.

Calming his breathing, Stirling hooks the back of the arrow on the string and pulls back.

He lets go and the arrow flies, skimming the trunk left of where he was aiming. Chunks of bark fall to the ground, leaving a wound on the tree.

Sighing, Stirling takes out another arrow and readies himself.

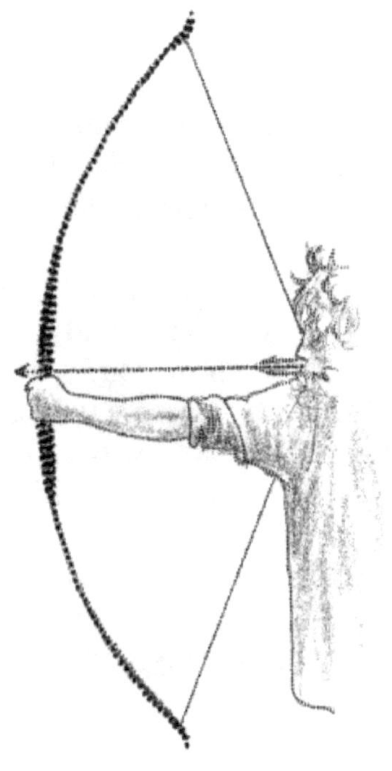

Forty-Six

The midmorning light shines through the mosaic windows of the throne room embracing the entire room with a radiance of colorful light without the aid of candles. Poised at the base of the throne's dais stands Amiria. Her leather riding gear has been exchanged for armor suited to be seen on display beside the king. Set aside from the public's eye, she has an exact replica of the armor she is wearing now made with metal in the shade of night. Extra padding had been added to silence the midnight armor as she slips through the shadows in secrecy on missions that if questioned, never conspired.

Over her cream-colored gambeson, she wears a red pleated brigandine, designed with soft velvet fabric lined with sheets of steel plates, her crest pinned above her heart. Her newly polished armor glints, reflecting the multitude of colors blanketing her from the windows. A gorget encircles her neck and collar bones protecting the vulnerable skin.

Pauldrons, shoulder armor etched with the Winged Cavalry emblem and gold start at her collar bone, extending over her shoulders onto her back. They run down her shoulder blades with three points, each lower than the other giving the appearance of wyvern wings.

Cowters cup her elbows sitting between the riveted rerebrace protecting her upper arm and vambraces on her forearms ending with her red brigandine gauntlets. On her upper thighs, she wears a pair of cuisse enclosing her whole leg but her grieves only cover the front of her calves tied over her leather-riding boots.

Her long hair is hidden inside the heart-shaped open-face helm with golden trim encircling her soft features. She is King Dietrich's favorite, his prized star to protect him through the night. She has convinced herself it's only because of her skills and mastery of the personally crafted longsword hanging from the scabbard on her hip. Out of her entire unit of seven Riders, he always requests her to be at his side. His personal shield, even when he has retreated to the solar to relax away from the public's eye.

She stands there feeling his eyes burning into the back of her head. She shivers, pinpricks rising along her neck to the base of her head. She never dares to turn around. She plays it off, ignoring the lust in his eyes, playing naive, pretending she doesn't notice. He's the king after all.

She needs to focus on her duties and her requirements. She should be honored to be chosen to stand beside the king. Every woman and man wants to stand where she stands. She can't take this opportunity for granted. She is meant to be here, she worked her entire life to be here, but all she wants to do is put stone walls, buildings, towns, and an entire forest in between them. Anything to hide from his prying eyes.

"Amiria, looking lovely as always," a deep voice calls across the room. The door nestled in the corner leading to the private sleeping quarters for her unit swings closed behind the young man. Living in the castle was a mandatory requirement given solely to Unit Larua. They are mere shouting distance away from King Dietrich, making them easily accessible for any urgent assignments.

She rolls her eyes as Calix, who has come to relieve her from her duties, struts across the room wearing matching armor.

"It's our uniform," Amiria snarls as Calix draws near.

She had learned the night of the banquet he was the previous recruit five years before her, a prodigy of his own which had gone quickly to his head. Not only is his mother the General but his father is Major Gautier, the one in charge their unit. He was born an elitist and remains entitled to it.

His skin, tanned and bronze, glows from the recent exposure to the sun. The wavy locks of thick dark brown hair hide beneath his helm showing only his crystal eyes. The armor accentuates his broad shoulders and narrow hips, a body the girls in the castle swoon over. His sculpted features loom over her as he stops less than an arm's reach away.

She glares up at him, her eyes dark and serious.

He grins a perfect smile topped off with dimples on each cheek saying in a suave tone. "How about after my shift the two of us get together? I know where to find some of the finest wine. What do you say?"

"Let me guess, in the Castle's buttery?" Amiria finds him absolutely. "No, thank you, Calix. I'd rather drink from the cities' runoff."

Revolting.

They are the youngest in their squad being only five years apart compared to ten-plus years for the rest of the average age in the group. Everyone slots them together. This is her assigned career, not her assigned marriage...yet. Who she wants to marry is one of the few freedoms the lower class has that she wishes was granted to her in this heavily controlled life. She could fall in love with someone from an acceptable class, but her father will have to approve. Everything is about bloodline. There is no marrying for love in this society.

She doesn't want to marry and start a family. He is everything she despises. He is in love with status and himself. He feels everything should be handed to him because of who he is and not if he actually earned or deserves it. He doesn't have feelings for her. He only believes he deserves to have her because they will make some sort of power couple. They will command the Winged Cavalry together, two unstoppable prodigies. He always gets what he wants and the fact that Amiria does not throw herself at him drives him mad.

"I at least deserve a reason why?" Calix replies, aggravated. He has been after her for three years and has never let up on his pursuit of her hand.

Amiria knows King Dietrich is watching them, so she has to refrain from using the words she feels accurately describe Calix and remain professional.

Stepping close she closes the small gap between them, only a finger's length apart. Standing on her toes, she tilts her chin up to his ear so he can hear her and whispers, "I said, no."

"You'll come around," he whispers back, smirking.

"Never." Amiria puts her weight back on her heels, her voice returning to normal. "I have important matters to attend to and you're wasting my time with your nonsense."

She pushes past him, their armor clashing as their shoulders meet.

Calix's eyes latch onto Amiria, his body turning as his head is pulled around by her. He doesn't take his eyes off her as she strolls across the floor of the throne room. The two men watch her as if they are competitors in a hunt and she is the trophy. Focusing on her boots clicking across the granite floor, Amiria desperately wants to bolt out of the hall. She holds back, forcing herself to keep a steady pace. She can feel their penetrating gaze stabbing through her armor, the chill of the blood running down her spine. She grabs the door of the throne room and yanks it open. A force unbeknownst to her pulls her head to check over her shoulder.

Calix raises his eyebrows with a smirk, but King Dietrich isn't watching her anymore. He has switched his priority; he wears an indistinguishable expression as he focuses on Calix.

Forty-Seven

With his hands busy kneading a lump of dough, Giles' attention changes to the door of the bakery opening, "Oh, Amiria. I feared you might not make it today."

Amiria wears a full grin as she closes the door behind her. She has changed out of her armor into civilian clothing consisting of a simple men's cotehardie tailored to her liking with a pair of black tights accompanied by her usual tall riding boots. She refuses to ever slip into a dress even though it will be a more suitable attire for a woman. Gowns were not designed to run into a battle at a moment's notice. Dresses aren't designed to run in at all and that just isn't her.

She had persistently returned to the bakery after that first time. She spent months gaining Giles' trust. At each stop, she would ask him how he is doing. She wanted him to know there are people out there who care. She wanted him to know not everyone in the Winged Cavalry was born without a heart, as the rumors state. She didn't know how to fix what had broken inside of him, but she didn't want him to mend his pieces back together alone.

In the beginning, he would stand on the other side of the table, afraid of her, and grunt his answers. She never wore any Cavalry emblems and kept her insignia out of sight, but he knew what she was. Then one day, he was leaning against the counter and didn't distance himself when she entered. He didn't smile, but he gave her real words as a reply. A smile grew on her face that day and their friendship began to bloom.

"Mr. Bakere, after three years, you would know by now I'd never miss my weekly stop. You do have the best biscuits in Lumierna. I should know. I've been sent all over the city." Amiria praises letting her shoulder bag, a simple leather satchel with a cross-shoulder strap, slide off her shoulder onto the table Giles is working at.

"It can't be better than the white bread baked in the castle? It's supposed to be purer than the darker bread we make down here," he remarks.

Amiria waves her hand. "Don't listen to them. They always say their stuff is superior, but it's not. You can taste the passion in yours."

"I'll take your word for it. You are my most faithful customer," he says, flattered.

Amiria's bag slumps over, revealing the contents of meat pies, fruit, and cheese inside.

"One of these days though, you're going to have to tell me who you always have your picnics with. I want to know who the lucky lad is," he states, motioning to the bag.

Placing the palms of her hands on the wooden table, Amiria leans forward rocking up onto her toes in a playful manner, "You know I'll never tell. A secret relationship is much more fun, but I assure you, you would highly approve of him."

Giles shuffles over to the shelf pulling a rye bread off the rack, a small smile escaping, "I know I've said this many times before, but ever since my son passed away, it's refreshing to have a young face frequently around here. Maybe in some other life, you two could have been friends."

She rolls back onto her heels and her expression softens. "Yeah, maybe in another life we would have been able to be friends." Amiria disguises her tone in an attempt to hide the vulnerability that had surfaced. "But that would be a weird friendship, a baker and a Winged Rider? Would it not?"

Setting the rye beside Amiria's bag, Giles playfully pokes her forehead. "We're friends, are we not? Or is it really only the pretzels that bring you back."

Amiria puts her hand on her forehead and playfully pouts. "It's definitely the pretzels."

Chuckling, Giles picks up a few biscuits from the nearby pile, adding them to her supplies. He remembers Stirling's strong admiration for the Cavalry and how he had thought of his son as a fool. He had chased his only son off instead of taking the time to understand him. If only he had been more patient with Stirling, he could have met Amiria for himself. She would have answered all his questions informing him of the true harsh lifestyle of the Winged Cavalry, teaching him it isn't the fantasy he believed. Then maybe, maybe his son would still be around.

At first, he hated the sight of her. He wished she would stop showing up. He wanted to be left alone, not reminded of the son he had lost. She would purchase her pretzel and depart, and he would get his wish. He would stand alone in the bakery so cold, no oven could heat it. He doesn't remember the point when he started eagerly waiting to see her, but as the week passed between her visits, he would fear something had happened to her. He feared the Cavalry had taken her, too. She was a sweet girl; she was the only person who asked how he was doing. The neighborhood news had moved on and so had the people, but he hadn't. He couldn't. He still hasn't.

He used to find it off that she traveled down to this lower

district when she had any bakery to pick from. She has the luxury of waltzing into the castle's kitchen and eating a bun pulled straight from the embers in the royal stove. But, she has chosen his shop, and now he has grown accustomed to her face every week. He has developed some sort of fatherly kinship towards her. She might not feel the same, but he will admit that if one week her face didn't light up his shop he would be heartbroken.

He can't place his finger on it but for some reason, she reminds him of Stirling.

Amiria slides the bread into her bag and slips the strap over her head so it lays across her chest. Her hand grips the strap holding it slightly away from her body. "Maybe one day life will be different. A life you can choose what to do with."

Amiria blushes, biting her tongue. She doesn't let herself speak in a liberal way outside the sanctuary of Stirling's cave. Ideas like this can get you thrown into the stocks. She is part of the Winged Cavalry; she works personally with and is entrusted by King Dietrich. Words such as these can be misconstrued as treasonous, but inside this bakery, she feels as if this is the only place in town she can let her walls start to lower.

She finds it amusing how she is comfortable saying these things even though these beliefs are what pushed Stirling and his father to fight to the point he chose life as a fugitive rather than remain here and live by the laws. Maybe it really did take the loss of his only child for him to understand the way of life needs to change.

Staring at Amiria, Giles swears he can see Stirling standing there right in front of him.

Maybe, he thinks. *Maybe, they're onto something. Maybe the rest of us are stuck living this routine of past traditions because it's easier than taking the lead and changing the future.*

This is not what he says aloud.

He avoids eye contact with her, muttering, "That's not something that can easily be changed. The system works. There's no need to fix something that isn't broken."

Amiria fumbles through her coin purse replying with an earnest tone, "It may not be broken on the outside, but has anyone stopped to check inside?" She places the coins gently on the table, "I'll see you next week Mr. Bakere."

"Hold on," he says, quickly reaching over to the shelf. "I almost forgot. I've got one more thing for you."

He picks up an object wrapped in parchment. "It's only gingerbread, but I thought you'd enjoy some on the house." He holds out the small package the size of Amiria's hand, offering it to her.

"Thank you," Amiria says, appreciative, holding her hand out to accept his gift. "Any particular reason for this?"

"No, just felt like it would add something new to your picnic," he answers quickly with a smile leading Amiria to the front door. He opens it for her, "See you next week?"

Amiria stops in the door frame returning Giles' smile, the same smile as Stirling's. "Always."

Like a protective parent sending their child off for the first time, Giles watches as Amiria hops down the stairs joining in with the rest of the crowd meandering from shop to shop who now know her as a familiar face. They show their respect with a rooted undertone of fear as they nod their heads and step aside, opening a clear pathway for her to walk through.

He leans his shoulder on the door frame letting the wood full of splinters and dents from generations of use hold up his weight. An uneasy feeling slowly sets over him like a thin sheet slowly wafting down to cover him after being tossed over the newly made bed.

Every week Amiria would always say, "I'll see you next week." She has always held true to her word. This time something feels off, as if the next time he sees her, it won't be for her weekly visit for her picnic supplies.

Forty-Eight

Amiria treads silently through the dense forest. To keep a noticeable path from developing, she made a note to change her route as often as possible to allow the plants and leaves to cover up any marking she may have left.

Over the last three years, she hasn't grown in height but her features are starting to become that of a woman's. The delicate features of a child, any roundness to her cheeks have disappeared. Her face is still soft though the angles in her jaw and cheekbones have become more defined. Her dark round eyes remain the same. They are fierce and will stare down death itself, but they are the type of eyes that for the right people will bloom with love and compassion.

Without turning her head, Amiria's ears perk to the sound of rustling leaves to her southwest. A single leaf floats gently to the forest floor, somersaulting as the thin object pushes through the air. The landing spot is near impossible to predict as the slightest breeze can alter its direction.

She can't predict where the leaf is going to land, but she

is always cunningly accurate in her prediction with people, whose heavier weight tends to move in a single direction.

The shadows overhead change, moving in a way not resembling leaves blowing in the wind or a small animal moving about. A smirk creeps onto her face pulling at the edges of her mouth as she takes a lunging step forward, bracing her stance. Reaching with both of her hands over her right shoulder, she firmly grabs the forearm of someone who had leaped from the trees like a wild beast.

Using the falling momentum of the attacker Amiria pulls their arm forward, catapulting them over her and slamming them into the ground onto their back, knocking the wind out of their lungs. Dust and leaves erupt into the air around them. She doesn't give the person a chance to catch their breath and she yanks on their arm swiftly flipping them onto their stomach and swoops into a kneeling position.

Her knee digs into their lower spine while she twists their arm behind their back.

"Okay, okay. I give. I give," Stirling shouts out in distress, his free arm slapping the dirt in front of him.

Amiria lets out a playful laugh releasing her grip and returning Stirling's control of his arm. She slides herself off his back into a sitting position beside him as he lifts himself and sits back on his heels, ignoring the dirt now covering the front of him.

Grimacing, he massages the now tender shoulder testing its capabilities of motion.

He has grown a significant amount over the years. He is no longer a scrawny child too tall for the little amount he weighs. He may have only grown a thumbs width in height but living out in the forest, he has grown physically stronger. His shoulders have become broad and his arms are strong from the years of hauling supplies and game to his cave. The boyish features of his face have hardened and sculpted into a young man as the lining of his jaw became more pronounced. Though many of his features have changed, his trademarks remain the same; his hair cut unevenly by a sharpened deer bone sticks up in a curly untamed mess, the downturn shape of his eyes as if he's always worried, and his nose is still a little too big.

The goofy smile he is giving to Amiria at this moment is another trait that will never go away or the way his hazel eyes seem to shine like a forest sunrise when he does. The three lined scars on his arm; grotesque, bumpy, and webbed, will never fade as if it is his personal insignia.

"One of these days I'm going to get you." Stirling jokes.

"How many times do I have to explain to you? It doesn't matter how good you get at leaping around this forest. You will never match nine years of military training and pretty much nineteen years of at-home personal training. Just admit you're never going to catch me. I was raised to defend and fight at any cost. You were raised to," Amiria's mouth curls, "To bake bread."

"You—I'm going to get you." Stirling pretends to be aggravated as he reaches forward in an attempt to snatch her but he isn't even close enough to grab her bag as she gracefully leaps backward out of reach.

"As I said, you'll never catch me, baker boy!" She mocks, bolting into the forest, her bag of food bouncing wildly at her side. The sound of her hysterical laughter disappears with her into the surrounding trees.

Stirling stumbles, his feet interlocking as he tries to hurl himself after her. He puts his hands out, catching himself before his face hits the ground, and jumps back into action. He takes off sprinting after her.

Running on the balls of her feet, the outside rolling inwards to her big toe, her heels never touching the ground, Amiria's boots are soundless. Years of stealth training cushioned by the pillows of soft leaves and pine needles thrown across the forest floor.

She can hear it behind her, the soft padding sound of

someone who knows these mountains like he knows his own home. Stirling is sprinting after her. She might be swift and nimble but his long legs give him the advantage in natural speed. He only falters in the fact that he doesn't know how to muffle the sounds of his steps, making his speed obsolete to someone with a keen ear.

Stirling abruptly comes skidding to a stop as an object catches his eye. Backstepping a few paces, he stands over a bag lying by a stump as if it had been caught by a branch and pulled off the carrier.

"She is bragging about all her training but then goes about dropping her stuff. So stealthy." Stirling mutters, tapping the bag with his shoe.

"Oof." Escapes Stirling's mouth as he is knocked forward with a sudden increase in weight coming down on his back.

He takes a couple of staggering steps forward regaining his balance as he gasps catching his startled breath. An arm comes around his neck with the other hand cupping the back. Pushing lightly, she presses his neck into her arm, enough to make a point but not enough to cut the blood flow.

Hunching forward, he tries to pry Amiria off his back, her legs wrapping around his waist, holding herself stable.

"That's how you attack from above. Did you know if I were doing this for real, you would be unconscious before you can count to three?" She says in a low voice close enough to his ear he can feel the warmth of her breath sending shivers down his spine.

The hairs on the back of his neck and arms raise as goosebumps form. He can feel the pressure of her body against his like a constrictive snake, a stunning creature giving you a deadly hug. Her heart full of adrenaline drums rapidly on his shoulder blades and gradually begins to slow to a steady rhythm.

She drops her arms, letting them fall gently in front of Stirling, dangling against his chest, "Will you carry me, baker boy?"

"C-Carry you?" he stutters.

"Yeah, to the cave so we can finally eat," she replies with a yawn, her eyes drooping. Seldom restful sleep caused by long extensive work shifts is catching up to her like a stampede. This is the first time she has asked Stirling to carry her, the first time she's asked anyone to carry her. She thinks of it as something a parent would do when you were a small child, but when you're born into the Winged Cavalry, you don't have time to be carried. You need to learn to hold yourself up.

"Um, okay," Stirling says shyly.

He raises his trembling hands, hovering them over Amiria's thighs. He can almost feel the fabric sending an electrical current tingling his palms. There is something fluttering around in his stomach making him nauseous. Then his heart, it's pounding all the way up into his throat, inhibiting him from breathing properly.

Taking a deep breath, his chest expands as far as it can go. His whole body is shaking. He holds in his breath, calming down, and slowly releases it, slipping his hands under her thighs behind her knees. Her legs unwrap from his waist, letting her whole weight rest in his palms. Lowering her head, she rests her chin on his shoulder, her head tilting and settling against his.

Heat rushes to his cheeks turning them rosy. He is glad Amiria is behind him, so she can't see the vibrant color on his face. They have been close friends since the day she found him in the cave all those years ago but close interactions not involving a headlock were scarce.

She is the same as trying to hug a wolf. They resemble their domesticated counterparts, lovable and by your side but try and pet one, and you've got a good chance of losing a limb. They're from a world of hunt or be hunted. She wears a frightening mask, but the mask is heavy and it is a relief for her to take it off. To drop everything and relax.

He can relate. He had worn a similar mask back when he resided under his family's roof. His mask was made up of the materials of a lie. But fabricated lies like woven wool begin to fray and unravel in time, and the mask will need to be discarded.

He still hasn't become accustomed to her touch. The light brush of her skin when they would accidentally bump or graze sends a heated pulse flowing through his body. It never became something he thought twice about. No, he only longed for it more.

Over time she slowly grew more comfortable around him and would lean on him or purposefully stand close enough to feel the warmth of his skin. He never found enough courage to do the same. He always waits for her to close the gap. He is afraid he will overstep boundaries; boundaries he isn't even sure if they are there. He is afraid of messing with the level of comfort and trust she has put in him.

Squatting down, he picks up the bag of food off the ground while trying to not drop Amiria in the process. He hands the bag up to her. She moves only enough to slip it over her head and arm before returning to rest her head on his shoulders with a yawn. Her eyelids are heavy as she shakes her head trying to wake up. Her attempt is futile as her eyelids close under their own weight.

Neither of them says a word as Stirling carries her to the cave. Resting with the rocking motion, Amiria is lulled to sleep by Stirling's stride. Being the rookie of her squad, she often stands the overnight shifts the senior members don't want, on top of all the special requests King Dietrich summons for her to accompany him on.

She never complains about the long and odd hours. She still finds time to spend with Stirling even if she has fallen asleep numerous times. He never seems to care; he just enjoys the company anyway. He would pull the blanket over her and tend to the fire making sure she was comfortable.

On the days she makes it out to the cave deep in the

mountain's forest is the only time she can shut her eyes and let the natural melatonin leak into her brain, so she can snuff out the candle of the outside world without worrying about alarms in their personal quarters sending them off into the night for another mission.

Ignis and Taika, who Amira had sent ahead so she could enjoy the walk in the forest, lift their heads simultaneously. Their large scaly bodies absorb the warmth of the sun in the clearing crowding the entrance to the cave hidden between the boulders under the beech tree forever frozen in the state of falling.

Stirling emerges from the shadows of the trees. Amiria, now sound asleep on his back, has her face resting in the crook of his neck. Her long dark hair spills over his shoulder, flowing around her arms hanging loosely in front of him, obscuring her slumbering face.

"What did you do to her?" Ignis asks, referring to her unconscious body.

"I didn't do anything. She's asleep," Stirling responds. "You think I'd be capable of knocking her out?"

"Yeah, you're right about something for once. You have a better chance of convincing the Cavalry not to kill you, than to knock out the king's star pupil," Ignis remarks.

"Ha. Ha. Ha. You're so funny." Stirling's sarcastic tone is obvious as he steps over Ignis' tail. "How about you stay out here and think about the harmful things you say to people."

"No, not people. Person. Just you. Aren't you special," Ignis teases in a cheeky tone. Stirling dismisses the insult with a shake of his head and submerges himself with Amira into the cave.

Inside the cave, Stirling makes his way over to the bed he has updated by laying large branches perpendicularly across two piles of logs stacked in a triangle. On top, he's added multiple deer hides for extra warmth and comfort. He had kept true to Amiria's request. He practiced the bow every day after she showed him the basics. It's miraculous how quickly you can master something when your survival depends on it.

He turns around facing away from the bed. Shrugging her off he gently lays her down into the soft pelts.

Stirring awake, she yawns, "Oh, we're here." She props herself on one arm, pulling the bag still slung around her off.

"Yeah, weird how you can magically travel while you're asleep," Stirling says.

He leans over placing his hand on her shoulder, helping lift her into a sitting position. She drags the bag onto her lap as Stirling plops down next to her snatching a pear out of the open top.

"I fell asleep again? I'm sorry." She apologizes. "Your father is doing well. He misses you as always."

"He talked about me again?" Stirling soberly stares down at the pear he's mindlessly fumbling back and forth between his hands.

Amiria nods. "He always talks about you. This time he mentioned again how we could have been friends. Though this time, I think he actually agreed with me when I said how maybe one-day things will change. Well, he didn't much as agree as in he didn't shoot down the idea saying it was preposterous. So, I take that as progress. I also get the feeling he still blames himself for your, um, passing."

The memory of blaming himself for his mother's death resurfaces in Stirling's mind. It had taken him years to finally convince himself differently. Even after, it still hung in the back of his mind, repressed until moments like this. Dragged from the back of the crowd to center stage.

When he had laid starving and dehydrated in the cave he believed would be his tomb he had blamed his father for his demise. This was his fault for not understanding. Stirling came to accept this was solely on himself and that there was no one else to blame. Like he always wanted, he made all the decisions in his life. No one made him choose this path that led him here. He walked here on his own.

His father is following the laws of the land, the Cavalry are only abiding by orders, and King Dietrich is only acting upon a system he inherited long before even his grandparents were born.

"Any cool missions recently?" he says, changing the topic.

The Winged Cavalry consumed the majority of her life, leaving only a scarce amount of free time, but Amiria did love her job. She is truly born for it.

She grins, leaning into Stirling, her eyes shining as she speaks. "Yeah, there was this group from Uviktiland. They managed to get past our borders and took up shop near one of the mining towns on the northeastern side of the island. I guess they thought we mined for Wyvernite crystals. Ha, guess they still haven't figured out the obvious. Well, they were being discreet and stealing an *almost* undetectable amount of other stones. But you know the king. He notices everything. He sure does love his documents. So, a few members of my squad and I had to go and exterminate them." Amiria sits back. "There are *some* things he does like to leave undocumented."

"That sounds pretty crazy," Stirling admits while taking a few bites of the pear.

He begins imagining himself hiding out in the woods at night. Silently stalking unaware victims like he stalks a deer. Waiting until the perfect moment to ambush the bandits and… his thoughts trail off, his eyes fixated on the half-eaten pear in his hand. His hands are rough and calloused from extensive manual labor; the hands of a builder, of a hunter, of a Rider, but were they the hands of a killer? Could they take the life of another even if they were the enemy?

"I guess it was crazy. Except for Calix, oh he irritates me so much." She says, shattering Stirling's thought process.

"He thinks he's being so charming and he's going to win my heart one day. He just, I just want to oooo." She finishes by pretending to strangle the air.

He hates hearing Calix's name. He is a gifted Rider the same as Amiria. Overly praised for merely existing and destined to rise quickly through the ranks because of his bloodline. Stirling's veins surge with jealousy. He doesn't know if he wants to hit him or shake his hand.

She manages to evade it, but he knows Calix is her father's top candidate for who he wants her to give her hand in marriage. Nobility doesn't always get the luxury of marrying someone they love but instead someone who will benefit the family and future generations.

Amiria is all Stirling has besides Ignis and it will kill him internally if he never sees her again. She speaks about how much she despises Calix, but he can give her the life he can't. They will be allowed to go out in public together, and announce their relationship to their family and friends. Have a home and children. They could stand hand in hand beside the king in charge of the entire Winged Cavalry. What can he offer her? A life of treason? Life in a cave hiding away, barely surviving and everyone thinks you're dead? Sure, she comes here on her day off for temporary escape but would she ever want to live day in and day out like this?

"What did he do?" Stirling asks because he wants to hear what negative things she has to say about Calix.

"The usual, undermining me because I'm a woman and thought I needed to stand back and let him handle the dirty work." Amiria grits her teeth while clenching the bag in her lap.

"Woah, hey take it out on him and not the food." Stirling says, slowly prying each finger off the bag until it's free from her crushing grip and sets it off to the side, "I thought you didn't like when people put you on the Cavalry pedestal, right Miss Prodigy?"

"I don't!" Amiria snaps, "It's different than not putting

me on this pedestal. He talks down to me like I'm his doll, and calls me his little bird, like I'm fragile and need his help. You talk to me as if we are equal. It's different. We're two people who enjoy spending time with one another."

Ignis and Taika pop into Stirling's mind. They were two very different dragons with two very different riders, but at the core, they were the same. They need to eat, sleep, and breathe. They are alive. They have thoughts and feelings about the world around them. The whole kingdom is full of people like Calix, especially in the noble class. Birthright is everything in their mind. Status is something you can earn but it is limited to your field. You can only work your way so far up the ladder until you run out of rungs. Some people's ladders start on higher ground with better support. His father has only begun to come to terms with how irrational the system is. People should be able to dictate their own lives, even if it is as simple as learning a new hobby or who they choose to spend their free time with.

Someone needs to stand up and prove to them they can. He isn't like Amiria though. He is not brave and selfless. He isn't willing to risk his life for the greater good. He is no one's hero.

The wooden frame shifts as Amiria scoots away from him. For a split second, a pang of hurt stabs him in the chest. She doesn't want to sit close to him anymore. The pang immediately turns to the flits of a sputtering heart as she lies down, resting the back of her head upon his lap. She scoops her hair from being tucked under her letting it cascade over his legs like a river dark in the night of a new moon.

His body stiffens. His back is straight as a board. His head tilts down at her, her lips slightly parting as if she has a question, and her eyes full of wonder as she stares up at him. They remind him of the night sky. As if they hold all the answers, but at the same time none of the answers because it is impossible to get there and learn the secrets held inside.

He knows the sunlight will reveal her eyes aren't black but a deep brown, the same as her dark hair when it is struck just right by the light it will reveal highlighted strands of almond.

He lets out a breath releasing the tension in his muscles. His shoulders hunch. He can't help but smile. She has a way of making his body confused. He will tense up at her close proximity only to end up relaxing under the touch.

"If you could fly anywhere, where would you go?" she asks dreamily.

With no hesitation, Stirling answers, "Southeast past Uviktiland."

"Southeast?" Amiria scrunches her nose, "But we don't know what's over there."

"Exactly, our maps show the Kingdom of Uviktiland runs along the coast and up along the north and northeast where all our trade routes are. But there must be more past that. The map lines drag off into emptiness. No nations, nor cities, not even mountainous regions or valleys. I'm curious about what's out there." Stirling's mind travels out of the cave across the ocean, a straight field of blue extending all the way to the horizon. "The world doesn't end even though it appears like it."

There is a heavy silence. All he hears is the distant waves crashing against the sea wall far below. He lowers his chin returning to Amiria. Her thick eyelashes lay feathered on her cheekbones, her soft breaths a whisper of a sound as her chest rises and falls. She appears peaceful, with a hint of an upwards curve visible in the corners of her mouth.

Maybe she will want to come live here with him. No, maybe she will want to run away with him. Somewhere where they can make up their own rules. Where there's the possibility they can finally be whoever they want to be. Maybe he can build them a house and they can spend every evening like this, the two of them talking until the sun goes down. Then they will curl up beneath the blankets knowing today, tomorrow, and every day after will be theirs.

His hand hovers over her hair, longing to feel the silkiness against his palm. He retracts his hand as if he had discovered she is venomous, placing it down to his side.

Just ask her, you idiot, he chastises himself.

He swallows the lump forming in his throat. Picking back up his hand, he gently strokes her hair. It'll be the two of them in a house he will make.

Forty-Nine

The warmth of the fire kisses Amiria's cheeks spreading across her entire body as she stretches awake beneath a blanket that had been tucked around her.

Stirling is kneeling beside the fire pit feeding the hungry flames another log from the pile he had split the previous day. The cave is soaked in a full shadow as the late afternoon sun moves to the adjacent side of the mountain. The fire casts a soft glow highlighting the tips of Stirling's hair like golden rays. It defines the structure of his face with shadows moving and swaying along with the crackling music of the flames.

"Amiria," he says, his eyes glued to the fire, her name rolling off his tongue like a song.

She pushes up, tucking her legs into a cross-legged sitting position. She loves the way her name sounds coming from his lips, sweet and delicate like it is his favorite word. No one else takes the same pride and care for it every time they speak it as he does.

"Yeah?" she replies groggily.

She glances over to see that Ignis and Taika have moved

their lounging quarters to the mouth of the cave. Ignis watches intently as always, his golden eyes gleaming with the reflection of the fire while Taika keeps her focus staring out of the cave, always on the guard.

Her gaze returns to Stirling, who is now staring at her, his face bursting with hope, "Amiria, I, uh..." He nervously rubs the sweat off his palms on his blue tunic that has faded over the years. "Will you—do you—" His fingers tap to his nervous rhythm.

"Stirling, say whatever it is already. What's gotten into you?" Amiria interrupts with impatience for Stirling's word fumbling.

Stirling closes his eyes and takes a breath. "Do you want to run away to the southeast with me?"

Silence.

"We can settle down somewhere new."

Silence

Stirling keeps rambling, filling in the awkward silence, "We can live in a house that I will build."

Caught off guard, her mouth hangs agape as they lock eyes with one another, the sound of seagulls echoing in the void between them. She can list a hundred topics guessing what he was going to say but this, this is not on her list. This is not what she was expecting to hear. She can't leave, she has a job, a family, and a life here.

The idea does pique her interest though. She has never felt at home in the castle. The only person wanting to talk to her is her paid handmaiden and Calix. She could say goodbye to strict laws, goodbye uniforms, and drills. Goodbye missions she has a chance of never returning home from and hello freedom. Hello to waking up next to Stirling with his goofy grin every morning. She twists the autumn-colored bracelet around her wrist.

Oh, what a dream that would be. All she has to do is say yes. Say yes, and all the suffering this Island has to offer will go away. Say yes and take his hand. Where else can she find happiness that is pure, besides these moments in this cave? Say yes, and this can be her forever. Say yes, and he can be her's forever.

"I can't," is what she ends up saying. "I would be a deserter. It would soil my family name. I can't do that to my father. Plus. They won't give up searching for me as they did you. I have too much training. I know too much. King Dietrich would rather kill me himself, getting his precious robes dirty than to let me walk free."

Of course, Stirling thinks to himself.

What was he thinking? Of course, she wouldn't want to run away with him. Why would she? She has the dream job working by the king's side and is sent on covert missions to protect the Isles of Wyverna. She lives lavishly, never having to worry about being cold or hungry. She is a respected individual with her place settled at the top. Who would give that up to sleep in the dirt in a world you don't even know exists?

"Sorry for asking. It was a stupid thought," Stirling says, with a quivering smile trying to hide the disappointment.

He had worked it up in his mind convincing himself that maybe there is a chance. Maybe she wants the same things in life he does. Maybe she wants *him*. He worked himself up so far, the fall is a devastating crash when he is struck down.

"You don't have to apologize. If this was another life, I would. I just—I can't abandon my position," Amiria says as she watches Stirling poke at the fire.

"Another life, always in another life. Why can't it be this life?" he says, dropping the twig he was using.

Amiria shrugs. "It's the hand we were dealt. But we can change it one day."

Stepping away from the fire, Stirling shuffles back to the bed and slumps down beside Amiria, his hands resting in his lap. "I don't want to keep waiting for one day. That one day isn't going to come unless I make it happen, and I would like it if you were by my side. This nation isn't going to change overnight, but I can change my world overnight by leaving."

She sits there checking him over. The untamed curls she's tried to keep at bay by cutting them when they get too long. The way the muscles of his back show through the worn tunic pulled taut against him as his broad shoulders hunch forward. He is no longer the boy she had met.

Her fingers twitch, desperately wanting to reach out and take his hand. To curl her fingers with his. She wants to jump up, yanking him with her as she yells to forget everything. Packing will only waste time. They will run away right then and there.

"Just be patient," she says, biting her tongue.

This isn't what she wants to say. She wants to leave with him. Why can't she say what she really wants? Her thoughts are saying one thing but the words coming out of her mouth are the opposite. What is she so scared of? The King? The Winged Cavalry? Her father? The unknown?

She reaches her hand, placing it on his shoulder, his cheek brushes against her fingers as he tilts his head into her.

"I *have* been patient. I've waited years," he mutters.

"I know." She hangs her head. "It's getting late. I've got to be heading home. I'll be back next week like always." She pauses, her gaze finding him again, "You'll be here, right?"

Stirling forces a smile. "Yeah, of course."

With her hand still on his shoulder, Amiria gives him a gentle squeeze before using him as support to stand up. Her fingers linger on the fabric longer than needed, subconsciously not wanting to leave his side.

"Oh, I almost forgot. Your father gave us a special treat. I asked him why but he said it would be a nice addition to my picnic. I don't really care for gingerbread so you can have it all."

He peers up at her stunned. "Gingerbread?"

"Yeah, do you not like it either?" she says.

Stirling's forced smile turns genuine, "Actually, it's my favorite."

"Oh," is all she manages to say. *Coincidence?* Amiria leans down trying to meet Stirling's gaze as he evades making eye contact. "I will see you next week then?"

Her intuition begins nipping at her insides. This goodbye is different.

"I'll see you next week," he mumbles.

"Please, please don't do anything rash," she says, letting her hand slip off his shoulder. "Stirling. I mean it."

He nods but doesn't meet her eye and curls his fingers into his palm to keep them from tapping. She will be able to read him, so he doesn't risk glancing up from the fire pit to witness the disappointment in her eyes. Turning away, she hides the self-loathing staining her face, her body betraying her soul, acting against her true wishes.

His lips turn downward, his head finally turning to watch as she walks away from him to Taika, who readies herself excitedly. He can't take his eyes off her. She tucks the loose strands of hair behind her ears and takes another glance back at Stirling who drops his gaze. Biting her lip, Amiria swings up onto Taika and pulls her goggles into place. The clicking sound of her belt buckling to the saddle echoes through the cave and screams in his ears, *Stop her!* Then at the sound of a short whistle, she is gone. Disappearing into the night, like a leaf carried away by the wind.

There is a rope tied around his heart and when she leaped out of the cave it yanked his heart right out of his chest with her. He desperately wants to take hold of the rope and pull her back to him. To convince her to stay the night with him. He wants to know what it is like to hold her tight in his arms.

"I'm going to take an educated guess. We're leaving anyway?" Ignis says as Stirling digs through the bag laying on the ground beside the bed.

He pulls out the wrapped item tugging on the string and tying it closed.

The wrapping opens, revealing the gingerbread. Stirling feels the tears catch in his throat but all that comes out is a single breathy laugh. The aroma wafting into the air around him sends him back to his childhood, his mother shooing him away from the fresh loaves as he attempts to nab one off the counter. He takes a bite savoring the flavor, unique in its own, sweetness with a kick of spice.

"I've wasted enough time here. It's finally time to make progress. Things don't happen on their own. What do you think?" Stirling finally says to Ignis.

"*Tell me, what's different? What caused you to suddenly decide to be proactive? You told me you were going to ask her, but why are we still leaving?*" Ignis questions.

"My conversation with Amiria. She asked me where I'd like to go, it got my mind rolling. I'm not going to spend my days hiding in this cave until I die here, alone and forgotten." Stirling says.

"You won't be alone."

"I'll have you, but what will happen when one of us dies before the other?" Stirling points out.

"*It's never crossed my mind,*" Ignis admits.

"And Amiria, she's not going to keep coming up here forever. One day she's going to find someone and have a family. I would prefer it if she came with us, but she's made her decision. I can't force her to leave everything behind for me."

"*Okay, you made your point. When do you suppose we should leave?*" Ignis asks.

"Tonight," Stirling says firmly.

"*Tonight!*" Ignis almost jumps up, "*That's a little short notice now, isn't it?*"

"Why do you have something planned for tomorrow?" Stirling throws out.

"*Well, no. I just need to mentally prepare myself for this,*" Ignis says as his excuse.

"It's our best option, now or never they might say. I've wasted years already. I can't afford one more day. Plus, I need to get as far away as I can before Amiria notices. I could tell she knew something was up with me and I don't want to risk her coming up here and stopping me. I don't think I'd be able to say no to her if she convinces me to stay."

"You feel bad if you force her to leave behind her life. But it's ok if she makes you throw away your chance of freedom to stay here for her?" Ignis points out.

"No, it's not okay. But she captivates me. I'd do anything to see her smile. That's exactly why I need to leave now. We need to leave and never look back." Stirling tells him. His voice turns somber, "But there is one thing I do need to do first. I want to say goodbye to my father."

Ignis is taken aback. *"Your father! Do you think that's a good idea? He thinks you're dead. He's grieved you once. Are you going to make him go through that again?"*

Stirling lets out a long sigh. "I know, but I want to see him again. I want him to know I am alive and I'll be fine."

Stirling leans over to the side of the bed closest to his wall and reaches beneath it, grabbing the bag and costrel Amiria had given him three years ago. He scoops up the bag left by his feet full of food, cradling them all in his arms as he stands up.

"You make a lot of rash decisions," Ignis comments.

"It's one of my main features. You should know this. We grew up together. I'm going to get all these bags tied to you before I head back to town so we can leave as soon as I return or if there is some kind of emergency." Stirling says, setting down the items beside Ignis, "You can come to rescue me."

He opens the old bag checking the contents; his goggles, a knife he had made from a sharpened bone and leather handle, scraps of shredded rope, a few arrowheads he had made, and a hatchet made of a sharpened rock. Besides the bow and quiver, these are a few of his only possessions.

"Do you think I should bring some of the pelts?" Stirling

scans the cave over his shoulder. He can't bring everything with him. He'll have to make it all from scratch again wherever he settles down.

"*I don't think rolling up a few and the blanket will hurt,*" Ignis suggests.

"I'll roll them around the bow and quiver. Maybe that'll protect it," Stirling says.

Stirling ties a leather rope he had made around each of Ignis' hind legs with a strap going over the top of his hips connecting them together. He rolls the bow and quiver each in their own pelt, tying them snuggly to the back harness along with the rolled blanket, bags, and costrel.

After double-checking his knots, Stirling turns glossy-eyed and stares at the cave that became his home even before he had run away; but every bird needs to eventually leave the nest.

Fifty

Stirling's slender figure slips along the shadows of the market streets, cutting through one of the many murky alleyways, barely a shoulder's width. He thinks back to the first day he went out flying with Amiria. How they walked through the narrow passage in the rock, the sky only a blue line above them. He looks up now, there is no starlit sky, only the underbelly of two building jetties merging into one fixture.

Nothing had changed over the years, the same shop signs hang over the same buildings since Lumierna was first formed, and the shops passed down through each generation.

He avoids taking a deep breath as the unpleasant aroma burns his nostrils from stagnant water, overflown privies, and miscellaneous items thrown out from the shops to gather in the city streets. The scent was never apparent until he had become accustomed to the fresh pine air of the mountains. Now the pungency of it is overwhelming and gagging him. Holding back the bile rising in his throat, he is perfectly content with never moving back to the city.

He tugs on the hood of the cloak he had made from deer hides. He had tanned and softened the leather with materials and tools he was able to assemble. Cleaning the skin with sharpened bones, then stretching it out by tacking it to tree trunks and softening it after covering it in the tanning solution over a low-smouldering fire. The stitching made from an unravelled rope is thick and uneven like large fault lines running its scar-like seams across an empty terrain.

The hood hangs low above his brow, casting a shadow over his eyes. He hopes to avoid detection and avoid the question of who he is. There is only a scarce amount of people who will be out at this time of night. Most families have finished supper and are turning in for the night to get ready for another hard day of work in the morning.

There it is. He stops in the middle of the street, the cold bakery looming over him, his fingers tapping rapidly at his sides. Index, middle, ring, pinky, middle, index. He stares immobile at the front door. The creaking baker's guild sign sun faded from years of exposure.

His pulse quickens. "Breathe, Stirling, just breathe. It's your own father. What's there to be scared of?"

Rolling his shoulders back with a deep breath, he holds it in and releases it slowly. Nervously wiping his hands off on his trousers, he walks up the warped wooden steps to the front door and reaches for the handle.

Giles sits at the table upstairs alone. The bench once occupied by his wife Jannell and son Stirling is pushed in close to the table, left untouched for years. Stirling's stool sits in its grooves by the window blanketed by a layer of dust shining in the moonlight from the opened window like fresh snow.

Tilting his head back, he takes a sip of his third pressed white wine, among the cheapest made.

He pulls the wooden cup away from his lips as he hears the front door creak. "Now, who would be showing up at this hour?"

He swings his leg over the bench, pushing up and away from the table. Exchanging his wine for the candle lantern resting in the middle of the table, he heads to the stairs. He listens attentively. His toes touch the next step and he lowers his heel down without a sound. Letting the single flame lantern guide his way, he cautiously steps down the stairs. He has no intention of frightening whoever is in the shop. He only wishes to explain he is closed for the night so he may resume his wine before laying his aching back to rest.

His free hand shoots to the wall to balance himself as he halts midstep as if he had reached the end of a leash teetering steps away from the bottom of the stairs. His chest constricting and contorting inside of him, squeezing all the air out of his lungs. Suddenly becoming nauseous, he falls ill at the sight of a man with sandy-colored hair curling out in every direction. His gold and green eyes reflecting the lantern light stare up at him wide-eyed like a frightened animal. This young man resembles a boy he wishes every day would come home to him, a boy he dreamt about walking through the bakery door. They would argue about where he had been and the chores that were neglected but he would be here, Stirling would be home. That reality will be nothing more than a dream. His son who he has never stopped missing is gone forever.

"I'm closed. There will be fresh products in the morning. Come back then," Giles manages to choke out after finding his composure.

"Sir," Stirling starts before deciding to change his wording. "Father—Father it's me. Stirling."

"Pardon me? I fear I have misheard you?" Giles says, his body beginning to shake.

"It's me, Stirling," he says, taking a steady step forward toward the bottom step.

"No, no, no, no," Giles says, shaking his head, "No, you stay back whoever you are. Stay back."

"Father," Stirling says, stepping forward once again.

"I said to stay back!" Giles begins to raise his voice.

Not lifting his foot high enough as he steps backward in sync with Stirling's advancements he stumbles back on the staircase, dropping the lantern to its side. The flame holds onto the horizontal candle wick as it flickers and wavers, casting moving shadows across the room.

"I—I said don't come near me. You're not my son. My son is dead," Giles pleads.

"Father, it's really me. The king has lied to you. I can explain everything," Stirling says hastily, trying to get his words out before Giles can interrupt him while putting his hands up, showing he has no weapons and means no harm.

Giles' hand shoots out in front of him in defense while his other supports his body on the stairs. "STAY BACK!" he shouts, beginning to slowly scoot up the staircase. His supporting hand fumbles blindly behind him to find the next step to pull himself away from Stirling. "Stay away, evil spirit. I have no deals to make with you! God has already taken everything from me." His voice quivers with fear.

Standing there baffled, Stirling is lost on how to proceed. He expected his father to be shocked and sceptical at first but after some reasoning, he would come around and believe him. What is being displayed in front of him is not his father is sceptical of him. His father is outright terrified of him. His eyes are frantic and dilated as if he is cowering from a monster.

Giles knows the shadowed object in front of him can't possibly be his son. Stirling is dead, and the only conceivable way for him to be here now in person is if he is a demon or another worldly creature is wearing his son's face. He doesn't want to know what a sick creature like that would want from him, but every folklore he has heard involving the damned never ends happily. They will ask to make deals or trades at the cost of life and souls while they wear the disguise of something trustworthy you will let yourself be vulnerable to.

Giles inhales sharply as Stirling moves to place a single foot on the bottom step. Before the step even has time to creak beneath his weight Giles leaps up from his reclined position halfway up the stairs and throws himself at Stirling in hysteria.

Stirling is paralyzed as his father comes barrelling down to the bottom steps pushing him in the chest with his bare hands. The combination of Giles' momentum and the thrust of his arms sends Stirling flying backward, landing hard on his back and sliding across the wooden floor.

Arching his back, Stirling gasps for air as the pain shoots along his spine. His father was never one to result to violence. He is always quick to lecture but he has never raised his hand to anyone.

Laying there in shock Giles towers over Stirling screaming, "Almighty and merciful God! I seek your protection! For evil has entered my home! Cover me with your presence and lend me your strength to protect myself from the wicked one!"

His face turns purple as he spits out more air than he is taking in. Stirling scurries backward using his elbows to drag his body, as his feet frantically kick to push him along, edging closer to the front door.

The yelling briefly stops as Giles picks up a wooden bread paddle lying near the stone oven. His mouth twists into a snarl as he raises the paddle over his head.

"Tell me what you are! Demon? Witch? WHAT DO YOU WANT FROM ME!?" Spit sprays from his mouth as he screams.

Stirling raises his hands in defense. "Father, it's me! Stirling! I'm your son!"

"Give up your lie, monster! My son is dead and so will you be!" Giles declares, his raucous voice pushing his volume to its limits as he swings the paddle downward at

Stirling who rolls over onto his belly, dodging the paddle as it slams down where he just was. It splinters into fragments leaving behind a sharp jagged handle still gripped in Giles' hands.

Frantic Stirling leaps from the ground throwing his shoulder against the door in a desperate attempt to flee his father. The wooden door gives into Stirling. The latch busts through the rotted wooden frame under the extensive force flinging it open. He grabs the edge of the door frame as he stumbles out onto the front steps. Tripping over his feet, he falls off the last step landing on his side on the dirt road. The door slams against the outside wall and swings back to a closing position at the same time a wooden handle is catapulted forward splintering the old wood.

Stirling lies in the mud staring up in disbelief at the cracked front door.

Neighbors stand outside their doors and lean out of their windows, wondering what the commotion can be about. They all stare at the boy hyperventilating and covered in mud. Their attention is grabbed as the front door to the bakery is kicked open.

"That's an imposter, a demon wearing my son's face!" Giles yells to his audience. Still on the ground, Stirling crawls backward in an attempt to gain distance between himself and his father.

He speaks up, defending himself to the bewildered citizens, "It's not true! It's really me! Stirling Bakere. The King has lied to all of you! I'm still alive!"

Dozens of sets of eyes stare at him. He turns in a circle in the center of the street searching, trying to meet a set that is open to understanding but none of them hear him. Their watching eyes are no different than knots in the wood, dense and unblinking. Stirling's frightened and pleading tears catch on his light eyelashes. Through the drops of liquid, an orange object in the sky catches his eye. The curious onlookers follow his gaze up to the stormy night sky erased of stars and moon.

An orange creature soars down from the clouds skimming across the thatched and wooden shingled rooftops. Horns begin to blow, sending an ear-piercing alarm echoing across Lumierna.

Stirling twists back around to his father still in the doorway. They lock eyes as the orange beast descends, his wings folding in to avoid clipping the tired and hunching buildings. He drops the final distance, his body crashing to the market streets with a significant thud. His knees bend to absorb the impact quaking and struggling to catch his weight. Regaining himself, he takes off into a gallop. Screams from women and children can be heard as the beast bolts past them, leaving a cloud of dust in his wake.

Stirling's face grimaces in anguish and heartbreak as he peels his gaze away from his father and takes off down the street in the direction of running away from the orange beast. Stirling's arms stretch out as the beast catches up to him. He grips the leather straps wrapped around the creature's scaly neck and arms, his feet lifting from the earth as it leaps into the air. Adjusting its wings to spread forward, compensating for the street's restriction as it ascends back to the sky.

Stirling watches as the people shrink below his dangling feet. He swears amongst the chaos and screaming, he heard his father calling his name.

Kelsea Koops

Fifty-One

With her goggles already strapped to her face, Amiria pulls on her opened face helm creating a black heart-shaped frame. She sprints down the spiraling stone staircase from the armory dimly lit by torches and slits in the walls barely wide enough to be called a window.

Her mission armor is a dark shadow of the armor she wears while standing post beside the king. Her hair sways from the bottom of the helm. Her boots click on the hard cold stairs behind her squad as she follows them to the stables where their dragons are kept separate from the rest of the Cavalry's.

She has been trained to decipher all the alarms and she knows this tone means an unknown dragon or wild dragon has flown over the city limits. She hasn't heard this tone since she was a child, since the wild dragons have learned to keep their distance if they do not want to be pursued.

The pitch and pattern of the alarm change. Amiria halts dead in her tracks. She isn't the only one. Her entire unit of seven stands immobile in the stairwell listening to make sure they are not mistaken about what they are hearing. They have all heard this alarm in training, but this is the first occurrence anyone in history has heard it being used for a real situation.

"Everyone! Get going! This is not a drill! GO! GO! GO!" Major Gautier shouts.

Everyone except Amiria and Calix resume sprinting, the alarm for illegal dragon riders ringing through their ears.

Amiria feels sick. She leans to see out the window not much wider than her face, the metal clanking against the stone as she presses against it trying to get a better view. Dread washes over her like a sudden downpour.

"Amiria! Hellooo!?" Calix says, ripping her away from the window by her shoulder. Her arms swing loosely at her sides like a rag doll as she is turned to face him. He leans in, filling her view; the spit from his shouting words speckles her face. "Get your act together, Amiria. Let's go!"

Amiria is silent, her mouth clamped shut. She can't find her voice. She can barely find her breath. Her mind is currently occupied with slowing down her racing heart rate. She can't let the rest of her squad see how this has shaken her. Swallowing the lump, she takes off running with Calix.

Fifty-Two

Stirling clings to Ignis. His body hanging off the side of him, suspended over the city below. The townsfolk now the size of the ants Stirling used to watch crawling in the grass. Ignis banks hard to the side, turning his body sideways so Stirling no longer hangs freely. He lays pressed against Ignis' ribcage, his movements slow and deliberate as he crawls up Ignis, swinging one of his legs off the side of his back.

Grabbing the buckle, he stretches it until finally loops through the ring on his belt. He grabs hold of the handles, Ignis taking this as his cue, he levels out carefully. Stirling, now secure in place, takes the opportunity to take in the sight.

"So this is what it appears like from above. It looks so— so fake. As if we aren't the ones at the height of clouds, but that's the regular ground and those are fireflies," Stirling says in astonishment at the winding dirt roads lit by torches and lanterns of citizens waking up to the sounds of the alarm.

Stirling reaches behind him, fishing through the bag tied to Ignis' hips, and pulls out his goggles. He runs his fingers over the etched design and pulls them over his face.

"I'm guessing that's not how you planned on it going? Not sure what you were expecting though. A good ol' father embracing his dead son or what?" Ignis says.

"I wasn't expecting an embrace, but I was hoping he would at least listen to me. Instead, he tried to kill me." Stirling hangs his head seeing his hands still trembling with shock. Closing his eyes, he represses the fresh-forming memory. Opening his eyes, he glances off into the direction of the castle and squints. "What's that?"

Ignis observes the triangle formation of seven dots ascending into the sky.

"That Stirling is our cue to go!" Ignis yells, pumping his wings as hard as he can, thrusting them up into the heavy cloud coverage.

Fifty-Three

Amiria flies at the tail end of her teammates in a "V" formation opposite Calix on his dragon the color of castle stone. Major Gautier, leading at the point, his dragon made from the brown shadows of the canyon.

"There they are!" Major Gautier shouts pointing up at the orange figure climbing its way up the night sky into the clouds, "We can't lose them in the coverage! Low-visibility searchlights are in effect! Order is to kill onsite!"

The whole team except, Amiria hollers in the excitement of the hunt as they race through the sky.

Stirling, you idiot. What were you thinking? Amiria fears.

Fifty-Four

No more than a fly on the gray ceiling, Stirling glances back down at the Winged Riders. They are faster than he is and gaining on him quickly. He was never able to beat Amiria in a straight-shot race and she is the least experienced member in the unit.

Becoming completely submerged in the misty air, his vision blurring as the clouds surround him. He spots the familiar beige dragon as his last sight of Wyverna.

He has no chance of outrunning them in the open air. They are the top Riders in the Winged Cavalry. They are a unit you don't get admitted to because you're a decent Rider with potential, no, they are the level of Riders the king hands picks to be his personal guard. The type who always wins or dies trying.

Of course, this is the team that will be sent out if an illegal rider is spotted. King Dietrich doesn't play chess to enjoy the game. He plays skewed to his advantage with extra pieces to ensure his victory. Stirling's only hope of making this out alive is to use the cloud cover to outmaneuver the team and make a break for the coast of Uviktiland.

The cool damp mist of the clouds wet his face and hair as they immerse themselves further into the gray world. Wiping the moisture off his goggles with the back of his hand, he squints, trying to improve his impaired vision. The air is so thick he can barely see Ignis's head right in front of him.

Each pump of his Ignis' wings climbs them higher. With each thrust forward, the air grows colder.

He blinks, the world is suddenly clear and he can see. The stars fill the night sky like the curious citizens filled the cities' streets. The moon low and yellow like the setting sun, hangs just above the clouds ready to greet them as they break free.

Spreading his wings, Ignis is an angel above the clouds. The yellow moonlight gives a new type of elegance to his feathered wings.

With steady beats, Ignis hangs suspended in the sky, the sea of off-white flowing below them. The uneven clouds create dips and shadows resembling the caps of waves in a rough ocean current.

"Ignis, is that lighting?" Stirling questions. The clouds below them begin to light up in flashes of orange and yellow light.

An eruption like an overdue volcano explodes from the clouds behind them, lighting up the area around them like daylight. Stirling can feel the sweltering heat against his back. It remains inside his leather cloak sticking his tunic to his skin. As the fire dissipates, a massive brown dragon, its features jagged and uneven like the face of a mountain, appears from the flames.

Stirling's voice climbs up from his lungs, clawing and ripping from his throat like an animal desperate to escape and save its life. "IGNIS! GOOOO!"

Before Stirling can finish, Ignis folds in his wings, letting his body turn, and dives back into the clouds.

His face contorting into a grimly sneer, Major Gautier pulls the reins of his mountainous dragon and dives chasing after them. He picks up his bull horn strapped around his armor with a leather cord. Sucking in as much air as he can, he puts the horn up to his lips, giving it a single extended blow. The sound pierces through the clouds, telling the rest of his unit the illegal rider has been spotted.

After his call is finished, his dragon sends out a small spurt of fire in the last known direction he had seen Stirling flying in, giving them the information on which they should continue their pursuit in the dense clouds.

Moisture continues to gather on his goggles making his already low visibility harder. He struggles to see, lost in the damp gray sea. His skin quickly cools from the scorching heat it had experienced. He can barely think as his heart pounds through his skull. He's lightheaded, his breaths shallow and sharp in the thin air.

"*Behind us!*" Ignis informs, twirling his body around before Stirling can even react.

Ignis' body hangs vertically suspended in the air. His wings pulled out straight behind him as his chest expands.

The belt looped around Stirling's waist digs into his skin as his weight tests the durability. His legs grip onto Ignis as gravity tries to pry them out of the poorly constructed stirrups. His fingers already pink and numb from the night air, far above the warmth of the land, grip the harness as if they are the only things keeping him from falling from the sky like a stone to the waters below.

Light glows deep inside Ignis' chest illuminating his bones and arteries, and casting shadows visible through his thick scaly skin. Stirling watches as the light travels up his neck, highlighting each vertebra. Ignis' chest contracts until the fire ignites from his jaws like a poisonous flower blooming beautifully for its unforeseen victim.

The clouds light up around them as if lit by a thousand

torches. Stirling squints, blinded as his pupils try to constrict fast enough to keep up with the sudden change in exposure.

Directly in front of them, a wall of fire forms matching the flames made by Ignis. The two blistering gas beasts charge at each other until they collide in the center, fighting and hissing as they morph into a sphere swirling with uncontrollable energy.

The glowing sphere hangs in the clouds like a red giant flickering in the Milkyway as two massive incomes of energy flow into it. Finally exceeding its limit, the ball of fire explodes in every direction sending out a wave of blazing heat.

Taken back by the fire, Ignis falls through the sky as the flames caress his armored skin.

Stirling's eyes are forced shut. Even through his goggles, the heat blasting against his face is too much to handle. He can feel Ignis' weight shift to be above him and the now familiar gut-wrenching feeling of freefall comes back to him like a punch to the stomach. The icy air pushes against his back, holding him pinned against Ignis.

Spinning his body upright, Ignis spreads his wings catching themselves. The tip of his orange feathers barely peeks out from the underbelly of the clouds like a shark's fin as he twirls.

Stirling clutches the handles in a terror he has never experienced. The entire harness has shifted, sliding over to one side of Ignis's body. His left ankle hooks onto the top of Ignis' back as his right leg and body dangle over the gray abyss. Struggling, he slowly pulls himself back to safety. Thankful the belt he had made remains buckled.

He is going to vomit. His whole body is trembling and not only from the damp air sinking into his bones, but the fear these clouds will be the last thing he ever sees.

So, this is battle?

He wants to curl in on himself, huddle up and hide warm by the fire in the safety of his cave. Somewhere death is not knocking at his door.

This is what the Winged Cavalry is trained to do. They don't have death waiting at their door. They have him following them around every corner. Then when it comes to it, to make sure their mission is complete and the kingdom is safe. They will willingly open their door and invite death into their home.

This life is not for him. The battlefield is not for him. This is not in his blood figuratively and literally. His passion and reason for living are to ride. But this isn't riding. This is surviving. There is no enjoyment of the flight this time. If he wants to continue flying with Ignis, he needs to make it out of here. He needs to make it to the shore.

Pushing through the clouds, Ignis strains himself to gain as much distance as he can before the Cavalry discovers their location again.

Fifty-Five

Amiria hovers in the thick clouds appearing to light up randomly with fireworks of orange, but they aren't random. There is a system they learned and practiced for this type of search. Everyone on the team owns a dragon who can emit fire. She had learned if someone was to bond with one of these types of dragons, it is a definite foreshadowing they will be offered a position in this squad or leadership in another area.

The Riders are only allowed to shoot fire in the same direction declared by the Rider who makes first contact with the subject. They will sound their alarm and spit fire in the direction they designate in hopes of locating the objective. To avoid the squad members from being struck by friendly fire, each Rider flies at their pre-assigned elevations and spreads outwards, covering the surface area of the sky.

Then there is the rule Amiria grew up learning as the way of the Cavalry life, attack and apprehend first, questions later. If a casualty or fatality happened, they are labeled as guilty since you had to pursue them to begin with. If innocent bystander casualties happen, you are to move on. They were harmed in the process of protecting the nation and it should be seen as an honor.

In their world, for the safety of the mass majority, it is assumed guilty until proven innocent. This is what she fears. They will attempt to catch Stirling even if it costs him his life. None of them will hesitate to put an arrow through his heart and let his body feed the fish. There is no trial for someone in his situation. It's an automatic death penalty. His only upside, if he is unable to escape, is he dies here on the battlefield and is not brought back to King Dietrich to be tortured and humiliated in front of the nation.

Her heart aches. She is experiencing a new concoction of emotions. This is not a normal mission where she can turn off what makes her human in order to complete the king's orders. This time she knows the perpetrator. He is her friend. He is someone she has become close with. Someone she cares about.

She is overflowing with rage at Stirling for conducting such an outrageous act as if he didn't even think what kind of impact this would have on her. In the center of her core, she worries luck might not be on his side this time. This familiar ocean might finally be his grave. She doesn't want a world where his smile isn't lighting up even in the darkest places. She is torn between wanting to break his bones for breaking his promise to her that he wouldn't go doing anything stupid and protecting him in her arms from the harshness of reality.

Uncomfortable, Amiria shifts her shoulders under her armor. Her quiver and bow rest above them, waiting to be brought into action. Her fingers itch to feel the elasticity and weight of the bow fight against her pull until she lets go and it springs back to shape, sending the arrow on its journey to a destination it never misses.

Her eyes closing, she prays Stirling is able to create

enough distance before he is spotted again. What if she sees him? What if it's her who he appears in front of? Will she take that shot? Who will she betray tonight? Who truly means more to her, the Winged Cavalry or Stirling?

Amiria slaps her hands against the sides of her helm. She dips her chin to her chest, squeezing the metal between her palms as pressure forms in her head. She can't stop the thoughts from flooding her brain and swelling against her skull.

What am I supposed to do?

Fifty-Six

Citizens stand scared and confused as they watch the night sky. Mothers hold their crying frightened children close, covering their ears from the blaring alarm. Fathers stand guard over their families trying to comprehend what is unfolding above them. Other than the people in Stirling's neighborhood who saw the unknown dragon swoop down and take a person, Lumierna's citizens are unaware of why the alarms are ringing and why the sky is lighting up. This can be the beginning of a war for all they know.

Giles stares numbly at the sky flashing like a violent storm made from a flurry of hell's fire.

"Giles, Giles Bakere." An elderly man says, his hand clasped on Giles' shoulder shaking him gently. Giles' eyes remained fixated on the sky in a hypnotic trance.

Barely audible over the crowd's cries and screams he whispers to himself, "Demon, it was demon, demon, demon, it was a demon."

"Giles!" The man says again, this time putting more

emphasis on his voice. Giles jumps, turning to him surprised as if he hadn't realized he had been standing there. "Giles was that your son? It looked a lot like him. Those blond curls." The elderly man asks his face puzzled and concerned beneath his wrinkles for his neighbor who is still pale from his encounter earlier.

Shaking his head, Giles' mouth hangs gaping. His jaw twitches as if he has thoughts to say but no way to form the words. Gazing back up at the erupting sky he wonders if this is real or if this is a nightmare. None of this is possible. His son is dead. His son is dead, and he can't ride a dragon. It's impossible. His son is dead. That was a demon and that was his hell beast.

King Dietrich couldn't have lied to him. Couldn't have lied to everyone. They trust their entire being to the king. Why can't he just live a quiet life as a baker?

Murmur ripples across the crowd with a strong wind. Each person spread their thoughts and opinions to their neighbor. Whispers circulate the rumors like wildfire during a summer's drought.

"Was that the baker's son? But he's dead. Witchery?"

"That had to be him, he ran out of the bakery. It looked like him."

"Where has he been hiding?"

"Was he held captive there this whole time? How did the Cavalry not find him?"

"What was that dragon? Is he riding it?

If that's not the baker's child? Who's riding the dragon?

Fifty-Seven

Stirling can't control his breathing, pumping air in and out of his lungs rapidly before he can process it, depriving his brain of oxygen. His heart rate is spiking uncontrollably. The edges of his vision are beginning to fade, a dark frame outlining his view slowly creeping across his eyes. His lips and fingers tingle. He's spinning. He knows Ignis is flying straight but he is spinning, and he can't stop. Everything is a gray blur around him like when he was a kid and spun himself in circles until he tipped over.

How far out over the ocean are they? If they weren't inside the clouds, would they be able to see the details of Uviktiland or would they still only see the endless darkness around them?

Staring down at his hands grasped to the handles Stirling's head bobs. His neck muscles are weak like a newborn. Everything seems to be pulsing as the world slowly disappears on him. The tunnel creeps in on his vision till he can barely see his hands releasing the handles of the harness.

His body slumps, his hands dropping to his sides as he hunches forward barely holding himself up.

He watches helplessly as the harness still latched to his belt comes loose from Ignis. The straps drag along Ignis' back, flapping in the wind as it appears Ignis is flying right out from below.

That's strange, he thinks as his body slides into the supplies packed on Ignis' hips.

He slips sideways, falling off Ignis' flank behind his wing. He flips through the air beginning his accelerating descent toward the vicious dark waters below.

The earthy orange figure in the murky sky fades away from existence as Stirling rapidly descends through the clouds. Ignis screams his name. His voice echoes in Stirling's head as if it is coming from every direction. He doesn't know which way is up and which way is down. He doesn't feel as if he is falling. It feels as if the wind is cradling his body, holding him stagnant, floating above the earth's surface claimed by humans.

He can't breathe or is it he has forgotten? The powerful wind races around him as if he is a stone resting in the middle of a raging river.

He is slipping in and out of consciousness, the black rim of his vision closing in on the last of his remaining sight.

Where am I? He wonders.

His body loses all sensation, his skin numb to the frigid wind, nothing solid to give him a sense of gravity, and nothing but gray mist to comprehend direction. He falls through the bottom of the clouds into the crisp clean air. With no land to be seen in the moonless night, the water and sky become a black dome around him and the gray clouds are the bottom.

He's going to crash through the dome's ceiling. He's going to crash through it and enter a void. He won't be able to call for help. She will pull him in close and drag him to her mysterious depths and he will cease to exist.

Stirling's mind finally releases its hold on reality and succumbs to the unconscious realm.

Ignis dives out of the clouds, his body a stark contrast to the metal-colored sky flickering like the light dying in the cooling embers. Tucking in his wings, he squeezes them as tight as he can into his body to bypass any air resistance. Desperately he tries to catch up with Stirling.

Ignis hates himself for not noticing Stirling had fallen off sooner. He was so preoccupied with eluding the Cavalry he couldn't feel the straps of the harness disappear along with the weight of Stirling shifting down his back. It wasn't until Stirling fell off, his foot kicking his side. By the time he turned around Stirling was already lost to the clouds.

If only Stirling had said something to him. Gave him some kind of warning. He had said nothing. His mind feels distant but not as if he was closing him off purposefully, as he has done in the past. Instead, his mind is pouring out of his grasp like grains of sand. The more he moves his hands to grab the fallen sand, the more he will lose.

He calls out to Stirling. Repeating his name over and over in a futile attempt to get a response. He can't let Stirling hit the water. This isn't jumping into a lake from a high rock. Falling from the clouds into the water will be no different than falling onto solid ground.

Stretching out his front claws, Ignis reaches. Slowly closing the gap between them.

Fifty-Eight

Hovering below the cloud line, Amiria's heart lurches slamming into her ribcage as she watches Stirling plummet from the clouds with Ignis tailing behind like a guardian angel descending from the heavens. Clutching her horn with a metal tip, she grits her teeth, pushing down the emotions raging inside her.

She desperately wants to extend out her hand to catch Stirling. To save him, to bring him back to the cave alive with her so they can sit close to each other by the fire as they did earlier today.

Once again, he had gotten himself into another problematic situation without weighing out the consequences beforehand. She can't keep saving him forever. Without her, he would have died in that cave years ago.

Helping him at this moment will be committing mutiny in the blatant view of the Cavalry. She has been committing treachery since she met Stirling. At this rate, the next time they are side by side it will be in the ditch King Dietrich throws their traitorous bodies in.

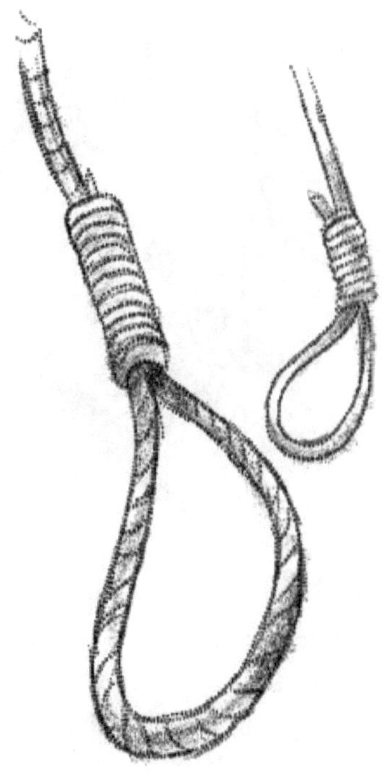

Fifty-Nine

Ignis' head passes Stirling's body first. His arms reach, searching for Stirling as he closes in on him. The tips of his nails graze the fabric of Stirling's cloak.

"Got him." He clasps his claws around Stirling's back, hugging him into his chest, Stirling's face pressing into the softer underbelly scales.

The water is racing up at them, ready to meet them head-on with a deadly collision. It is too late for Ignis to turn and pull up. If he tries to spread his wings out now, at this speed and distance from the water, he will risk breaking them by crashing into the water with them fully extended.

Resorting to the only option he can think of in the short amount of allotted time. He covers his chest and stomach with his wings encasing Stirling safely inside. Ignis' head tucks into his body for protection letting his body roll into the harsh impact, his shoulders striking first and his hips and tail last.

Ignis refuses to let Stirling go as the rough waters rip

around them, twisting, turning, and tugging as it rushes to fill in the empty pocket displaced by the mass of Ignis' intruding body.

Gasping, Stirling breathes in sharply as he's awoken by a slap of cold water. His lungs are met with liquid overly saturated with salt. He chokes as the water fills his lungs, each cough only bringing in more. His goggles sit crooked on his face exposing his eyes to the salt water stinging them instantly.

Disoriented in his surroundings, Stirling squirms. He finds himself immobile and blind in a world with no air and no light. His lungs scream for oxygen and he begins thrashing himself against Ignis, pushing on his chest trying to free himself from his suffocating situation. Ignis squeezes tighter, afraid Stirling will wiggle free and be ripped away from him with the current. He needs to find his barrens in which direction is the surface.

Air bubbles escape from Ignis' nostrils running down his face and neck, wriggling and morphing as they push upwards, rising through the liquid.

"I'm still upside down," Ignis realizes, turning his head to face his tail, his body following the path as he swims through the water, swaying back and forth like a snake.

Ignis' head breaches the surface extending out above the water on his long neck, his mouth gaping open as he takes in air. Leaning back, he allows his body to float up to the surface, exposing his chest with Stirling limp in his arms.

Stirling can feel the cold breeze nip at his drenched body. He tries to breathe in the fresh air. Nothing. He's still drowning. He is above the water's surface but he is still drowning, his lungs full of water as he gasps for the air all around him. It taunts and mocks him as he suffocates.

Turning white, Stirling weakly taps on Ignis' chest with his fist, only producing gurgling sounds as he tries to take in the air. Ignis panics. He doesn't understand what to do or why Stirling is still having trouble breathing when they are no longer underwater.

In a frantic attempt to help him, Ignis picks Stirling up with his large claws gripping around the entire width of Stirling's upper arms and shoulders. He shakes Stirling, whiplashing him back and forth.

Stirling throws up the entire capacity of his lungs in water.

"You're alive! You're alive! I was so scared I lost you," Ignis says, dropping him back down onto his chest, relieved.

Stirling continues to cough, his lungs straining to breathe properly. "Not today," Stirling wheezes.

Sixty

Amiria hasn't moved from her position beneath the clouds. She pretends to keep watch while the rest of her team searches the proximity of the clouds. The metal tip of the horn rests on her bottom lip, waiting to give a call if she has any form of a visual.

"I swear to God, baker boy. If you die before you even make it to the shore. I'll resurrect you to kill you myself," she grumbles.

The sound of a horn blaring through the night from the Rider positioned above the clouds gives the signal he still has no sight. Amiria watches the midnight water with an orange speck swimming away from the life they knew. Her lips wrap around the cool metal, and she takes in a deep breath holding it until her chest hurts while she decides who she will betray tonight.

She thinks of her future, armor shining in the throne room, a metal for apprehending the first illegal rider. Admirers will praise her courageous efforts, her father will finally be proud of her.

Kelsea Koops

Her dream shatters as the vision expands to Stirling's neck in the king's hand, the life slowly draining from his eyes. Giles alone in his bakery with a reopened wound and having to mourn his son for a second time.

Her breath hitches, puffing air around the tip of the horn. Steadying her emotions, she sucks in air through her nostrils and releases, giving off the signal she too has no visual.

Sixty-One

Stumbling in the shallow surf, Ignis carries Stirling sprawled over his back up onto the sandy beach of Uviktiland.

They are far from the port town of Vistjaldenne, the faint flickering in the distance of the large torches in the harbor. The Winged Cavalry is still in pursuit, believing they are hidden in the clouds since their looks outs on top and bottom have had no visuals of the perpetrator. As they move away from the island, they have more sky to cover, lowering their chances of finding Stirling as the distance between each member grows.

"We still need cover." Stirling croaks, his throat sore from the salt water and coughing. His teeth chatter as he continues to speak, "Let's at least make it to the tree line before we rest. We're lucky there won't be any dogs or foot soldiers this time, not until they are granted permission from the king of this land."

Ignis manages an exhausted nod, his feet slowly dragging through the sand leaving behind a trail.

Barely passing the first trunks, Ignis collapses to the ground, his chest heaving as he catches his breath. His scales and feathers are already beginning to dry from the short amount of time they've been on land.

Stirling, with the harness still attached to him, tumbles off Ignis onto the soft dirt. His clothes are soaked through and clinging to his skin. His body vibrates as he tucks his knees into his chest, pulling himself into a fetal position.

"It's—so—cold," Stirling says through his shutters, his jaw locking up with the convulsions of his body.

"A fire won't be a good idea," Ignis reminds him.

"I know." Stirling agrees, knowing it will give away their location.

Forcing his shivering body to unravel, Stirling peels himself apart. Instead of only unlatching the harness from him he undoes his entire belt instead. His trembling fingers, pruned and numb, make it difficult to take off. He slides it off, letting it plop to the ground beside his hips.

Slowly rising to his feet, Stirling pulls off his goggles sitting crooked on his face, and tosses them beside the harness. Removing his cloak, he slings it over a thin tree leaning over in the shape of an arch. Reaching over his head, he grabs the back of his collar and tugs off his tunic and undershirt.

"Why are you doing that? Don't clothes keep humans warm?" Ignis asks, his head drowsily lying on the ground.

"Clothes take too long to dry. They'll keep me wet and colder longer," Stirling explains. He holds his tunic out in front of him and rings it, twisting the fabric free of water.

A painful throb pulsates through his hands as the skin stretches over his knuckles. Almost dropping the fabric, the pain across the back of his hands becomes apparent. Spreading from the bottom half of his fingers down to the back of his hands are severe burns. His skin was seared off, leaving oozing red with the edges singed white. It is as if his hands waited for him to notice before releasing the full extent of his pain now radiating up his forearms. His grip loosens with the shock of his wounds and the tunic slips from his hands. His hands become rigid, stuck in the open position.

Stirling is brought back to the day Ignis wounded his arm. He remembers the white-hot pain and the sight of the glowing iron pressing against his skin, melting it closed. How he could smell the cooking skin. His stomach knots, making him want to puke.

"*You okay?*" Ignis asks curiously, tilting his head.

"No, I got burned pretty badly. Even the air touching it hurts. I'm guessing it's from when you had the fire showdown and when that happened." Stirling says, nodding his chin at the charred harness sprawled on the ground, the front of it eaten away by flames.

"*I took most of the blast, and I'm okay,*" Ignis says.

"You also have naturally armored skin," Stirling points out. "Uagh." He winces as he leans down to pick up his tunic. His hands are unforgiving of any movements he makes.

He semi-shakes some of the dirt loose and tosses it over the tree with his cloak.

Stirling breathes, readying himself for the pain he knows he's going to endure. Careful not to bump the back of his hands, he slowly drops his trousers down to his medium-length braies that come to the middle of his thigh. Stirling curses and pulls his arms in close as the pain refuses to subside.

"I guess we'll get some rest for now, and we'll start moving at dawn. We'll have to stay on foot for a while until we think it's safe to fly again." Stirling says, shuffling his shivering body back to Ignis. "I wonder if any of the stuff made it."

Stirling tenderly unties the water-logged bags, rolled hides, and blanket off Ignis. His fingers barely want to move, the tendons disturbing the burned skin. Stirling sighs as he inspects the bag of food. The bread, cheese, and meat pies are destroyed. They are no more than a soggy lining on the inside of the bag. The pears and apples are in no better shape; they exploded as if someone struck them with a blunt weapon. He turns the bag inside out, letting the contents litter the ground. The wrapping of the gingerbread his father made lays at his feet.

He never got to finish what may be the last time he ever eats his father's baking.

He opens the next bag and is thankful to see his tools have made it. He hangs the bags and his blanket up on the branches to dry.

Stirling unravels the hide encasing the bow and the one around the quiver.

His head hangs, dropping with his hope as the bow breaks in half in his hands.

Large splinters run along the once beautiful wood. With his confidence at the bottom of the ocean, he opens the quiver.

The arrows remain inside the quiver since he had tied it closed but the majority of them are broken in some way. The quiver had caved in on them as if it had been crushed with a large rock.

Amiria had given these to him.

Stirling sets the bow and quiver off to the side. Not only did he break a gift, but he also lost all his food and broke what will help him obtain more.

Depressed, Stirling crawls over to Ignis, who raises his wing, inviting Stirling to hide underneath. Stirling huddles against Ignis, cradling his stinging hands. Ignis closes his feathers over Stirling as the only form of protection from the night.

Sixty-Two

Taika's talons tear into the side of the mountain as she pulls herself inside Stirling's cave, her tail slithering in behind her, disappearing into the shadows and out of view from any of the Winged Riders.

Amiria slides off Taika's back, her movements slow as if her limbs are pushing through water muddied thick with sorrow. The sounds of her boots and armor echo in the vast empty pocket hidden away deep in the mountains. A place she ran away to. A place where she was happy. A place where he was always waiting for her.

He left her behind. He asked her to come along, but she has a duty, a responsibility. She wanted to go with him. She desperately wants to escape this restrictive life, and never see those people in the castle again, but he sprung it on her. He didn't give her a chance to prepare herself. He left her behind with no intention of even saying goodbye. Did she mean anything to him?

Amiria stares down at the cold ashes of the fire pit.

Remnants of the fire not long ago, warm and homely, provided them light as they sat together for what she now knows was the last time. She remembers the way his hair glowed like a halo around his head.

Anger surges through her—screams of abandonment escape from her lungs. Taking a lunging step towards the fire, she whips her foot forward, kicking as hard as she can. The inside of her foot clashes against the rocks piled into a circle sending a few rolling into the ash and coals. One rock jumps away from the rest, landing near Stirling's bed.

Ash clouds into the air, her fists clenched at her sides. She breathes heavily as the cloud settles into dust on the cave floor.

Still pent up with rage, she steps around the fire pit, scooping up the rock. Squeezing it, she curses under her breath, "How could you leave me here? You think you had it worse than everyone else. You think you were forgotten about, doomed to die alone in this cave. That no one cared."

Amiria chucks the rock out over the cliff's edge. "I CARED!" she yells as the rock disappears, her eyes wet with tears she never lets fall.

Turning, she kicks the wood branch supporting the wall tented over Stirling's camp. The branch snaps where her foot makes contact. It buckles under the weight, snapping in half, it tilts the wall off balanced to one side. The remaining support slips out from under the wall slamming down on top of the bed. The triangle of stacked logs beneath it rolls out flattening everything to the ground.

She can't see it in the dark, but she can hear it. The sound of pages fluttering. She squints into the darkness around the wall lying by her feet.

Amiria tosses a few logs into the pit without bothering to fix the rocks. She meets Taika's eye and nods her head to the logs.

Taika extends her neck out to the fire. The spikes lining her jaw barely skim the cave floor. Her chest glows dimly

373

like a newly lit candle. She exhales a soft breath. The light travels out of her chest, along her neck, and across the logs. The hot breath ignites them instantly.

Turning back to the bed, Amiria investigates the sound. She kneels, going all the way down to her elbows to peek underneath the wall hanging about fist high off the ground as the bed structure prevents it from fully touching.

She still can't see anything. She lifts the wall enough to clear the bed and pushes it off. Stirling had removed all the pelts, leaving behind only the pine and rush. Amiria searches through the plants for the source of the noise. Aggravated and impatient, she begins heaving the long pieces of wood away. Each landing on top of the wall while pine and rush fly out into the air, carpeting the area.

There lying below where the bed are two items; a poorly constructed journal with no cover, only paper bound with a string, and a wooden dragon.

She pauses, staring at the contents. She snatches up the journal and begins flipping through the pages. She opens the first page; they are crudely drawn picture notes. Notes Stirling took while watching her class.

She tears each page from the journal as she turns the pages. She doesn't care that they fall to the ground and pile at her feet like autumn leaves.

He learned everything from her and this is how he paid her respect? Dumping her here like his old forgotten notes?

She stops and yanks off her gauntlet to see the leather bracelet at the bottom of her vembracer. The cave echoes with the clang of metal as she lets the gauntlet clatter to the stone floor. She uses her teeth and pulls the knot free.

If he found it easy to forget her than she will have no problem removing evidence of his existence. Then she can return to her regular duties--her structured life.

She momentarily stutters as she turns to the fire. Is that

what she wants? Does she have any other choice?

No...she doesn't

Exending her hand out over the fire she watches the hungry flames plead and wave their hands eagerly for her offering. Her metal fist trembles in the flickering orange glow but refuses to uncurl. Making small jabbing motions as her chest begins to constrict she can't command her hand to open.

Hand still clenched she drops it to her side and screams into the night.

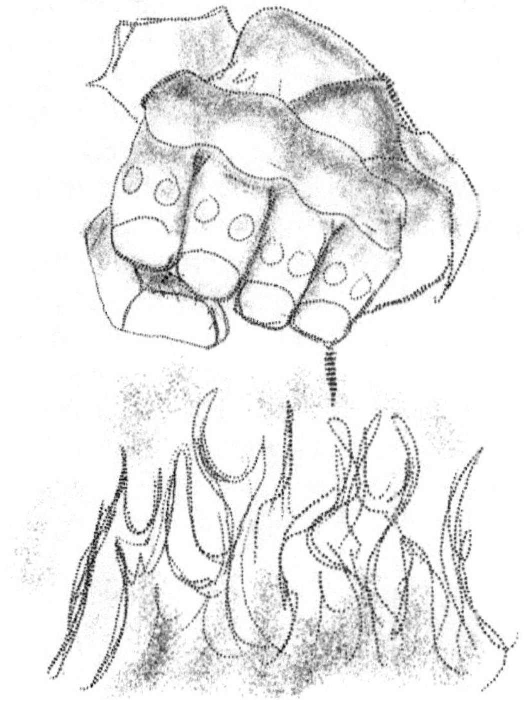

Sixty-Three

S tirling always believed the coldest part of the day is just before the sun starts to turn the horizon a deep gold and the stars slowly begin to fade away to wherever it is they go during the day.

His bloodshot eyes strain to open from both the exposure to salt water and lack of sleep. They sting as he rubs them with his forearm, his hands too sensitive to use. He didn't dream at all during the short night. He couldn't fall into a deep enough sleep between shivering and startling awake at every sound emitted from the surrounding trees.

He tries to focus his blurry vision on the coastal trees beyond the gap of Ignis' wing. His eyes water and refuse to stay open. He pushes against the wing and shimmies out into the open, his body shuddering at the touch of the early morning air.

With only one eye opened, Ignis watches Stirling groggily.

Ignis doesn't need to say what he is thinking for Stirling

to understand. "I know, but we have a long day ahead of us. We need to start covering as much ground as we can. The further we get, the better our chances. Maybe we'll reach another ocean. Maybe this land stretches forever. Either way, let's find out." Stiffly, he shuffles, dragging his feet over to his clothing hanging dry on the tree.

Shivering, Stirling slips on his trousers, tying the waistband tight around his hips. The fabric is as frigid as the air around him.

"*To the Southeast?*" Ignis yawns.

"To the southeast," Stirling confirms.

Sixty-Four

O yez, Oyez, Oyez!" the Crier shouts, ringing his bell, gathering the murmuring crowd's attention, "The boy who you may have witnessed illegally riding an unknown species of the dragon will not be publicly announced. He and the dragon have been shot down by King Dietrich's top Winged Riders. Both perished and were lost to the water's grave. The riding of a dragon without wearing the mark, no matter the species, is a treacherous crime and is punishable by being drawn and quartered without trial. The act of practicing any trade that is not marked as your insignia is punishable by hanging. Guards are now permitted to access any home and shop without the consent of the owner, according to King Dietrich's orders to maintain security in the kingdom. No more information will be given at this time. God save the king."

Blending in with the rest of the townspeople, Giles stares, listening to the crier. *It was a boy? The boy is dead?*

People begin to chatter amongst their neighbors in hushed tones out of earshot of the city guards, "Who could it have been? Why won't they tell us?"

"I bet you it really was the baker's son. I saw him leave the bakery with my own eyes."

"Impossible. He died years ago."

"He ran away, but the body was never returned."

"Where would he have been living this whole time? The forest? He definitely would have died."

"Then who was the rider?"

"Was it a lie that the boy died those years ago?"

"Is he really dead now?"

"Hush, do not speak against the king's word. People will hear."

Giles can't take any more of the whispers. He turns, pushing his way out of the crowd to return to the comfort of his bakery.

"There goes the baker."

"He must know something."

"It was his son."

"It was his son."

"It had to be his son."

Giles slows as he reaches his bakery. A man in his late twenties wearing formal attire, a long tunic cinched at the waist with a full gear belt, leather bracers, and riding gloves. The Winged Cavalry's emblem embroidered on his sleeve stands out like a black splotch on white parchment. The man stands bored, holding onto the reins of three horses with red and purple caparisons, a fabric cloaked over the horse with a significant color and pattern.

Three, Giles thinks, now hyper-aware.

One step at a time, Giles convinces his feet to move toward his bakery.

"Is there something I may help you with?" Giles asks the Rider holding the reins.

The man's eyes dig into him like an icy pickaxe. "Do you go by the name of Giles Bakere?"

"Yes, sir," Giles replies.

The man smiles, but his eyes remain cold. "Good. My colleagues are waiting inside for you."

What more do they want from me? Giles wonders as he walks up to his front door.

The Rider's stare sends pin picks down his spine. He opens the door with a fresh crack where the broken paddle it the night before.

Calix and a senior member of his squad with hair starting to gray on the sides, Dicun, stand in the bakery. Calix is holding the broken paddle, examining it while Dicun leans against the table with his arms crossed.

Both of the men's eyes land on Giles as he closes the door nervously behind him.

"You were waiting for me?" Giles asks.

Dicun steps towards Giles, his face a permanent scowl. "We're inquiring about some information about your son, Stirling Bakere."

Giles tries to hide it, but his emotions are obvious. They are stamped on his forehead for anyone who mentions his son's name like the insignia tattooed on his arm. He gulps, terrified of their presence.

"Would you like a seat?" he manages to say.

"There's no need. We shouldn't be here much longer," Dicun turns him down. "Mr. Bakere, are you able to tell us the last time you have seen your son?"

"Around three years ago, the day he ran away," Giles responds with a quiver of uncertainty in his voice. In an attempt to play casual, he slowly steps toward the table in the middle of the room. Dicun keeps his chest facing Giles as he passes, discreetly stepping back and replacing Giles' old position blocking the exit.

"We have witness statements reporting they saw you and what appeared to be your son Stirling Bakere exiting this bakery last night. There seems to have been some kind of—" Dicun reads the front door, "Altercation. Do you recall any of this, Mr. Bakere? If it was not your son, then who exited your bakery last night and took off on an unregistered dragon," Dicun demands.

Giles, weak in the knees, leans against the table, staring at them in disbelief. He thought he was done with interrogations. He thought he was past all the questions about his son when those guards came to his home, informing him of the news that Stirling was dead. They were the ones who wrote the report that his son had perished from a fall in the mountains.

Turning ghostly, he utters, "My son is dead."

"Mr. Bakere, we have multiple witness accounts," Calix points out, setting the paddle down on the shelf.

Giles slams his hand on the wooden table in distress. "My son died three years ago!"

Calix grabs the arm Giles slammed on the table and places his other hand on the back of Giles' head. In one motion Calix rips Giles' hand free of the table and pushes his face down against the solid wood.

Giles continues to shout, "You are the ones who told me he was dead without letting me see him! He was my only child and I didn't even get to bury him! Whoever the townspeople saw last night was not my son! It was a demon because he was never buried on hollow ground!"

Dicun squats down, lowering his face to Giles' still pressed against the table. "We're going to need you to refrain from raising your voice at us. Or we will arrest you for threatening a member of the Cavalry. They've got a special place for people like you."

Calix leans, putting his weight on Giles' head, pressing his face harder against the table. "I'm not believing this crap of it being a demon. Tell us, baker." Calix spits the last word. "Now, tell me. Who was it?"

Why does it matter who it was? They said they killed him. Why won't they leave me alone? Giles wonders. Spit runs from the side of his mouth, caking the flour to his lips.

Plumes of white dust float from the table as he huffs, struggling in the Rider's hand.

"I don't know!" Giles cries out broken.

These are the people Stirling had so desperately wanted to be. They are the reason he is dead. They were unable to accurately conduct their job in finding him and returning him home. They declared him dead. Now they are here, with the glint of murder in their eyes. These people aren't our guardians. These people are our nightmares.

Before releasing his hold on Giles' head, Calix drags his face down to the edge of the table. Giles, no longer holding up his weight, collapses to the floor with the help of an unfriendly hand. Frightened like a small child, he peaks up at Calix and Dicun, his mind flashing back to the boy who lay terrified on this floor last night. The way he wore fear-filled eyes, but not the way he is now, staring up at strangers threatening his life. The boy had pleaded up at him as if someone he loved and trusted hurt him, shattering him into pieces.

"Mr. Bakere, you need to tell us the truth. Otherwise, we can take it as you are withholding information and we have ways to extract the information from you. So, I'll ask you one more time. What do you remember from last night?" Dicun stresses, his figure towering over Giles.

"It was dark, I only had one candle lit and I dropped it. He was tall with curly light-colored hair. He was wearing a cloak, so I didn't see his mark," Giles stammers. "He-he—" Giles stops. "He looked a lot like my son, Stirling," he tells them, "but Stirling is dead! My son is dead!" Tears begin to trickle down his cheeks as he murmurs, "He's dead, he's dead, he's dead."

Dicun turns to Calix. "We're done here. I've got what I need."

Calix's face twists as he sneers, "Sir, he has admitted nothing."

Dicun steps closer to Calix, their chest almost touching. He leans in and speaks, barely audible in his ear, "Watch your tone, child. You obviously know nothing." Dicun straightens back up and says clearly, "We're done here."

He glances down at Giles. "Clean yourself up, Mr. Bakere." He pushes past Calix, who is seething.

Calix talks through his teeth down at Giles, "You're lucky he's here, baker."

Giles collapses, lying on his back as the door slams behind Calix, and sobs. He cries over the loss of his son. He cries for the idea he was alive, and he loses him again. He cries for the love he never got to show him, and for the father, he should have been to him. He cries for his wife, the love of his life and the one person who would have prevented all of this from happening.

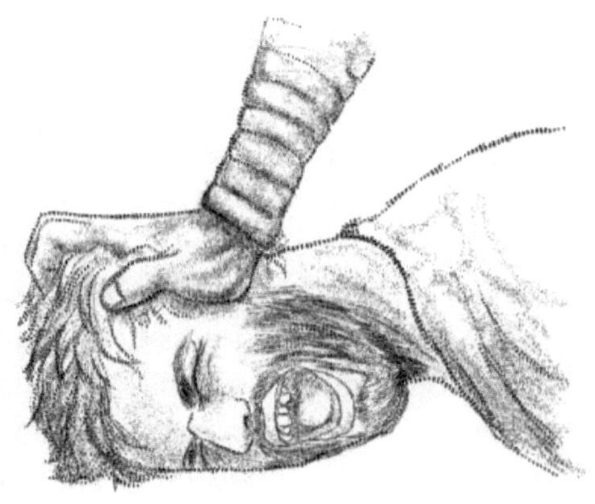

Sixty-Five

Inside the antechamber, Unit Larua sits patiently around an enormous yew wood table with a runner stretching from one side to the other colored with the Winged Cavalry's coat of arms; red and purple quartered with their insignia in white across it. A candle chandelier made of wood and dark metal hangs above the table. If Amiria lets her eyes gloss over, the chandelier blurs out of focus, and the excessive amount of candles blends into one large ball of fire floating above them. Torches mounted to the walls light the tapestries of honored Winged Riders and weapons through the ages.

On one side of the table, Amiria sits in the last seat before the end. Calix poised beside her with his arms crossed. The member who stood outside the bakery holding the horses named Everard sits across the table from her beside Eda, the only other female on the team in her late twenties. Her blonde hair is pulled back into a short braid reaching to her collar.

Dicun sits on the other side of Calix directly across from Armundus, the most senior member of her squad besides Major Gautier; he tends to remain silent, his features a statue. Amiria has only spoken a few words to him over the past few years.

At the end of the table, King Dietrich sits at the head. Her father, out of her peripheral view, sits across from Major Gautier beside Dicun.

King Dietrich glares down the length of the table, eyes stopping on each of the members of his personal guards sitting stiffly with their shoulders pulled against the back of their seats, none wanting to meet his eye.

"You disappointed me last night. I am making the assumption the fugitive who should have been brought down has made it to Uviktiland. Tracks in the sand leading into the tree line had been spotted this morning by scouts. Because of your failure, I now have to include other squads in this investigation since you can no longer be trusted to complete your assignments alone.

"I should fire all of you today, but I don't have time to find a new team of Riders possessing the same talents you are so luckily to be gifted in. You have caused me embarrassment because, as much as it pained me, I had to send a letter to the King of Uvikitland requesting permission to search his land since we couldn't control what we know now as a single boy. This permission won't come for free. You've cost your kingdom a lot of resources. Let that sink in. Remember who this falls back onto—" He stops as the members stare down at the wood grains of the table, feeling the weight of each stone King Dietrich is personally setting on their shoulders.

He resumes, "The citizens shall believe the fugitive has been shot and killed, any further information is classified and anyone prying for answers on the topic will be arrested. We don't want anyone getting any sort of ideas. If any of you leak even the smallest amount of information, you will be charged with treason and sentenced to death. I don't care what *talent* you have. I don't stand for mutiny. I will be splitting you in half to lead a specialized reconnaissance team.

"Armundus, Eda, and Everard you will be joining the first team, team requaero. You will be taking two units of my picking to survey Uviktiland. You need to gain all intel you are able to on where this fugitive can be hiding. You will begin operations build up immediately on how to survey the landscape and configure an accurate map of the land. You will be dispatched as soon as I get the response letter from their King.

"Dicun, Calix, and Amiria, you will remain here. You will be joining the secondary team, team perimo. You will be making contact at the rendezvous point that is not yet determined. Team requaero, you will decide on a designated location deemed safe and secure. The location you will send back with a runner. Team perimo. You will take their intel and you will locate this fugitive and kill on site."

King Dietrich pauses again as Amiria's squad refrains from squirming under his heavy presence. "You will be deploying to check in all directions, north, east, and south."

Amiria's fist clenches in her lap beneath the table, the memory of her and Stirling sitting in the cave still fresh in her mind. *"If you could go anywhere, where would you go?"*

"The southeast."

"Permission to speak, sir," Amiria exclaims.

The entire table all shifts their gaze in silence to Amiria. She feels like she's stuck on display in the stocks for everyone to gawk at. Without moving his head, Calix's gaze drops down to Amiria's hands still balled into fists. Field Marshal Rey shoots a warning in his daughter's direction.

King Dietrich smiles deviously. "Permission granted, Ms. Rey."

"I have a strong belief this boy will not travel south or

southeast. It will be a waste of men to send them in those directions," Amiria suggests.

"Oh? Now, why do you say that?" King Dietrich says, intrigued.

"I've been made aware I am of the same age as the fugitive. He is young and inexperienced. We don't know what the world to the south and southeast is like. It is a mystery. We live a perfectly structured life here. Nothing is ever unknown to us. We know exactly where to go and what we should be doing. So, a whole uncharted world? That sounds frightening to someone who has most likely never even left this section of the island before. The most reasonable direction he would go in is Uviktiland's mountainous range in the north. It is something semi-familiar and gives him an excellent cover. Those mountains themselves need a whole team to cover," she proposes, keeping her breathing steady.

King Dietrich sits back, his jeweled hands intertwined and resting on his flat stomach. His eyes follow the flow of her black hair that flows over her shoulder and down her chest. His eyes flit over to the young Gautier at her side, who's distracted by something in her lap or the ground. He returns his gaze to Amiria's eyes, pursing his lips he ponders to himself over the information Amiria has given him. "I will take your words into consideration."

The eyes of Amiria's squad members stab into her repeatedly. She can't meet any of their eyes, afraid they will read the lie on her face, read the pages revealing she was the one who cost them the mission, the one who purposefully committed mutiny.

Calix watches discreetly as Amiria swallows hard, her hands still clenched beneath the table.

"Field Marshal Rey, Major Gautier, we have more to discuss. The rest of you are dismissed, return to your quarters till further notice," King Dietrich instructs.

Outside the antechamber in a large hallway lit by the

afternoon sun shining in through tall thin windows with the top of each one rounded in an arch, Amiria is the last to exit the room. She softly closes the door behind her and trails the group as they begin their loud obnoxious chatter.

"How much are you willing to bet I'll bring that boy's head to the king?" Dicun says to Armundus.

Armundus gives Dicun a sideways glance. "Nothing."

Everard pushes forward, joining the conversation. "That's because his demise will be by my own sword. I've got the best swordsmith money can buy, sharpening it right now. I'm also on the first team. So, you won't even get the opportunity."

Eda links her arms around Everard's, "You men go ahead and kill the boy as gruesomely as your heart desires. My eyes are on that dragon. I want to see what those feathered wings look like up close. They will add such a lovely color to my room. Plain walls can be so cold and dreary. It'll surely brighten it up," Eda chimes, her eyes sparkling as she fantasizes how she will use them.

"Why are you so sure we need to kill the dragon?" Calix asks. "It is a new species. Do we not want to keep it?"

Eda scoffs, "Do you know nothing? If this traitorous boy *bonded*—" Her facial expression twists with disgust as she says the word. "—with this dragon. Then this dragon will fight to the death to protect him. Obvious information. If you were the top of your class, I'd hate to see how the rest of you tested."

"Watch how you speak to me, Eda. Just because you are my senior by a years, it does not give you permission to do so. Remember where my family stands to yours," Calix growls. "If anyone is going to bring that boy's head to the king, it'll be me and when I take over for my father, you will be taking orders from me."

Amiria doesn't follow the group as they turn right at the end of the hallway. She can't stand listening to them anymore. The way they speak about Stirling as if he is some sort of game. As if they were a group of hunters and he is the buck they want to bring home to display on their mantle.

Feeling sick to her stomach, Amiria turns down the opposite corridor. The thoughts of her teammates finding Stirling runs through her mind. She hates him for abandoning her, but she doesn't want her friend to die. He wouldn't last a minute in hand-to-hand combat against any of them. He has no special training, no special bloodline. He is only human. His crime that is punishable by death? Nothing but wanting to be something he was told he couldn't. He isn't some sort of monster that needs to be slayed.

"Amiria Rey, now where can you be off to?" Calix slyly calls out to her.

Rolling her eyes, Amiria refuses to acknowledge him and continues walking. Calix slowly jogs after her.

"It's rude to ignore someone," he says, catching up to her. Amiria slows to a stop as he steps in front of her.

"What do you want?" she bites.

Calix steps closer to her as he talks. In return, Amiria instinctively steps away backward. "Thought we could spend some time together before we deploy to new lands as a team." Amiria's back bumps into the colorfully painted wall. Calix presses his palms against the wall on either side of her head, trapping her in place. "It's really good to get to know your partners."

"And what makes you think I'm interested in getting to know my partners?" She raises her eyebrow.

"Because then we can really know each other, inside and out." Calix grins a mischievous smile.

He shifts all his pressure to his left hand, freeing his right.

He picks up a portion of Amiria's hair, letting the dark silk slide through his fingers until it reaches the end, where he stops and plays with the soft strands, "You seemed pretty sure of yourself back there when you told the king about the fugitive not going southeast. Is there something you're keeping from me, my little bird?"

Amiria grabs his hand, "I know if you don't let go of my hair, I will be forced to cut your hand off for indecently touching a personnel of a higher family status."

Amiria slips under Calix's arm, pulling it behind him with her. With his arm wrenched behind his back. Amiria slams him against the wall, "But I'd hate to upset the king by staining his nice floors with the blood of someone like you." She pushes off him, stepping back a safe distance out of his reach.

Calix spins around, his back still leaning against the wall, "I will have you eventually."

Amiria pivots on her heel, her hair whipping as she turns away from him. "I'd rather die." She calls out over her shoulder.

She can feel his stare like burning arrows piercing her as she holds her body urging her to run back, forcing it to calmly walk away. She slips around a corner, prepared to take a breath of relief but instead freezes as she hears Major Gautier call out Calix's name. *He sounds furious.*

Flattening herself against the wall, she scoots to the edge and peaks around the corner.

Calix stands up straight from leaning against the wall and turns to face his father. He is the spitting image of the Major, as if he is a younger clone, with the same dark hair and crystal eyes.

Major Gautier's eyebrows furrow. In a blur of movement, he backhands Calix across the face. His knuckles connect hard against Calix's cheekbone, whipping his head to the side. He doesn't move, his head staying where it was forcibly positioned by his father's hand.

Amiria gasps silently.

Major Gautier leans into Calix, his voice the deep rumble of a thunderstorm. "If you ever embarrass me in front of the king like that again, I will disown you." He spits on the floor at Calix's feet, "If that is how you will perform during the most crucial missions of your life, you do not deserve to carry on our family's name."

Calix doesn't move, his eyes directed at the floor as he mumbles, "You failed too. You oversee us."

Major Gautier becomes enraged, grabbing Calix's face, his hand cupped under his jaw, his claws digging into Calix's cheeks as he forces him to look him in the eye. "Do not speak against me. Do you understand me? Fail me again, and you're gone. I have more children to succeed your mother and me. You're disposable, just like he was." Major Gautier releases his grip on Calix with a throw of his hand.

Calix sidesteps to keep his balance.

"Look at you, you're pathetic. Twenty-four and still haven't wed. You'll be lonely forever. You need to get your life together Calix." He lowers his voice for only Calix to hear. "Get the Rey girl on your own before I have to arrange it. Because I'm starting to reconsider that your younger brother has a better chance."

Calix whispers half to himself, "I don't like her because she's the next Field Marshal."

Missing the tail of the conversation, Amiria slinks away before anyone notices she was eavesdropping. Amiria feels like she should be happy to see Calix getting what she believes he deserves after the way he treats her and everyone else as if they are no more than objects. But she isn't glad. It was solely her fault, yet her father isn't upset with her. Of course, her father tends to be too busy to pay much attention to her, even to be disciplined.

Justice isn't as sweet as she thought it would be. It is sour, and she wants nothing more than to spit it out.

Sixty-Six

The sun is beginning to lower in the sky, striking the back of their heads as they continue forward. Stirling pushes through a large thicket and turns back to face the sun. He holds his thumb up horizontally to the sky, measuring the distance between the sun and the horizon.

The land had flattened out compared to the mountainous region he spent his life in. Other than being high in the air he has never been able to see such an expansive distance before. He grew up shadowed by leaning buildings, towering pines, and mountains that disappeared into the clouds. It gives him an almost dizzy feeling, the feeling of eternity, the land a limitless stretch in front of him, never to end.

The sun has no mountains to hide behind, stretching his day longer than he knew possible.

The land is magnificent in its own way, with rolling hills made of gold speckled with imperfections made of clusters of thickets and oak trees. There is a limited cover, but that includes the lack of coverage in the cloudless sky for the

Winged Cavalry to sneak up on him. No one is following him anymore.

"Can we take a break under that oak tree up ahead?" Ignis asks, dragging his tired feet.

"Are you done already?" Stirling jabs.

"We've been walking all day after a restless night. What do you expect? Next time you can swim across the sea while I ride on your back," Ignis rebuts.

Stirling scans the sky behind them. "Okay. We haven't seen any sign of the Cavalry since last night. Either they went in the wrong direction, or they are still waiting for permission to search. We can take a nap, and at nightfall, we can take to the sky and really cover some distance."

The oak tree's branches spiderweb out to the prairie in all directions. A few of the lower heavier branches succumb to their own weight and rest on the leaf-riddled ground, giving the tree an almost cave-like appearance.

Ignis throws his body down on the ground at the base of the trunk sending dry leaves and dust into the air. Brushing off the small oak leaves that landed on his head, Stirling crashes, exhausted, next to Ignis. He ignores the minor irritation the oak leaves cause as their sharp edges poke through his clothing. He is more focused on the pain still radiating from any movement of his hands. He lifts the dressing he made from tearing the hem of his tunic stuffed with the yellow flowering plant, St John's wort, a little trick he picked up from visiting the flower lady's hut with his mother.

"How do your hands feel?" Ignis asks.

"Awful, just moving my fingers is excruciating. I hope they don't scar too badly. They're pretty gross," Stirling says, setting his oozing hands down in his lap.

"Your arm is already gross," Ignis adds.

"Thanks. You're a real confidence booster," Stirling replies sarcastically.

"*How far are we going to go?*" Ignis yawns.

"Like I said before. Until we can't go any further. I want to make sure we're never found," he answers.

"*Even too far for Amiria?*" Ignis brings up.

Stirling feels the spike in his heart. "No," he says, lying down.

Rolling over, he turns away from Ignis and mumbles, "Nothing is too far for Amiria."

His eyelids close, shutting away the light like the sun closing in on the horizon. He misses her already. It hurts knowing there is no more. *See you next week.*

Running toward your dream isn't easy and it doesn't come for free. You often must give up what is precious to you, something of equal importance in your heart. Learning to make difficult choices is what will make you stronger and succeed in the end.

The twinkling sky dimly lights the landscape with a soft glow. The golden hills are now silver waves. The tree rustles as Ignis pushes through the branches with Stirling stepping out into the open night air.

"*Are you sure this is going to work?*" Ignis questions.

Stirling takes a sip of water from the costrel slung across his chest, then tugs the strap of supplies still worn on Ignis' hips.

"It's going to have to. We've got no other choice," he says, hanging a single strand of leather tied together from the remnants of the damaged harness around Ignis' neck. "I'm going to need to hang on like my life depends on it…Well, it does."

"*Yes, but don't you remember when you first tried flying like this?*" Ignis reminds him.

"Yeah, but I'm better now. That was six years ago," Stirling reassures.

He finishes the knot and slips on his goggles. Holding onto the leather strap, Stirling attempts to pull himself onto Ignis' back. The strap spins, pivoting around Ignis' neck.

Stirling's footing slips with his body's support giving away beneath him he falls forward. His face squishes against Ignis' side, slowing his fall to a stop.

Sighing, Ignis lays his body down on the ground with his legs tucked beneath him. His back is now waist height with Stirling, who rubs the imprint of scales on his face. Shaking his head, he presses his palms against Ignis's back, swinging his leg up and over, straddling him.

Looping the T-shaped hook through the metal on Ignis' harness, he locks himself in. Pausing, he stares down at his injured hands, pulling up the sleeve of his undershirt to analyze his mutilated insignia. Physical scars to remind him of the days his life was altered, the path changing and contorting into something unrecognizable. A life path with new twists, turns, and multiple directions. He walks it lost without any guidance. This is what he wanted, was it not?

Bringing his attention upward, he takes in the bright and silent night. The wind rolls across the plains, giving life to the hills as they dance under the stars to the melody of crickets.

Stirling smiles. "All right. I'm ready."

Epilogue

Slender fingers nervously tug on the sleeves of her dress, a constant fear they have ridden up and her insignia is viewable. The girl is young, just reached adulthood. The stains on her hand-me-down apron surpass her in years. Hiding her face, she watches her feet walk through the well-lit night. She hopes she didn't wait too long after supper. The last thing she wants is to anger someone by waking them up.

Her eyes bounce up now and then, checking her surroundings. Even if there is another person in sight, coming to an automatic conclusion about her true intentions is close to nonexistent. She only needs to lie, saying she was having supper at a friend's house and is returning home.

Still, the thought of being questioned by a guard quakes her nerves.

She tugs the ends of her sleeves with sweaty palms repeatedly, her heart pounding with each step as she walks up to the front door of the wax-chandler. Rubbing the sweat off on her apron, she contemplates to herself. She can hear the shuffling of feet just beyond the door.

It's now or never, she tells herself.

Lifting her hand, she raps her knuckles against the door, her eyes growing wide with anticipation. She hears the meandering footsteps getting ready for bed stop. With a hesitant pause, they tread lightly to the front door of the shop.

The front door creaks open just enough to allow the woman inside to poke her head out. Her frizzy hair, graying and pulled back into a knot. "It's a little late to be knocking on someone's door. We're closed anyway."

"I'm not here to shop," the girl blurts.

"Then what brings you to my doorstep at this hour?" the wax-chandler asks.

"I'm the cordwainer from a couple of blocks west of here. You've bought shoes from my family's shop," the girl explains.

"I know who you are, but that doesn't explain what business

you have here," the wax-chandler snipes.

The cordwainer checks the street behind her.

She leans in close to the wax-chandler with her voice barely a whisper. "I was wondering, if there is any possibility, you might be able to teach me how to, um, how to make my own candles and soap?"

The wax-chandler's face is stricken with horror. Grabbing the cordwainer's arm, she yanks her inside the shop, closing the door swiftly behind her. In a hushed tone, she lectures, "Are you out of your mind, child! You know that is illegal, right?"

The cordwainer cowers. Her face turning red, she crosses her arms in an attempt to make herself smaller. Wishing she can slip through the cracks of the floorboards beneath her feet. If the wax-chandler tells anyone she even asked for such a favor, she will be hung.

"I'm so sorry. Please forget I was ever here. Please, I'm begging you. Don't tell anyone what I asked you. I'm the oldest child and I need to help raise my siblings," she apologizes, her body flushed with embarrassment and fear.

The corners of the wax-chandler's eyes wrinkle as she observes the young girl. The cordwainer shifts nervously on her feet, brushing away the tears forming as if she can hide them.

Scratching her head, the wax-chandler takes it all into consideration. She shifts her gaze around her shop, organized neatly with her product to the opened window.

"You're going to call the guards, aren't you?" the cordwainer worries. The wax-chandler releases a long drawn-out sigh as she steps over to the window.

 "No my dear, I am not." She closes the shutters and turns back to the cordwainer. "You're a fool for coming here. Your siblings and your parents rely on your assistance. Yet your acts of defiance can lead you to death."

He learned how to ride a dragon—why can't I learn to make a candle? The cordwainer wishes she had never come to this shop.

The wax-chandler rubs her temples. "Maybe I'm just an old fool too. Anything we say from here out should be barely loud enough to count as a whisper. Our conversations are for our ears only." The cordwainer perks up, her eyes widening. The wax-chandler continues, "I'll teach you, but only on one condition."

She can't control herself. "Anything! What is it you want?"

The wax-chandler smiles gently. "I know you make new shoes, but can you show me how to repair my old ones?"

Returning the smile, the cordwainer states eagerly. "I can."

Check out a free short story on my website
kelseakoops.com

Jannell and Faerydae's love story.

Kelsea Koops

Acknowledgments

I'll start with the obvious, my family and my husband. My mom, for showing excitement for me by making a reusable bottle with pages from my book. My sister, for letting me read to her my roughest drafts and knitting me a stuffed Ignis. My dad, for taking the time to read the rough drafts, the final product, and being my number one fan. My husband, for dealing with me constantly talking about my book, hounding him with questions, and hovering over my laptop. I will, of course, love to thank my in-laws, who love my book no matter what.

I have to give a special shout out to some of my best friends. Taylor who helped me name my protagonist, Jessica who helped proof read, and Sophi who helped edit my book. That girl would sit in the cold, raining PNW forest with me while camping as we took turns reading the book out loud and making adjustments.

I'm also going to give thanks to my editor Belle Manuel. She was the one who helped change my book and characters for the better.

Then I'm going back to the roots, where it all started. I will not mention the place I had worked but let me say graveyard was so dull that I started writing this book. I will never forget those I worked with at the place that shall not be named. They supported me when the book was nothing but scribbles in a journal. They listened to me as I told them my idea and encouraged me to go for it. Four and half years later and its finally done because of their initial support.

Now I won't neglect to thank the later years. I had left that initial job and began somewhere else. My coworkers and supervisor watched me write furiously in my rough draft notebooks and type on the computer during down times. Instead of my supervisor telling me to put the notebook away and my coworkers getting upset that I was distracted at work, they supported me. Constantly asking me how my progress was going and putting positive vibes that I will one day finally complete it. Here it is guys. Except, I will still be typing at work because there's no stopping me now. So, you're stuck with me still click-clacking away, but after all these of watching me type, you must be used to it now.

Thank you, everyone.

Kelsea Koops

About the Author

Born and raised in Thousand Oaks, California, I had changed what I wanted to be when I grew up numerous times like any child. Looking back through all my schoolwork and old notebooks, I loved story writing. The evidence was there, but I just ignored it. End of high school, I took that interest, believing I wanted to be a screenwriter. I wrote a full-length movie, but I didn't enjoy the lack of detail. I love writing detail, really building a mental picture of the world. I dropped out of college before gaining an associate degree and went straight into the workforce. I attempted to write another movie for the fun of it but never finished it. Looking back now, I don't know why I didn't just write those as books.

At 21, I had entirely given up on the idea of being a screenwriter but still liked writing as a hobby. I wrote a short story for only me to read, and it wasn't until I was 25 that it occurred to me to turn it into a full-length novel. Scars of Lumierna is the result.

When I'm not at my full-time job hovering over a computer, or at home sitting on the couch with my computer. I'm out camping, with my computer. With a rooftop tent mounted to my four-wheel drive Toyota, I love taking long drives through the Olympic Mountain's logging roads, even some roads that my car shouldn't be going on, and I had to do the sketchy backup and turn around. At the end of the day, my friend Sophi and I would pick a spot, make a fire and work on my book. There is no better place to work than in the middle of the forest with no one around except your best friend, some dogs, and the sound of the crackling fire.

Connect with me online at

Tiktok kelseakoops_author

Instagram kelseakoops_author

kelseakoops.com

www.ingramcontent.com/pod-product-compliance
Lightning Source LLC
Chambersburg PA
CBHW031154010826
48971CB00012B/137